The LOBSTER PRINCESS

MICHAEL BLATHERWICK

Paperback: ISBN 979-8-9867772-7-6
eBook: ISBN 979-8-9867772-8-3

Library of Congress Control Number: 2024918876

First paperback edition: October 2024

Development Editing: Julian Greystoke
Additional Editing and Proofreading: Megan Sanders
Cover design by Vivien Reis
Cartography and map design by Paige Connelly
at paigeconnellyillustration.com

Jackowick Publishing
Trenton, NJ 08620
michaelblatherwick.com

For Uncle Chuck, the King of Maine

Temple of Ascalon
Ice Lake
Himmelhavets
Kingdom of Swan
Merchant Town
Ribbed Beach
King's Plain
Kingdom of Löbfolk
South Islands
Lighthouse
The Western Contiaent
The Great Sea

Books by Michael Blatherwick

Photograph Chronicles Series

Photograph and the Atomic Juggernaut (Book One)
Photograph and the Daughters of Invention (Book Two)
Photograph and the New Wheeled Order (Book Three)

The Lobster Princess, Apondra's Tale

The Lobster Princess (Book One)

Song of the Lobfolk Children

"He of the Blue, He of the Old,
His tale unsung until it's told!
Words of wisdom, words of good,
Protects the sea, protects the wood!
When darkness fell across the land,
He lit the way with claw and hand!
He saved our folk, then disappeared,
Defeated all the things we feared!
The end of days, the longest night
His courage gives us hope and light!
We do not fear the Undersea,
For Azcalaw will always be!
Azcalaw! Azcalaw!"

Chapter 1

Happy Birthday

APONDRA. WAKE UP, my dear. Today is the day we have decreed as your eighteenth birthday."

At first, the white light between the thick velvet curtains stabbed Apondra's eyes. The feather-filled duvet, tucked high under her chin, smelled like marigolds and apples, washed by hand in a mixture of pollens and fatty soap by the king's staff. Apondra closed her eyes again and smiled, laying one arm over the bed coverings, palm up, for her father to hold. She tightened her grip around her raggedy plush lobster, well-worn after eighteen years, which rested in the crook of her other arm.

"Is it time for my birthday story, Father?"

"Yes, my princess. Many years ago, when the queen died suddenly, the king, who of course is me, was heartbroken and without an heir. The queen was not yet able to bear a child, so her passing left the king very distraught. Not only was she his queen, but she was his true love. Her dark eyes were like the rolling tides at night outside your windows. Her words were poems, perfect words pieced together in gentle rows, like music and love. Even the utterance of my name made my heart leap." She felt his thick firm fingers on her hand.

"That always makes me sad when you speak of her, Father. Don't lobsters mate for life?" She opened her eyes again. Her father, her adoptive father, King Abbasdah, sat next to the bed. His face was unremarkable for his species, but so handsome to Apondra. His smooth and spotted light-brown head, unadorned by his crown, shone over his black eyes. Where her face had a small round nose, his was devoid of a proboscis, only a tapered maw ending in a set of short, segmented antennae, his "dinner dusters" as he called them, surrounding his small mouth composed of segmented lips and two short mandibles. His large claws, high on his shoulders, rested at his sides under his dark red royal cloak. His other arms, a total of four as opposed to her two, extended in pairs from each shoulder joint; it was common for lobfolk to let their claws hang unused like wings as their forelimbs provided the usefulness of opposable thumbs and fingers, hands just like hers. Under his royal apron, his four legs folded under his chair and his stubby tail ending in a wide fin flapped on the floor whenever he adjusted his height, which he did now to finally answer her question. He smiled and placed his hand on her cheek.

"Mating for life? That's folklore, my dear. Old human sailor tales. Matron fables. Superstitions, myths, and legends, these are all rooted in some shard of evidence. We do not mate for life, but lobfolk do feel love, some say the most intense love in the world as we can be very long-lived. And this love can cause us such grief and pain when we lose it." He ran his fingers through her thin brown hair. "So, when my wife passed, two thoughts burned like a raging fire inside of me. First and foremost, my heart was shattered. Second, I had no heir. When the vizier and I found a basket of branches floating in the tide on the beach one morning, we knew it was a miracle in need of rescue. A child, a human child, who could heal my heart. A miracle, indeed."

"Father, was I really a miracle?" She raised an eyebrow, and the corners of her mouth pressed tiny folds under her high cheeks as she smiled.

"Well, we did pray to Azcalaw. You were not well when we found you. But our prayers were heard by Azcalaw of the Blue, and your body healed."

She squeezed her rag-lobster. "The children in my classes whispered that he was my true father, Azcalaw."

"That is untrue, Princess," a deep but soft voice interrupted from the opposite side of the room, the royal lobfolk vizier. "But we did thank him and praise him. Praise Azcalaw."

Apondra nodded, signaling for him to continue.

"Magic." The vizier adjusted his cap (although Apondra did refer to it as his "beanie" in jest as a child). "Some did speculate that you were born from the magic of the sea." The vizier stepped forward from beside the bedroom door, his dark gray robe and matching tunic flowing around his claws. "You are, quite simply, a human girl born of humans. But nonetheless, eighteen years later, we now celebrate your royal ascension."

"We have time for ceremonies later," the king chided. "For now, let me enjoy my role as doting father. Where was I? Oh yes, Princess, your arrival! Some said that you were the dying hope of a merchant family, set adrift as the ocean swallowed them whole."

Her parents were human, this was a fact, but she admitted enjoying the attention when lobfolk would whisper if she was indeed one of Azcalaw's miracles. Apondra now looked at her folded hands in her lap. "I have heard some of the rumors, that my arrival was an omen, that I am an abomination of the waters."

"Hush," said the king.

"I have heard that magic was lost the day I was found. I'm not a fool to these specula—"

"Magic," the vizier interrupted, "is still in this world. Ignore those fools. Magic is all around us, but it is not a fruit you can grow and pluck from a tree in an orchard. Magic is not chosen, it chooses." The king looked to the vizier with sad eyes. "As the Grand Vizier of King Abbasdah, my magic has been gone for many years, but not the wisdom I obtained when I could wield it. I am still a vizier of renown."

"That you are!" Apondra smiled. She brushed her hair across her forehead and uncovered her brown eyes, reminding herself to ask for a new shell comb for the kingdom's only resident with hair. "I am so grateful to have the love of my father, and your guiding hands, Vizier."

"And someday," said the king, "you will use love and wisdom to rule when I am gone. Love and wisdom. Mercy and hope. These are the true powers wielded by a king. Or a queen."

She clapped her hands in excitement, then extended them to the vizier.

"And now your turn! Tell me the story again, as you do on each of my birthdays. You both remember such different details."

"Such a demanding princess," scoffed the vizier, running a finger through his antennae in mock recollection. "I was just about to start my version of your tale. One morning, a cool day in the fall when the leaves began to turn amber, gold, and ruby, the king, while on his morning walk, stopped at the edge of the bay. He emerged from the tree line and found a baby, pink and shivering, crying on a tiny bed of soggy pine bark and woven branches that had washed ashore. He knew from the moment he saw her that his heart could love this orphan child, as his court was now empty of wife and progeny. He leaned over and delicately, with all twenty of his fingers, picked up the babe. She immediately stopped crying, as if she knew that this 'strange' fellow before her would protect her. Why, he had never seen eyes so deep and wonderous, like melted chocolate. At first, the king took pity on this creature." The vizier stopped, as he did on each of her birthdays, to poke her limbs. "She was malformed with only ten fingers, two arms, two legs. Her skin was smooth, and he feared that she had molted too early, or perhaps she would not at all. Suddenly, a flash of realization. This was not a lobfolk, but a human baby, something he had never seen before. But her beauty was too fine, too fair, for him to leave her to die.

"His attendant whistled for their escort, and the royal cattle mounts arrived, a regiment of kyloes pulling chariots adorned with royal red swatches and cloths. The king swaddled the baby in his own cloak as they rode back to The Castle of Wooded Stone, *Castle Homarus*, where you live now. The vizier, that would be me, of course, examined the babe further and determined she was indeed a human. While we have had our cautious interactions with humans over the past several decades, keep in mind that a human child, let alone a human infant, had never been seen in the kingdom, and so should be set free back into the bay to be with her own kind. The king protested. The baby's eyes portrayed an emotional capability unlike the warriors of men, or beasts of the wild. She was so similar to us, yet so different."

The king handed Apondra her favorite robe, a long thick weave of blue and white felt and fleece. She glanced at the vizier; he averted his eyes as she slid from her nightgown. Only the vizier and her father were allowed in her presence when she changed, one of many insistences by the king to let her live "by her culture's norms, including modesty," so that she would learn proper behavior when emissaries and merchants from the nations of men visited their tiny kingdom. She smiled when she had finished tying the belt of her robe. "Go on, Vizier!"

"Thank you, Princess. Well, as the king and his vizier debated what to do with the child, the tiny girl reached up and stroked the king's long brown antennae hanging on each side of his mandibles. She cooed, and his heart was truly whole.

"Once she was of age to speak and walk, the vizier and the king immediately began her education. She learned the lobfolk lore, our history, and most critically, the firm lines between fact, fiction, and the speculative fog in between, for she was to be raised as a critical thinker and considerate decision maker, her most important skills should she ascend to the throne.

"Her name, *your name*, was chosen by one of the townspeople when we presented her publicly for the first time. A young albino lobfolk, an eager student who spent his free time in our grand library, offered the name 'Apondra' because he liked how it sounded. Nothing more. As Grand Vizier, I noted that a child from beyond our world would bear that burden of her uniqueness in every aspect of her life, so we agreed it was appropriate. And so, on that day, you became Apondra."

As the vizier concluded, Apondra walked to the window and looked at the clouds, underlit by the rising sun to the east, creeping over the tall pines and junipers between the castle and the ocean waters to the east. She examined her hands in the sun; tanned fingers, four on each hand plus a thumb, and tiny hairs that glinted on the backs of her hands and her forearms. Her arms, only two, were each attached by the shoulder at the side of her torso, just like any other human. She looked at the king, Abbasdah, her father, and his four arms sprouting from the sides of his chest. His shell and arm coverings were brown, like the vizier, but ringed by a creamy hue along each edge when a plate or segmentation joined another one. The curve of his spinal shell showed his age, as was common among the elder lobfolk, and he avoided talk of his final molting. It was assumed his last shell had already passed, but perhaps he had one more in his life cycle.

She was entering her 18th year since her discovery, now a woman in the eyes of the laws of the royal court, ready to attend to the full matters of the lobfolk. *Her people.* King Abbasdah stood behind her and again ran his fingers through her long brown hair, the color of dark, wet wood washed on the beach. Unlike the chaff of the sea, her hair was light and thin, straight and clean, washed with a soap made of lichens and lilacs (she truly loved the scent of lilacs above all the other flora). His antennae ran over her face, an intimate gesture for lobfolk with their kin. "You are my daughter," he cooed. "I love you as if you were my blood. Every day has been a joy to see you rise and take your walks to the library for your studies."

A prideful smile came over his face, met by her own. "Father, every day I am grateful you rescued me from the water weeds at the lip of the Great Sea. But I know you are hiding something."

The dark orbs of his eyes glistened. "Aye. I am hiding from time. You are no longer a child." From the shadow of the doorway, the vizier clattered forward on his four legs. He brushed aside his robe, revealing his two great claws, each without a "thumb", lost years before she was born and failing to regenerate due to the vizier's age. He extended them in a gesture of respect for the princess.

"Fair Princess Apondra, on your eighteenth birthday, you are now the Eave Queen, adjacent to the House of King Abbasdah. You are not of his blood, but you are of his word, claw, and hand, an official of the Court of Abbasdah. We have already sent an announcement party to the surrounding lands, and an ambassador party left last month to cross the Great Sea. Our royal artists provided each ambassador with your portrait sketch, of course."

Her smile faded, not because of the sudden impending celebrity status from her birthday announcement, but from anticipating the question she asked frequently, suddenly more urgent now that she was officially joining the court.

"How is your health today, Father?"

The vizier answered instead of the king. "The maladies of longevity have returned. We fought it off with our herbals and the healing kelps of the deep bay, but I fear we cannot halt time's inevitable swim toward the Undersea."

The king sighed. It was now that Apondra saw new cracks in his shell, tiny airborne flakes drifting away in harmony with the draperies, touched by the breeze. He was certainly long-lived and well-worn by battle before her birth. Over the past several months she had observed his breathing becoming more labored, his official schedule of duties reduced or delegated to other officiants. The aging process that overtook him was more akin to the gentle weathering of a stone to the sea than a blight creeping up the bark of a young sapling. She denied his mortality and pushed the thoughts down, again, into her chest.

"Perhaps I will ask Ken the librarian to do further research into restoring his vigor."

The vizier placed a finger on his lower mandible. "Perhaps. It may be too big of a challenge for a bookish *hermit* to source and secure such a remedy."

"He's not a hermit," Apondra protested. "He just likes to stay in the library. As do I! And if anyone is smart enough to uncover a hidden remedy, it's Ken. With my help." She curled her lips into a proud smile.

"Oh, is that so, my beautiful genius?" said Abbasdah. "What is required? Name it and I shall send the lobatorium guards to obtain it."

The vizier protested, a common occurrence by Apondra's tally when her father offered resources too freely. "The knights of your lobatorium cannot … manifest a remedy, nor do they have the numbers to scour the countryside picking berries and herbs or uncover lonely mages with potions hidden in tree stumps."

Abbasdah stroked his chin feelers with two of his hands and twiddled his fingers on the other two. His cape flicked back to reveal his own large claws, scarred and damaged, but still functional. He clacked the claws in thought before brandishing a peaceful smile.

"Later. All of this can be discussed later. Today is Apondra's day! Daughter, do what pleases you this afternoon, after court, of course, before we have your celebration dinner. Now, we shall depart so you can finish dressing, for today is your day. Happy Birthday, Princess."

"Will I have time to visit the library before court today?"

"You always seem to find time, my dear."

The courtyard of the Castle Homarus, the Keep of Stone Woods, bristled with activity as lobfolk merchants and petitioners swarmed the intricately patterned pathway of faded gray pavers. The outer walls stretched three stories high, mountains of black bricks and stones lined by both living trees and solid carved vertical logs. Birds fluttered from branch to branch in the live sections of the keep, an osprey sitting in its nest made in the corner of the front battlement. The moss masons bought their lunches and supplemental tools from the merchant square before heading off to attend to the never-ending maintenance of the outer layers. Apondra loved the clickety-clack of their feet countered by the dull pounding of claws as the impatient masons slammed their giant appendages ahead of them to vault forward. To make life less intrusive, the king had decreed that no one need stop and bow for the princess as she skipped to the library, but occasionally one of the elder lobfolk would pause and announce, "Eave Queen, make hail and way!"

Apondra shielded her eyes for a moment. The courtyard, still bright despite the now overcast sky, echoed with the clattering of feet and clacking of shells. She rarely noticed the noises of lobfolk locomotion anymore, sometimes feeling special that she could move silently around them on her "squishy" legs. Her long green skirt and favorite gray wool sweater kept her warm as she skipped among the vendors.

A man, human, looked up from his dealings with one of the merchants. It was not common to see men directly buying goods inside the walls of Castle Homarus, but Apondra did not give them much thought. This one, a dark bronze man of the islands of the far south with long, finely braided black hair flowing over his yellow tunic, caught her eye today, as it was even less frequent to have such well-traveled visitors. She smiled and waved briefly, as this is what she thought an Eave Queen should do, greet all travelers and possible emissaries.

"Good day, friend! We are grateful for your coin!" she yelled.

"Fair one," the man replied, "you should leave and come with me back to my island! I will gift you with treasure, and you will have plentiful children!" He flexed his arms; large, peaked biceps decorated in gold rings and black tattoos. A guard of the lobatorium, a female adorned in draping chainmail, stepped between them.

"You will speak respectfully to our Eave Queen," the guard hissed. Apondra saw the guards' hands rest on the handles of each of her side daggers.

"Knight Diggins," Apondra said, placing a gentle hand over her guard's own. "I'm sure he is just being friendly."

"Indeed, I am," said the man. He knelt before her, his broad white smile beaming before he returned to his standing height, taller than her guard. "As a matter of fact, *Eave Queen Apondra*, I am here to present a gift from my kingdom to you on your birthday." He motioned for two of his attendants to step forward, both of similar dress but with shaved heads bearing a thin strip of hair running along the crown of their heads. They presented a leather box to their leader, who carefully reached inside and produced a small matching leather book, no larger than his hand.

"What is this?" Apondra unfolded the pages, each one blank, but a different color, with flowers and leaves pulped into the fibers. "It's so intricate, and so beautiful!"

"It is a journal, Your Highness. In my kingdom, the dreams and wishes of women are revered, and my queen wishes you to have this, to write your story beginning with your birthday today."

Apondra stood, spellbound, until the academic synapses in her brain could connect all the clues. "Why, you're King Qimmah! From the Kingdom of South Islands! And your wife is the queen, of course!"

Diggins aligned herself shoulder-to-shoulder with Apondra. "A king who slings his words of childbearing when his queen is not present? You are a shameful ruler!"

Qimmah knelt again, only this time to Diggins. "My Lady, shield maiden of the lobatorium, in my kingdom, the queen wears the crown on the throne. We greet all royalty of foreign nations by offering ourselves in marriage. It is a symbol of conquest by peace, love, and the bonds of parents and children."

Apondra placed her hand under Qimmah's chin and gestured for him to rise. "You see, Knight Diggins, the unified kingdoms of the South Islands were also abstainers from the great wars of men and lobfolk. They negotiated the final treaties alongside the crayfolk, our brethren from the south. Your brethren, that is." She winked at both. "And we are forever grateful. So, I must endure this ritual every time you visit, isn't that right, King Qimmah?"

"Now that you are the Eave Queen, yes, every time." He placed the journal back into her hands. "But this, yes, this is your gift. Your father has bragged of your literacy, and we look forward to you filling this book. It will become a treasure worth more than any trinket we could bring you." He raised a finger and flicked a coin to the lobfolk merchant at the table behind him. "Speaking of trinkets, I almost forgot to pay for this, for my wife." He reached into his shirt and revealed a tiny silver lobster pendant. "Do you think she'll like it?"

"I have one like it myself," she replied, revealing her own charm around her neck. "Here." Apondra untied her cord and handed her necklace to Qimmah. "Two pendants. One for you, one for her. And a reminder of our kingdoms' shared cooperation." She placed her hand over her now bare neck. "Lobfolk believe that jewelry is like a barnacle, a living thing that moves from host to host. It is a good omen to give it away to one who will take care of it."

Qimmah leaned in close, as if to kiss Apondra on the cheek, but instead whispered in her ear. "I still have trouble discerning the male and female lobfolk, Princess. Can you—"

Apondra held up a slender finger to his lips. "Females? Thinner claws. Fatter tails. But as you are well-versed in diplomacy, as a king, you can always ask one of your guards to, you know, ask on your behalf. Lobfolk do not take offense."

She bid him good day and continued toward the library, proud of her first accidental diplomatic encounter. Diggins shuffled behind her, now making her presence much more obvious as Apondra's bodyguard.

"I will have to stay closer to you now that you are officially the Eave Queen, Your Highness. I am used to slinking in the distance like a long shadow as per your father's wishes. And I apologize for—"

"Nothing to apologize about," Apondra laughed. "I appreciate that you have receded in the past so that your watchful eye did not become a hawk nesting on my head, but now, we'll adjust and adapt. That's what a wise ruler should do, right? Adjust, and adapt!"

Past the main merchant square, opposite the great hall of the king, Apondra caught her breath. The steps into the library loomed before her. The long single slabs, individual stones brought by workers a century ago, were chosen for their unique gentle curve, allowing the lobfolk tails to not drag as they ascended. As a child, she would run at the stairs, leaping as high and far as she could to count how many steps she could clear. Today, she contemplated her record, now at six steps, and instead chose to walk one at a time, behavior befitting a future queen.

The inside of the library foyer housed the legendary armor and valiant weapons of past champions before leading to an anteroom of indices, cabinets of meticulously organized and notated cards for each of the books. Beyond the cabinets, worn tables of varnished pine, and a long counter of ash and swamp wood, a staircase led down into the earth and to the endless volumes of books where Apondra would lose herself for hours. As she stopped in front of the counter, a lobfolk with white-shelled limbs and an ivory head dutifully dusted the armory, as he did every day before auditing the indices. His pink eyes flashed from antiquity to antiquity, his mouth moving as he spoke to himself with a high-pitched muttering. He rubbed the sleeve of his faded blue-gray robe on the corner of a glass display case.

"Excuse me, gentle sir," Apondra said in a singsong voice, "would you know where I could find the head librarian? He's a rather annoying fellow, loves to brag about all the things he's read, and I hear he once stole a cow."

The albino lobfolk paused his task and scratched his head with his duster, a bundle of fresh willows. "Well, I heard he was invited to a monarch's birthday party but instead he drank a flagon of wine to knock himself out so that he wouldn't have to tolerate a blathering princess." He tossed the duster at her head. "Happy birthday, Appy!"

Apondra rushed forward and leapt into her best friend's arms. Diggins shook her head and picked up the duster. "Must you do this every single time?"

"Oh, Diggy, let us have our things!" Apondra laughed. "Maybe someday you'll have a best friend, if you smiled once or twice."

"My brother is my best friend," she scoffed. "There are so many lobfolk children outside the castle in the village, but each day my duty involves the safety of the two overgrown children." Diggins bowed. "Your Highness. *And Ken.*"

Ken rolled up the sleeves of his robe and fluttered his duster against a large square shield, dented with deep scratches but otherwise undecorated. "Apondra, it's time," he said with a flourishing antenna display, "for a quiz!

Name this please." She loved his pop quizzes, and she clapped her hands as she spouted her answer.

"The Bounty Shield. Named for the defense of the weak harvest during the sixteenth tidal cycle. The drought had stunted the crops, and it was decided to protect the food so that the young would not starve." She pointed her finger into the air to emphasize her next point. "This disruption to the ecosystem goaded many hungry herbivores into attacking our crops, which then attracted their predators, the omnivores and the carnivores."

"Keep going."

"The farmers asked the lobatorium, specifically the Legion of the Nines, to protect them from predators during the final week of harvest. The Bounty Shield was passed from hero to hero of the lobatorium as the great weasel Hammerhiss slithered through the high grasses. He was on his way toward the final crop of wheat, and also the hares and birds fighting with the farmhands as they gathered the last of the grain. Then, Hammerhiss attacked! The lobatorium fought, and, as each hero fell to the dirty giant predator, the next hero used the shield to hold the line until Maka the Bold arrived.

"And tell me about Maka the Bold."

"He was a strong lobfolk, but new to the guard. He applied defensive tactics and rallied the remaining fighters to protect the farmhands, and then charged Hammerhiss, with his shield leading the way. He fought with his last limb to fell the great beast and won. But it cost him his life."

"Good," agreed Ken. "And …"

"… a painting of the feat hangs in honor over the throne of Abbasdah, a reminder that we are to fight to the end for our future." She lowered her head and sighed. "Such an adventure."

Soft footsteps approached from behind. Apondra turned and saw Diggins staring deeply into the crevices of the artifact.

"He was of my family, Maka the Bold." She thumped all four of her fists against her chest and then clacked her long, thin claws. "His bloodline lives."

Apondra nodded. "Yes. His bloodline lives in you, good knight." She immediately felt the hollowness of her words, knowing her father's bloodline died with him. Abbasdah was her father, but she was not his kin. Her excitement for her birthday overshadowed her existential peril: what right did she truly have to rule these people, these lobfolk, a land of history and heroism and duty into which she merely "arrived" one day?

"Appy?" Ken touched her shoulder, then leaned close to her ear. "You're drifting. Again."

"Again."

"Things?"

"Yes." She cherished the intimacy and trust of their single word language as best friends. They met officially when she was barely five years old. He was ten, but already in training as a junior librarian due to his family's wishes to protect him from cruelty and stares at his albino shell. They bonded fast as two outsiders, and she worked to keep pace with his ferocious ability to learn. Only they themselves were allowed to call each other the mocking names of their conditions, lessening the blows of the real world. He squinted at her.

"I know that look, soft shell."

"I … am not sure. I don't know what is ahead for me." She rolled up her sleeves before crossing her arms. "I am going to sit in the royal court today."

"And you have doubts."

"Yes."

"Do your best, that's all you can do. And in the end, that's all anyone expects you to do, especially your father." He leaned forward and tickled her forehead with his antenna, his best attempt at a kiss. "Good intentions, good deeds. That's what defines a good ruler." He stepped back and spread his claws wide. "Come over here, Diggins! Share in the love and give me a hug! Then tell Apondra what a good ruler she'll be!"

"No." Diggins crossed her upper arms and rested her lower hands on her dagger handles. "And yes, my Eave Queen, you will be an excellent ruler. I know this." Diggins looked at her feet. "I see this every day in your growth."

Ken smiled and clacked his claws. "Is that a compliment from the grumpy knight? I think it is, Appy!" He puffed his chest, skittered back behind the display case, and produced a large box. "My friend, my eave queen, when you are done with your royal birthday proceedings, I have, in here, a new book which we shall read together! Happy birthday, Appy!"

"Thank you, Ken!" She kissed him on the forehead and saluted Diggins as she skipped out the library doors.

Chapter 2

The Courtyard and the Library

APONDRA SCANNED THE vendor stands from atop the library's porch steps. Her favorite lobfolk vendor, Dell P'Kah, came every other day with his table of sea sweets and salty kelp chips, fresh from his roasting pans. Although the merchants usually set their wares and goods in the same locations, it was common for their booths to rotate to accommodate new and temporary vendors from the northern trading routes. She skipped down into the square and inhaled the mixture of meats, fruits, flowers, and awful stinky cheeses, searching for a lonely whiff of his treats.

"There!"

A shot of sugary cupcake tickled her nose. She spun around a fish vendor and saw Dell, carefully arranging his cakes with three hands, his fourth hand preoccupied with stroking his short antennae.

"Where do I put the ham and butterscotch cake? Hmm. Ah, good morning, Princess Apondra! Or should I say, happy birthday, Eave Queen! Oh, I have just the right delectable for you!" He reached under his assigned table for the day and retrieved a folded white cloth. He unwrapped it with devilish eyes, revealing a small, red, square cake. A new smell captured Apondra's attention.

"By the seas, what is that?" she said, reaching for it without asking. She caught herself being too greedy, too *childlike*, and folded her hands in a proper gesture. "May I try that?"

"Of course. I made just one, to test it. If you like it, I'll bring full trays starting next week. 'The Eave Queen's newest delight!' That's how I'll brand it!" He proffered the spongy pastry. "It has heavy vanilla and buttermilk, which, might I add, is rather hard to procure from the kyloe cows, and I used a special pollen to tint it red." She bit into the moist confection, noting the exquisite new combination of flavors. "It's like a … soft cloth … I imagine this is what fine silk would taste like, if one could eat a scrap that fell from one of the trader boats." She licked her lips to gather the errant crumbs. "Or perhaps the taste of … velvet."

"Ah, yes! That's what I'll call it! Red *silk* cake!" She offered a coin, but he shook his head. "This was a sample, a gift, and also an honor for the Eave Queen to taste! Your smile is payment enough, Princess."

"You've been saying that for ten years, Dell!" She slipped the coin under his tablecloth, number-side up for luck and prosperity, as he turned to grab another tray of cakes. She knew he would find it later when he packed up for the day, as he was a neat and tidy baker without equal in the entire kingdom.

She licked the sweet oils off her fingertips as she bounded up the wide grand stairs of the public hall, each long step, like the library, slightly bowed to accommodate the lobfolk's hefty bodies and stubby tails. With her sugar rush now pulsing through her blood, she found the hop-hopping of her locomotion an invigorating joy, one last time before adulthood. Her excitement welled in her chest thinking of today, to finally sit next to her father for the royal court and hoping that she could find at least one case where her intelligence would prove useful counsel to the subjects. *Her subjects*, she reminded herself. She reached inside her bag and withdrew a piece of curved coral wrapped in a spiral of white ribbon, her official tiara, and placed it on her head.

The guardsmen opened the two wide wooden doors bound in thin bands of iron, and she thanked each of them individually as she slowed her gait. A bit winded, she quietly tiptoed along the side of the hall, then up to the dais, a single-step platform at the far end. The king had proclaimed that the old dais was too high and projected an air of distant superiority, but the single-step design he commissioned would establish the roles and rules of a subject and ruler without condescension. She wished that someday she could be as thoughtful as she slid into her short-backed chair to her father's left. The vizier sat on his right, his royal logbook and seagull feather quill at the ready.

Knight Diggins rang the commencement bell, and the first of the assembled lobfolk stepped forward, a farmer in his apron, but also his formal cap, shaped like an upside-down bowl woven of dried stalks which he removed before the king. He spoke softly and pleaded for help repairing a stockade fence for his sheep, as his son and daughter were both ill. He held up a broken pincher claw, a reminder of his work ethic. King Abbasdah nodded.

"Request granted. One soldier will be dispatched today. And I will send herbs tomorrow to aid in your claw regeneration."

The next requests fell into a similar vein; a farm's broken millstone, a mariner family's fishing nets lost in a storm, a grain miller's waterwheel that needed to be moved upstream, and a dispute between two neighbors over a fallen tree across their property line. Apondra relished hearing all these stories, little flashes of life outside the walls of the king's court and the outlying fields of their tiny kingdom. She had visited outside from time to time, but the daily life on the farm, or travel beyond the forests, somewhere *out there*, fertilized the seeds of adventure. If a good ruler fixes the issues brought to the court, then a *great* ruler must be proactive and venture forth into the world to prevent an event from occurring, Apondra concluded. She imagined her father must be bored with such small matters, but his age now prevented him from going forth into the kingdom. He was still a great ruler, she concluded; he always flittered his antennae as a blessing to each of his subjects after granting his judgment and his aid with a genuine happiness earned knowing that he could help.

And how could he memorize all their names? Apondra repeated the details of each subject who presented their grievances to the king. He treated the entire kingdom as family, and by proxy, these were her cousins and aunts and uncles now, nieces and nephews from the further coasts and further fields. The vizier, scribbling madly on his seaweed paper scroll, documented the requester, issue, task, and proposed resources, grumbling every so often as he made a mistake and scrambled to dip his quill into the ink and scritch-scratch over an erroneous entry.

The grievances would run for a full two hours, as per the public schedule, with all citizens miraculously attended to by quick clarifications and swift judgements of the king. Apondra slumped, wondering how she would fare if she were thrust onto the throne and adorned with his crown. She adjusted her coral tiara. Practice, she deduced, was her father's power, seeing no shortcut to his trove of wisdom. Another ring of the bell indicated the formal end of the event, and any remaining lobfolk filtered out through the doors. The hall now sat mostly empty, save the royals and their attendants on the pedestal.

"Well," the king sighed, "did I do a good job, Apondra?" He laid a hand over hers and closed his eyes, his antennae fluttering over her cheek. "And what was that wonderful, sweet aroma I detected on you? Another of Dell's treasures?"

Before she could respond, a chaotic clattering exploded into the hall.

Two lobfolk, dressed in cloaks woven from thick brown yarn indicative of the northern mariners, rushed toward the king. His guards stepped forward and were met with no resistance; the mariners immediately stopped and bowed. One of them, the assumed elder due to his size and weathered claws, spoke.

"Good King Abbasdah, Eave Queen Apondra, my name is Korren, and this is my son Stikker." He looked to the vizier. "I'm sorry, Grand Vizier, I do not know your name."

"I have no name, as vizier of the court of Abbasdah." The vizier crossed two of his arms, the others at the ready with his writing implements. "You may continue."

"Well then. Greetings, *Grand Vizier*. We have come from Ribbed Beach. We have an urgent issue that cannot wait." Korren bowed again, then stood with a labored breath, shaking small grains of sand from his skirting and tunic. "If we could bend your antennae."

"'Urgent' is a word that is invalidated by overuse and abuse," the vizier scoffed.

"Let's hear their request," proposed Apondra. The vizier tilted his head. The king nodded.

"Thank you, Eave Queen," continued Korren. "A large sea creature, we believe a whalekin, has washed up dead on our shore—"

"This is not 'urgent,'" interrupted the vizier.

"It has been eviscerated by the jaws of a larger beast," said Stikker, glancing at Apondra, then back to the vizier. "We know of no creatures larger than a whalekin, aye, nothing in the sea even comes close to their size, or the size of our vessels. And, as a result, all our mariners are fearful to staff their bob-boats and set sail."

The vizier folded all four of his hands. "*This* is urgent."

The king stepped down from the dais and placed two hands on each of the mariners' shoulders. "If this is true, yes, quite urgent. A mere clawful of days of lost fishing at this time of year can cause a significant impact on our supply." He lowered his voice. "Has anyone been hurt or killed?"

"Nay," said Stikker. The younger mariner hesitated and then continued. "Not yet. Not that we know of. But we know the largest of our deep fishery bob-boats is missing, and another is due back tomorrow. If this sea beast is still present, I fear for their safety, as well as our harvest of fish and seaweed."

"Father," Apondra said, "I've never heard of such an event." She scratched her head, almost tipping her tiny crown. "Could this be a rogue whale?"

Abbasdah ran his fingers through his antennae. "Perhaps a pack of orcas? Or another aggressive whale? We can see if we can dispatch a harpoonist team."

"Your Highness," said Korren, his voice receding, "with all due respect for your wisdom, this was not caused by any beast that any of our village have ever encountered. Nothing in my lifetime on the sea could have caused such an injury to a whale. It was like a wolf taking a bite out of a rabbit."

"Or a boat," said Stikker. "The round hulls of the bob-boats are made to slip out of the jaws of most whales." He held his hands out, as if grabbing an imaginary ball or pumpkin. "This was something much bigger." He crushed the imaginary sphere.

"Apondra," called the king, "your afternoon studies are now to research the largest sea beasts in the library. Gather all you can." He nodded to his other counsel. "Vizier, check the mythologies."

The mythologies? What use would they be? Apondra parted her lips, then reconsidered her inquiry. This was an unprecedented attack, something *very real and very large* had killed a whale, and their largest fishing boat was missing. Surely, the mythology tomes would be useless; there was no such thing as a sea serpent, or any creature larger than a whale.

She needed facts such as anatomies, hunting patterns, prey and predator relationships. This was her specialty; she now had the very important job of applying logic to the problem and took a moment to rethink an immediate action.

"Father, what can we offer these mariners now?"

"For now? Light food after their hurried journey, of course, but they can make it back home to their village before supper. I will dispatch a first watch in the morning to Ribbed Beach; six of our best swimmers on the harpoonist team will stand at the ready in case we need to rescue anyone from the boat that is yet to return. And perhaps our spear marksmen can be dispatched as well to provide a presence and convey to the people, and to the Ward of Ribbed Beach, that we are taking this seriously. Then, Apondra, after your research, I will decide the next step." He gestured to one of the guards to accompany the mariners through a side door to a smaller supplemental dining hall. "And let us provide these two lobfolk with extra meals to bring home to their families. We can provide that comfort as well."

When the doors had closed behind the visitors, Abbasdah sat down on his chair. Apondra curled her legs underneath her skirt as she settled on the stone tiles of the floor in front of him.

"I know that look, Father." She watched as his claws slumped on his shoulders, his eyes downcast, his mouth half-open. "You wear a wonderful mask in front of the people, but now I see the face of worry."

"I do worry. There are burdens of the crown that I pray you will never know. The soul of every lost lobfolk is the responsibility of whoever sits in this chair. I pray for the safety of the missing vessel, not just for the potential impact on our food stores, but for the affected families." He lifted the metal ring off his head and placed it in his lap. "Apondra, head now to the library. I'm afraid we will need to postpone your official birthday ceremonies. Your task is of high importance, for if the most remote possibilities are true, we are all in terrible danger."

She raised an eyebrow at his last words. "I'll do my best, Father."

"Ken, where are you?" Apondra ran through the hall of antiquities in the library foyer and with a triumphant swing tossed her leather book parcel onto the floor. Ken leapt up from behind a wooden cabinet, spilling a list of index cards onto the floor.

"Can you please enter like a civilized lobfolk once in a while?" His white hands quickly scooped up his cards. "This will take me all afternoon to reorganize!" He placed a handful of cards on the table and nodded to the open door. "Hello, Diggy."

"Librarian. Hello. Again." Diggins nodded as she entered before setting herself onto a stool next to the door. "Apondra has me running like mad today, so pardon me for sitting."

Apondra rushed over to Ken as his stack of cards again slid off the table. "I'm sorry! Here." She lifted the edges of her skirt to create a make-shift basket. "Put them here and I'll lay them out on the tables." Apondra did not want to waste any time in her quest for information, but her father always taught her to be polite and make amends when she caused irritation to others. Her mere existence was a source of consternation for a handful of the lobfolk, but luckily Ken knew what it meant to be an outsider in his own way. As an albino, he drew the stares of the commoners when he ventured out from his self-imposed internment in the library years after the death of his parents.

"So, you're very early for your evening studies," Ken huffed. "Are you following an especially impulsive curiosity?"

"I'm on a time-sensitive research mission for my father. I need to look up anything we have on great sea beasts."

His antennae stood straight up. "Sea beasts, you say?" He placed the cards on a table and walked over to the public display for the great relics and antiques. He stopped in front of the Bounty Shield and paused. "Sea beasts."

"Correct. A whale, very large whale, washed up on the Ribbed Beach. And a large, er, bite had removed its belly, according to the villagers. Father seems to think this is of urgent importance. I need to find everything I can!"

Ken's focus remained on the shield. He crossed all four of his arms and circled the relic in thought. "An unknown beast. Let's put all the possibilities on the table, figuratively and literally." He glanced at the index card pile. "Is it possible that we are dealing with something previously thought of as a myth?"

"That's what the vizier is proposing. I think he may have a bit of salt-water in the brain. He's looking in the royal mythologies. But why should we think of a myth? This happened, this is a real event! A real creature that did this, that's a fact."

"Because, Appy, myths are often based on fact, even if it is a misperception of truth that cannot be understood in the moment. And large sea beasts have been distorted by myth and legend since the dawn of time, across all cultures that work and know the waves."

"Alright. Let's think for a moment." Apondra began to sift through the stack of cards. "The old zoological texts."

"But why those, Appy? They're just the old fables of misinformation before we studied and completed the current encyclopedia of animalia."

"Because, my fellow lover of academic research," she said with a wink, "if we are looking for something that could be based on a myth, wouldn't it make sense to chase the old accounts? Maybe there's something that was missing or misreported and thus ignored. Even whales were not fully understood until first studied." She scratched her temple. "And hunted."

"You're a clever girl."

"Only when presented with a good academic challenge! Now let me into the lower archives, I just need you to unlock the tunnels." She glanced over her shoulder, waiting for Diggins to stand.

"I don't think you'll need me to be your shadow while you're with your friend," Diggins said, placing her spear against the wall. "My duty is also to judge character, and this one sure is quite the character."

"A joke, Diggy? Careful, you might develop a charming personality." Ken whisked over to a large iron ring on the wall, adorned with a set of ornate silver keys. "Today certainly is full of surprises. Appy, if I may reframe your investigation for you, in the interest of critical thinking, what exactly are you investigating?" He pointed the key ring at her with authority. "You seem so set on making this an intellectual adventure."

"Ken, I told you, I'm investigating a large sea beast!"

"One that attacked a whale." He tilted his head and raised an antenna, goading her for an additional deduction.

"Yes, a large beast capable of attacking something the size of a whale." She paused, her face flush with a mixture of embarrassment and excitement. "Sea vessels are also the size of a whale." She pulled the cuffs of her sweater over her hands.

"Yes, that's what I was beginning to think here. You seemed so focused on this being an animal, but for all we know, this could even be some kind of new warship. This is a puzzle, but one I'm invested in. I'll grab the nautical disaster records and see which ones coincide with any mysterious or unsolved reviews by the Board of Mariners. Here." He handed her a wooden rod as long as her arm, topped with a shell wrapped in thick, soft cloth, and then the key ring. "Use this pomp to turn on the lights, and then go deep into the tunnels. Whales are of course at the end of the alphabet in the far shelves of the zoological section. I'll be along as soon as I clean up these cards."

"Of course. Thank you!" She grabbed the implements and hastened to another staircase tucked in the back of the hall that descended into darkness. She reached up with the pomp and tapped gently on a large water-filled cube of glass hanging in the stairwell. The bioluminescent algae inside awakened from their slumber, as did the small eel who lived inside with them, providing a symbiotic circle of plant, animal, and animal waste. The greenish-yellow glow lit the way down to the bottom, where she tapped the pomp on another water lantern next to a door.

Apondra had only ventured here a handful of times, as the archives contained many old and fragile items that were deemed too important for her younger hands to hold. The massive room was almost as large as the footprint of the entire castle and courtyard; in the chaotic centuries long before her birth, the vast structure was built as a hiding place, especially during the first war with humans, so that the mothers and spawn could be safe during birthing and maturation. Her father laughed when he explained it to her, and her questions about what she would do someday when she had a child. Two of the old breeding pools, stone-rimmed inserts in the floor, wider than she was tall, remained in the front of the underlibrary beside two long empty tables. She glanced briefly at her reflection in the pools, brimming with more glowing algae, and thought of the silent springs that kept the water full and cool, and the children born here in past eons, one of which may have been an ancestor of her father. A rightful heir may have been born here, she thought, as her reflection broke with the thrashing of a small eel, igniting new bursts of the yellow and green glow.

The books were arranged by Ken and his predecessors into several sections: mathematics, science, grammar, artisan craft guides, botany, and zoology. The lobfolk insisted on keeping old and outdated books, so that the new texts could always be reexamined with a critical eye as science, literature, and history advanced, but were rarely revisited. Ken also noted that the redundant and outdated texts were a failsafe in case of another war or disaster. The historical logs occupied the majority of the underlibrary and were presented in the front. Apondra dove deep in the dark aisles toward the bestiaries.

"Volcano shrimp … vultures … water whisperers … ah, here we go!" She gently lifted the large tome for whales. Next to it, another hefty book labeled as the second volume also caught her eye. She grabbed that as well and hastened back to one of the long tables by the birthing pools.

"Let's see, predators, food chain competitors. Hmmm." She paused as a dark thought passed over her imagination. "Let's not rule out 'cannibalism' from this. That's what Ken would do."

As she spoke his name aloud, the clacking of his feet echoed from the stairwell. His stubby tail thunked on each step behind him as he hurried. "Apondra! Apondra!"

"Ken! Ken!" she replied mockingly with a smile. "What on the seas are you so excited about? I've barely opened the books. Please don't tell me you already have a solution."

"I had a thought, a fear in fact." He rushed past her with rhythmic percussive footfalls to the bestiary. "What if it's both?"

"Both? What is 'both'?"

He returned with a tome, one she knew well from her childhood. The cover depicted a large skull with a terrifying beak and immense incisors. *Animals No More* read the title. He splayed it open and shuffled the pages madly.

"Princess, I was thinking about the possibility that something man-made took down this whale. It seemed unlikely to me as we haven't seen many innovations in sea warfare for centuries, nor the hostilities of an armada."

"Go on."

"Then, I thought about someone pretending to be an animal, like disguising a ship as a sea beast. Unlikely, very unlikely." His antennae danced in a frenzy with his increasing excitement. "Whale bones have been found on the beaches for centuries, found in old crafts and relics from all kingdoms, yes?"

"Yes," she said, grabbing one of his free arms and tugging at his elbow. "Please, tell me what you're thinking! I'm nearly dying from suspense!"

"I'm showing you my thought process, my academic accomplice. Now, it dawned on me that whales have no predators that we are aware of, at least in the modern world."

She yanked at his arms that worked through the pages of his book, barely holding in her laughter that concealed mild annoyance. "Ken! Tell me! What are you thinking?"

"What if the animal is something that *was* real but is now a *myth*?" He slowed his pace as he leafed through the yellowed pages. "An animal we only know from legends and fossil records? What if something extinct is no longer extinct?" His mandibles stretched into a smile, and he turned the book to her face. "One of these."

She stopped and studied the pictures she had seen as a child. Apondra enjoyed imagining the great deceased beasts, the immense reptiles and mammals, the precursors to their smaller, modern-day versions. Even the lobfolk had an ancient ancestor, the large paleolobsters that broke off from the common lobsters that still lived in the sea. Her fingers traced the images on the page, not of a lobster, but another sea beast that lived on through much smaller modern-day heirs.

"A turtle?"

"A saltwater snapping turtle, Appy. But one of immense size, feasting on whales, it would be a match if one still existed. And they did exist long ago. Even now, our river snappers can grow quite large when left unmolested." His eyes twinkled. "We can claim we know what may lurk in the furthest depths of the Great Sea, but we must admit a possibility of uncertainty to modern academic arrogance. We do have the claims made in the old legends, after all."

"You don't suppose a rogue beast like this is still … alive?"

"We cannot rule it out. The lack of evidence—"

"—is not evidence." Apondra rested her hand under her chin. "Hmm."

"And we must be humble, as scholars," he said with a dramatic pause and a twinkle in his eyes, "that we know more today than we did yesterday, but not as much as tomorrow."

"You know I love your brain very much."

"As do I, yours." He grabbed a stack of clean papyrus from a shelf, a baleen quill, and a bottle of ink. "Now you get to work on these, write what you can. I'll gather the notes on nautical disasters. I assume you can read them tonight or on our journey tomorrow."

"Our journey?" Her eyes widened.

"Appy, we could be among the first to lay eyes on evidence of a previously extinct beast! We must travel out before dawn. Why, imagine if some evidence is chewed away by hungry sea gulls, or a merchant who finds a giant tooth or claw that he wants to grind to a powder for some love potion concoction or cure-all!"

"But what about Diggins?" She crossed her arms, frustrated at the thought of her own guard objecting to their investigation or, simply, slowing them down.

"That's why we'll leave before dawn, and," Ken said, glancing deep into the bowels of the subterranean room, "I have a plan."

"Alright, then. An hour before dawn, I'll meet you in the hall upstairs." She kissed him on the forehead and grabbed her notes. "Adventure! Academia! Oh, this is what I've dreamed of doing for so long!" She read a distracted look on Ken's face, as his pink eyes darted from side to side. "What's wrong?"

He stared down at the birthing pool, the algae swirling and glowing as the eels splashed in a playful frenzy. "Oh, you know. A day away from the library is one less day to read. There's never enough time to read everything."

Apondra tucked her fresh notes into a folio of thin bark wrapped in coarse cloth, which she then placed into her satchel. The water lamps dimmed slowly as if to announce her time in the underlibrary had expired. She leapt up the stairs, two at a time, and bounded into the library's main hall, Ken slowly climbing behind her as he fumbled with his own book satchel across his body. Diggins had disappeared from her sentry in the room, instead replaced by the vizier, sitting on the stool, a worried look on his face full of frittering antennae and a long wooden spear in his hands.

"My Eave Queen, I have requested a full guard for your escort."

"Where is Diggins?" She moved toward the window next to the door but was blocked by the vizier's claw.

"Guarding the door from the outside," said the vizier, standing slowly. "A small unsatisfied crowd has gathered." Apondra scoffed.

"And this requires me to have an escort?"

He held up his hands in defense. "This is not a pleasant assembly. Word has spread too fast of an 'attacking sea beast' and some of the dissenters in the populace, especially the older lobfolk, have noted that this coincides with your 'birth date' and assumption of the full title of Eave Queen. Larold, the Ward of Ribbed Beach has freely disseminated this information, as he's no fan of your position in the royal court." The vizier sighed, then clutched the spear closer to his chest. "I deal in politics, as well as legends, and unfortunately the populace still wields both to fuel the fires of superstition and false narratives."

"Wait, is this my fault?" The commotion outside grew, voices jumbled into an indiscernible chant of mistrust.

"Well," he said, flipping his hands left and right, "some are whispering that you're an omen, some say the sea beast is an omen, some say you are both omens, but nonetheless, your protection is now our primary concern."

He lowered his voice again and leaned in close. "It only takes one claw to tear the net and spill the fish, so to speak. And I swear to Azcalaw above that I will not let you be torn."

"I'll talk to them," she stammered. "I'll speak to them." She saw denial in the vizier's face. "I'll tell them what we're doing and explain how I'm serving them. I'll reason with them!"

"Reason is not appreciated by those who worship a blue lobster god and demand action," he said in a whisper. "Your father is ill, your legitimacy is questioned, and some would rather take all of this as a sign to appoint a new king, apparently as soon as possible." He breathed heavily, his voice straining with a rare tinge of fear. "It is dangerous for you to leave through the front door without a full escort in the short term until we can disperse these grumpy old lobfolk."

"Then how am I to leave when the lobatorium you have ordered for me is not here yet?" She stomped over to her bag and rustled through her books, unsure what exactly she was looking for, then dumped the contents on the floor. She shook her head and began to repack, leaving a few duplicated items such as extra scarves and writing quills out of her slightly thinned-down kit.

Ken reached over to the display in the center of the room and picked up the Bounty Shield. "Ahem. It is in accordance with our laws that the highest non-noble who is not a member of the royal court shall be acting head of the Eave Queen's royal guard in times of peril." He mounted the shield onto his large left claw. "And apparently, I am the only non-noble, my Eave Queen, and the vizier is of the royal court." Ken exhaled loudly. "And Diggy is outside handling the cranky old claws." He handed her his satchel full of papers. "The vizier's probably better with a spear than I am, anyway. And taller."

Apondra swallowed hard. How could any of her subjects, no, her countrymen, be so upset with her? Was she so isolated and insulated to not see how her presence could be such a disturbance? An omen? She looked at Ken, her friend, standing behind the mighty shield but cowering as a row erupted outside the library's external door. The vizier stood, hands on spear, his misshapen and scarred claws extended in defense on each side of his body. Her existence was now putting her friends in peril for reasons, or lack of reasons, she could barely comprehend. She felt afraid, for the first time, of her subjects.

"What are we doing? Are we just walking out through an angry mob?" She crisscrossed the satchel bags on each shoulder across her body. "Or hiding until our escort appears?"

"Neither, my Eave Queen," announced the vizier. "I believe Ken here has a familiarity with what I'm proposing. We are leaving through the library's darkness."

Ken lifted the shield slightly in front of his face. "That's how we were going to sneak out tomorrow morning." The vizier crossed his two arms that were not brandishing his spear. "Sorry, Vizier, we were going to sneak out to Ribbed Beach."

"I will scold you properly when you return," the vizier said with a scowl. "For now, we focus on escape." He grabbed Apondra's hand and pulled her down the stairs, followed by Ken, back into the darkness.

Only one of the birthing pools still glowed from the algae, casting light a few feet into the rows of tomes. The vizier took the lead with his spear, followed by Apondra, and a huffing Ken in the rear, clenching the Bounty Shield. *Lobfolk are not built for stealth,* she noted as they clicked and clacked deeper into the dark. They traveled further into the bowels, beyond the zoological guides and bestiaries. She could barely see, only halting when she ran into the vizier's back.

"Oomph," she gasped, "why aren't we lighting our way?"

"Because if we do," said Ken, glancing to the head of their pack, "they will know we were here by the fading algae. Am I correct?"

"Yes. Hush, please," hissed the vizier. His fingers tapped along the stone wall, the tone uniform until the dull clicks deepened, indicating a hollow. He pushed at the wall, and a pure dark abyss opened before them, a secret passage. Another soft tap and a tiny glass ball, barely bigger than Apondra's hand, glowed with a green and yellow light. "Only the royals even know of this passage. And Ken, I assume." He tapped the algae lamp again. "Remarkable. I hoped they would still be alive."

The root-lined passage reeked of wet rotting leaves and moist clay. Small puddles of standing water spilled over the centuries-old stones each time Apondra missed as she leapt from rock to rock on a path intended for the strides of four-legged lobfolk. In some sections, pillars of living wood extended from floor to ceiling, formed by trees older than the castle itself. By Apondra's internal sense of direction, the group now crossed under the outer walls of Castle Homarus. She wondered when the last time was anyone passed through this escape tunnel, perhaps during the last war against humans or the brutal blizzard of last century. She turned and saw Ken sprinting to catch up.

"Sorry, I was closing the secret door. I pushed a piece of soft root into the frame to, you know, jam it in case someone tried to find and open the door."

"Good," said the vizier. "Now, listen carefully. When we emerge, we will be a distance from the castle, somewhere in the interior of the forest to the north beyond the King's Plain. I will return to Castle Homarus and let the king and Diggins know where you are, and where you are going. Hopefully the crowd outside the library will begin to disperse out of boredom, and we can formulate the formal response to your whereabouts, as you have 'officially taken the initiative to investigate the whale carcass' because you're not an omen." She detected a smirk on his face in the low light.

"Right," Apondra panted, already short of breath from the hasty escape. "And where are we to actually go?"

The vizier reached his claws up and pressed on a wooden panel. It yielded to his effort, and he motioned for them to ascend.

"My Eave Queen, you are still going to investigate the whale carcass at Ribbed Beach, of course." Apondra and Ken exchanged glances. The vizier pointed back up to the subterranean escape hatch. "There's no better ruse than the truth. Let's hope some of the villagers there will be a little more receptive to your presence since they were the ones who actually asked for aid. And what better way for you to prove your devotion to your lobfolk subjects and that you are not an omen of ill tidings than by being proactive?"

"Right, and what about me?" Ken asked.

The vizier handed his spear to Ken. "You said you're the guard, so guard her. With your life." He tapped Ken on his claws. "Diggins will be right behind you once I relay all of this to her. In the meantime, just keep the Princess within a claw's reach at all times."

Chapter 3

To Ribbed Beach and Back

APONDRA'S BOOTS CRUNCHED the first crisp leaves of autumn as she crept quickly and carefully over the white stones and moss of the woods. Her familiarity was with the trails and roads, not the underbrush. Ken's shield led the way as he held the rogue brambles and branches out of her way, stopping occasionally to assist her as she pulled a thorny vine out of her sweater. Her leather slip-ons and thin socks, already damp from the mosses and mud, would need to be removed as soon as possible once they found a place to rest. The darkness of night had descended quickly, and the lights of the castle torches were far behind them now.

"Everything is fine. Fine, fine, fine," muttered Ken. "You didn't bring anything to eat by chance, did you?" Apondra shook her head, then broke into a wide smile.

"Oh, just a moment! I have sweets!"

"Fantastic. We'll set up a little camp past that embankment and see what we can ration."

After counting her cupcakes, four, and splitting one in half, the two companions settled down into a rut between two large rocks. Each placed a bag of books under their heads, and Apondra curled up against Ken's arms. She removed her shoes and socks, then tucked her feet under her skirt for warmth, curled against her legs. She watched a tiny glowworm inch across a twig a bit further than an arm's length away.

"Ken, why would people … hate me?" She had trouble forming the words, and hearing them escape from her lips upset her enough to birth a single tear down her cheek.

"There are many reasons why."

"What?" She spun around, mouth agape. He drew back in surprise.

"My words were not chosen wisely, Appy. What I meant was, some people will find any reason to not like something different from themselves." He twiddled his white fingers.

"Because I am a human?"

"Well, that is one reason. You are royalty, but you are also not of the royal bloodline. You have people kowtowing to your education so that you do not have to work the fields or toil at sea." His voice trailed. "I am an albino. I am from a well-off family of scholars who have never broken a claw on manual labor. I have nice small accommodations because of my job."

"And you take care of my education."

"Yes," he sighed. "I cultivate and prepare the individual that some say is an illegitimate heir." He smiled, his pink eyes barely visible in the dark, but she could see a sheen forming on their surface. "Some lobfolk don't understand how I could possibly call you my best friend." He wrapped two arms around her shoulders and pulled her in close, followed by two hands gently on her waist, the firmness of his shell pressing against her sweater. His pale claws arched forward, almost entirely enclosing her as they wrapped over her back. "We don't choose our friends. They just become part of our lives."

"Inseparable."

"Indissoluble." Ken glanced away.

"Good word," she said, stroking his scaly hand.

"Thank you." He reached back and pulled his cloak around her.

"Ken, do you know how to make a fire?"

"I'm an academic, not an adventurer." He looked around their make-shift bedroll of branches. "I would need a flintstone, or some sticks and twine, maybe some lint…"

"We'll make do, I suppose." She exhaled, searching for a trace of her breath in the faint moonlight. "We'll be fine for tonight, but let's put that on our list of things to learn."

The pair of scholars rose early, just before sunrise. After stuffing dry leaves into her shoes and donning her damp socks, Apondra shared a tiny breakfast of cupcake with Ken and continued north to the village on the main road. They veered off the path at a faded road sign that pointed to a long wooden split rail fence made of slightly rotted mismatched wooden beams marking the perimeter of the Ribbed Beach hamlet. They stepped over and under the beams and immediately faced a foul smell blowing from the sea. Beyond the tree line, the rocky sands came into view.

"That's quite an interesting perfume, Your Highness," Ken joked. She sniffed at her sleeves and nodded in agreement.

"I could use a proper bath," she said. "But I believe that poor fellow up ahead is the cause."

Her suspicions were confirmed as they emerged from the tree line, unnoticed at first by the pack of lobfolk surrounding the enormous gray mound on the sand, dotted with seagulls picking at the exposed abdominal cavity of the once mighty mammal. Further along the beach, a bob-boat of anglers landed, stabilizing its large spherical hull with long pontoons the length of a tall spruce. The sailors on deck lowered the pair of sails while a group of anglers emerged frantically from the surrounding surf, carrying large but mostly empty nets over their shells. Apondra pressed her hand against her brow and squinted against the bright sun above and the beams reflecting from the sea below. The anglers kept their distance from the dead whale, one of them waving his claw and cursing into the wind.

"Yuck," exclaimed Ken, holding two hands over his mouth, "what a horrible scene. And those anglers should be pulling heavy nets full of fresh catch. Those nets have barely one barrel of fish in total. I'm sure this dead thing and whatever killed it have spooked their harvest. And their effort." He opened his notebook and scribbled with a piece of charcoal. "If they miss just one month of netting fish, this could cause a severe rationing in the food supply for this ward." He scribbled again. "The math gets much worse the longer it takes to resolve this."

One of the assembled lobfolk held his claws in the air, waving for their attention. "Who is that?" he shouted, then suddenly bowed. "Eave Queen, welcome to Ribbed Beach! This is quite an unexpected visit." A small group repeated his gestures, while a handful of the crowd moved to the side, crossing arm over arm over arm in disgust. A green lobfolk, smaller in size than the others, spoke with discontent.

"Eave Queen, I request on behalf of the monitoring council of Ribbed Beach that you depart. Your royal presence has been noted; however, we would prefer to side with caution. This omen, here," he tapped the dead whale with his claw, "is not of our choosing. But we can choose to ask you to return to Castle Homarus. May Azcalaw protect you on your travels home." She saw one of his hands reset to his belt, next to a short sheath. Apondra opened her book satchel and presented one of the tomes.

"Good sir—"

"Councilman Teelok."

"—Councilman Teelok, we just ask for a few minutes to walk over to the carcass, inspect the damage against the information inside this book, and then we shall return as we came. We ask for no hospitality or resources." She licked her lips and tasted the salty mist. "Except perhaps some water." Teelok handed her his hipflask with a neutral expression on his face.

Ken proffered his own book. "We shall not set foot off this beach, if that will alleviate the superstitious ones in your village."

"And who are you, *albino*?"

"I am Ken, the librarian and historian of the court." He dropped his spear and shield as he adjusted his booksack.

"Not much use in a fight, eh?" Teelok placed all of his hands on hips. "Hurry then. I can offer no specific protection from any rogue actors."

Rogue actors? Apondra's mouth hung open, aghast at the implications. Who among them would risk civil penalties for impeding her mission or harming her? She hastened her pace, glancing over her shoulder at the far away outlines of lobfolk just beyond the head of the beach by the entrance to the town's square. Ken nudged her along and they arrived in front of the whale's body.

She had only seen a whale in person from a distance, once, during a tour of the lighthouses. At one stop, she had witnessed the majestic spectacle of a breech as a family of humpbacks spun and leapt out of the water in their timeless dance. It was difficult to completely gauge their immense size from that event, but even then, she could understand how the whales and seafaring folk needed to keep their distance for the sake of each other's safety.

Apondra placed her hand on the side of the carcass' bulk, leathery and slick with an oily residue. She pulled her sweater over her nose as she peered into the body cavity, careful not to let her skirt touch any of the viscera. Ken scribbled notes on a paper with his charcoal as he flipped the pages of his reference book.

"Appy, look here. The internal organs are gone, most likely due to a combination of the attacker's appetite, the attack itself, and of course the drifting across the sea." He looked back and forth, then back and forth again between the whale and the tide. "Hmm. Sea levels dragged it here. After mid-nightfall if the seasonal tide charts are to be followed. If it came up during the day's high tide, the townsfolk would have seen it coming in. Therefore, based on the report of the mariners at council yesterday, this was here for about a day and a half. Maybe two days total since it was attacked. Any longer and we would see more decay and scavenger damage." He pointed into the cavity. "No crabs or our lobster brethren made their way in while it was at sea. A very short timeframe between the attack and the present."

Apondra learned so much from his tutoring about critical analysis and problem solving, but now she saw it in action; a rush of excitement despite the gravitas of the circumstances. She poked at an exposed bone with her own charcoal writing stick. "This? What's this?"

"The rib cage. You know that, Appy."

"No, I mean this section here."

She dragged her stick along the rib, stained pink over its earthy yellow hue. The charcoal slipped into a groove that ran down the rib, growing in width and depth, until it reached the bottom where the rib had been sheared.

"Hmm." Ken placed his book in his satchel and retrieved a different tome. "That rib damage is consistent with the ragged skin and muscle tissue." He pointed to the opening and shooed away a gull pulling at the gristle. "Teeth usually puncture first, Apondra, then tear. This is more of a 'gripping' first and then a tear."

"The attacking creature held it first?"

"Yes and no. It held it, but with its beak." Ken lifted his book and showed her an illustration. It resembled a turtle, its shell craggy like a broken cliff face, its mouth a pointed and nasty snout ending in a beak. The artist had depicted the jaw as open, revealing no teeth but a slinky and wretched tongue. The front legs showed powerful slightly webbed phalanges ending in hooked talons. Ken pointed from the claws in the picture to a set of punctures by the head and tail of the whale. "This, dear friend, is a snapping turtle. And *that*," he said, pointing to the open whale body, "is indeed the work of a very large one."

"How large?"

"How big is a myth?"

Teelok interrupted their investigation. "A myth, as they say, is as large as the mouth of a liar." He gestured to the trail leading back to the woods. "And an omen is as large as the cavernous depths of a scared mind." On the opposite side of the beach, a small cluster of a half dozen lobfolk marched toward them, carrying fishing spears and garden rakes.

"We should be leaving soon," Apondra said, her heart pounding in her chest at the sight of the mob. "Are they going to attack me? Tell them we are going back!"

"I think they are more interested in … *them*."

Teelok leaned close and grabbed her arm. He pointed wordlessly down the beach at three shapes, lobfolk, dressed in matching blue robes. Their antennae protruded from under their azure hoods. They raised their arms in unison at the sea and clacked their claws.

"Who are they?" whispered Apondra.

"Zealots," said Teelok. "A cult from the far north, just below the Kingdom of Ice Lake. This," he said with a sweeping gesture toward to the dead whale, "is something they prayed for."

"They prayed for the evisceration of a whale?"

"No," said Teelok. His voice shook as he looked out at the sea. "They prayed for *that*."

Apondra looked out over the blue-green water, into the relative calm of the sea. A giant boulder bobbed in the gentle waves, a rocky and jagged protrusion like a tiny island unattached to the sea floor covered in dark browns and deep green blotches. It moved slowly, parallel to the shore, moving from the south back north. For a moment, it paused, floating on the waves, then suddenly sank, diving below the surface with a large frothy splash. She gasped.

Teelok turned back to the cultists as the trio raised their claws and shouted undecipherable moans of joy. The lobfolk on the shore screeched and screamed, gesticulating wildly at the ocean.

"Teelok? What was that?" Apondra said. She drew shallow breaths as she tried to reconcile the image from Ken's book with what she just saw.

"Something that made those blue fellows very happy, but from where I'm standing here next to you, it looked like a very large shell."

"A turtle shell," she said, her breath barely escaping her lungs as fear mixed with excitement. "Wow."

Ken sidled up to her, his face deep in the pages of his book, and poked Teelok in the shoulder. "What did I miss? And who are those fellows down there in the blue robes?"

"We must get back!" Apondra grabbed Ken's claw and pulled it. "A turtle! A giant turtle! In the sea! And those cultists! Something very bad is happening!"

"Slow down, Princess!" Ken followed as she stomped up the beach toward the woods. Teelok passed her and tugged her toward their exit path. She fumed.

"I am a member of the royal family! You do not get to handle me like this!"

He whispered in her ear, his eyes wide. "I sincerely apologize, Eave Queen, but this is not a safe situation for you and your albino guardian here, and a complicated one for myself, as my moves are under the watchful eye of the Ward of Ribbed Beach, Larold. I need to show strength to my village and escorting you out is, sadly, one way I can do that."

"I don't understand!" She struggled but did not break free from his hand. Ken's footsteps continued behind them in his attempt to catch up. Teelok relaxed his grip.

"Princess, listen carefully, please! I instructed my son to leave a basket of food just inside the forest, and a fresh blanket as protection against the chill. I beg your forgiveness for my handling of you." He finally released her arm but continued to walk next to her. "I have a duty to my townsfolk. *Please.* I accept any punishment that the king levies against me once you report my handling of you." She turned to look into his eyes, sad but stormy. "Please help me keep up this appearance for now, for the sake of the village, before the fishermen and farmers divert their energy from providing what little food they can to gossiping and planning insurrection based on superstition." He broke away. "Those blue-robed cultists are going to make things more complicated to keep the peace."

"Who are they, Teelok?"

"Trouble. Trouble does not need a name."

She nodded almost imperceptibly and quickened her steps to outpace Teelok, as she found herself now comforted by his quiet words. Apondra slouched, portraying sullen body language to help his ruse.

Their steps quickened from walking to jogging as she and Ken reached the woods, a spark of fear hastening their footfalls. Once they were beyond the beach, the path took a sharp turn, where a small green lobfolk waited next to a tree. He held a brown wicker basket containing a folded parcel of what she assumed was food. He handed this and a rolled blanket wrapped in coarse string to her and bowed. "We wish you well." He held out a small silver ring on a necklace made of twine. "For you, Eave Queen. It was my mother's before she was called by Azcalaw to the Undersea."

"Your hospitality and deeds will be recorded in this tale," she said with a smile. "But I cannot take your gift. Your name, young lobfolk?"

"Teeron, my Eave Queen."

"Thank you, Teeron, Son of Teelok."

Ken nodded toward the next turn in the path. "*Eave Queen*, this way please. We must bring all of this to the vizier." He peeked at the basket. "Except for whatever's in there. I'm quite hungry."

Beyond the twisted, leafless branches of the lower tree limbs arching over the road, Apondra and Ken spotted the pack of royal lobfolk guards in marching formation. Among them, she first recognized Moe Murr, one of the lobatorium in his shimmering chainmail, acting as the leader, scanning the woods with his dull brass monocular. He placed the instrument into his belt and waved to Apondra. She returned his salutation with a sigh of relief.

"Moe! You are a sight for sore eyes! We traveled to Ribbed Beach, and then we saw the—"

"Eave Queen, *Princess*, we must make haste and return you to the castle. Your father is worried sick!" His normally firm demeanor was replaced by a pleading she had not seen in him before, as one of the stoic members of the high guard. Ascension to his position required not just a valiant battle personality, but a shrewd mind that could separate emotion from duty. His eyes hardened as he looked beyond him to Ken.

"Good day, *bookkeeper*."

"Hail, Moe. Good to see you. How is your sister?"

"*Diggins* is fine. She had a skirmish with a few farmers outside of your little bookshop—"

"It's a library—"

"Ahem. Your place of employment. But she's well, thank you. She was sent to Ribbed Beach to follow you, so she should be on her way back once she discovers you have already come and gone." Moe tapped his monocular spyglass with nervous fingers. "Ken, you will stay in the rear of the procession. We have little use for your lack of prowess in the front." Ken slumped his shoulders and retreated. Apondra looked back from her spot, third behind Moe and another guard, and shrugged.

"I don't see why you need to be so cruel sometimes when you provide orders." Apondra pouted.

"I am not being cruel," said Moe, scanning again with his monocular, "I am pragmatic. Is that the correct word, Your Highness?"

"The 'bookkeeper' could confirm that," she said dryly as she caught a slight smile stretch across Moe's face.

"I apologize for not being as friendly as my sister."

Apondra held back a laugh. "That's alright."

"Nonetheless, Your Highness, we are going to take you in through the front gate. It is not stealthy, but since you are within our formation, no one shall dare to slander you."

Slander? How have the subjects so rapidly escalated this false narrative of me being some kind of omen? I must talk to the vizier as soon as possible!

The small caravan quickly approached the mouth of the merchant trail and exited the forest. The walls of Castle Homarus rose a short distance away across the King's Plain, the mighty trees embedded in the stone walls now visible. Before the gate, a small group of no more than a dozen lobfolk turned to face Apondra's company, bearing trowels, fishing rods, brooms, and other tools of their varied trades.

"Not much of an arsenal," Ken chirped from the rear. "But please do make sure that I'm not skewered by an errant soup spoon or breadboard."

"You will be fine, bookkeeper," bellowed Moe. He channeled his voice to the crowd. "One side, with haste! We return with the Eave Queen, Princess Apondra." A lobfolk carrying a pair of tongs stepped directly in front of the procession.

"She is not our queen! She is an omen now that her nature has been revealed! We will not yield!"

Moe stepped in front of the protestor, headbutted him, and stood his ground as the protester fell backward onto his tail. "Yield."

Apondra gasped and clutched her chest as she witnessed Moe's treatment of the peasant but was rushed inside before she could protest. *How could he do this to a fellow lobfolk? They are our kin!* Her heart shrank.

"I am no one's kin," she whispered.

Inside the castle walls, her guards hurried her inside the main hall. As soon as he saw her, Abbasdah rushed to Apondra and embraced her with all his arms, his great claws clasped like a shield behind her back. "My daughter, this has been a very surprising and trying ordeal. So much is happening all at once." Apondra looked up into his eyes, hollow under his crown. A tiny flake of shell poked out from underneath his royal headpiece.

"Are you molting prematurely, Father? Is this from stress?"

"A coincidence." He lifted the crown, revealing a spidering cracking that dulled the shine on his head. "As you know, I am … not as young as I once was." He attempted a frail smile.

"Oh, Father!" she cried, running her hands along his smooth face, up until the rough edges nicked at her fair palms. The vizier stepped out from behind the throne to wave away a small cadre of guards. Ken ignored the command, only stepping back a few paces, then bowing to the vizier who now spoke gently to the princess.

"Apondra, we all know that he has not been in the best health for some time now. We have seen the signs, which is why it has been urgent to keep up with your royal education. We are not in crisis," he said, his antennae drooping as a sad look swept over his face, "but appearances of distress can sometimes be all it takes for the populace to hurtle toward chaos."

Another guard unit ran through the throne room and out into the courtyard. The vizier paused, glanced at Ken, and raised an inquisitive antenna. Ken raised his own in response.

"Vizier, what is going on?"

The vizier held up his hands to shush Ken and stared into the distance, cocking his head. "Come. Quickly. I hear a commotion coming from the castle gates."

Apondra, her father, and Ken followed the vizier up a side stairwell that led out to the walkway at the top of the bulwark. They traversed the length of the side of the castle as best as they could, the vizier holding Abbasdah's arms as they walked, and then turned to the platform above the main gate's great arch. From the battlement they could see across the clearing of King's Plain all the way to the woods. They waited for Abbasdah to reach them before anyone spoke.

"Father, there!"

Apondra reached out, pointing to the small group gathered midway between the castle and the merchant trail that bisected King's Plain. Her finger shook; a dread of the unknown, greater than her imagination of the beast that felled the whale, flooded her spine with a dry chill, icicles into her veins. She strained to make out the details of the dark form not yet in focus.

"Father! What is that?"

"This is most unexpected, Apondra. Everything is happening all at once."

"What do you mean? What is that coming from the woods?"

The king sighed and placed a hand on each of his daughter's shoulders. "Men."

Chapter 4

Desperate and Disparate Emissaries

"HELLO THERE!"

At the midpoint of King's Plain, a man in weathered chainmail and a short deep blue cape climbed down from his paint horse, splattered with pure white and honey brown spots. His five companions dismounted on his signal: four armored soldiers in matching blue and white capes and tunics with chainmail armor, sheathed longswords on their waists, and someone Apondra surmised to be their squire, wearing less armor and a shorter matching cape of the same color blue as the rest of the party. The squire handed a blue bag with noticeable weight to the leader and waved to the castle with a short flag of blue emblazoned with a white outline of a swan in flight.

"Father, they seem friendly," Apondra said. She waved back from the wall before her father held up his hand at her.

"Daughter, this is a moment of extreme diplomacy. We haven't been visited by soldiers of men since …" His voice trailed off in recollection. "It has been a few years."

"But we have seen men, many humans have visited often. Why King Qimmah was just here!"

"Yes, but we haven't had visitors like this, *soldiers*. And not from the Kingdom of Swan across the sea." King Abbasdah crossed his arms and puffed his chest. He looked to the vizier who matched his pose.

"My king, they are armed, but no ranged weapons. Wait, I do see one longbow attached to one horse's kit. One archer." The vizier relaxed his posture. "This is not the negotiation entourage of a war party."

The contingent of men split, the four soldiers staying with the horses as their leader and the squire approached on foot. Apondra peeked over the lip of the wall and saw a cadre of six of their own lobfolk soldiers break off from the defensive line, headed toward the supposed ambassadors.

"Halt," hailed King Abbasdah to his lobfolk. "Let them come closer to us."

The humans closed the distance to the castle with a steady gait. When they reached the lobfolk guard, the leader paused and held up his hands. His squire leaned over and unfastened his master's sword belt, the sheathed weapon dropping to the ground with a clatter. The unorthodox presentation gave pause to the king's assembly. Apondra peered over the battlement as her father addressed the visitors.

"Humans, I am King Abbasdah, Monarch of Castle Homarus, Keep of Stone Woods. This is my daughter, Apondra, Princess of the Shore and Eave Queen to this kingdom of lobfolk. Tell me your names and your business, please."

The leader cleared his throat and beamed a broad, warm smile, running a hand through his wavy brown hair. Handsome, *for a human*, athletic, and younger than she would expect for someone holding a rank of seniority for his party, he bowed and nodded to his squire to follow his lead.

"Good King Abbasdah, I admire your diplomacy and forces. I am Gunnar Brekke, First Cavalier of the Kingdom of Swan. This is my squire and hand, Tomas. We come with urgent news and a request for your … counsel."

Counsel? Apondra found the word enigmatic. She tugged at her father's sleeve and whispered in his ear. "This is odd, yes?"

"On multiple levels," sniped the vizier, eavesdropping. "My king, I suggest Apondra and myself go to meet this cavalier. You are well guarded from them up here, and bringing a human along in our group may confuse any ruse he is using, if he is indeed here with some deception."

Abbasdah looked to his daughter for approval. "Do you think this is a wise idea, Eave Queen, to meet this human directly?"

"I think so, yes. Because of what the vizier said, and because I should …" She searched for a word or phrase to prop up her confidence; nothing came to mind. "I should do this."

"Then I shall remain. Apondra, you are young, intelligent, and eager, but remember that, for now, the vizier is much more knowledgeable in the rules of diplomatic engagement. If he gives an order, follow his recommendation."

The princess and vizier descended the stairs to the gate. As the great doors creaked open, just wide enough for them to slip through, she noticed the squire standing at attention, his face almost childlike, smooth skin, blue eyes, and brown hair like her own. He looked to be about her age, but her estimates were not to be relied on by her own admittance; she had few examples to measure him by, only the aged traveling merchant men she had met who visited the storefronts in the courtyard.

The cavalier strode forward, removing his gloves for a handshake. He was older than the squire, but now that Apondra saw him up close, she could tell their ages were not too far apart. His eyes sparkled with a more radiant blue, his features firm and accented by a thick jawline. She noted his shoulders were broad, and he looked … *strong.* His muscles were larger than many of the merchants she had seen in the market, his belly not as round from too many salted meats and seaweed sugar cakes. She blushed as she shook his hand and caught herself staring.

"I am Apondra, Princess of the Kingdom of the Lobfolk." She cleared her throat. "Eave Queen, officially, as of my birthday yesterday."

"It is a pleasure, Princess Apondra," he replied with a wink. "Happy birthday." She blushed, forgetting she had been introduced by a shout from the wall minutes before. The vizier broke their meeting.

"Good day, Gunnar Brekke, First Cavalier of the Kingdom of Swan. I am the Grand Vizier. And you are an uninvited guest, but a guest, nonetheless. Speak your quest that has brought you to our land. *Uninvited.*" The vizier crossed his pairs of arms, drawing the attention of the squire. "Are we your first lobfolk, young man?"

"Aye," said Tomas. "Well, in formal introduction, face to … face. I have seen your kind from a distance." He smiled, tugging at his tunic slightly to even the hem. "It is a pleasure to meet not only you, but someone of your prestige, wizard."

The vizier smiled. "Vizier is not the same as wizard, but I am just as formidable in the war of the mind."

Gunnar smiled. "Noted, wise Grand Vizier. We have urgent information and as I said, we request your counsel."

"Then speak, human."

Gunnar gawked. "So we are not going inside? Or rather, somewhere with perhaps a chair and table set for even an informal meeting? I have important items in my parcel to show you." He held up his blue bag. "Important *evidence.*"

"Of what, Cavalier Brekke?" asked Apondra.

He opened the bag and withdrew a large piece of metal, a rough cylinder with a circumference larger than an apple, bent into a U-shape the length of his forearm, sheared on one side. She received it and almost immediately dropped it, the weight far heavier than she anticipated.

"I'm not sure what this is," she said. "It appears to be some kind of broken … device?"

"Eave Queen, and Vizier, that is an anchor, or rather, *was*. It was attached to one of our merchant ships that returned to port badly damaged. While moored offshore, a great beast attacked the vessel and severed the anchor. Tomas, the drawing, please?" He motioned to the squire who withdrew a leather tube from the bag. Tomas opened the end of the cylinder and revealed a parchment.

"This is a drawing made by one of the sailors, Your … Majesty?" Tomas stuttered.

"Apondra is quite alright."

"Apondra," Tomas repeated.

"*Princess Apondra* will suffice," said the vizier.

She unrolled the parchment and gasped. The vizier leaned over her shoulder and traced the lines of the illustration with his finger. A long, hooklike beak adorned a sinister face. The head sprouted from a large round shell, knotted with horny growths and spikes across its back. One claw rose out of the ocean, a fist ending in webbed claws. It was as she had seen in the old tomes: a monstrous snapping turtle.

"When was this?" asked the vizier.

"Twenty days earlier," said Gunnar. "And we are not a kingdom with a large navy. We are mostly of the land, but our merchant ships and small fleet are now grounded. We lost three ships already, the fourth damaged as you saw from the anchor fragment." He swallowed hard, a trace of fear crossing his previously brave face. "A war ship, equipped with harpoons and poisons, left port to hunt the beast. The pieces washed ashore the following day."

"Survivors?" Apondra asked. Gunnar only shook his head.

"We will starve if we cannot access the sea for trade, and we have lost a disproportionate number of able-bodied sailors. Our travel here on a swift boat large enough to accommodate us and our mounts was a risk, but necessary as ordered by our king and queen. We seek your knowledge and help."

"These are not concerns to us," snapped the vizier. "Your situation is unfortunate, but you must make do. We cannot provide more than three wagons of food stock to assist your kingdom as a gesture of goodwill. We have our own to take care of, you must understand."

Apondra opened her mouth to speak, but the vizier held up a hand. She was confused how he could be so cold when her father had always ruled with the edict of helping all, helping anyone in need, that the needs of the many were always more important than the individual. Or in this case, would not one tiny kingdom want to assist another if they had the means, especially if they shared a common adversary in the sea between their lands?

Tomas cleared his throat. "Good Vizier, we are not asking for food, or even arms." He glanced up and down at the vizier's anatomy. "And you have more arms than we do, so to speak. But we seek information."

Apondra raised an eyebrow to Gunnar.

"What my squire is asking is, can you provide us with access to any texts or lore regarding something, or someone that we think can assist our pursuit of knowledge? We have no written records to fall back on, only the elders of our counsel and their oral history of a dark time, an era when the sea was ruled by a beast of the same description. A beast of the same nature decimated the fleets of many kingdoms, including yours, we are told by the legend keepers. The sea beast was felled by a mighty … warrior."

"Entity," corrected the vizier.

"Correct, an … entity. We are told of the name of a great entity, not entirely of your world, not entirely of ours. A great warrior, some would say a god, who slew the sea beast."

The vizier gestured to examine the anchor fragment. He rotated it in his hands, running his fingers over the severed ends. He handed it to Tomas, as well as the re-rolled illustration.

"Cavalier. You speak of Azcalaw. Our hero of myth. Many worship his name, but he belonged to no kingdom. Your legends of him are yours, and ours are ours."

"Yes! Yes! Azcalaw!" Gunnar's eyes lit up. "We would ask for your help in finding him and pleading for his aid. Surely if this sea beast is allowed to continue its path of wrath, it will doom both of our lands to a slow death by starvation!"

"You know of Azcalaw?" Apondra grabbed Tomas by the hand. "Do you know the songs? All our children do!"

Tomas politely removed himself from her grasp. "We have, um, done some research. Gunnar?" He turned to the Cavalier. "Am I saying too much?"

"No, my friend." Gunnar lightly held Apondra's hand but looked to the Vizier. "At the time of the attack on our ships, a person of interest was seen down at the docks, a *lobfolk* of interest. Dressed in a blue robe, his face painted with garish lines."

Apondra gasped. Gunnar continued, unaware of the true meaning of her reaction.

"Vizier, our guards took in this lobfolk, and he told us of the return of your folk hero, Azcalaw. He assured us that Azcalaw was no myth, but sleeping on this side of the sea until he could be summoned back to the world."

"That's quite a leap of faith," the vizier said, pointing a claw in the air. "Taking some fanatic for his word."

"I was not privileged to interview this lobfolk. Our king and his vizier met him in private, and our vizier deemed the words to be true."

Apondra swam through the questions that rushed through her head. Did the vizier of the Kingdom of Swan use magic to interrogate the lobfolk?

What would that entail? Why did her own vizier lack magic? What kind of evidence would prove a children's story to be fact? She reflected on the encounter at the beach, and the surreal images of the whale corpse and the giant turtle shell beyond the waves.

She placed her thumb under her chin and spied Ken on the fringe of the assembly. He shrugged and held his claws in the air. She nodded.

"Vizier," she said, "why not? Why can't Azcalaw be real? If he has persisted in variation of legends in their kingdom, across the sea, couldn't it be based on a root of fact?" The vizier ignored her and turned his back.

"We cannot help you, Gunnar. You may enter the courtyard with your men. Leave your horses outside, please. I will have them attended to. We shall feed you and your men, as it is the polite thing to do, and we are a polite kingdom. Then you shall leave."

Apondra stood, crossing her arms and turning up her chin at the vizier. "Azcalaw is a character from children's books. I read the tales as a child; he is a mighty hero." The vizier held a steely gaze. "Are you now admitting he is real? Can we not search the archives and provide our visitors with information, at the very least?" She held his forearm, her eyes darting back and forth in plea. "Why will we not help them?"

The vizier continued his silence as they entered the courtyard; the king's staff already appropriated a hewn oak table and benches for the visitors and the royals. The vizier clapped and pointed, demanding sustenance from the selected vendors who remained in the courtyard. A familiar face, Dell the baker, brought a tray of his new cupcakes and loaves of potato bread and placed them on the end of the table, smiling at Apondra. She grabbed the vizier by the arm again and pulled him away from the impromptu feast.

"What secret are you keeping from our visitors, and from me?"

"I will not hold secrets from you," he said, his eyes shifting from her to the guests at the table. "I promise, as you will come to understand, that there is a time and place for any secret to be drawn into the light."

He placed his hand over hers. "I promise, Apondra. When the time is appropriate. *I promise you.* And if there is one lesson you need to learn from this diplomatic event, it is that a kingdom asking for 'aid without trade' is either hiding an ulterior motive …" His voice faded. "Or the danger is larger than any political boundaries."

The squire and cavalier moved through the small crowd to take their seats. Gunnar placed his napkin on his lap and his gloves under his seat, with Tomas mirroring his actions.

"A feast undeserved, I thank you," said Gunnar. Apondra saw his politeness and her heart … skipped a beat? Was this the feeling of sudden swoon she had read in the old romantic novellas obtained from the kingdoms of men in the library? He was handsome by her own admission, the feeling of wanting to look at his features, to talk to him, to be near him. She seated herself on the opposite side of Tomas. He glanced at her and nodded before starting to whisper.

"Your Highness, my role as squire involves observation on behalf of my master, and I have been observing *you* observing *the cavalier* quite a bit." He averted his eyes from her, glancing at his folded hands. "He is handsome and without a bride, but his heart is not available. At least not for now." He unfolded his hands and set them on the sides of his plate. "I … look out for my master. And I just wanted you to know so that we can focus on this mission without distractions." She noticed his own tiny smile and his glance darting up to her face. "A princess is distracting by her nature, especially, well…" His voice trailed off for a moment. "You have very nice hair."

She blushed and fluttered her eyelashes. "Your … observations … are appreciated. And thank you for such a compliment." Apondra snapped back to the task at hand as the dull thudding of bowls heaped with hot breads bounced onto the table, interrupting the small talk of the gathering. *Duty, I must focus on my duty,* she affirmed, presenting herself as a royal authority and diplomat, and attempting to pass on recommendations like a good ruler. *Like my father.*

A loud bell rang twice. The attendant lobfolk around the table stood still, prompting the humans to stand in unison. King Abbasdah descended the staircase from the front gate as they rose, nodding and waving. The vizier rushed to his side, and Apondra watched him whispering the details of their meeting that she was sure her father eavesdropped from atop the battlement. Abbasdah shuffled more slowly than usual and sat at the end of the table, next to Gunnar.

"Cavalier Gunnar, esteemed representative of the Kingdom of Swan, I must agree with the counsel I have received. We are not going to be able to provide you with any information."

"Father, why not?" shouted Apondra, slapping the table, surprising both her guests and herself. "You raised me to value honesty and disclosure, in diplomacy and in family. What is the truth regarding Azcalaw and why will you not speak of him?"

The king sighed, deeply. He looked across the assembled group and picked at the cupcake on his plate, scraping off the iced topping until the raw red spongy cake sat naked in the center.

"When you uncover a thing, you cannot hide it ever again." His voice changed to a low raspy growl. "And to reveal the truth of Azcalaw is to perhaps unleash a greater darkness in an attempt to squelch a lesser one."

"But father," Apondra cried, "this makes no sense. Azcalaw is a folk hero, a hero that comes in our darkest hours! Why is this tall tale so dangerous?"

The vizier held a cautious finger and pointed it at Apondra. "Because it is based on facts. And buried under those facts is the complicated truth and heavy prices paid by generations before us, generations of man and lobfolk."

Gunnar stood. He drummed the table with his fingers, surveying the assembled lobfolk and humans. "We, men of my kingdom, have no choice. Many will die over the winter if we cannot supplement our livestock and crops through our mariner's trading ships, and for those who survive starvation, we will be no match to stand up to any other kingdom with its eyes on our access to the sea, our land, and our treasury." His cordial tone darkened. "We do not have designs on your land from our side of the sea, you know that." He glared at Abbasdah. "Our ancestors, mine and yours, had the wisdom to end wars for our mutual benefit, and the Kingdom of Swan honors its truces. We have done so with your kingdom for decades. And, we should expect likewise from you, Your Highness, to honor the word of man."

"Do not insult us, Cavalier," said the vizier. His claws rattled above his head. "We may look strange, like simple beasts to you humans, but we are an intelligent and emotive society, a highly educated and moral civilization, and yes, we honor words." He looked at Apondra, her eyes narrowing as she observed the volley. The vizier continued, pointing at her. "We took in one of your own when she was abandoned, and our king raised her as his heir. We know love and compassion," he said with a huff. "This is who we are. We are lobfolk."

"Then dammit, if not for us, do it for her." The cavalier's voice softened again, a compassionate return to his calmer demeanor. "I apologize for my outburst. Even in our kingdom, *your* act of fatherly love is told as a lesson to our children, teaching them empathy, love, *family*. Did you know that? Remember why, King Abbasdah, you chose to save this child and make her your kin." His gaze did not stray from the princess. "Because your heart was filled with love, and empathy, and you saw a greater good in the world around you. Please, help us." His breath rose and fell with loud gasps. "We have lost men and women in our attempt to slay this beast. Families have been broken by our feeble attempts at attacking it. *Families*. Please."

A silence fell across the table and muted the courtyard. Abbasdah sat back in his chair, unmoving. "You appear to be a man who cannot hide deception when he lets emotions get the better of his speech. I can see why your king and queen sent you specifically to make this plea, Gunnar." Abbasdah lowered his head. "I hear your words. You are a man of honesty." He twitched his antennae in thought. "I hear them, indeed. So let me state, in front of man and lobfolk, that I am making this decision. It is on my shell to bear. Vizier? Collect the journals of lore." He sighed, glancing at his daughter. "*The shellbound texts.*"

The vizier stood, his face tense, antennae rigid. "I oblige, my king."

"Daughter, bring these men to the guest lodge. Squire, you may attend to your horses and corral them with our cattlemounts. I will designate one of our lobatorium guards as your aide. All others shall remain in these walls for the interim."

The soldiers and Gunnar followed a pair of guards to a lodge entrance in the rear of the courtyard. Apondra caught Gunnar glancing over his shoulder, a quick smile that she returned in kind. Her father's hand on her shoulder startled her.

"He seems to be a good man, Princess. But be cautious."

"Do you not trust him?"

"I trust him. That is a man of honor, and he is motivated by compassion. It's your young heart that you need to watch."

She blushed. Apondra hooked her arm into her father's and walked to the grand hall and throne room to await the vizier's return.

From her bedroom in the high tower, Apondra would often look out the window, across the courtyard, past the bulwarks, and into the outlying village on the side of the castle, observing the thatched roofs and smoky chimneys of the lobfolk, and imagining the evening chores inside the homes. She loved to catch a stray whiff of some hearty stew on the breeze, or a spicy sauce's fragrance peppering the wind, but tonight she smelled nothing from their hearths. A few lobfolk walked together to the longhouse, presumably for a drink while their house partners tended to their chores. Like their sea brethren, they maintained long monogamous relationships, but did not truly mate for life by some invisible law of nature. Many chose to do so, but it was also accepted to switch partners after a lengthy period of commitment. She had heard that men, humans, were similar in this way regarding marriage and love. The words of the squire bounded inside her head, that the cavalier, Gunnar, was not open to love at this time. He was handsome, and seemed kind and smart. Surely, he would have no problem finding a bride. She glanced at her desk, custom made for her size and anatomy, and the journals neatly stacked on top.

"I'll get back to you all in a little while," she said to no one, running her hand along the ancient wood frame of the window. A knock on the door interrupted her daydreaming. "Enter, please."

Ken opened the door and took one step into the room. "Requesting further entrance, Your Highness?"

"Oh hush with the formalities, friend. Please, come in!"

Ken hurried through the open door over to her desk and deposited another set of books. "This is all I could find on short notice, Appy. Very scant references to Azcalaw as a historical figure. Of course, there were several dozen books of children's poems and the like about him." He itched his white elbows, a nervous habit she observed many times when he had taken a fancy to a deep thought and dug deeper inside of it. "Do you even know what Azcalaw is?"

"A legend, a story to tell children at night, a fairy tale to entertain the scouts and merchants on their long journeys across the mountains or into the sea?"

"Well, that yes, but do you know *what* he is?"

"A giant blue lobster, or lobfolk. But not rarer than an albino, you know," she said with a wink. "We do see blue lobfolk from time to time. At least in these parts."

"If I could blush like you, I would," Ken replied, fanning his antennae. "But actually, he is quite rarer than I am. He's not just a big blue lobfolk. He's an entirely different species based on the scant descriptions." Ken reached into his satchel and retrieved a rounded-edge book, bound by two flat shells for the covers. "This is the shelltome I was told to retrieve." He scurried to her door and closed it.

"Where was it from?" She ran her fingers across the smooth pearl-like shell halves, tied neatly by fine string, like a silk spun by the sea worms from the pools by the northern shores. "It's beautiful."

"This is something from one of the underground alcoves of the library. Unfiled. And unaudited in my index cards because it is too frail to place upright on a shelf." He laid it on her bed, then picked it up, tilting his head for permission. She nodded and he set it down. He untied the string and delicately opened the pages.

"So what is this, exactly?"

"It is a book, of sorts, but in actuality it's a collection of journals. I like the word 'omnibus' if I had to properly categorize it. Anyway, this was stolen from our now brethren lobfolk in the north before we were allied, but it is not *their* journal. It is the journal of an even older line of warrior king lobfolk, and contains short passages of text, including some by humans that attempted settlements before the unification of the kingdom. I think this would be a situation where history is indeed written by the victors, but the losers had something much too important to be erased from the record." He flipped to a page in the middle and turned it for her to see. "These shellbound tomes are very rare, and often kept hidden by those who come across them. Here, please read this."

She traced her fingers under the letters of the words, square and crude compared to the refined fonts of the royal texts, but still legible:

Aught Arbor

> *I have spoken to Azcalaw! He is a terrifying beast, and yet no beast by the strength and prowess of his intellect. Azcalaw permitted me in his court, myself and four of my spearmen.*
>
> *His face is what I remember most vividly, a terrifying visage. His is not the head of any lobfolk I have seen before. A soft nasal appendage above a slim orifice lined with sharp individual teeth like a shark or sea snake. His eyes, pools of glowing white adorned with a black iris. His skin, he had skin! Patches of flesh surrounded and bound these features, all hued in light blue, and topped like a hard cake. His claws attached to each shoulder by human arms that widened from claw to torso, plated in the dark blue armor of his shell. He was no lobfolk of any kind ever seen. Dare I say, at two mounts high, he was a gigantic human, but also a lobster. Yet neither species should claim him.*
>
> *His speech was deep, a hypnotic humming that commanded even silence with his long, slow breaths. I asked him what he was, and he grasped my best spearman with one claw. He lifted him as if a minnow and threw him to the ground.*
>
> *"I am the time of time forgot. I am the place of place forgot. I am born of thought, but the mindless know me. I am beyond this world's nature."*

Apondra grasped Ken's hand and turned away from the words. "What is this thing? This is not Azcalaw!"

"Go on."

She ran her fingers slowly under each word of the terrifying text.

> *I spoke respectfully as one would to a god or demon. I asked him for aid to help us in our time of need. He sat motionless for several minutes, but I dared not move as his eyes never stopped looking*

at my own. He finally ended that eternity of fear and clacked his claws together.

"You are no more important to me than the chum that the scavengers devour. But I am bound to this land, and the sea, by the dawn of time. If the balance is destroyed, so am I. And perhaps that is the only way I can find the end of time and final rest."

A second spearman, our loremaster and vizier, stepped forward. He cast a blue dust over Azcalaw. The beast-god laughed, then severed our loremaster's head with a thrash of his claw!

"A parlor trick!" he bellowed. "I am disgusted by this feeble attempt to control my mind."

He grabbed my remaining spearmen and cracked their shells, feasting on their meat! I fled in fear and disgrace, knowing that not only had I led my soldiers to their death, but that I would return to my kingdom, a harbinger of doom.

"Ick," Ken said, shaking his arms. "I think that may be a bit of embellishment. Cannibalism of one's enemies is only seen in the most primitive villages. And why would the chronicler have stayed to watch Azcalaw snack on his compatriots?"

"Hmm." She read the words again, twisting through the author's voice to see if she could uncover something new. "Perhaps it was a survivor adding to his account, spinning a taller tale so he would not be branded as a coward for running."

"You've been reading more of the war histories than I thought." Ken winked. "Let's continue. This later chronicle is what first caught my eye. I'm not entirely sure if the author was a human or lobfolk from the north."

Aught Twice Frost

We are in the thirtieth day of the blizzard. I have seen families eat their dead. I fear that we who remain are just here to witness the end of times and document the trials for another world's legends.

I saw him today, Azcalaw! He walked through the street, his head higher than the rooftops of the vacant houses. He wore a cloak of writhing eels, each outer layer slowly freezing and dying, leaving a trail of dead sea snakes in his wake. I prayed and begged for him to leave, but watched his titanic form make its way to the ward's hall. He pulled the gate from its mounts, and after several minutes inside the hall, he left as he came, plowing through the snow and carrying a burning barrel as a torch in each claw.

I ran to the ward's chamber and saw him motionless on the floor, barely able to speak. I asked what had happened, and he spoke words I shall never forget, even if my life is to end before dawn:

"Azcalaw will save us, for he is our god king. But to pay his price is to condemn the entire county to a slow death." He then whispered a horrible task into my ear...

In the morning, I did as the ward instructed, and rounded up one hundred of our young, the youngest as instructed by Azcalaw. We bid our children farewell, never to see them again.

The snows abated during the day, and the night air rose above the ice point for the first time, ending the frost, and remaining there until the beginning of our crop season. We survived, but our souls were defeated, knowing he had taken our children forever.

Apondra ran her fingers over the torn spine where several pages had been removed. Ken gently retrieved the shelltome and tied it closed.

"Appy, those missing pages have never been found. I assume another kingdom or ledgerman wanted them destroyed." Ken stroked his chin. "Or those pages held some other intrinsic value. Hmm."

"And the children of that village?"

"Nothing of note."

"The people? The lobfolk?"

Ken lowered his head. "Gone. A lost society. While many believed it was simply conquered by the north, some say it was swallowed by the mountains. Others say it was abandoned out of fear, the descendants emigrating into the other kingdoms." He paused. "Including ours."

She placed her thumb under her chin. The words scrolled past her mind's eye again. And again. She reread the text and imprinted the words into images, each time constructing another detail. A sudden idea burst through the imaginary pictures.

"The old vizier, in the story. He had a blue dust. What was that?"

"If I told you it was magical dust, would you—"

"—call you crazy? Yes, yes, I would, if I had read this a few days ago before a dead whale washed up on the beach and we glimpsed a turtle the size of a mountain floating in the sea." She paced around her bed. "But whatever it was, it existed. In the story. It was specifically noted by the narrator. Perhaps we could try to find this magic dust, or replicate it?"

"So that we can blow it into Azcalaw's face and be beheaded? Yes, that sounds like a marvelous plan." Ken crossed his arms and pouted. "Apondra, the things we are researching are challenging the very nature of logical thought. Perhaps we're not the best suited individuals to pursue this endeavor."

"Perhaps that is why we *are* the best suited. Our collected knowledge is indeed our greatest weapon; we are logical. And literate. We are not wizards or warriors who are looking to fight our way through this." She held his hand and rubbed the thin crust of his shell that enclosed each of his fingers. "These are certainly not the hands of a knight, *Sir Ken*."

He chuckled and tucked the shellbook into his bag before he bid Apondra goodnight with a short bow. She halted him as he approached the door.

"Friend Ken, why *would* these books not be discussed?"

"What do you mean, Appy?"

"These shelltomes. They were hidden in plain sight, holding secrets."

Ken tilted his head, lifted his bag, and handed it to Apondra. "Until someone asks if something exists, does it exist at all?"

"That's quite … grandiloquent?"

"I'd rather say ominous."

He lightly tapped the bag containing the shellbook in her arms. "Why don't you keep this for now. Let's keep passing this secret around a little longer."

The morning provided little reprieve for Apondra's tumultuous mind. She could barely sleep, imaging Azcalaw as a "beast god" based on the scant description in the tome. A man and a lobster, but not a lobfolk, something more human and yet inhuman. And the size! Twice that of a steed? His head above the rooftops in the village? The details loomed larger than the images she heard as a child; there was something … terrifying … about the possible reality of a real life giant. She read tales of titans from the myths of men, but now she wondered if the seeds of fiction were sown from facts. Or was it the other way around? No matter, she thought, it was time for breakfast with their human guests from the Kingdom of Swan.

Upon descending to the throne room, she was met by a new set of smells, uncommon for the morning meal. Turkey meat and pan-seared potatoes, green peppers, and sweet apples, these were foods she often married to the midday meal, or supper. The long table stretched ahead of her, and the men from the Kingdom of Swan sat laughing and joking with the royal lobfolk butcher. She took her place by the head of the table, the men diligently asking the butcher about seasonings and preparations. *This is quite wonderful*, she thought, *a meeting of foreign lands united by cooking tips!* Apondra smiled, her attendant placing slices of hot potato bread and sweet meats on her plate. Her face turned to a frown as the vizier made his presence known.

"Clear a place!" he commanded, his arms overflowing with papers and scrolls. "This is not a social hour!" He slammed the scrolls and wooden paperweights onto the tabletop. His tired black eyes slowly met each of their faces as his voice growled. "Is no one here moved to urgency by that which brings us here together? Our shared crisis?"

Gunnar stood and carefully pushed the plates and cutlery aside. "Apologies, vizier. We are of course readying our spirits for the difficulties ahead."

The vizier huffed, antennae fluttering. "Hold this parchment down." He unspooled a large sheet of new papyrus almost as wide as his reach, stained with fresh ink blots as well as jagged lines of cartography. Another pile of smaller, older maps was laid on top by his ink-stained hands.

"What's this?" asked Apondra. She had never recalled such a frantic energy from the vizier.

"This, my Eave Queen, is the journey ahead to find Azcalaw and request his aid." He circled a castle image with his fingers. "I have been up all night compiling the old maps, combing the atlases, and researching folklore. We are here, of course." He smudged an inky mark next to an image of the castle. "And I believe the entirety of the journey needs to be somewhere here." His pointer finger drifted north, through forests and mountains, over a river city, and then circled an area in the north, beyond a small square keep at the foot of a range of mountains just below the Kingdom of Ice Lake. "None of the tales make any deviation from this region. This is the domain of Azcalaw."

The mention of the name brought the table to silence. The vizier leaned over to the cavalier, without menace but with darkening authority. "I will require your undivided attention."

"You have it." Gunnar rested his turkey leg on his plate. "Continue, please."

"I had to challenge one of the old merchant sailors late last night, one who was not keen on the visiting human presence here, in order to obtain one of the key pieces of this map. I shall not deceive you; he wanted you gone as soon as possible, and it was that assurance that precipitated his final decision to donate his oldest sea map to us, stored in his family's archives. So we should hold up our end of the bargain and leave promptly to seek the facts as well as the Temple of Azcalaw when I am finished." He stared at the cavalier again. "And your prompt departure when this is done. A deal is a deal, and lobfolk hold to our word."

Apondra detected another storm cloud in the vizier's words, his verbal lightning landing at the feet of the humans.

"Where is the king?" asked Tomas, scraping the last of his oats from his bowl. "Should he not be a part of this?"

"The king is feeling his age this morning," the vizier said, softening his tone for a moment. "Apondra, I am sorry to have passed over this in my haste and state of extreme fatigue. You can, and shall, visit him before you go. He is just slow, it is not serious, but also, he is not of mind to lead the planning after I gave him an herbal remedy. Diggins is at the king's bedside now. He is in good claws."

Tomas stood, looked to Gunnar for permission to speak, and cleared his throat. "Vizier, if I may, I have two concerns. Firstly, are we to assume you do not have the men or means to mount an attack on this gigantic sea beast in the interim? And, secondly, why should the princess come with us?" Gunnar raised an eyebrow, acknowledging the validity of Tomas' line of inquiry. "No disrespect to the princess, but what would she bring to this mission?"

"Squire," said the vizier, "we are a tiny kingdom. It puts us at a great risk if we follow the Kingdom of Swan's example to attempt an attack, as noted by Gunnar, to try to pursue this beast and suffer foolhardy losses, *as you have*, without a plan." Apondra cringed as the vizier spoke his judgement of Gunnar's land. "We do not maintain a large army of conscripts. Both male and female lobfolk share in our tasks, our work, our defense, as well as our governance and education."

Tomas clenched his fists on the table; Gunnar placed his hand on the squire's and smiled.

"Vizier, I would assure you we had a well-trained and executed naval exercise, which is why, after the failure, we knew we needed to ask for the assistance of those who most likely know the sea and its denizens better than us humans."

"Such a diplomatic reply, well thought out." The vizier stroked his antennae. "To your squire's second question on the inclusion of the princess, she is the *Eave Queen*, she is both our king's heir and of your species. That will be invaluable in possible diplomatic situations, as the king will not be able to take this journey in his given state. The council will of course take care of the daily management as needed. And, to complete my reasoning for sending Apondra, I have guided her academics and I assure you, she is the smartest *human* at this table."

Apondra blushed. She slowed her bites of her breakfast and set down her fork. She noticed the men had placed their utensils at the top of their plate when finished, something she hadn't learned from lobfolk manners. She did the same and folded her hands in her lap. Her father's health was top of mind, but these little rituals helped her place her focus in the short term on their quest. *A queen needs to separate the heart from the mind.* A light touch on her shoulder reassured her. Ken had entered and now stood by her side.

"Vizier, tell us of the journey," she said, sitting up with her back arched.

"At first glance, the route along the shore will take longer, but will be safer and more predictable as we have the most cartographical information along here." He traced a line in and out of alcoves and rocky outcroppings that dragged north. "However, time is our enemy, and you will need to utilize the inland route and merchant trails as much as possible. In the event of an emergency, the group shall move to the shore. 'Leave no doubt to the route' and you shall arrive one way or another." He placed his book into Ken's hands. "Take this, librarian."

"Vizier? What am I to do with this?"

"Take it with you; your knowledge will be needed as well on this expedition. You will need to continue the research as you travel, as I do not have the time to complete all the work on the finer details of the apocrypha and history of Azcalaw."

"I suppose I'll pack my books, then," Ken said to no one. "My cold weather cloak, my sleep blanket, my bags of tea leaves for the morning meal …" The vizier spoke over him.

"Cavalier, squire, librarian, Eave Queen. You shall take your respective units. I have already asked the market merchants to assist in preparing rations; any who volunteered goods will be given a special placement in the courtyard for the next Festival of the Moon Cycle." He rubbed his eyes. "I have not slept yet. Please respect the work I have put in, including choosing foods that are suitable for lobfolk and human tastes."

"That's very considerate," said Tomas.

The vizier glowered. "We are a righteous and equitable race." The squire shrank back in his seat. "As I was saying, the supplies are ready. Your horses outside have been fed, and our kyloes should be ready within the hour." A confused look from Gunnar led the vizier to clarify. "*Kyloe*. Our long-haired cattle steeds."

Gunnar beamed. "Well, that is interesting."

"Not to me," mumbled Ken. "I've never been on a kyloe, and I'm happy with that."

"You'll ride with me," Apondra chimed. "My life is in your hands, friend!"

"I should say the other way around," Ken replied. He glanced at his own stubby tail under his robe. "You have the option to ride a horse. I don't."

"Good Eave Queen, may I continue?" The vizier, noticeably agitated, still respected the decorum of the court. After her agreeable nod, he placed a wooden saltshaker on the square structure on the northern end of the map.

"Here. This location is the last population center of the civilized lobfolk beyond our kingdom, *Himmelhavets*, the outpost town. We shall use this as our waypoint for any final letter exchanges. I shall send information forward, and when possible, you shall send information back. Any of the deceased may be left here if for some reason they cannot be buried immediately." A cold silence from the room followed. "I am just being pragmatic."

"How much danger are we in, Vizier?" Gunnar stood and attached his cape. "I am carrying the burden of your princess' safety in my mission. *Our* mission."

"We have been told that at this time of the year, we should not see any hungry beasts starved for food or crops. Bandits and vagabonds should be minimal in the rural north. You'd be more likely to be attacked by a swarm of bees than anything else." He smiled and tapped his fingers on his claws, producing a loud, dull, *tak-tak-tak*. "And the odds favor lobfolk over humans in that instance."

After carefully rolling the maps back into tight scrolls, the vizier placed them into a leather tube and handed it to Ken. He gestured for the group to exit the hall, except for Apondra; he gently touched her forearm and whispered, "Your father awaits, make haste."

⁓

To Apondra, each step up the castle stairwell stretched further apart, each footfall louder than the beating of her heart in her temples. Now that she allowed herself to relapse from the king's daughter to her father's daughter, her thoughts raced with apprehension. At the top of the stairs, she jogged around a tight turn until she found herself in front of his ornately carved dark wooden door. She caught her breath and turned the T-shaped iron handle.

"Father!" she called as she bounded inside. Abbasdah sat upright, his lower half covered by a fine purple linen sheet. Naked of his crown, Apondra saw the flaking transparent pieces of his scalp shell, an uneven molt that traveled down his face and under his eyes. Diggins sat in a chair on the other side of the bed, her spear leaning against the wall. Apondra caught a flash of sadness in Diggins' eyes as she nodded at the princess and the king.

"Daughter," Abbasdah said in a frail voice. "I think this is just a final shedding for me, but this one has put me in undue distress." He held up his arms, still thick with a luxurious sheen on their plates. His fingers betrayed him, twitching and trembling slightly as he grabbed her hand.

"Father, please rest. I understand the shedding and molting can be a physical effort."

"The vizier debriefed me early this morning on the proposed journey," he said, ignoring her plea. "And he advised me. I am not well. Our lobfolk bodies were meant for longer years than your own, but our downfall can be swift and unexpected."

A crushing fist clenched her heart. This was too much for her, the crisis of the sea beast, some of her own subjects calling her an ill omen, and now her father's declining health. Perhaps the dissenters were right; perhaps she was not fit to rule. Apondra pushed the thoughts down, adding to the sourness in her stomach, and held her father's hand.

"Father, I can't leave you this way."

"Apondra, the many outweigh the few. This is how to lead, not rule. *Lead.* Why do you think our vizier does so much around here? Because he voluntarily takes on the burdens of those around him. Because he knows it will all be for the best when it works out. *When*, not if." He smiled, his old antennae around his mouth lightly crackling with the motions, tiny flakes drifting to the bedsheet like snow. "And what can you do if I pass away? Mourn. Laugh at the memories. Sing to the birds at every dawn that your father loved you. None of these things involve anyone else but you and your heart."

She sobbed at his words, laying her head on his bed. Such kindness and calm in the face of his own mortality, all from a father in name who rescued her from a sandy beach. His peaceful consolation touched her again, like the time she first learned to ride a chariot hitched to a kyloe, when she fell off and broke her wrist; Abbasdah quietly held her as the guards summoned the vizier, and never once did the king show anything but a smile to his daughter as she cried and howled in agony. Abbasdah now patted her on the head.

"Go. For your people, our kingdom. And for these strangers who have asked for help. Be kind, be smart, be safe, and be cunning."

She felt a soft hand on her shoulder. Diggins.

"I will be with you, not because of my king's will, but because I serve you, Eave Queen."

"Thank you, Diggins."

Her father smiled. "When you return, you'll tell me all about your adventures. I will easily hold off the tides of time and the Undersea until then." He pulled his sheet up to his chest and touched his forehead, another flake of shell sticking to his fingers. "Now go, go! Be the daughter I raised. Be the Eave Queen!"

Chapter 5

A Journey by Horse and Kyloe

WITH A SOFT bristled brush, Apondra smoothed the shaggy amber hair away from the dark eyes of her kyloe. The steer's long horns, wider than its shoulders and nearly white, save stains of grass and dirt on the tips, glistened in the sun. She loved them, cattle once bred in the highlands that flourished in the hills and streams of the land surrounding the kingdom. She often wondered what they would say if they could talk. Her mount snorted, nudging its large head against her sweater. She dug her hands into the tufts of orange-brown hair on his flanks and scratched him.

"There, there, Teacup, we'll be on our way soon." A pair of lobfolk completed tightening the harness straps attached to the wicker basket chariot behind Teacup. Ken poked the basket before putting his satchel of books in the front cubby.

"This is safe, I assume," he said. "I've never ridden in one, as I've mentioned. Did I mention that?" He twiddled his thumbs. "If you have anything reassuring to say to me, this would be the moment."

"Ken, I've been on a several rides with my father across King's Plain and the meadows that surround the town. Teacup here is my favorite. He's very gentle. And very obedient. He's always listened to me ever since he was a calf. I trust him, and he trusts me." She winked. The clip-clop of Gunnar's horse announced his approach to their assembled convoy.

"Can these … cows … handle the terrain?" Gunnar asked. His horse, larger than many of the horses she had seen from visiting parties of ambassadors and traders, made its way next to the chariot, stopping without any command cue from its rider. "It seems an odd choice. We have some herds of these cattle in the highlands north of the Kingdom of Swan."

"They do love the hills," Apondra said, and added a quick, light tap to Teacup's shoulder. "And they are built for endurance. My people have used them for centuries as our guides. They have a second sense for water sources." Gunnar's face held a tight frown. "They're called *kyloe*. This one is mine. His name is Teacup."

"Then I hope Teacup will be happy to join our journey." He held his hand out for Teacup to smell. Gunnar's face relaxed into a subtle smile. "Gentle. And happy."

"He is, I'm sure of it." She patted down the straps around the steer's shoulders. "What is your horse's name?"

"This is Rose. Don't let his name fool you, he's a fighter, a bold stallion."

Ken shuffled next to Rose and bent over, examining the underside of the horse. "Rose is an interesting name," Ken interrupted. "For a male horse, that is."

"He's named after my daughter." Gunnar lowered his head. "She passed, with her mother, shortly after we were wed."

"I'm sorry." Apondra reached up and pet Rose's mane. "That's a lovely idea, a tribute."

"It reminds me to fight. For good."

Apondra settled into silence, respecting that Gunnar had chosen to disclose such a personal wound. She suddenly saw him as a father, not just the hand of his king, with a hollow in his heart. Due to his youthful appearance, she suspected that Gunnar's tragedy was at a young age, barely an adult, which meant that his daughter Rose must have died … very young. She ran the back of her hand down Rose's shoulder.

"I should estimate that I was adopted at about the same age as Rose when she passed," she said, immediately covering her mouth and lowering her eyes.

"Just a babe," Gunnar said. He took off his riding glove and extended his hand. "You know, these are the little moments that I've learned help to bond a regiment. When we learn things about our motivations, and care for our fellow men," he paused, looking to Ken, "and lobfolk, we are more invested in each other's success."

She shook his hand, firm with a calloused palm. She had not realized how warm his skin would feel. *These are the things I do not have with the lobfolk.* She held it for a long moment and ran her thumb across his knuckles. He withdrew politely.

"I have no recent recollection of touching such a weathered hand," she said with a blush. "I embarrass myself by gawking. I apologize. That's not very fitting of royalty."

"That's alright," he replied. He pointed to a band of gold around his finger. "This is for my wife. Although she is gone, I believe our souls are bound forever. Tell your father I have no intention of asking for his daughter's hand." He winked. "As much of a prize as you might be to some kingdoms with bachelor princes, Eave Queen. My heart was given away long ago."

Gunnar kicked Rose slightly and moved to the front of the now assembled convoy. Ken clattered into Teacup's chariot, banging his claws against the basket.

"*Beautiful* Eave Queen, if you are done flirting, it's time to go."

"I was not flirting! I was bonding. Bonding with the *regiment.*"

"If you bond too much, you'll become glued. Come on, let's get Teacup going."

After stepping into the chariot and taking her place in front of Ken, she flicked the shoulder reigns. Teacup slipped in line behind the horsemen and ahead of the other four kyloes. Diggins stood in her chariot, her brother Moe talking to her quietly, resting his hands on her hips. Apondra observed, discreetly, as they pressed their foreheads together, locking their claws, their antennae touching each other's face in a sweet sibling gesture of goodbye, betraying their gruff exteriors. Moe finally turned away, head high and spear set over his shoulder. Diggins whipped her reigns and her kyloe chariot trotted past the group to the front of the line next to Gunnar.

"Let's away!" Gunnar shouted, taking the lead with a quick trot.

Apondra watched Tomas on his horse, also brown and white like Rose, darting up and down the line as he checked on each human soldier, always the attentive squire. He settled in on the right side of Gunnar as they marched forward through the outer field of the King's Plain onto the merchant path. Tomas glanced over his shoulder more than once, and each time that she caught his eye and waved, he smiled and ducked his head, his cheeks red.

The convoy continued at a brisk and steady pace into midday. The wild grasses bled into taller brush, dotted by yellow cattails from hidden ponds and small white flowers along the edges of the path. Tomas now looked to the east, watching the remnants of the shore winds as they touched the tops of the foliage. A rippling wave rolled through the yellow and green stalks of grass with each small gust, a dry scent touching each rider. The squire fell back to Apondra and Ken's position.

"I'm surprised that I can't smell the sea anymore. It was so prevalent on the journey to your castle."

"Wait until we get to the mountains," Ken noted, rolling up a map. "I hear the springs smell like ice."

"That's an interesting phrase."

"I'm full of interesting phrases. If we stay alive, you'll hear plenty." Ken scanned the fields. "According to the maps, the merchant path we're on diverges; one branch leads northeast to the long route along the shore, and the other will be our break northwest into the forested foothills." Tomas nodded.

"Ken, what kinds of dangers are in our way?"

"Oh, bandits for sure, as the vizier told us. But I think your knights' presence and our combined show of swords and spears would be an immense deterrent. Anyone who recognizes the princess would be foolish to attack. She's actually quite safe, such is the reputation of our good King Abbasdah!" He crossed two arms over his chest and raised the other two to the sky. "Good is respected in these lands, even by the thieves."

"And what of the animals of lower intelligence?" asked Tomas. "Do they respect good?"

"Well, some of them do, I suppose, in the sense that if we do not pose a threat to them or their offspring, we'll be on our way without incident. And we won't have to worry about any large carnivores, or omnivores, emerging from hibernation at this time of year looking for a fast meal." Ken rubbed his chin. "This is one reason why the merchant trails are placed where they are; safe routes away from ideal places for nests and dens and the like."

At the head of the party, Gunnar raised his hand to signal a halt. The horses and kyloes stopped in unison as the trees ahead arched over the trail's entrance into the next section of the woods. A lone lobfolk in a tattered gray cape stood in the middle of the path, leaning on a long and broken branch, leaves still attached to the top. In another hand, he clutched a small harp on a strap, as was common for traveling minstrel lobfolk. Apondra noted the misshaped bulge under his cloak and leapt out of her chariot basket.

"Apondra!" called Gunnar as she raced past him. Diggins dismounted her chariot and stormed behind her. Apondra hurried toward the mysterious traveler, followed by the footfalls of the cavalier. The traveler's cloak slid off his back, revealing only one large claw, and a dark wet stain on his opposite shoulder where his other claw should be.

"Your claw! What happened?" Apondra asked, coming to a breathless stop in front of him. "You need medicine! Healing!" She looked at his mortal wound, her eyes welling. "I'm sorry," she whispered, "I don't know what to do."

The traveler lifted his head, his eyes dull and gray. "Turn back," he hissed. "This path is no longer safe. I was attacked." He began to slump forward, steadying himself with his branch. "I beg you, turn around."

Gunnar slid to a stop, placing himself between Apondra and the stranger. "What or who did this to you?" He wrapped his hands around the lobfolk's arms, easing the burden of the tree branch staff. "I have you, friend. Please sit, be still."

"Vicious creatures, hunting where they shouldn't be." The traveler coughed, a dark wad of spittle coating his hand as he covered his mandibles.

"Your name," Apondra pleaded, "let me send word to your kin."

"It was Balew. My name was Balew. Now it is a single note in the song of eternity."

The branch that he used as a cane fell out of his hands and his body fell to the ground, his harp following with a short cacophony of notes. He was dead.

Tomas scampered up to the body, examining where the claw had been removed. "This is not a clean cut. It was torn off. See the rough tissue here and here." He lowered his head. "He was doomed to bleed to death, there was no way to save him."

"We should assume a beast," said Gunnar. "No man, or I would guess lobfolk, would be able to tear it off in one pull. A weapon would cut the limb with more precision." Ken and Diggins joined the circle around the dead minstrel, the librarian placing a hand over Balew's face.

"Excuse me, this is one of our kinfolk and he has died. There is a protocol we need to respect." He tilted the deceased's head and lifted an edge of the blood-stained cloak. "However, your forensic examination is correct, squire. This gentlelob has been brutally attacked by a beast." He waved back to the party. "Quickly, a burial."

Gunnar replaced his gloves. "A ceremony, now?" He grabbed a flat rock and began to scrape at the soil.

"No, no, no," replied Ken. "If this was by a beast, we need to *bury* the remains, lest we attract scavengers, or the very predator itself who did this." He paused and folded his hands. "We respect the life of this deceased traveler, Mister Balew, and hope he had no family that would miss him." He rummaged through the traveler's pockets. "Nothing of value."

"Ken!" shouted Apondra. "Pickpocketing? How rude!"

"My dear Eave Queen, I am looking for *anything*, like a keepsake or other identifying trinket. Something with a family crest? Or at least to mark his grave. All we know is a single name. What would you do?"

"Well, not that! Something more proper than hanging bait for a passing thief to steal!"

Ken scanned the trail. "Pick some of those white wildflowers and we'll make a nice little garden marker."

"You've spent too much time with the vizier," she huffed. "You've learned how to be pragmatic at the wrong time!"

"Princess. *Apondra*." Gunnar paused his digging and wiped a fresh coat of sweat from his brow. "He's right. We need heads and hearts to succeed on this mission." He resumed digging with his piece of flat stone. "And Ken is being a *head* right now."

Apondra shielded her eyes and scanned the fields. A lone osprey came into view, then left after his circling examination of the party. The shallow grave in progress by the soldiers took shape. Again, she looked to the sky, now noticing two large black birds, perhaps vultures, silently spiraling up and down, gliding on outstretched wings. She adjusted her focus back to their stopped procession of horses and kyloes.

"New formation." Apondra wiped a tear from her cheek. "We alternate horse and kyloe. The musk of the cattle is a part of their natural protection, and it may diffuse the scent of men and horses a bit. In the event of an attack, or a vagabond in the road, horses go left, kyloes break right to widen our line. We'll also appear larger to an oncoming beast."

Gunnar laid the traveler's body into the hole and covered him with the bloody gray cloak. "Princess, you've got quite the mind for tactics."

"I read something like that in an old fairy tale, or maybe it was a war journal. I can't recall right now." She smiled at him, her still wet eyes glancing away. "I'm making this up as I go."

"That's what we all do." He smiled back and brushed his gloves. Tomas placed a circle of white petals over the grave. "A good tactician reassesses and adapts." Gunnar picked one of the white flowers and blew it into the wind. "We adapt."

⁓

The merchant trail broke to their left, west and northward, slowly rising on a gentle slope as the party entered the woods. Apondra recognized the tall juniper trees and pines, but new foliage filled the gaps in her line of sight as well as her imagination. Ken reached over her shoulder to snatch a low hanging branch as the chariot rattled over a root. She touched the needles on the tip of the branch, shaped like a tiny vibrant green caterpillar.

"Ken, what's this one?"

"A type of hemlock," he suggested. "I'd need to study further as to which specific variant. Many hemlocks are useful for medicine as a counter-toxin, especially for dermal infections for the unshelled beasts." He sighed, anticipating her next questions. "Lobfolk derma layers are our shells. This will not be able to help your father. The vizier would have already tried that."

Apondra lowered her head, still trying to understand how her father could become so ill so fast. It didn't make sense as he was in near perfect health recently. She pulled her hands inside her sweater sleeves, now aware of the chill of the forest around her, hidden from the sun's warming rays.

"Ken, what kind of toxin would hemlock be used against? If a toxin or poison was given to someone, that is?"

"I know where your questions are leading," he said. Ken snapped Teacup's reigns to signal him to pull harder up the slope behind Rose and the Cavalier. "You wonder who would poison your father," he said, smiling and placing one hand on her shoulder, his others gripping the reigns. "Conspiracy, even rooted in truth, grows wickedly before twisting into a briar of lies."

"Did you just make that up?"

He nodded. "Appy," he said, "don't be distracted by conspiracy here. Your father is, well, getting on in his years. There are things you can't just fix by being clever." He sighed. "You've never lost anyone close to you before, and if it is his time to travel to the Undersea, it is his time. My parents died when I was quite young, and I'm not very good at this type of counseling."

She looked at the hemlock sprig in his hand. Ken was right; she had never given serious thought to her father's passing. Her friend was trying his best to reign her in from a wild squirrel chase that she manifested without any evidence. Apondra took the hemlock from his hand and snickered.

"Here I am, living the hyperbole of going on a journey outside of my father's walls."

"Oh, Appy. You still find a way to sparkle through your melancholic and introspective thoughts."

The path leveled off at the top of the next bend; a flat stretch of well-worn trail drove straight as a spear through the woods ahead. She looked over the side of the basket and observed the hoof prints and wagon wheel ruts on each side of the widening path, one set veering suddenly off the trail. Gunnar drew his sword ahead of them and pointed to the leaves and needles on their right side.

"These marks show that two merchants passed side by side here, then one went off the trail. And it was recently." He held his sword high, blade parallel to the ground to indicate a stop. The horses and kyloes halted side-by-side. Rose snorted and stomped.

"Easy, friend." Gunnar hopped down, sword still in hand, and stepped off the trail. "There."

A hundred feet from the path, Apondra recognized the wheels and boxy shape of an empty horse cart. She dismounted the chariot, motioned for Ken to stay put, and joined the cavalier as he stepped over the sparse bramble off the trail. Gunnar placed himself in front of her.

"Too late to tell you to stay back, Princess?"

"I suppose so. What do you think?"

"Someone abandoned their cart, but not by choice." The silence of the forest was broken by their footfalls and the screech of an owl somewhere above. "An owl? Before nightfall?" His jaw tensed. "Nocturnal animals do not behave like this unless there is danger."

"Day owls," Apondra replied. "They chase the mice and hares during daylight. The rodents of course would be looking for their own food. Grains, seeds, leafy things." She grabbed the cavalier's sleeve. "Or our food."

Next to the cart, a body lay motionless, a human. A sack of foodstuffs had fallen open beside him, and a small pack of mice ran out as the cavalier's feet thumped the ground. He poked the bag with his sword to ensure the vermin had departed, then pierced the sack and lifted it in the air. A metal coin fell through the hole.

"If it was a bandit, they're not very smart. Or thorough."

Apondra examined the coin. An imprint of a bird, no, *a swan*, on one side. She held it to the cavalier, her eyes narrowed. "Your kingdom's coin."

"We don't have merchants inland here. Normally." He clasped the coin and placed it in his pocket, then corrected his manners. "Apologies, would you like this?"

"Give it to your squire. He works hard."

"I will," he said. "But I question why this merchant would be out here, with our coin. It's a bit baffling."

Diggins stepped into their huddle, spear pointed upward at the trees. "Human, remember these merchant routes are not of any kingdom. Barter and trade will shuffle coins from hand to hand until they can be exchanged at a bank, such as in the merchant town." She silently studied the sky. "Your coin is not common here, that is true, but uncommon is still a valid explanation."

"Perhaps a first-time merchant, which would explain how his wagon was ill-prepared for the hostilities of your lands." Gunnar froze; he put a finger to his lips and listened to the stillness.

"Our land is not hostile," Diggins whispered. A hooting day owl startled them as it swooped down, the red-feathered tips of its wings blazing against the browns of bark and dried leaves. It landed right at their feet and seized a mouse. With a tiny screech, it flew up over their heads, prey in its talons, its red-brown underbelly feathers fluttering over their heads.

"Aggressive," said Gunnar. "What was that you were saying about hostility?" He steadied his hand on Diggins' shoulder.

"Only when they are hungry," Diggins said. Apondra crept between the two soldiers to examine the dead traveler. "We should turn him over."

Diggins prodded the corpse with her spear to comply, twisting the body onto its back, revealing the hollow of the merchant's chest. A large hole, torn out in ragged chunks, sent a wave of nausea through Apondra's stomach and choked her throat. She had never seen such gore on a human or lobfolk, the exposed insides only viewed in drawings in her anatomy tomes. It was similar to livestock and other animals she had studied, but darker in aroma and dread. Gunnar pushed his boot into the deceased's shoulder to roll him face down into his original position.

"Animal. Hungry. But not hungry enough to eat the whole man. Perhaps it seized just enough to feed its young." Gunnar crept to the merchant cart and examined the contents: full barrels of honey ale, a few hefty baskets of metal working tools, and a smaller basket filled with spools of fishing line. "Nothing of high value, but value, nonetheless. It was definitely not a bandit that attacked this man." He bit his lip. "A beast, for sure. Your Highness, back to the group, please. I'm afraid our safety must be prioritized over burying this poor soul."

He took her hand with urgency as they ran back to their convoy waiting on the merchant trail. Ken and Tomas continued a deep conversation, huddled over their map as Gunnar helped Apondra into her chariot. Diggins silently retreated to the group, walking backwards, spear still in her hand. Apondra watched how Diggins and Gunnar complimented each other, silently understanding a soldier's protocol for escort and defense. There are things one learns without books, she mused. Diggins finally rejoined the caravan and tapped her spear on the chariot.

"Ken, where does your map say we can afford to stop for the night to camp? These woods are not safe."

"Good question, Diggy. If we continue on this road through the late evening, which is not helpful for my anxiety, mind you, we should come to a hilltop where the trees are clear. The path widens again and there should be an established campsite for merchants. We may have good company there."

"That will aid our numbers while we rest," said Gunnar. "Any marauding beasts will be less likely to attack if we increase our party size."

Apondra recognized an intensity in Gunnar's commands. He did not dismiss anyone else's contributions, and then acted, defining a plan without revealing the specific threats he saw in his mind. She wanted to know more, but also understood the urgency of action to give them the most daylight for travel.

"Hup, hup, Teacup!" Apondra clutched the reigns, following closely behind Gunnar and Rose. Ken reached into the back of the chariot and the cubby holding their kitbox secure against the bumps in the road.

"Appy, do we have any torches stashed away?"

"No torches until we are stationary," shouted Gunnar. "Our eyes will adjust as the sun sets. Fire may draw inquisitive beasts toward us when we are moving."

"But what of a campfire?" Ken protested. "Will we not set one, or two or three, when we reach the merchant clearing?"

"The commotion and our numbers at the camp will help deter the beasts, assuming there are other travelers. At the same time, we can also hopefully make use of fire pits to hide the light of flames. Being out in the open will give us our best protection to watch for intruders. They don't like to attack in the uncovered areas."

"'They?' Who is 'they'?" Ken dug into his bag.

Another day owl swooped down, examining one of the lobfolk guards before fluttering back into the high boughs of a hemlock tree.

"The giant weasels, of course." Gunnar kicked his heels into Rose to pick up the pace.

"Oh, of course," muttered Ken. Apondra turned in the chariot basket and handed him a bestiary from the satchel.

"Page one hundred and sixty, weasels," she said with a broad smile.

"Weasels. Of course." Ken reached into his belt pouch and retrieved a piece of buttered sweet loaf. "If we're going to be ripped to shreds by a wild weasel, I'm going to eat my desserts before dinner."

"I'm glad you have priorities," Apondra said. Ken flicked the pages of the tome between bites as the caravan sped along the path against the dying rays of sunlight slicing through the forest.

The group rode in silence through the waning hours of the day. Tomas guided his horse from the front to the back of the line from time to time, checking on the caravan members and offering water from canteens or dried fruit and smoked meats to lobfolk and humans. Apondra observed no prejudice or preferential treatment; he served all as his superiors, including Diggins, and if anything, he smiled more at the lobfolk guards to demonstrate his eagerness. Canteen in hand, he pulled next to her chariot.

"Eave Queen, some drink?"

"Please Tomas, just call me Apondra."

"Princess Apondra—"

"Just Apondra." She smiled, prompting him to blush. Ken tapped her on the shoulder.

"I think he fancies you," Ken said.

"Ken!"

Tomas' face ruddied further, still noticeable in the dusk light. "It's alright, Your Highness," admitted the squire. "It's a pleasure to be on this mission for the benefit of our two kingdoms. You remind me of someone very fair that I once knew."

She cocked her head. "Was this someone that you fancied before traveling over here?"

The squire lowered his head, his blush gone. "No, I could not. She was my lady to serve, but the bride of my lord." His eyes darted toward Gunnar, silently scanning the woods from his saddle.

"Oh." Apondra observed Rose and his rider pull ahead slightly. It was still not her place to ask for more information, to try to understand the duty of a man who had lost his wife and child but continued to lead with confidence and respect. Tomas acknowledged her silent inquisition.

"He's a good man. I would serve him to my death." He hung the canteen back on his hip. "If you are thirsty, just ask." The squire directed his steed to the back of the caravan and handed a canteen to Diggins.

The merchant trail broke through the tree line as the sun passed the horizon. Gunnar halted the group with his sword, then held it at the ready. Ahead, a pair of small fires on each side of the trail denoted the clearing. Shadowy forms moved in front of the flames, curved backs of lobfolk on one side of the encampment, humans on the other. The segregated groups did not interact. Teacup sidled up to Rose, and Apondra dismounted the chariot. She smoothed the front of her skirt, then tucked her hair behind her ears and straightened her coral crown. She rubbed her palms down the front of her skirt again.

"I should go first. I'm a diplomat of the lobfolk and a human and I can be useful."

"No," said Gunnar, "you should conceal your royalty, for now. We do not know the intentions or reputations of the parties ahead. I will go with Ken."

"Me?" said the startled librarian. "Why not one of our guards? Diggy looks like she would enjoy menacing at strangers for a bit."

"The lobfolk will accept you as you are." Gunnar pulled his cloak over his pauldrons. "The humans should be presented with a nonthreatening … individual. They could perceive me as a captive if I go with a lobfolk solider and am wearing my crest and colors from a foreign sovereign nation."

"Hmph." Ken grabbed his satchel and handed it to Apondra. "Take care of my books if I am roasted for a feast."

"Oh hush," she laughed. "You're a very learned lobster. You'll be quick-witted to aid the cavalier." She grabbed her ribbon-wrapped coral headpiece and slid it inside her bag.

Tomas pulled his horse by the reigns into their huddle. "We should proceed together, all of us. Present ourselves as much at face value as we can. They could suspect something if some of us stay back. And we'll all be together, if there's any trouble, that is."

Apondra agreed. "Yes, let's do that. What say you, Cavalier?"

Gunnar nodded, albeit reluctantly. "Aye, it is the best plan. Everyone dismount; we approach in two columns, side by side. Lobfolk left, humans right."

The guards obliged. The horses at the human encampment ahead snorted, tied to stumps set back from the firepit. A large wagon, filled with crates and chests, sat further back, topped by an archer who stood as soon as he saw their approach. His entire visage bathed in the light of the campfire reflected the same deep brown hue; his boots, pants, and shirt almost perfectly matched his skin, eyes, and the stripe of hair over the crown of his head. He nocked his bow but did not draw. His voice echoed as he shouted.

"This is a common place. There is no conflict here. What soldiers enter from two nations together?"

Gunnar unfurled his cloak to reveal his full armor. "We are two nations, yes, lobfolk and the Kingdom of Swan, passing through on mutually beneficial business." He paused. "We carry no goods or wealth."

The lobfolk encampment approach in unison, their kyloes grazing on the edge of the clearing. A brown, striped-shelled merchant tapped his staff on the ground for attention.

"These humans have told us there have been sightings of bears encroaching on the territory of the weasel beasts. We would be grateful to have you join our numbers for the night but also ask you to contribute a sentry to our security."

"You shall have it," replied Diggins.

"And," the archer interjected, leaping down from the wagon, "you will gather wood from the edge of the forest for the fires. *Your* fires. We have none to contribute to your camp."

"Agreed."

"And one more thing," said the archer. He grinned, a wide smile of brilliant white teeth. "Your confidentiality is requested. That is the way of the merchant and rule of our road. Your business is yours, and ours is ours." He stared at Apondra. "But company such as yours is quite welcome in my camp, of course."

"I don't like your tone," said Ken, stomping ahead of the cavalier. "Do you know who I am?"

"I do not, shellfish."

"I am K'Ken Darloch Ambertide, sorcerer of Castle Homarus! If I choose, I will call the clouds of storm and draw the very lightning from the sky to strike you down." He reached into his pocket and pulled out a buttered sweet bread. "With one bite of this dragon bone, I will spit fire upon you!"

The archer glared at Ken, then the princess, and finally the cavalier, who cocked his head and nodded. The archer placed his bow over his shoulder. "We want no trouble, albino." He offered his hand to Gunnar. "I am Sharpe, and that is all you need to know further about me and my merchant clients."

"I am Gunnar. Thank you for your advice, Sharpe."

Walking down the path to an empty encampment, Gunnar leaned over to Ken. "Quite the show you just put on. I'm not sure that was necessary?"

"I panicked. Just a bit. I didn't like how he looked at Apondra." Ken shook his tail. "There are few benefits to being an albino lobster, except that most people have never met one before. So I fibbed. In the interest of our safety." He twiddled his fingers. "I hope no one asks for a magic trick."

⌇

The embers of the campfire flared as Gunnar tossed another log on top of the pile. The hilt of his sword glistened in orange glow, catching Apondra's eye. She looked at the decoration now that she was close and could see the details of two wings branching away from the sheath, the neck and head of a swan etched on the blade.

"That's beautiful," she said, cradling her small bowl of onion and potato stew in her hands. "Was it made just for you?"

Gunnar smiled, his stubble casting tiny, jagged shadows across his jaw. "It's from my wife." Apondra nodded, reticent to say anymore. He squatted next to her, unsheathed the blade fully, and held it toward the flame, balanced inches past the hilt on his fingers. "My wife's family. Generations of smiths. The men made weapons and tools. The women made jewelry, torch sconces, chandeliers, the items of high value. When I received my appointment as First Cavalier of the King, they pooled their money to buy the steel to forge the blade." He sheathed it. "My immediate family was too poor to contribute. Farmers. Working stock. The royal guard of Swan is recruited from all trades."

"That's lovely. Ours as well. Anyone can join if they are fit to serve."

He smiled as he stood. "Although I am a widower now, her family is still my duty. I serve the kingdom, and kin, though they are not of my blood, just the same. From what I understand, we have that duty in common, you and I."

"Yes, we do. Family is the people that raised you." She paused. "Those who love you."

"And we love them even when they pass beyond this life, sailing into the Undersea."

In her dreams, Apondra tried to see the faces of her birth parents, a futile exercise, but one she allowed herself often as a child. Did they have her hair, her eyes? Were they good people? It mattered less and less every day, when she woke and felt the embrace of her adoptive father, the lobfolk who raised her. With a small stick, she poked at a log teetering on the edge of the fire, guiding it back into the heart of the flames.

"Princess, I'll be right back." Gunnar lowered his head and stepped away from the firepit. "It's my turn for patrolling the camp. I'll relieve Diggins. She's been working nonstop." He nodded, and she reciprocated. As he departed, Tomas took his place, kneeling next to Apondra at first, and then setting himself on a log. His right leg stuck forward at an odd angle.

"Goodness, Tomas! What happened?"

"I guess I should just get this over with," he said with a grunt. He rolled down his right boot stocking and lifted his pantleg, revealing a wooden calf and several thin leather straps. He unbuckled them and detached the lower leg, the round stump of his knee wrapped in a cloth sock.

"Does it hurt?" Apondra asked.

"Aye, only after a long day on my feet." He withdrew a clean sock from his sack and replaced the one on his knee. "When we're outside, such as this, I have to sleep with it on in case of an emergency."

"That's terrible." She studied his movements, quickly changing the sock to conceal the scars, then reattaching the wooden leg. Flick, clip, pull; he tightened the straps and rolled down his pantleg. "Who made that for you?"

"I made it myself." Tomas gently tapped his heels together. "The ankle? I created a pin like a hinge, and leather bumpers to allow natural angles. I think it took about three design tests to get it right."

"You're quite clever. I can see why you were chosen to serve the cavalier."

"We don't choose who we serve." He poked at the ankle with a stick, cleaning out a clump of mud.

Her heart ached for his affliction. She had known several lobfolk who had lost limbs, mostly the fishers and soldiers. Sometimes the limb grew back, sometimes it did not, such as the vizier's claw stubs. The vizier said it was a complicated set of biological rules and situational circumstances that determined if, when, and how a lost limb returned. She sipped at the last of the stew water in her bowl and licked her lips.

"May I ask, Tomas?"

"You may." He smiled, his face orange and smooth in the campfire light. She thought it a tragedy for someone so young to be crippled. *Not that any age is acceptable for such an injury.*

"Well, ahem, how did it happen?"

"I was a stableboy from a poor family. We were neighbors to Gunnar's kin, the Brekke clan, and I worked in their barns for payment in extra food. One day, one of the cattle broke through the stockade and raced into the barn. My leg was trampled, pulverized. The cavalier, before he was a cavalier mind you, carried me on a horse and rushed me into town. The doctor did what he could. I was very lucky." He sipped at his own fresh bowl of stew.

"That's horrible. I'm sorry that happened to you."

Tomas nodded. "One of the king's guards witnessed Gunnar's skill on horseback, his heroism in bringing a broken boy from the fields into town for aid. He recommended Gunnar for the guard." Tomas peered into his bowl of steaming broth. "If not for me, Gunnar Brekke, First Cavalier of the Kingdom of Swan, would have never been discovered. And, in that same moment, any hopes for me becoming a guard someday were dashed."

"I can see that no one would want to hire a lame knight." She bit her lip, ashamed of the words she chose. "I'm sorry, that came out wrong! I apologize, Tomas."

"It's alright, Princess. Because can you guess who would hire me? *A cavalier.* As soon as Gunnar had his appointment, he directly petitioned the king and demanded, yes, *demanded*, that I be taken as his squire." He glanced beyond the edge of the campfire's light, where the shadow of Gunnar slowly circled, scanning the woods. "One tragedy created two paths of fulfillment."

"And what of his wife and child?" Again, she recoiled at her words. Her eagerness for answers was overcome by her own self-diagnosed rudeness. "I'm sorry, again. I should not be so nosy."

"Why don't we say," Tomas paused, rubbing his chin, "that it is your royal right to inquire about the background of your allies." He swallowed the rest of his stew. "A sickness, nothing more. That was the cause of Gunnar's sorrow. The sickness swept through the kingdom quickly. Many became ill, unable to work until they recovered. But, although few died from it, his own wife and child drew the unlucky lot. For a cavalier, to be defeated by an enemy you cannot strike with a sword is devastating." Tomas turned his bowl in his hands. "He dug their graves in the rain, since it was required by the local doctor to have the dead buried quickly, forgoing a proper ceremony." He sloshed the remaining stew in his bowl, sipped, and stared into the fire. "I helped him dig the plot for his child. I wish that on no one."

"Horrible." She placed her hand on his knee. "I apologize for asking."

"He wanted to put their bodies to rest for their journey to the Undersea as soon as possible to still his mind."

"Did that work?"

"No. He still feels the pain. He cries for them both at night, alone. A broken heart cannot be mended to what it was before." He rubbed his right leg. "It can be fixed, but it will never be the same. There is always a scar."

"You have quite a way with words." She blushed, unsure if her compliment would be regarded as flirting. She suddenly found herself enjoying his company almost as much as her long lessons with Ken in the library.

"Being a squire is an education. Some see it as a glorified stableboy, but I rather enjoy it. There is value and self-worth that comes from work. My callouses are my experiences, my knowledge." He held his hands out to the fire. She withdrew hers into her sleeves, ashamed of her soft pads and fingertips.

"Well, you seem like a fine person to travel with, an invaluable companion for this adventure." She nodded toward Gunnar's dark shape as he disappeared beyond the camp. "Both of you. Fine people."

A rustling in the grass and a snapping of twigs behind them startled the pair. Sharpe emerged from the shadows, bow in hand. He held a gloved finger to his lips.

"Shhh. Look to the north end of the clearing," he whispered.

Apondra and Tomas turned slowly, following the form of Gunnar walking on the outer edge of the encampment, barely visible in the moonlight. The crackling and hissing of the logs on the fire was met by the creaking of the archer's bow as he nocked an arrow, fixated on Gunnar's position.

"What are you doing?" hissed Apondra. "Stop it!"

Sharpe closed one eye and ignored her.

"Sir!" The squire staggered to his feet. "Are you mad?" He reached for the dagger in his belt.

"Stay still, fellow travelers." Sharpe exhaled and released his bow. The arrow flew over the campfire and into the dark behind Gunnar. A sudden screech and wailing followed. The cavalier spun and slashed, the flash of his sword barely visible. Another loud cry and then silence. Apondra grabbed a rock and ran into the dark toward the noise.

"Apondra! Princess!" called Tomas. "Come back!"

Her eyes strained to adjust now that the fire was behind her. Details of Gunnar came into focus, his sword, his belt, his cape flaring back over his shoulders as he stood over a hairy lifeless mound, slightly larger than a man or lobfolk. When she reached him, he flung his hand up to stop her progress.

"Eave Queen, return to the campfire!"

She looked down at the deceased creature. Tall as a bear, but thinner, its long neck pierced by Sharpe's arrow, and a slash across its chest from the cavalier's blade. The dead beast on the ground was one she recognized from her studies: a giant weasel, an apex predator. Its oily black nails curled into fists in its death pose, a slight stink of rotted eggs leaving its carcass.

She had never seen one in person, alive or dead, and she feared it even though it posed no threat in its current state.

"Princess, back to the camp!" Gunnar grabbed her by the arm and hurried her back. The other guards and Ken emerged from their tents and sleepsacks, weapons in hand; Ken wielded a walking staff as he rubbed his eyes.

"What's all this?" he said, noting the princess' crude weapon. "A rock?"

"I don't have a blade! It was the best I could do!"

"Here!" Tomas handed her a cooking knife. "Better than a rock."

"Fine," she said, accepting it. Gunnar and a human guard ran to the other two merchant camps, rousing them from their slumber. Improvised torches burst to life around each group, sticks shoved into the dirt, or tool handles wrapped in torn cloth and lit ablaze. Sharpe quickly moved to the top of a supply wagon, bow drawn, scanning the outer circle.

"Cavalier!" he called out. "Look to the east!" He fired his bow over their heads, landing in another shrieking beast's chest. Gunnar charged the wounded weasel, felling it with a single stroke.

"Princess! To the archer's position! High ground! High ground for defense!" Gunnar retreated to the collected group, his sword glistening with dark blood. "Everyone, backs to the fires! Squire! Untether the mounts! They're sitting like bait!" He unclipped his cape and swung his sword at a shape in the dark. "Everyone, you are all allies right now! Fight for your fellow traveler!"

Diggins stepped forward, spear in hand, and paused before charging another dark flash before her. "Wretched beast!" she cried as she plunged the spear through the weasel's chest.

A pair of weasels tackled a horse as Tomas untied the reigns. He stumbled back, dagger in hand. One of the beasts turned from the horse's neck and lunged at him, only to meet the spear of one of the lobfolk guards.

"Have your death, you hairy demon!" the guard yelled. He swung his massive claws at the weasel, knocking it to the ground. With his free arms, the guard grabbed the end of his spear, still lodged in the weasel, and pushed it through the beast; the tip burst through its back.

"Thank you, sir," said Tomas.

"Get up and fight with me!" The lobster knight turned and suddenly cried out, both claws yanked from his shoulders by another weasel. The monster slashed at his face and chest, then shot upright, frozen. The weasel's chest burst as the head of Diggin's spear emerged from its ribs. She stood triumphant as it fell forward, dead.

"Protect my princess, Tomas!" Diggins yanked out her spear and swung at another weasel, its foul cry of pain roaring across the camp.

As Apondra watched the melee unfold from her vantage point atop the wagon, she clutched Sharpe's back. "To the west! Save the squire!"

"If my aim is true," Sharpe said, firing off an arrow into another weasel's head. It bared its bloody teeth as it fell dead next to Tomas.

"Archer, to your right!" She called the directions, and he in turn nocked his bow and fired into the dark at the shapes that were neither human nor lobfolk. She watched as the bodies of merchants slowly littered the other campsites.

"There should not be this many, and they should not be this far from their home!" Sharpe yelled. "And I am running low on arrows quickly!"

"I'll fetch them!" she replied. He turned and grabbed her arm.

"Listen to me!" He bit his lip. "Go into the fray, but not the empty spaces that are dark; that's where more will be lying in wait. Stay in the light. Don't stop to assist others, you can't help them, they're just as untrained as you. If you die, I am useless." He reached back and felt the three arrows in his quiver. "Get me five. Five more."

"Five. I can grab five."

She leapt off the wagon and rolled in the dirt. Another cry from one of the knights, another scream. Her heart pounded in her chest, her throat already dry from frantic panicked panting. She ran along a trail of torches toward the first weasel body, an arrow protruding from its side, a sword slash to its neck. Her hands slipped on the shaft of the arrow, wet with blood. Apondra fumbled in her pocket to find the cooking knife. *I must not be scared*, she assured herself, sliding the knife next to the arrow shaft to free it. *One.*

"Ken!" she called as she ran to the next body. From the corner of her eye, she caught the glint of his white shell, reflecting orange and yellow flames as he swung a fiery log to keep a weasel at bay.

An arrow sailed over her head, past Ken, and into the animal's chest. She leapt onto it as it fell, ripping the arrow out. *Too quick!* The weasel convulsed and slashed at her with its claws, its nails catching the loose wool of her sweater and pulling her into its arms. With a shrill scream, she stabbed it with the arrow she had just liberated from its ribs.

A flash of silver next to her was followed by Tomas, his dagger plunging into the weasel's head.

"Thank you," she said between breaths.

"My duty." He nodded and grabbed her hand. "Back to the wagon!"

"But Sharpe needs more arrows!" She scanned the encampment, figures dashing in and out of the shadows. Ken reemerged and scurried to a fallen torch and shoved it back into the dirt. "Ken! The archer needs arrows! Help me retrieve them!"

"The torches are being extinguished! The weasels are knocking them down and putting them out!"

"Do both! Torches and arrows!"

"As the Eave Queen commands," he said dryly, scuttling over to another downed torch.

She spun on her heels and ran in a looping arc back toward Sharpe, hand-in-hand with Tomas. She saw his face, gripped with fear, his teeth clenched as he pulled her along, but his presence still gave her strength with his sheer willpower, trying to run and hop with his wooden limb. She reached down as they passed another furry carcass and yanked an arrow's shaft from a beast's back, one that had broken into the inner circle. Her sleeves caught on the rough edge of the archer's wagon as she attempted to climb, falling back to the ground.

"Three arrows!" she yelled, handing them to Sharpe's outstretched hand.

"Make that six!" called Ken, circling the wagon with his hands full.

"I take it you lied about being a wizard," Sharpe snarled, his arrow sailing over the head of a weasel on the fringe.

"I'm not proud of that in this particular moment." Ken lifted one of his arms and displayed the Cavalier's discarded cape. "But I am a very smart individual."

Ken clawed to the top of the wagon cart and stretched the cape between his claws. "I know that normal weasels and owls are not the best of friends, so without further ado … HOOOOO!"

Apondra howled with laughter as Ken flapped his claws and the cape, hooting in a loud voice. The weasels in the inner ring froze and stared at the wagon.

"HOOOOO, I say! HOOOO!" Ken stomped his feet and slapped his stubby tail, turning in a circle.

"Keep them focused," snarled Sharpe, drawing a bead on the closest weasel, staring dumbfounded at Ken.

With a blazing roar, Gunnar charged from between two torches and slashed the weasel's back. His sword spun with him as he pivoted to the next frozen beast, cutting its head clean from its long neck.

"Keep going, Ken!" Apondra clapped.

"Weasel!" shouted Sharpe, turning to the side of the wagon. He nocked an arrow and pulled the bowstring back, firing at the wiry animal. It spun and caught the arrow in its arm, sending it into a rage. It spun again and knocked over a set of torches, extinguishing them immediately.

"Wretched beast!" yelled Gunnar. He ran past the wagon to another weasel, racing full speed at their makeshift fort. Gunnar lifted his sword over his head.

And froze.

An arrow pierced his chest, just above the armor. He fell forward, slowly, into the maw of the weasel.

Apondra screamed and turned to face Sharpe, frozen in his firing stance. "WHAT DID YOU DO?"

Sharpe dropped his bow, his hands trembling. "I missed."

She leapt off the wagon, tears streaming down her face, and sprinted to Gunnar's side. His blood painted her hands as she fumbled with his armor in her attempt to remove the arrow. She stopped when she accepted the truth, he was dead.

"Oh no, no, no," she whimpered. *That idiotic rogue, foul archer,* she screamed in her head. *How could he make such a mistake?* She cradled Gunnar's head for a moment, his eyes rolled back, mouth agape. A hand grabbed her by the collar of her sweater.

Tomas.

"Run!" he yelled. He pushed her back toward the wagon and scooped up the cavalier's sword. The weasel leapt but was met by the bloodied blade and the fury of Tomas' rage.

"To darkness with you!" Tomas screamed. He slashed again, and again, his face puffy and red, his lips violently shaking with each exertion. The beast's limbs fell to the earth, and a puddle of ruddy mud covered the squire's boots.

Ken and Apondra returned to his side; the white lobfolk with a spear, and the human girl with her cooking knife.

"He was my friend," Tomas said quietly, his voice barely audible.

Sharpe climbed down from the top of the wagon and picked up a pair of blazing torches. He stabbed them into the ground, starting a circle of fire around the wagon. Apondra stared at him through her tears, an anger festering inside to match the growing intensity of the flaming ring. He acknowledged her with a nod.

"They won't cross the flames. Help me."

Ken and the squire plugged the gaps in the ring, surveying the scene. Dead giant weasels interspersed with the bodies of merchants, lobfolk and human, and the guardsmen. A huffing and neighing in the darkness drew their attention.

"Teacup!" Apondra ran and hugged the scruffy steer as he shuffled into their midst. She nestled her head into his fluffy forehead, wiping her tears on his coarse and dirty hair. Behind him, Rose trotted up to Gunnar's still body. The horse nudged him with his nose, and then dug a hoof into the dirt next to him.

"Easy boy," Tomas reassured the horse. He grabbed the bridle. "I've got you. Come to the wagon, Rose."

A shadow moved behind one of the fires. Apondra clutched her cooking knife, then dropped it once the form moved into the light.

"Oh Diggy," she whispered.

Diggins dragged her body forward through the dirt. She looked up, her mouth covered in blood, her claws cracked and hanging at odd angles. She stopped and lay in front of Apondra, unable to roll over on her side despite her efforts.

"Eave Queen," she whispered, her breaths shallow and short, "tell my brother. Tell Moe that I will see him on the great beach in the Undersea."

"Please don't talk this way," she said. In her heart, she knew that Diggins was slipping away, her wounds too great to overcome. "You have served this kingdom as a legendary hero." Tears streamed down her face, blurring Apondra's vision as she reached for Diggins' free hand.

"It has been an honor to serve you," Diggins replied. "Tell my brother that I love him. Tell Moe that Diggy loves him." Her head dropped to one side, the light leaving her eyes. A whining wind grew inside Apondra's head, eventually blocking the snaps and crackling of the blazes around the camp. Ken's hand pulled her away, back toward the wagon.

"Appy, back to the group." His fingers rubbed her shoulder, and his voice cracked. "She was a great lobfolk. And my friend as well."

They sobbed as they retreated. The three humans and Ken braced their backs against the wagon, one on each side. Apondra clutched her blade's handle with both hands, pointed toward the unknown dark of the woods. With every breath, dawn grew closer. Rose and Teacup settled into slumber inside the ring of fire. The crackling flames whispered into the night as they each took turns dozing to sleep, occasionally startled awake by an unknown sound drifting on the wind until the sun rose.

A fine mist of fading fog greeted Apondra in the morning as she wiped the gunk from the corners of her eyes. The smell of cooked meats filled her nostrils, as well as traces of ash and burnt wood. A passing musky scent of weasel fur returned her to the present situation. She rolled to her side and watched Ken and Tomas silently cooking their meals. Just beyond the ring of burnt torches, Sharpe sat on the ground with his back to the group, his bow resting next to him. She stretched and stood, brushed the ash and bits of leaves off her skirt, and stomped over to him.

"Morning," he said. She replied with a slap to his cheek. Her eyes burned.

"How could you do that?" she cried, a new set of tears running down her face. "How could you?"

Sharpe held up his hands; they trembled, his fingernails crusted with dirt and ash. "I buried him before dawn, the cavalier. I'm sorry."

"Gunnar. Gunnar Brekke. That was his name." She thought of slapping him again. "What were you thinking?"

"It was the heat of battle, and I missed!" Sharpe shouted. "Do you think I honestly meant to kill him?" He attempted to stand but fell over. He grabbed his bow. "I'm sorry."

"Well, no wonder your friends didn't help us." She wanted to hurt him with words, but cruelty did not sit well with her as she tried. "They must have known you were not to be relied on."

He slowly scanned the far reaches of the campsite. "Those who didn't die must have run away. The ones I knew were my clients, not my friends."

"What will we do now?" Apondra said. "We're out here, alone. And we have so much further to go." She began to sob again. "What will we do?"

Sharpe pointed to the smoldering pile of embers that constituted their kitchen. "Eat something. Gather your things. We'll hitch up your chariot to the steer and you can head home."

"We can't head home, we're on a mission … to save our kingdom." She sighed and covered her face with her hands. "We're on a mission."

Apondra settled next to Ken and quietly grabbed a piece of bread and a salted meat from a hot stone on the edge of the fire pit. Ken leaned over and placed a hand on her shoulder.

"As objectively as I can put this, and bear in mind I've spent too much time with the vizier, we would not be alive, none of us, if not for our combined efforts, including the archer. I don't think he'd have remained here this morning if he was a scoundrel." He sipped from a cup of breakfast soup and glanced at the solitary archer still standing in self-exile. "He's a not a bad person. That is one of the few measures that we have of this stranger, but I believe it is an accurate one."

She nodded. Tomas had already set off, working on packing Rose's saddlebags. He wore Gunnar's sword and sheath fastened to his belt. As he bent over, a glimmering golden sparkle dangling from his neck caught her eye, Gunnar's wedding ring on a string. The calmness of the squire performing his duties, Ken's reassuring words, and the distraught state of the archer told her that she needed to force stability in her own emotions if she was to be of any use.

"Squire Tomas?"

"Yes, Eave Queen?"

"Your dagger. May I have it? Temporarily, that is. It's probably better than a cooking knife." She held up her tiny blade. "I suppose you will be using the sword from here on out."

"Do you know how to wield it?" He paused. "In battle?"

"I can learn. I will hire you; I can pay."

"That's not necessary."

"You are without a lord," she said, her voice breaking. "As a member of my royal house, I will take you as my squire." She steadied herself, already missing the devotion and protection of Diggins. Tomas had proven himself as far more than a competent squire; his attentiveness was driven by his bond with Gunnar. She assured herself that Diggins would approve of her choice. "You will not be without purpose."

He nodded. This poor young man had just lost his mentor and protector, as well as his friend. She could find a way to bring him some comfort, but she knew she did this as much for herself as for him. Sharpe finally entered the clearing and began to sift through the wagon's remaining contents.

"We have plenty of food stuffs, clean blankets, and these." He handed a pair of blue pants to Apondra. "These are more practical for you."

She nodded and slid them up under her skirt before removing the bloody clothes. Now was not a time for formal modesty, but she did note the squire and Ken turned away as she changed. She shook out her sweater before slipping it back over her tunic. Sharpe handed her a belt, his eyes downcast.

"Oh no thank you, archer, these fit alright."

"It's for your weapon."

"Oh. Right."

She fastened the leather belt and short sheath around her waist under her sweater and slid the squire's dagger into it. Sharpe slunk back to the wagon and placed a pair of heavy canvas sacks at her feet.

"These should be enough to get us north to the merchant town. From there, we'll go our separate ways. And here." He placed a tiny, stitched bag in her hand. She opened it and peered at the silver coins inside, flashing him a confused look. "That would have been split between my merchant employers and myself. You can use that to hire a guide, or a ship to take you back south from the merchant town's port." He glanced at Tomas. "I will assume that I am not welcome to join your party for the long term."

Tomas' jaw tensed. "You can lead us to the merchant town, correct?"

"I can. And I will." His voice trembled lightly as he ran his dirty hand over his short patch of hair. Apondra pulled him to the side and lowered her voice.

"I don't think you'll be welcome to ride on Rose with the squire, and we do not have room in our chariot. Ken is a bit larger than you and I."

Sharpe whistled. A horse, black with white legs and a white blaze between its eyes, stepped out of the woods into the clearing.

"I have a ride, *Domino*. He's mine. I don't tether him whenever I camp in case I need to escape. And it gives him the mobility to not be bait for beasts."

"Do you often need to escape from camps when you escort a merchant?"

He tethered another bag on the back of his horse. "Sometimes." He placed his bow across the saddle and mounted Domino. "But I will stay. We all owe each other our lives, and I have to make some sort of amends." He looked down at the saddle horn. "I promise this to you all."

As Sharpe slowly plodded ahead, Apondra and Ken mounted Teacup's chariot and pulled next to Tomas on Rose; there was no sign of his own horse, so she assumed the worst. Ken reached over her shoulder to pull out his map. "What would happen if we turned back?"

"I'll be seen as responsible for having our own guards and a council from the Kingdom of Swan slaughtered." She swallowed hard. "It will all but confirm that I am an ill omen."

He placed a hand on her shoulder. "Then we go forward, my Eave Queen. I'm just as afraid and unsure as you are. We are in over our heads, but our task is to find Azcalaw." His antennae settled lightly on her cheek. "I am so scared, Appy, but we go forward and trust our abilities."

She felt the handle of the dagger on her hip. "And what abilities do we have?"

"We are bookish, we interpret facts. And I will always choose the mind over a sword if I were to enter a battle."

Chapter 6

The Merchant Town

SHARPE CONTINUED HIS sentry, seated on Domino, not speaking since they departed from the scene of the slaughter. Teacup grazed quietly on the mix of bromegrass between patches of orange stones breaking through the foliage, only stopping to lift his head and check on Apondra and Tomas seated on the other side of the trailhead. Apondra waved at him; he stared back, chewing a mouthful of grass. She thought for a moment that Teacup smiled before he lowered his head for another mouthful. With a brisk shake of his head to ward off a tiny swarm of flies, Teacup meandered back to the road and stood silently next to Rose. Tomas nodded toward the animals.

"They seem to be fast friends," he said. Apondra nodded, tearing a piece of salted meat into two, offering one half to the squire.

"Indeed, they are. Here. Eat." He accepted her generosity. She could see beyond the squire's sunken eyes into the pain and loss of his lord, imagining his pain must be what she felt when she allowed herself to dwell on Diggins. "Squire, you have a job to do. As do I." She laid her text across her lap. "I'm still confused by the giant weasels. They shouldn't be this far from their territory, nor in such large numbers." She flipped the pages again. "There's nothing in here about this type of hunting pack scenario."

"That's because it shouldn't have happened," Sharpe said with a low growl, dismounting his horse. "The weasels are apex predators. Like bears, they are one of the chevrons of nature's mountains."

Ken, returning from the path to their right, shook his head slowly. "There are no wheel or hoof paths of recent note to the northeast, thank you all for asking for my scouting mission's results." He scratched his head. "Archer, did you say, 'chevron'? That's quite a specific word. Are you a learned person?"

Sharpe looked to the sky. "I have learned many things as a sellbow while escorting men and women, and the occasional lobfolk, along the merchant trails."

Apondra's eyes widened. "Then what else do you know about the giant weasels?"

"I know that because they are large predators, they have to spread out. Each one must have several miles of territory and prey to sustain their … clan?"

"Gang," said Ken. "Or boogle. Or pack." He accepted a strip of meat from Apondra. "I like 'boogle' since it seems to fit more alliteratively with the old tales of their magical nature, shapeshifting and all of that."

"They are not shapeshifters," corrected Sharpe. "That is just a tale told to children, to make them fearful of the real magic in the world. But some do live in burrows, even at their size. People have seen live prey escaping out of their holes and assumed it was due to a shapeshift." He looked toward the fork ahead of them. "As I was saying, they are predators. Only something affecting their food would push them away from their burrows or nests to hunt in larger packs."

"Boogles," Ken said, waggling a stick of meat at Sharpe.

"Boogles, fine." Sharpe took a few steps to the less traveled path bending northeast. "This is the way to the merchant town, or rather, the shorter way. The weasels may be more common this way, as the trail touches the edge of their hunting grounds." He glanced back at Apondra's lap. "You know what they say about books? There are more blank spaces on a page than ink. The real world fills those gaps."

Apondra closed the text and placed both hands firmly on the cover, pressing her fingers into the leather. She was a learned person, her head full of facts and lessons, but now that she had been out in the real world, and seen things like death firsthand, she realized how little she actually knew. Her mind was indeed full of blank spaces to be filled, whether she was ready or not.

"Eave Queen," said Ken, "we should make our way soon. I vote, despite my general aversion to danger and the unknown, that we take the path to the northeast, the road less traveled of late. We are unlikely to encounter any nefarious individuals, and we can hedge our bet on getting to the safety of town sooner."

"I would agree," voted Sharpe.

Apondra touched Tomas lightly on the shoulder. "What say you?"

"Me? My station does not allow me to counsel."

"Your station is that you are a member of our party, and you get a voice." She flashed a firm but friendly smile.

He looked up, his jaw tensed. "I say we go northwest. But I am outvoted. No more bloodshed."

Sharpe tightened the packs on his horse and yelled back to the squire. "Your concern is noted." He mounted Domino and circled the group. "As the person with the most familiarity with these lands, boots and hooves on the ground that is, I would say that our chance of conflict is reduced by spending the least amount of time traveling. Everyone mount up when you are done your meals."

"He's become rather bossy," Ken hissed at Apondra.

"I think he wears his guilt on his sleeve and is overcompensating to win back our respect." She packed her books and stood in the chariot. "If he was being truly selfish and acting in pure self-interest, his reputation as a caravan escort was just ruined by the attack, and he is looking to earn our endorsement at our destination. So I say that even at that level, he's our best hope of getting through this. For now." She sighed, a tear sliding slowly down her cheek.

"Appy?"

She wiped her face with her tattered sweater sleeve. "I don't want to be afraid. But I am."

"I'm afraid, too. But if we stand still, fear will overcome us."

Sharpe waited for Teacup and Rose to join his side next to Domino before leading the tiny convoy down the path to the right, heading northeast.

⚘

The red spruces rocked silently as the wind increased. No birds in the air, no rodents or deer on the ground. Apondra felt a cold blanket of quiet pass over her. She pulled the collar of her sweater up over her mouth and nose, eyes darting above the hem back and forth searching for any signs of life. She did not expect to come across a large animal such as a moose in this void, but not even a tiny rodent or insect emerged. Nothing. Even a hunting party would be preceded by a ripple of wildlife rushing to escape their traps and blades.

Nothing.

Sharpe held his bow above his head to halt the group.

"The tree line breaks ahead. Do you see the light and the clearing?"

"I do," acknowledged Ken.

"The woods should be unbroken until we come upon the town. Something is wrong." He swung his quiver from his shoulder to his hip. "Slow pace."

The horses eased their gait, followed by Teacup and the light creaking of the chariot's wicker. Within several yards, the trail abruptly ended, dropping off with a hard edge as if a giant spade or trowel had cut it in two. A channel as wide as the Castle Homarus courtyard cut perpendicular to the beaten path. Apondra stepped out of the chariot and crept to the edge of the gigantic gulley, looking left and right, west and east. Her inspection revealed nothing but dried mud and fallen trees strewn in each direction.

"What could have done this? It's as if a boulder just rolled through the woods." She pulled her hands into her sleeves.

"A *gigantic* boulder," corrected Ken. He crept over to the edge of the channel and stepped down into the large rut. "Hmm. It's dry, packed hard. We should be able to cross." He took several steps forward into the destructive wake, kneeling to examine a distinct trough, several feet long, as deep and wide as his claws. "Appy, look here. These are tracks."

Tomas and Sharpe followed their mounts, then Apondra without Teacup who stood on the lip of the path still attached to his chariot. The gigantic gashes repeated further across the rut to the east and west.

"These are indeed tracks," said Sharpe.

"What did I just say?" Ken crossed all of his arms and flapped his claws. "I may not have ears, but my antennae function better than yours, archer."

"Hmph." Sharpe jogged several yards, following the prints, then returned. "They go in one direction. I don't recognize the animal that made these. I'm not sure whether they were going east toward the sea or away from it to the west, but we should best hurry in case it comes back along the same path." He glanced at Teacup. "We can either lower the cattle's cart down or try to roll some of the fallen logs to make a ramp."

"We may need both," said Apondra. "Lower the chariot down here, and then build the ramp up on the other side. We don't have the strength to pull it up on our own, and I don't think Teacup would be able to maneuver ascending as well as descending while strapped to it." She bit her lip, still listening to the silence created by the absence of any wildlife. Any chirp or squeak would have calmed her nerves.

"I'm on it," interrupted Tomas, running toward the other side of the rut and the break in the woods where the trailhead resumed, his limp more pronounced now that Apondra was aware of his false leg.

Sharpe turned to Ken. "I'll stay here to help with Teacup. You have more arms and can carry more wood than I."

"That doesn't mean I'm strong," mumbled Ken. "But I'll do what I can."

Within an hour, the crude ramp was built, and Teacup dragged the cart up and onto the reclaimed merchant trail. Apondra grabbed her notebook and a piece of charcoal.

"Sketching?" asked Ken.

"Yes. Evidence of what we saw for scope and scale. If this was done by the giant snapper that was observed at Ribbed Beach, then the land is in just as much peril as the sea." She tapped her charcoal on her chin. "If nothing else, we can let the merchants know. Perhaps they can even build a bridge or boardwalk."

"Individual merchants," interrupted Sharpe, "will not be invested in helping others with the route. They won't dip into their profits to buy lumber or labor for the free use of others." He turned to face the darkness in the woods ahead. "Even worse, they might use slaves."

Ken's antennae twitched. Apondra saw this as a sign that his curiosity piqued. "Archer, do they really employ slaves? That's against the laws of our kingdom."

"This isn't your kingdom out here." His eyes darted from the path forward to the path behind them. "And yes, slaves are used by some."

Tomas gripped Rose's reigns and took the lead into the forest. "If we cannot have uplifting or constructive dialogue, we should have none," he said, his tone gruffer than Apondra had recalled in any previous conversations. "Gunnar told me that morale can be worth more than full bellies." He touched the hilt of his sword. "We are losing daylight."

Ken and Apondra followed in their chariot as Sharpe and Domino slunk back to the rear of their tiny caravan. The sun fell sooner than they had hoped due to the time lost crossing the giant rut. Apondra strained her eyes, peering into the darkness spreading through the trees like a fog.

"Should we camp?"

"We have just a handful of hours until the merchant town. We should arrive at midnight. If we camp, we do it now and then wake and ride right at dawn," Sharpe replied. He looked at the head of their procession. "Squire, what is your decision?"

Apondra smiled.

"Archer," Tomas replied, "I say we stop. But it is the princess and her safety that should have final say."

"Your counsel is appreciated," Apondra said, "and I would agree. The animals are likely tired. There is a small brook running along the trail here, several feet into the woods. So we stop, we let the animals drink and rest, and we camp on the other side of the brook."

"I should say," interjected Ken, "that we build a tiny fire. We don't need to ring ourselves, but it will be chilly."

Sharpe dismounted, along with Tomas, and they walked together to the side of the trail. Sharpe spoke first.

"I did not think lighting a fire for a party of four would be such a complicated decision."

"Merchants will see us from the trail," said Ken, "and stop for company or comfort."

"Animals may be drawn to our scents," replied Sharpe. "The water will break the scent trail on one side, and the fire's smoke and our animals will make humans and lobfolk less detectable."

"Hmm. Wet logs." Apondra shivered, not from the cooling forest but the looming fear of the wilds. "We make the fire, then once we have embers, we keep them fed with wet logs. That will reduce the light but keep us warm, as well as create smoke."

Sharpe nodded. "It's the best we can do. Two of us on guard, two of us sleeping. Or trying to sleep." He checked the ends of his bowstring. "I doubt any of us will rest easy."

Ken tossed a food sack at their feet. "Well, let's start the fire and start eating. I can't worry as much when my belly is full."

The travelers packed the campsite just before dawn and continued on their way. Apondra listened to the trees, smiling to herself when she heard the first hoot of a day owl, a good sign that the animals deemed the forest as now safe, or at least safer than it was when the large rut was dug by whatever giant beast or snapping turtle had plowed through. Ken and Tomas engaged in functional conversation about the road and the chariot's possible maintenance, driven by Tomas describing his experiences crafting with leathers and softwoods. Sharpe sat quietly on Domino, his shoulders slumped as he scanned the sides of the road more often than the path forward.

Ahead of them, smoke rose above the tree line in blacks, grays, and whites from various pyres. Apondra could barely separate the scents of woods, foods, and kilns as the aromas beckoned through the branches. The trail widened, and the quartet exited the forest.

The chimneyed peaks of inns, bakeries, and wall-to-wall cottages ringed the outside of the merchant town. Behind the single- and two-story buildings, large storage halls, three stories high, stretched back toward the river that bisected the tiny metropolis. The masts of the largest ships rose above the warehouses, and between the gaps in the buildings, a smaller ship floated silently down river toward the inevitable maw of the ocean. Ken pulled his cloak over his head.

"I am a lobster out of water," he quipped. "And a rather obvious one, at that." He displayed his white hands. Apondra looped her index finger around his and smiled.

"You are just another ordinary merchant here. Let's gather information and send our sellbow on his way."

Sharpe dismounted and tied Domino in front of an inn, a green-shuttered house bearing a broken sign that read "Twisted Nickel". He paid a small old man a coin and waved to the group.

"Our mounts are safe, this is our groom," he said, nodding to the old man. "And we have a room on the second floor accessible from the back. Lobfolk-friendly stairs are a feature of this inn. Let's lock up our things inside."

The room itself provided adequate comfort. Four generously sized beds, two on each side, and a high-silled window for privacy. They placed their food and remaining supplies on and underneath the long table in the middle of the room. Apondra set her bag of books on her bed on one side of the window, and Ken did the same. Tomas silently took the bed closest to the door and tapped his wooden leg to catch Apondra's attention.

"If anyone needs me, I'll be down in the tavern."

"Time already for a drink?" smiled Sharpe.

"Information," Tomas said without a smile in return. He rattled a small bag of coins attached to his belt. "I'll gather the news and see what the townsfolk know, if anything, about the beast that caused that giant rut we came across."

"Ken!" Apondra shouted, "I have an idea! Let's see if we can find a book merchant!"

"Eave Queen," he replied with a hint of reprimand in his voice, "we did not bring money for shopping."

"But maybe we'll find something about Azcalaw! We may cross paths with some texts from the northern lands, or even Ice Lake!"

"Here." Sharpe stacked a set of small silver coins in Apondra's hand. "I know you are good for the credit. I assume you'll repay my loan once you return to your kingdom." His eyes narrowed. "Correct?"

"Yes, of course!" She did not like the shadow in his tone and told herself to spend some time with him, alone, to get to know him better in case he chose to travel further with them. It was clear to her that he felt a swirling storm of guilt, greed, empathy, and protectiveness, changing every hour. She did trust him now, she knew that, but the extent of that trust was a line she needed to find and then redraw.

After a quick snack of dried blueberries, Apondra and Ken ventured into the depths of the town toward the central river. The mixture of weathered gray stone, fresh white wooden walls, and mismatched shutters from building to building implied a town that rebuilt itself over centuries of wear. The current street, covered in freshly placed stones, abruptly ended as it intersected the old potholed main avenue. Immediately they noticed a mixture of humans and lobfolk as they navigated closer to the docks. The large warehouses of crisscrossed wooden plank siding bustled with activity as workers dashed in and out of doorways and paddocks with sacks and pushcarts of foods. A team of lobfolk wearing thick canvass capes carried beams of fresh cut lumber on their shoulders to an awaiting horse cart. Apondra caught herself admiring their silent strength, working class members, hustling back and forth to earn their wages. Ken clawed at the corners of his cloak.

"Is it okay if I feel intimidated by their size? Those are some very large specimens, if I do say so."

"They are strong, Ken. They do this all day, every day. I can't imagine how many times some of these lobfolk have molted as they grew." She allowed herself a short smile. "All for the glory of their kingdoms and the benefit of their families."

A husky singsong voice replied from over her shoulder. "They do what they're told, or they'll be resold."

She turned and saw a tall thin human wearing a cloth apron over his leathers, his wet black hair combed over his tan skull and falling over his shoulders. The lines in his face betrayed an otherwise youthful appearance and vigor. At his side, a coiled leather whip hung on his belt hook.

"Hello, sir. Who are you?"

"Quartermaster. Those shellfish are my minions. They work for me." He crossed his arms and nodded. "The best at what they do."

"They must be highly skilled laborers, no?"

"They sign on for three years in exchange for food and lodging, and when they are done, they earn their coinage."

"Slaves." Ken lowered his claws to his sides. "That's slavery."

"Indentured servants." The quartermaster sneered, revealing a mouth of yellowed teeth. "Judging by the rather intricate knit of your wool, fair lady, I'd say you're far from your estate." He touched her sleeve, his dirty fingers feeling the material. He withdrew a handkerchief and wiped away the stain on her sweater. "Apologies."

She crossed her arms. "Why would these lobfolk agree to such a contract? And what happens when their years are finished?"

"As I said, they earn their coin in the end. Many of these workers are lost, abandoned by families or their compatriots. Some are criminals. But without coin, you can do nothing in this world." He whistled to a group of lumber carriers and tapped his whip. "When your basic needs are taken care of, that lump sum in deferment is enough to buy freedom. A house, a field for crops, or a boat," he said. "It may take them a few tours of service, but I pay my wages. I'm not like some of the other quartermasters."

"Can someone buy their freedom?" Apondra placed her hand over her pocket and the coins she received from Sharpe. "How much?"

"So many questions! I suppose freedom could be purchased, but you'd have to pay double their wages; repay their owner, and then compensate their service time."

"Oh." She slipped her hand back into her sleeve. The quartermaster glanced over his shoulder.

"Not everyone will be as accommodating as myself to strangers. I run a fair business; others do not." He lowered his face closer to hers. "Keep your head low. And your friend here, keep him close by your side. If you run into trouble, tell them you know Dale, Quartermaster of Dock Nineteen." He held out his hand.

"I think he wants a bribe," Ken proffered.

"It's a handshake, friend." He pointed to his open palm. "No concealed weapon, thus my palm is up. Be wary of your ignorance to the merchant ways. Any other questions will cost you."

"You've been very kind, and I thank you. But why?" She bit her lip and reached for her coins.

"I recognize a potential client. A good businessman can sense wealth. You can act demure and innocent, fair lady, but the tailoring of your clothing and your smooth skin tell me you have never labored in a field or mill. I can smell the wealth on you. *Royal wealth.*" He leaned closer. "I attract the hardest and most loyal workers through my earnestness. Other quartermasters are profitable through abuse and deception." Dale smiled, his stale breath blasting her face. "One coin, please."

Apondra shook his hand and then retrieved the smallest coin she could feel in her pocket, then a second one. "Where would I find a book dealer, if such a place exists here?"

He examined the coins and smiled. "Go to dock *nine*, downstream. *Nine.* You should see an art and antiquities dealer's place of business. Tell him Dale sent you." He flipped the coin into the air and caught it. "Names and endorsements go far in this town. *Your Highness.*"

With a wink, he turned and strode back to the docks. Apondra and Ken moved shoulder to shoulder and headed to the lower dock numbers. She pulled her sweater's collar up over her mouth as Ken scanned the crowd.

"Your reputation precedes you, apparently. We need to buy you a cloak, or a hood, or perhaps a large hollow gourd for a mask," Ken quipped.

She scanned the booths and approached a textile merchant's stand. She pointed to a piece of red and black striped fabric that hung on a nail on the side of his table.

"Sir, that scrap, I'll buy it."

"For you, m'lady? Just a smile will suffice." The man handed her the triangle of cloth and folded it. "I can't sell pieces so small for sails or bedding."

She thanked him, dropped a coin on the counter, and quickly wrapped the cloth over her hair and around her face. It was thankfully larger than she expected when she unfolded it, and she tucked the edges under her hair into her collar.

"Stealth," said Ken.

"Anonymity."

"Better word."

A large wooden circle with a crudely painted "9" hung by two black chains under the thick, brown-bricked arch. The workers and their goods now reflected buckets of metalware, decorative pans and vases, candle holders by the dozen, and rolled scrolls of cloth or parchment. Several humans and lobfolk wandered amid the workers, some carrying black clubs and adorned in matching blue-striped sashes.

"They might be security for the valuable items," Ken noted. "It's much more profitable to steal a silver cup than a pine log if you're a dockworker. Probably more portable as well."

A crack of wood against wood startled Apondra. One of the security men smacked his club against a pole, rallying a circle of guards to a lobfolk carrying a large sack. A guard struck him in his stomach, causing him to double over and loosen his grip on a tiny silver plate concealed under his work apron. A second worker took the sack from him as the guards pummeled the thief with their clubs. One of the lobfolk guards shouted.

"Quartermaster! Come for severance!"

A pair of hands lifted Apondra from behind and moved her to the side. A mountainous lobfolk with black and red stripes painted across his claws strode forward and grabbed the thief by the arms. He placed a black coin into the thief's hand.

"Your toll token. Pay for your exit by land or by sea. Your wages earned have been forfeited. BANNED FROM DOCK NINE!" his voice boomed.

Ken grabbed Apondra by the hand and pulled her behind a stack of barrels. "So this is how 'indentured servitude' works? This is horrible." He glanced behind them where a lobfolk dressed in light blue robes, followed by two more in dark blue robes, made their way to the thief.

"Repent," yelled the light blue leader. He threw back his hood, revealing a face painted with crude blue stripes across his brown shell that dribbled down his antennae. "Repent, thief! Pay us your black coin of shame and we shall bring you on the journey to salvation. Board our spiritual vessel and we shall take you to your peace as we wait for the end of times."

Ken placed a hand over his face. "Oh, this is rich."

"Shh, let me hear what this zealot is saying."

She pulled her scarf higher over her nose and crept closer to where the blue-robed lobfolk confronted the quartermaster and the guards. The thief cowered between the two parties as the painted-face spoke.

"I am Tenor, high priest of the clan of—"

"I know who you are, Tenor," snarled the quartermaster. "No one wants to hear your drivel. Steal this slave's coin with your empty promises and be on your way."

"My dear sir," said Tenor, his hands splayed across his chest in mock offense, "we are here to save this poor little clam so that he can nurture the pearl inside himself. Have you not seen the glaring signs that we are witnessing the first act of the end of time?" He flailed his arms skyward, his disciples imitating him. "The seas have opened, the lands shall tear, and the skies will fall! Elementals from each of the worlds will judge us unworthy! Only by the grace of he who rules us all shall we—"

"Enough!" The quartermaster poked him with the handle of his whip. "There are yards of punishment attached to this handle. Get out!"

The thief extended his hand and placed the black coin into Tenor's own. He stood and raised his arms.

"By his name, I am saved! I pledge to him the rest of my days!"

Tenor held the coin above his head, pointing three accusatory fingers at the crowd. He locked eyes with Apondra; she gasped.

"Those who reject our divine leader will not be saved." He tilted his head.

Apondra blinked; a chill ran down her spine. Tenor's eyes sparkled blue, almost white, for barely a second, boring into her fixed gaze before he concluded his speech.

"The lost magic returns. And so, this world shall be torn apart."

His robed disciples and their recruit locked arms with Tenor, and hurried back under the dock's archway, disappearing into the crowds beyond. Apondra could not shake Tenor's stare, and the piercing glow that still lingered like a cold shiver deep in her bones. She pulled her scarf tight and trembled, forcing herself to refocus her thoughts. *I need to confront the quartermaster before he resumes his tasks.*

"Excuse me, but who were those … religious … folk?"

"Religion?" The quartermaster scoffed. "They're thieves. They attempt to rescue those who are exiled, steal their ferry coins, and then who knows what after that." He waved his hand to shoo her away. "Cultists of Azcalaw, fools."

"What?" She grabbed his arm as he turned. "Azcalaw? Where do they come from?"

He whipped around and stuck his finger in her face. "I don't have time for you, young lady. Now be gone!" He stomped away, whip in hand, and whistled at a group of men carrying a small sculpture. Ken pulled her back to the side of the busy causeway.

"Eave Queen," Ken whispered, "we can follow those priests, or whatever they are, if we make haste!"

"We are not trackers, nor are we skilled spies!" She huffed as her scarf drooped off her head. "And you stand out like a sore claw!"

"And you stand out like a tulip in a stone field!"

"Your sarcasm almost sounded like a compliment."

"Well, you see my point." His eyes darted. "You draw attention, even with your face covered. I don't see any women here, let alone one 'so fair and lovely as you'. We can always send Sharpe to snoop around for these cultists. Based on the quartermaster's familiarity with them, I assume they come here often."

"Sharpe is looking for a ride to get out of here. I don't think that's an option we have on the table."

"Sharpe can be bought for coin," Ken said, tugging at her coin purse. "And tuck this away! You're just asking for a thief to steal it!"

"Sorry. Good point."

"I make good points quite often." He smiled. "Now, you head to the antiquities dealer's shop. Stick with what you know, which is old dusty books!"

"And what about you?"

"I'm going to follow the blue-cloaks."

"I thought you said we weren't spies!"

"*We* are not. But I want to observe them if I can and see where else they go for their little street sermons. Then, if we can enlist Sharpe's help, we'll have a good trail of crumbs for him to follow."

"Hello?"

Apondra opened the door of the art dealer's warehouse and immediately stepped back. Before her spread a staggering series of open wooden shelves, row after row of roughcut timber attached to flat boards and metal pins, a chaotic storage array of various heights and widths. A flagpole mounted at the front and middle of each row designated a color and a number, some sort of organizational method she couldn't immediately understand.

"May I help you, miss?" slithered a voice above her shoulder. A lobfolk, his shell covered in black and red spots, unfurled his black cloak and stepped around her. A crisscrossed pattern of leather straps and belts adorned his body with dozens of pockets, loops, and pouches equipped with writing implements, strings, and scissors. He removed a small paper pad and flipped through the pages while dipping a baleen pen into a tiny ink vial that hung around his neck. "Name, please." She pulled her scarf away from her face.

"Apondra."

"Full name. I require it for my client logs." He dipped his pen into the ink again. "My book of business is almost as valuable as my wares." He eyed her up and down, pausing as he scrutinized her sweater. "Well?"

"My name is Apondra ... Inkly. Oh, and Dell said to mention his name." She could think of no other alias, still stunned by the immense size of the warehouse. He flickered his antennae and scribbled.

"And what are you here for?"

"Books? I am looking to purchase books."

"What kind?"

"Histories and myths?"

"What era?"

"Come again?"

He retrieved another notepad, flicking through the pages even faster, then stopping abruptly. "Modern, First War, Oceana War, Early Kingdom, Pre-Kingdom, Mythical Errata, Mythical Proper, or Ice Dawn?"

She wished Ken was here.

"Ice Dawn?" Perhaps starting with the oldest books would be the most useful strategy, as the more recent histories and myths were well documented in her own library back home at the castle.

"Light Blue Banners, section twelve. Do you need a cart, or did you bring your own slave to assist you?"

She puffed out her chest. "I don't use slaves."

"Whatever," dismissed the book merchant. "You're heading to the far corner of the warehouse. Do not disturb the scribes. Please and thank you." He closed his cloak and shuffled down the first aisle.

"Thank you, sir."

"Clem. Call me Clem, Lady Inkly."

She placed her thumb on her chin and reviewed his instructions. The spectrum of colored flags had no particular order, but she spotted the light and dark blue pennants at the end. A short walk and a quick turn at the end of the rows placed her in the light blue shelves.

The books were extraordinary, both in number and appearance. Not only were there multiple titles beyond her imagination, but each one sat with a dozen or so copies in each stack. When the few book merchants came to Castle Homarus, they only brought one copy of each selection. Of course there must be somewhere they all live, like a family, sitting on shelves together! Her heart raced as she lightly touched the spines, each one with unique wrinkles and stitches sewn by hand. Some bore beautiful leather skins stretched over wood or metal plates, while others lay on their side as simply bound parchments with a cloth wrapping. But the books! So many books made her question if she were to die in this very spot, would it be the most wonderful place to haunt.

She counted the sections as she passed each of them; nine, ten, eleven. As she approached the twelfth, she froze; a rhythmic scratching and clawing crept from the next aisle. Apondra stood on her toes to peer through a break in the book stacks and saw several tables, each set high with reams of fresh-cut paper. Women, human women, sat hunched over sheets of papers, their hands stained with ink, scribbling madly. She listened; a mumbling rhythm, a humming, hovered over the desks. A tall pair of women in red skirts and shirts slowly waded between the transcribers, reading from their own books in unison, their voices animated and clear, but low enough that the noise barely met Apondra's ears.

In flawless unison, the transcribers flipped their sheets of paper over, dipped their quills in perfectly syncopated motions, and continued to write. *So this is how books are made?* She hoped the transcribers were paid well for such important work, then realized the likelihood that these were the slave jobs available to women. She comforted herself with the thought that at least they were literate, educated by default throughout their tenure, and labored indoors away from the elements.

"Don't disturb them," hissed Clem in a harsh whisper behind her. "One mistake can cost us many coins as well as ruin their workflow rhythm. Or, even worse, ruin a book." She nodded, afraid now to speak. She pointed to a shelf in section twelve, and he nodded.

The first books Apondra examined were basic histories of the earliest eras, mythologies from oral traditions handed down for generations until the dawn of literacy and the written word. Stories of great beasts or gods slicing each other open to create various pieces of the world, epic love tales, and fables of morality. She could lose herself in here, she thought, but she needed to hasten her search. She reached higher and lower on the shelves, scanning the titles and reading the first handful of pages as she slid books in and out of their slots. *Nothing of use, at least using this method.* The merchant watched her carefully, and she made sure that each book went back to the proper shelf, respectfully replaced so that the covers would not be damaged. He finally crossed his arms and clicked his mandibles to get her attention.

"I have a feeling you are looking for something less … common," he whispered.

"Yes, more obscure. I'm looking for histories about Azcalaw."

The merchant placed his finger on Apondra's lips. She recoiled. "Lady Inkly, say no more, and say nothing. Come. You may count your coins silently along the way."

He led Apondra to the end of the aisle and turned down a short hallway in the back of the warehouse. At the end of the corridor, Clem gestured to a thick wooden door, bound with enormous brass straps. He opened it with some effort and led her inside; a dark office and vault lit by a handful of candles. Along three walls, tall locked wooden cabinets featuring large glass portholes decorated with gold and silver trim stood silently. He opened the first unit with one of the many keyrings hidden under his cloak.

"Miss Inkly, would I be correct to assume you are looking for something of a very delicate nature, something unique?" She nodded, her eyes still adjusting to the dim room.

Clem's hands crept deep into the shelf and retrieved a book; he flittered his antennae and smiled as he presented it to her. The covers were large, flat, white shells, almost pearlized, shiny and oily in the flickering light. If she had not known better, she would have assumed it was the same shellbook that Ken had shown her back in her room in what felt like a lifetime ago. He opened the cover carefully and showed her the table of contents. Each chapter title was a single word, crafted from a language she had never seen before, except for one she instantly recognized.

Azcalaw.

"I've seen one of these texts before! What is this?" she said, reaching for the book before he snatched it away from her.

"A book, seized by a conqueror many generations ago. It is a log of the deities of a people long forgotten. But this is not just a book, it is an *antique*. To own such a thing is to buy a piece of art, as it is one of a kind." He held out two of his hands and rubbed his fingers together. "I doubt you have the coin to purchase it, but you can purchase a transcription of the chapter. I find this to be an agreeable business model that I offer to nobles, and scholars such as yourself."

At this moment, Apondra suddenly realized they were not alone. A woman, or rather, a girl about her own age, sat motionless in the corner by the dull light of a candle on a tiny desk next to her stool. Her face was pale, her brown eyes lifeless, her shoulder-length blond hair dirty with the split ends touched by ink. As she stood, Apondra noticed a tight necklace, a shackle, but made of a substance like black glass glinting in the flickering light, fastened to the girl's neck.

"How much?" Apondra asked, her voice shaking as the girl continued her unblinking stare. "And how soon?"

"Sixty coins. You may pay half now and half when you pick it up. Any time after sunrise."

Her hands trembled slightly as she counted the coins in her purse, glancing at the poor girl in the corner. *Is she still a girl, or is she a woman? How long has she been here?* The details didn't matter as Apondra focused on how much suffering went into the books she loved, the merchant town, and the hundreds if not thousands of people indentured to the mere act of commerce. *If I cannot save them all, I will save one, and it will be this one.*

She handed over thirty coins, leaving just a handful in her tiny sack, and steadied her voice. "Sunrise. And I want this slave girl to be here when I pick up the translation so that I may thank her for her work." She swallowed. "Someone should appreciate her."

Clem stepped back, his antennae viciously swirling against her proposal. "My dear … Apondra Inkly, was it? … this girl is not a hardened slave.

She is a gifted transcriber. The things she has read, the information she knows of ancient lore is far more valuable than any slave wage or ransom."

"Why would you tell me this?"

"Because, *Apondra, Eave Queen of the Kingdom of the Lobfolk*, I know who you are. Your disguise is very weak." She felt shame in her faulty ruse, as she pulled her sweater over her hands. He placed a hand on her shoulder. "As a dealer in fine arts and items of antiquity, I have personally delivered some exquisite items to, and on behalf of your father, King Abbasdah. The last time I visited your court was a few years ago, but I remember seeing a young princess, *a human girl*, running through the hall with an armful of books." He smiled. "I am a merchant, and it is my business to get to know everything about my clients, including their family, to solidify those professional relationships. Besides, you don't forget a beautiful face, nor an inquisitive mind." He turned back to the girl in the corner. "This one, her mind is full of the greatest beauty and sadness you will ever know."

"Is that why you keep her chained?" Apondra slapped away his hand.

"Temper, girl. You may be royalty in your kingdom, but only the trust of strangers who know your secret keeps you alive in this town. That girl, over there, she is my responsibility. Illegitimate kings would slaughter to know what she knows." He knelt, bringing his head below the eyeline of both girls. "Your father is a good king. I know you are not here as a spy. Plus, as I've said, your stealth skills are quite lacking."

"How much for her? I can have a chest of coins sent in exchange for her." Her eyes darted between the merchant and the girl.

"I am not for sale," the girl said, speaking for the first time with a rhythmic baritone. "I am here because I choose to be here, despite what Clem may say." She stood, her ragged dress and thin ink-splattered shirt flowing with her short steps forward. "I do not require a liberator." The girl took the shellbound book and flipped to the middle. "I have already transcribed this chapter once before. You don't know how to wield the words within."

"And what does that mean?" asked Apondra.

"This is a book of imprisonment of those who lived in days before recorded time."

"My dear," said Clem, his volume rising, "please still your tongue."

"I'm sorry." She slunk back to her stool.

"Wait." Apondra grabbed her coins from the merchant's hand. "You, girl. What is your name?"

The girl bit her lip. Clem shook his head. "She has no name. She is just another treasure in this vault."

Apondra lifted her chin and counted her coins. "Girl. This is for you. Tell me, now, what you have read. Merchant, I will give you your final payment tomorrow at dawn in full. No written translation is needed, if she can orally tell me contents." As she placed the coins into the girl's hand, she felt a small tingle, an icy pinprick that did not pierce the skin, in the tips of her fingers. For just a moment, Apondra thought she saw a blue spark under the coins. The girl looked up, her jaw tense, her eyes flashing. "What was that?" Apondra whispered.

The girl interrupted with a small shake of her head and forced the coins into Clem's hand. She spoke again. "Lady Apondra, you will pay for services rendered, even if you cancel the transcription. I will tell you what I have read, pampered princess." She looked at her merchant captor. "I'll just need an hour with her, Clem. This is easy money."

Clem slowly nodded. "One hour for sixty coins." As he reached for the doorknob, Apondra spied his wristlet slipping out from his sleeve, a thick band made of black glass like the one around the girl's neck. He closed the door behind him as he returned to the warehouse.

No sooner had the latch clicked, the girl leapt to her feet and grabbed a wineskin from under the table. She tossed the cork on the ground and drank the entire contents, then turned to Apondra and grabbed her wrist. "Alright sweetie, this is the part where you liberate me."

"Can't I just pay Clem?"

"You are such a foolish girl for someone so bookish by the first impression you've presented here. Listen. I am being forced to learn the secrets of the texts so that he can eventually offer me to the highest bidder, a king or bastard heir looking to rule the kingdoms. Information is power, and he is building me into a priceless weapon!" The girl fiddled with her neck shackle.

"So why don't you leave? Can't you escape? I see no chains."

The girl looked down and lifted her soiled skirt to reveal her legs covered in long black painted lines, intricately woven through patterns of circles and ovals. Apondra thought at first it was an abstract garden, but then realized the images were chains.

"These are runes. *Runes of binding*. They are linked to the cuff around my neck and the one Clem wears on his wrist. I cannot travel far from his cuff. When he wants me to stay put, he just hangs his wristlet on the outside of the door." She gazed into Apondra's eyes, a dominating stare that burned with a newly ignited anger, *and a flash of blue sparks*. "I cannot remove my own runes. They block me from casting *any* of the spells that I've read and learned. Only someone else can say the words and release me."

"Are you saying that these are … magic?"

The girl nodded once, her focus shifting to the locked cabinets behind Apondra. The princess turned slowly, estimating the number of books inside, how long it would take to read them, and then turned back to the girl. Her eyes showed a truth in her words and a plea for help.

"These are all spells, books of spells. I have learned many of them, memorized the words of languages I don't even understand. Long ago, the first spell I was tricked into learning was to bind myself to him, to Clem. He tricked me into reading it aloud."

"So, what can I do? We have less than an hour."

"I've played many scenarios in my head, and, finally, he made one mistake. When he revealed your identity as a princess, I realized that you might have the leverage to save me. But some spells, they work in very unique ways." Her voice drifted. "Some may only be spoken by a caster. He did not realize that my binding could be broken by using the voice of someone who can *channel* the spell." Apondra heard a desperation and perhaps an accusation in the way she said *channel*.

"I will help you, girl, but you must help me. It is the reason that led me here. There is a terrible danger that is coming, one that threatens all kingdoms. That's why I am here to learn about Azcalaw."

"Alright, help-for-help. Agreed." The girl dropped her hem to hide the binding runes. "I will tell you the unbinding spell. You will recite it as I speak it, exactly how I speak it. When it is over, we will need to run and sneak aboard the next ship leaving the docks."

"Wait a moment. My companions are at the Twisted Nickel on the edge of town. When we escape, we'll hide there and leave in the morrow after I pay the merchant."

"You're still going to pay him?"

"I have my word to uphold?"

"*Your word?*" The girl's jaw dropped. "Really?"

"If he doesn't suspect me, I can provide some cover, or additional time, for your escape. Plus, he knows who I am! He can put a claim out to my kingdom for unpaid debt!"

The girl dragged Apondra to the stool and forced her to sit on it. "Fine, whatever. We can work that out later. For now, we don't have much time. Please just listen to me. Carefully." The girl lifted her skirt again and closed her eyes. "Repeat after me, match the syllables exactly as I say them:

A girl is born, her heart is wide, her mother's touch, her simple pride

Her pain is felt, by chains of flesh, to bind her now, il qua gahk nesh!"

Apondra repeated the words, mimicking the unknown sounds at the end of the spell. "Anything?"

The girl opened her eyes. A thin, almost imperceptible, blue mist floated between Apondra and the girl, the same color as the spark between their hands, and the sparkle she saw in Tenor's eyes when the blue-cloaks recruited the thief outside. The patterns on the girl's legs began to move and swirl, pulsing like veins, black and then blue, then black again. Slowly, each branching tattoo receded down her legs, disappearing into her shoes.

"Apondra! Quickly! Get off the stool!"

As Apondra stood, a black circle, a shadow darker than deep night, manifested on the floor beneath her. Thick inky tentacles bled from the floor, inching their appendages up the stool's legs. The tendrils clutched at the stool's crossbar, gnashing thorny vines against the wood.

"What is this?" Apondra leapt, her back pressed against the wall of cabinets.

"Since you spoke the spell, and I spoke the spell, your words undid it, but mine … cast it again. I didn't think that part through."

"What?" The blackened tendrils smashed the stool against the wall, slithering madly around the blackened spot. "You've created this thing here?"

"Give me a minute," the girl said in a raspy whisper. "I need to think." She paced over to the closest cabinet and tried the lock. "Wait, I've got it."

She held her hands out, palms up, and closed her eyes.

"Telling tales, whitened sails, pressing time against the vales,

Undo the time, undo the hand, ill nich bana, embrada shand!"

Apondra watched in disbelief as a blue glowing spiderweb bloomed from her own chest, sucked into the girl, a cold wave rushing into and then out of her lungs. Again, the azure fog spread, this time from the girl toward the floor. The tentacles froze, inches away from Apondra. White flecks of ice began to form on each tentacle, traveling down to the black puddle that rippled until it turned white with frost as well. The girl swung her leg and stomped on the frozen form, shattering it. A second shatter followed, as the shackle binding the girl's neck cracked and fell to the floor.

"What was that?"

"A spell of entropy. I've never tried that one before."

"Well, you certainly know some useful spells."

"Only what I can remember."

"And those words, the words at the end of each, what were they?"

"Look, I don't have time to explain the finer points of the sacred spell languages, *Princess!*"

"*Apondra* is fine. And I don't know your name, girl."

The girl tucked her hair behind each ear. Her cheeks shone pale and smooth, like the fine porcelain Apondra saw in the market back home on the dolls from the merchants of the faraway islands. "Diana. Just Diana."

"*Diana*, I promise I'll get you far from here."

The latch on the door rattled.

"He's back!" whispered Diana.

The vault door opened with a slow creak, followed by the tapping footfalls of the merchant. Diana leapt onto her stool, pushing Apondra to the side.

"Girl, what is this?" Clem said, scurrying across the room and kicking out her seat. As she landed, her skirt lifted, revealing her now bare legs, free of the binding runes. She clutched her neck. Apondra saw the fear in Diana's face as she realized Clem could now see that she was free from her bondage.

"I'll be leaving now!" Diana clutched the leg of the stool and swung it at his chest, knocking him on his tail. Apondra stepped back, aghast, then quickly tried the cabinets. *Locked.* On the small transcription table, she eyed the shellbound book and grabbed it with one hand, sliding it under her sweater. She then clutched a wad of Diana's shirt.

"Run!"

The girls leapt over the stunned merchant and bounded out of the office and into the hallway. Diana tugged Apondra to the left, directly through the rows of transcribing women.

"Words! Words everywhere!" Diana yelled, sweeping a pile of papers into the air. With silent acknowledgement, Apondra did the same, whipping a whirlwind of parchment in their wake. Clem stumbled and slid on the sheets as he attempted his pursuit in vain.

"Look what you've done! Extra dinner and a purse of coins for whoever stops those girls!"

A pair of lobfolk slaves dropped their boxes of parchments and lumbered between the girls and the exit doorway, claws bared above their heads, clacking in menacing tones.

"Can't you cast another spell?" Apondra shouted, dodging one of the massive limbs.

"That's not how it works!" Diana replied, dodging her own adversary's clutches.

A thin whizzing buzzed through the air. An arrow shattered as it impacted a shelf beam several feet from Clem's head.

Sharpe stepped through the exit doorway, his bow drawn.

"Take one step closer to Her Highness and my aim will be true," he shouted. Ken tumbled in behind him, catching his breath.

"Eave Queen, come!" Ken shouted. He held his walking staff like a sword, swatting at the lobfolk slaves. "Shoo!"

"That girl is my property!" growled Clem, drawing a dagger from one of his many pouches. "Give her to me, intact, or pay her cost. This is business, not piracy!"

"We're not here for piracy, we just came to retrieve Apondra for supper!" said Ken. "What will reconcile the damages?" He rummaged in his coin pouch.

"Ten. Thousand. For the damages and for my slave girl."

"Oh. Well then." Ken closed his pouch. "Would you take a deposit of ten coins and a sweet cake?"

A timid familiar voice joined the fray. "Or this." Tomas stood behind the group, holding Gunnar's silver sword, point down, toward Clem. "It's the steel of Gunnar Brekke, First Cavalier of the Kingdom of Swan. It's worth far more than ten thousand."

Apondra gasped. The look in Tomas' eyes, unselfishly giving this token of his master's duty for the life of a girl he did not know, moved her nearly tears. "Tomas, you can't!"

"But you must," hissed Clem, gently touching the sword. He ran his fingers up and down the blade, smiling at his own reflection in the mirrored surfaces. "To come across a sword such as this by any means other than battle would be considered theft."

"It was my master's blade." Tomas paused, glancing at Sharpe. "In his last battle, he killed over a dozen giant weasels, saving the life of Her Highness, Eave Queen Apondra. I swear this to be true, and by my right as his squire, I grant it to you, in exchange for this girl, a clearing of our debt, and safe passage out of here." His hands shook as he extended the blade closer to Clem. "These other slaves here, and my fellow travelers all bear witness to this offer. Accept the deal."

"You do understand, squire, that if you wish to repurchase this from me in the future, it will cost you far more than you will ever see in your lifetime."

"So be it, but it is mine to exchange. For the girl. Now let her, and Princess Apondra, walk free." Tomas swallowed hard. "Take this sword and validate this contract. *Take it.*"

Apondra's hand tightened around Diana's, her pulse fast and hot in her grip. Although she could see the sweat on Tomas' brow, the nervous quiver in his lips, she also saw the heroic selflessness in him, instilled by his master's tutelage. Gunnar's ring glinted as it hung from his neck.

"Take it," Tomas commanded.

Clem again ran his fingers down the blade, then over the hilt, picking at the fine lines of the expertly smithed and engraved swan wings. He held it above his head and watched the sword reflect the flickering candles and torches from the walls and tables. "I have come out far, far, ahead in this deal." He sneered, his antennae arching at cruel angles. "Far, far, ahead." He gently placed the blade on top of a nearby table. "Diana, your notes are in the cabinets?"

"Yes."

"And translated to the common language?"

"Yes." Apondra could see Diana's fingers crossed behind her back.

"Then I will find another poor girl, one less treacherous, and continue my business." Clem glanced at Apondra. "There will always be another slave."

She glared at him. "But today, this one is free."

Clem extended a hand to Tomas. "The deal is done. All have witnessed." Again, he sneered. Apondra watched Tomas' jaw tighten as he shook the merchant's hand. She could see the conflict and pain in his eyes but knew this was a young man who was willing to do difficult things when they were the right things to do.

The merchant's other slaves receded, allowing the party to leave through the open doors into the market. The sun began its descent behind the mountains in the west. Ken pulled his cloak over his head as Apondra looped her scarf over her face. He reached an arm around her and Diana on each side.

"Stay close, we'll discuss this all later. To the Twisted Nickel as fast as we can."

Sharpe walked ahead of the group, bow in hand, and Tomas held the rear. Apondra felt the handle of the dagger in her belt and stopped their procession.

"Squire, here." She handed him the sheathed blade. He nodded silently and placed it on his hip.

"Thank you, Apondra."

Diana stepped to Tomas and kissed him on the cheek. "Thank you," she whispered. "You are a good man."

He nodded, blushed, and pointed to a sign at a cross street ahead. "We'll turn here, then double back, in case that dirty merchant sent anyone to follow us."

Diana shook her head. "He won't. He's a scoundrel, but a businessman first. Without his word as a binding contract, he would lose all his wealth, and his customers. Even the more nefarious ones."

Apondra huffed. "He's a slaver. That's all I need to know to not have any remorse about liberating you. You are a free person now."

"I liberated myself, you were just a *vessel*," Diana said, pulling at a clump of her hair crusted with ink. "All I ask of you now is for a proper bath and then I will go my own way."

Sharpe exhaled loudly as they reached the front stoop of the Twisted Nickel. "I was not able to secure transportation." His hands on his hips, he lowered his head to Apondra. "I'm sorry. Give me until tomorrow."

"That's alright, archer."

A sturdy old man with a short white beard emerged from the inn wearing horse-riding gloves and a tight leather hat often used by couriers across the kingdoms, waving a piece of paper folded and sealed with wax. "I was told to deliver this to an albino. I've been waiting the better part of the day to hand this directly to you." He tapped his foot. "I assume that is *you*, good sir?"

Ken looked over both his shoulders. "Yes, that would be me. Thank you." The courier continued to tap his foot. "Oh, right. Have a coin. Thank you." Ken paid the gratuity and then held the wax seal on the paper for all to see, revealed in the light of the porch lamps. "It's the seal of our king, Abbasdah."

"Well, open it!" shouted Apondra. Her glee was met by the breaking of the seal by Ken and a stern look.

"Oh dear," said Ken. "It's written in the vizier's hand. Your father is alive, but no better than when we left. And a gentlelob named, Larold, the Ward of Ribbed Beach, has been provoking the royal council to declare the kingunable to perform his duties." His eyes narrowed, two of his arms itching his elbows. "Larold has been in opposition to Teelok, the lobfolk we met at the beach, and is putting forth his name to lead the king's council and whatever that would entail."

Ken folded the paper and tucked it into his cloak's inner pocket. His downcast eyes told Apondra that he had some deeper thoughts and doubts, but perhaps this was not the time to discuss, especially after the day's events. If it was true that one of the council was trying to usurp her claim to the throne, there was little she could do out here, so far from home, except to try to find Azcalaw and save the kingdom. After a quick glance at the other members of the party, her knees buckled, as her spirit sank from the weight of the day's events on top of her growing burdens.

"I'm going to need to sit down for a while, I think."

The party arrived at their room and Apondra promptly led Diana to the bath chamber at the end of the hall. She waited outside as the lobfolk staff maidens brought hot water, and she tipped them each with a coin from the shrinking pile in her purse.

Apondra waited quietly as Diana bathed. The muffled splashes through the door provided a respite from the discordant streets, so much louder and chaotic than home, and the explosion of activities at the merchant warehouses. Her fingers trembled slightly as she looked at the dirt under her nails, a bit nervous now that she was confronted with another reality of how far from the castle she was. *A bath might do me some good*, she concluded, an activity that replicated some normalcy from her life as a noble.

She knocked lightly and opened the door. Diana sat on a stool next to the bathtub, brushing out her hair, a warm light blond like finely spun gold. Her shoulders and back were laid bare, revealing several long purple bruises from shoulder to shoulder, in stark contrast to her almost pure ivory pallor. Apondra tried not to stare at the first human woman she had seen in this state other than herself; she blushed. Diana pulled her robe over her uncovered skin.

"You can bathe if you like. I'm done."

"I would, um, like a moment of privacy?"

Diana turned her back. "You know, technically, you didn't *liberate* me. You just purchased me for a sword." She pulled a pair of socks over her feet. "Your squire brought these for me. Fresh wool." She wiggled her toes and smiled.

"He is a good man. A young man, but old in many ways." Apondra pulled her sweater over her head. "So, if I have technically bought you, then I declare you a free person. Is that how I officially liberate you?"

"We've exchanged enough wordplay to establish my freedom, I suppose. I'm guessing slaves in your kingdom go by different laws."

"We don't have slaves. Not in my kingdom," she scoffed.

"Open your eyes, Your Highness," Diana huffed. She pulled her slave tunic over her head and shook out the large wool sweater on the floor. "Every kingdom has slaves of one sort or another. Some just don't know it."

Apondra dipped her head into the bath, a metal tub supported by a ring of bricks. Her hair floated on the surface, absorbing the dying warmth. Her tears mixed with the remaining bubbles of soap and dirt on the surface, her hate for the merchant town boiling over, this wretched place that revealed too many secrets she never knew or never wanted to know. She let her thoughts drift back to her father, lying in bed, his loving hands holding hers. A tap on her shoulder startled her; Diana loomed over the tub.

"I'm going downstairs to eat. If I don't see you, I'll bring something back to the room for you. Your Highness." Diana shut the door, leaving Apondra to stew in her own thoughts in the now dirty bathwater.

Chapter 7

An Abrupt Departure North

Tomas pulled up a chair to the corner booth inside the Twisted Nickel, seating himself next to Ken and Diana. Sharpe had disappeared for the evening to continue his quest for transportation, much to Apondra's relief. She wrung out one last clump of wet hair as she took in the smells of the other travelers' plates and meals, an occasional foreign spice drifting into her nose.

Diana glanced out the window at Teacup and Rose, tethered outside in the yard under the watchful eyes of the tavern guards. Domino wandered alone in the paddock next to them, mirroring his owner's solitude a little too on-the-nose for Apondra's taste. She wanted the animals to at least be friends.

"That's an extraordinary beast, that steer," Diana remarked.

"I could say the same about you," Ken replied, "given what Apondra told us. The extraordinary part, not the beast part." She pushed her fork across her plate through a shrinking pile of fried potato slices without acknowledging his words. Ken lowered his voice. "Diana, tell us what you know of magic."

His last word lingered for a moment, barely audible above the banter and clinking glassware of the other patrons, at least those that remained after the dinnertime rush. Diana eyed the crowd and put down her fork.

"Magic is like air. Or rather, a smell in the air. You can't grab it. You can't hold it. But its scent is more pungent for some and varies in strength." She sipped at her half pint of ale. "And sometimes it disappears."

Tomas joined their conspiracy. "We have one, a magic user, or rather, a court sorcerer in my kingdom. He's our vizier. He says it takes decades to learn and wield, and only the chosen few are born with the power. Only a dozen or so other magic users live across the countryside, usually in exile. Many are reclusive fellows, hiding in the wilderness, except for Agnew, the Hermit of the Wetlands."

"Why is it that hermits are often so well-known despite their proclivity for isolation?" Ken quipped.

Tomas glanced over his shoulder. "Perhaps as a warning to others to stay away." He fixed his gaze on Diana. "A magic user is a potentially dangerous weapon, but you know that."

"That's somewhat true," Diana said. "The bit you mentioned about learning magic. But the privilege of wielding it is also tied to time, in a way." She laid a cloth napkin on the table and dipped her fork tines into her brown sauce. She drew a line across the cloth with her utensil, a waving pulse that bisected the center fold. Then, like the veins of a leaf, she drew branches birthed from random points of the main line. "This is magic." She licked her fork clean and dipped it into a yellow gravy on Ken's plate. "And these are magic capable people." She let the fork drip dots of yellow across the napkin, some on the lines and branches, others, in empty areas. A lone dot fell on the main trunk on her crude condiment sketch.

"So, are some touched by magic and others not?" asked Tomas.

"Yes … and no. The main line here is time. Magic flows through time. At some points," she tapped the branches, "magic flows out into the world." She circled a yellow dot on one of the branches. "If a user is touched, at that place and time, they can use it."

"And the dots not on the branch?" asked Ken.

"See this one here? In some cases, someone is born who is magic sensitive, but they are not able to wield it because, well, wrong branch. *Wrong time.*" She touched a yellow dot stranded in the middle of a white expanse. "And in rare, rare moments, someone is born of magic." She dipped her fork in the gravy again and circled the lone dab on the main trunk. "These are the unique individuals, such as Azcalaw. Or one of the other deities. Or legends."

Ken sat back and fiddled with his antennae. "So, you are on a branch? And how did Apondra set you free?"

"I was able to tap into the magic, despite my bondage, through a conduit. *Apondra* was the conduit." She tapped the dot sitting in the white void. "So this person, this conduit, can be used by someone on a branch." She drew a line between a dot on a branch and the dot in the empty space. "The weaker magics can be used this way. That's what the old texts have taught me."

"How did you learn all of this?" Ken prompted her.

"I was found by the merchant, Clem, and a paid consultant, a tracker who was a magic sensitive conduit. Clem placed me in the reading room when I was five. I was then bound at age six once he realized my potential." Diana placed her fork and knife back on her plate, crossed. "I am nineteen now, I think. I had a lot of time to learn, to decipher the old legends, and learn the sacred words that were seeded through thousands and thousands of books."

"Azcalaw," whispered Tomas, "what do you know?"

"A myth. A child's tale now, but a superstition to generations of ancestors, men and lobfolk, long dead. But every myth is rooted in fact, or misinterpretation of fact." Ken smiled at her words, but she did not return his expression. "So at one point, yes, a being named Azcalaw was real. And that is what I know of magic."

Apondra studied Diana's face in earnest as the spellcaster quietly resumed eating the remnants of her meal. The exposition sounded truthful, but Apondra looked for some reason for Diana to deceive or conceal more of the truth that only she knew.

"Diana, where will you go in the morning? I mean, if you have nowhere to go, please join us. You can help us find Azcalaw. Assuming he is real, of course."

"I think this is an appropriate time to use the phrase, 'a fool's errand', because that is what you are all on. There's nothing more to Azcalaw than a criminal cult that takes advantage of the poor and indebted."

Ken carefully sipped his soup, wiping a dribble that fell to his chest. "Blasted human spoons. Diana, back to your knowledge of magic, I'm curious if—"

"No more magic talk." She picked up her plate and licked it clean, wiping the errant juices from her mouth with her sleeve. "This is delicious." The group stared back at her as another dribble of brown sauce crept down her chin. "You all understand this is my first time of significance outside of that wretched place, yes?"

Ken folded his hands. "An animal raised in a cage knows nothing but the cage. You are no animal, despite your plate manners."

Diana picked up her glass and downed the remaining drink in one large gulp.

"I'm going to bed." She pushed her empty plate to the middle of the table and stood, teetering as she slid out of the booth. Tomas watched her stumble past one of the patrons, leaning on him to right herself and then out the tavern doors.

"I'm going to make sure she gets to the room safely." He slid out of his seat and jogged to catch up with her, passing the bar matron who approached the table with a small plate holding a cupcake.

"Are you the person paying for the meal, good sir?" she asked Ken with a wink, placing the cupcake in front of him.

"I don't really have a choice here, do I?" he said with a sigh. He plinked a small pile of coins on the table.

The ceiling of the bedroom stared back at Apondra in the dark; she couldn't sleep. Next to her, Diana snored through her drunken state. Apondra gently rolled her new companion on her side, taking another inventory of her roommates. Ken slept on his stomach, as lobfolk do, and Sharpe lay on top of his sheets, bow in hand, dozing. He and Tomas decided to take turns for half the night each, standing watch over the animals, not fully trusting the tavern guards. It also meant they spent as little time in the same place as each other, defusing their underlying tensions.

Apondra threw her arms to her sides on the cool sheet. The moon's white light peeked through the clouds now, enhancing the details in the room; their sacks and bags in the corner, a pitcher of water and smudged drinking glasses on the table, and a handful of unlit candles in the wall sconces. She sighed and stood. *I think I'll go see how Teacup is doing.*

The night air chilled her breath, barely visible in tiny whisps when she exhaled. Teacup snorted at the sight of his owner, eliciting a tiny giggle from Apondra. She had picked him out personally as a young calf, the runt, but also the softest babe covered in his young orange-brown coat. His colors darkened with his age, but as she ran her hands over his flanks, she could sometimes catch a burst of orange hairs, like tiny flames igniting inside of him.

"Hello, sweet friend," she said softly, rubbing his nose.

"Hello," replied Tomas, startling her. He stepped out from behind Rose, dagger prominently displayed on the front of his belt. "Sleep eludes you."

"Yes, it does," she said. The charming chirps of night birds in the woods filled the background with light harmony. "How goes it?"

"Well, the guards seem to be doing their job. They're wandering around here somewhere. And sober," he said with a wink. "Always a plus when it comes to hired hands."

"You have experience with these types of employees, I assume?"

"Yes, quite a bit." He smiled at her, then looked at his feet. "When the cavalier and I are traveling—were traveling—we often used whatever lodging we could find. In the more remote villages, the security teams leave much to be desired. Even a bribe for 'special treatment' is not always respected." He dragged his false foot across the dirt. "I remember once, in the south, we stayed at an inn that was staffed exclusively by drunk elderly women. The menfolk were sailors, so the women ran the town. They fawned over Gunnar. We had such special treatment until they learned his heart was still betrothed to his wife's soul." He held Gunnar's ring on his necklace, smiling as he ran his fingers over the fine gold.

Apondra smiled back at him. His shoulders slumped, tired from the night's watch, tired from the night before, and tired, she assumed, from the weight of losing his master. She now hated that word, *master*. His sense of duty was unwavering in her eyes, a protector and aide, and now she saw him as a friend, someone who entrusted her with his small stories and vulnerabilities when no one was around.

"You know, I am grateful you're here." She placed a hand on his shoulder. "I'm not very good at this adventure and traveling business. So thank you for staying."

"I am duty bound."

She moved her hand to his wrist. "I am duty bound as well, to protect and care for my kingdom. And therefore, bound to any people who care for mine." Her mouth felt dry. "But there's no sense of duty when it comes to friends. It's more like an instinct." She swallowed. "A feeling."

They stood silently, both looking at the ground between them. A quiet came over the small patch of grazing ground, leaving just the sounds of their animals breathing and her breath as she shuddered in the chill. Silence.

Where are the birds?

"Listen!" she whispered. "The night birds! They've stopped! Not a single note, shriek, or hoot."

He stepped back and clutched his dagger handle.

"Tomas, do you hear—"

"Shhh!"

At first, nothing. Then a bird chirping, squawking, frantically screeching as it burst from the top boughs of the trees. A cacophony of hollering and wailing songbirds in a massive flock poured forth from the forest, flying overhead and over the city in a formation so dense that it partially blotted out the moon. Apondra covered her ears from the shrill cries.

"What is it?" she yelled.

"An emergency! Our animals! Untether our animals!" yelled the squire.

The trees creaked and groaned, followed by loud snaps in the distance, then the deep crunches of trunks being sheared in half. Thunderous percussive stomps pounded like war drums, a deep slow rhythm approaching from the darkness. Apondra frantically attached Teacup's chariot, her hands shaking as she fumbled with his straps; the squire pulled Rose and Domino toward her.

"Princess! I'll hold the animals, you run inside and gather the others!" he yelled, the thunder ascending into a rolling wave of shattering and exploding trees. Apondra turned to the inn's door and found Sharpe at the ready, bow in hand, arrow already nocked.

"What is this?" he yelled. His face froze. Even in the dark, Apondra guessed his features had turned pale.

A final louder explosion from the woods, a hundred yards north along the tree line, birthed the head of a large beast, its titanic beak pointed and black like a hawk, its eyes small and glowing yellow like two ominous lanterns. The leathery head loomed bigger than a house, followed by a twisted short neck covered in shiny slime. With another lurch, the creature pulled itself forward with large stumpy claws, each talon as long as a horse, muscular limbs that shot out of its jagged and stony shell. The colossal snapping turtle roared, a breathy rattling noise that would frighten even a ghost. It turned to glare at the group, both eyes fixed on them with an unblinking deadness.

"What do we do?" whispered Apondra.

"I have no idea," replied Sharpe.

The giant beast whipped its head away from them and surged forward, smashing into a row of buildings further down the lane. Screams pierced the night, followed by bursts of illumination as fires spread from broken lamps, fallen candles, and cracked hearths. The massive shell, higher than the buildings, cast a fearsome silhouette, like a gigantic, serrated blade to be wielded by an elder god. Apondra strained to see further across town, toward the river, and the beast's current trajectory.

"It's going to smash into the warehouses!" she cried. Ken and Diana entered their circle, each one carrying a heaping armload of their bags and belongings.

"We've got everything," Ken yelled, tossing the bags of books into the chariot. "We need to run, now, in case that thing turns around!"

"I don't think it will," said Sharpe, pointing at the extended wake of destruction. "It's heading right into the river."

The words had no sooner left his mouth when a series of tall masts protruding above the warehouses tipped and fell in unison, indicating the beast had entered the water. By Apondra's estimation, the river in that section was barely wider than the creature's shell, and every boat would be utterly destroyed as it swam downstream toward the inevitable ocean. A warehouse on the edge of its path burst into flames, followed by popping explosions from the nearby buildings.

"All of those people," Apondra whispered, "they're dying. Slaves stacked in boarding houses. I pray they can escape."

"These are things we do not know for certain," interrupted Diana. "Many live outside the merchant town, especially the slave camps, but yes, there will be death down there."

Tomas mounted Rose and pointed his dagger away from the town. "Eave Queen, we must flee, now! We should be far from here if that thing doubles back on its path."

"Where would we go?" she asked. She shook her hands, then grabbed her own wrist. Gunnar, Diggins, all of the guards from their caravan, all of these faces flashed before her eyes. "Where can we run?"

"We continue," Tomas shouted. "We go north, toward the very edge of the kingdom. Ken, we can follow the northwest merchant path to Himmelhavets, the final outpost, correct?" The squire reached down and pulled Diana onto his horse. Ken tossed the last sack into the chariot as he helped Apondra to her spot then searched the sky for a navigational star. He pointed up, then traced a line down to the dark horizon.

"Yes, to the north and then west. The tales of Azcalaw begin and end beyond the outpost. As sure as we've all seen that *thing,* we can be more assured that there is some truth behind Azcalaw. Or at least, that's the hope we'll cling to."

Sharpe leapt onto Domino, turning away from the group. The archer held up his reigns to signal a retreat, then pulled them lightly to face Apondra. He glanced at Diana, his jaw tense. "If it needs to be said, I have no intention now of leaving you all, as you'll be lost without my help.

Daybreak is in over an hour, so let's proceed with caution in the dark. The instant that dawn's light shines over the mountains, we will ride as fast as our mounts can take us." He winked at Apondra. "Or at least as fast as Teacup can go."

"Oh, he'll go, alright. He's faster than he looks." She clutched the reigns and whistled, the kyloe lumbering forward, one step at a time, pausing to sniff a patch of clover at the edge of the grounds.

"I think 'fast' is a relative term," Ken said with a shake of his head. Apondra adjusted Teacup's reigns and whistled again, the trio of beasts trotting and stumbling forward into the night, chased by the fading echoes of fire and screams of the merchant town. She glanced back at the ruinous landscape, glowing with runaway fires as centuries-old buildings burned in mere minutes, and she imagined the books now lost, the transcribers locked in their quarters, and the slaves who may have gone to sleep thinking tomorrow was the day their indentured servitude contract ended, never to wake again. Her breath shook as she began to sob.

"All of those people. Gone."

Ken embraced her from behind, stroking her hair with a trembling hand. "Just look away, Appy. Look away."

⁓

Heat from the late morning sun bore down on the travelers. Apondra tied her sweater around her waist, examining her tunic and the off-white stains under her arms and on the center of her chest. She sighed and reached forward to pat Teacup on his haunches.

"We'll stop soon, friend."

Ahead, the trail broke through the tree line across a short crag of gray rocks dotted with lush ferns that thrived in the edges of the forest's shadows. Beyond, a wide field of grasses stretched to each side of the beaten ground. With a short whistle, a lobfolk in the field wearing a wide straw hat that covered his shoulders hailed the group.

"Hello, travelers! Please don't spook my sheep! I've lost two already in these grasses, and only recovered one!"

A bleating chorus broke from the right, announcing the flock trampling the grass as they heeded their shepherd's whistle. The party stopped and dismounted; Sharpe shielded his eyes as he scanned the field.

"There! I see a movement in the grasses. Looks like a sheep."

The shepherd waded through the field toward the gap, crying with joy as he picked up the lamb.

"Oh, thank you!" His flock dutifully followed him into the clearing next to the path. He reached into his shoulder bag and offered a leather flask. "It's fine wine. I won't have any coins to thank you until I sell the wool, but please, have a drink."

"Don't mind if I do," said Diana, swigging the flask. She wiped her lips on her forearm. "That's better."

"I'll pass. Thank you, kind shepherd," said Apondra. She petted one of the rams that had made Teacup's acquaintance. The ram bleated softly, a gentle creature with a blackened face and dull white wool. His short horns indicated a youthful age, and his eyes looked at her with a sweetness that made her miss home.

"He's a prize, that one," said the shepherd. "He helps me with the flock. Very smart. Very unusual."

"Hmmph," Ken huffed, surrounded by curious sheep. "I think these ones here have taken a liking to me." He gently pushed one with his staff.

Tomas and Sharpe broke away from the group, scanning the grass.

"How many more are missing?" asked Tomas. "I see one more moving over there beyond the lilac patch."

"They're all here now, all twenty," counted the shepherd. "Eighteen, plus the lamb and the ram."

"Are you sure?" said Sharpe. He slipped his bow off his shoulder, watching the movement in the grass heading toward them. The long blades shook, then twisted as the concealed form darted to the right.

"Yes. All here."

The flock of sheep replied with a loud bleating and began to scamper in a circle around the group. The ram took the outside ring, pushing the sheep closer to Teacup, standing steadfast in the midst of his new wooly friends. Apondra and Diana joined Tomas and Sharpe.

"There! See it?" shouted Tomas, unsheathing his dagger. The movement in the grass zipped right, then left, drawing closer in a slithering, arcing path.

"Shepherd, have you got any more to drink?" asked Diana, leaping over to his side and grabbing the flask. "Trust me, I'm more fun when I drink."

She downed the entire contents and wiped the drops of red wine on her palms, her hands twitching. "Do you smell that?" Diana whispered.

A dirty stink floated across the path, a musk like rotting straw and sweat. Sharp grabbed an arrow; Tomas passed his dagger between his hands. Ken scurried into the chariot and stood as high as he could on a bag of books.

"There!" Ken shouted. "Look out!"

A giant weasel reared up from the grass on the edge of the path. It hissed and bared its fangs, its triangular head covered in dark brown and black fur. Sharpe steadied his bow as Diana held up her hand.

"I've got this," she growled. She grabbed Apondra by the sleeve and dragged her to her side.

"What are you doing?"

"Using you, channeler."

She strode right toward the beast, Apondra in tow, provoking the weasel to stand on its hind legs to a towering height above all their heads. Diana's hands constricted over an imaginary ball in front of her chest as she shouted.

"Air to wind, wind to heat, innoch solanales immol!"

A cold gust of wind swept over and through Apondra, culminating in a blue mist that enshrouded Diana. A burst of azure flame exploded from the spellcaster's hands, launching a volley of steaming potatoes at the weasel, knocking it on its back.

"Potatoes?" yelled Sharpe as he fired an arrow into the beast's shoulder.

"It was supposed to be fireballs. I've got this," commanded Diana. She held her hands up and shouted again at the weasel.

"*Sand and soil, serpent's coil, illi conta!*"

A thick black vine sprouted from the path, wrapping around the weasel's throat. The creature snarled with the little air it could breathe, its limbs thrashing until Diana cast another volley of flaming potatoes, scorching the writhing beast. Its limbs finally relaxed, dead. Diana stumbled over to the shepherd.

"Thank you for the wine. I cast better when I'm drunk." Tomas caught her as she tripped and fell forward.

"Well, that's reassuring and frightening at the same time," he said. Apondra nodded.

"How does that work, exactly?"

"Don't know," Diana said, her speech slurring. "There's something about courage and belief that makes the spell work. Belief. So, the courage from the alcohol helps." She sat on the ground and put her head between her knees. "There's something about wine that gets me intoxicated almost instantly. Magic is weird." Her head rolled from side to side. "I may throw up; those spells were not easy."

Ken hovered over her, madly flipping through the pages of one of his tomes. "I have so many questions, so many! Diana, can you tell me—"

"Why potatoes? I got one of the words a little wrong," she said, gurgling. "I've been studying for years, but only actively practicing for, well, since I met you all." The shepherd's ram trotted up to Diana and bleated in her face. "Uh, you're welcome?"

Ken threw his hands in the air. "Well, that's just wonderful! Dear newborn mage, if you need any words for your spells confirmed, please just ask me! You know that I am a librarian, yes?"

"I do now." She burped. "But that's a little challenging during the heat of battle. 'Hey, white claws, what's a good word in the old languages for something deadly?' It's not practical." She reached over and grabbed a potato, flipping it between her hands. "Still hot." She bit into it and immediately spit it out. "Tastes like dirt."

Apondra knelt next to her and sniffed at the discarded potato. "Why did you grab me? What was that?"

"It's like … a feeling. You're attuned to magic, and I can, you know." Diana mimicked scooping something into her hand.

"No. I *don't* know. What is *that*?" Apondra took her turn to mimic holding an imaginary object.

"Like a conduit. I can suck more magic out of the world through you. I can do it on my own, but you're like, I don't know, a lighthouse that signals the magic and then I grab it more quickly through you."

"That's unsettling."

"I don't make the rules." Diana hacked and convulsed. "Here it comes. Nope, it's gone. I thought that was going to be vomit for sure."

The shepherd approached slowly, then took one step back as Diana coughed again. "Thank you, spellcaster." He pointed to the road ahead of the group. "There is a fork just ahead that runs parallel to the forest. It's not the merchant trail, which leads into the sugar maple grove, but you won't make any other shelter before nightfall if you continue this way." He whistled for his flock. "There is lodging down that side road, a good place to stay for the night. As you can see, you don't want to be in these woods in the dark."

Ken unfolded his map. "According to my navigation, the outpost town, Himmelhavets, is only a half day's travel from here."

The shepherd held up three fingers. "Your map is wrong, sir. Three days, at least. And my flock moves at a quick clip for most of the day." He picked up his curved staff and rucksack from their hiding place under a pile of loose brush. "Safe travels."

"Well, that's a fine twist," noted Sharpe, mounting his horse. "Three days? That's just fine."

Sharpe extended a hand to Diana and hoisted her onto the back of his saddle. He looped a belt around their waists to hold her upright and took the lead toward the tree line. As Sharpe's hand slid to her thigh to hold her steady for a moment, then back to his reigns, Apondra tapped Ken on the shoulder.

"I think he fancies her," she whispered.

"That's not the only incident of attraction on this journey," he replied. "Tomas keeps glancing back at you, Appy."

"He's just checking in." She blushed.

"I disagree. Happily."

⚬

Dusk fell quickly, as did their arrival at the tiny inn at the end of the day's travels. No sign named this place, a simple two-story house with a smoking chimney on each side. The covered porch and animal paddock were built from old wood, slightly crooked and gray from seasons of exposure, covered in patches of thick green moss as was the roof of the building. A short elderly man with deep brown skin and gray wisps of hair on his balding head waved to Sharpe.

"One of my countrymen! Hello friend," he yelled, opening his arms wide to Sharpe as he stepped down with short limping steps.

"Hello, countryman. We're looking for one night of lodging, and feed for our animals."

"Sure, sure, sure! My boys will handle that. Come in, we have a couple other guests, so food is already being prepared for supper!"

Apondra entered first, examining the clean rustic features that contrasted with the weathered outside appearance: finely stained and oiled wood furniture, smooth patterned floors, and shining pewter mugs hanging above the bar and serving counter. She found the little details charming, buoying her spirits on this now tragic adventure beyond the castle and her home village. Two men, hunters or perhaps trappers, sat at a table on one side of the large room. In the middle, a wide empty table welcomed them, already set by the innkeeper for the new guests. On the far side, just before the staircase, a trio of lobfolk in blue robes huddled around a plate of fried potatoes. She narrowed her eyes, recognizing the garments of the cultists she encountered in Merchant Town. The robed diners immediately looked up and hailed.

"Hello! I see one of our kin in your party!" said the first, a stout lobfolk with blue painted lines on his head. "You look familiar, albino. What is your name?"

"Ken. Just Ken."

"Well, *Ken*, we are certainly glad to see you. And I do think I have seen you before." He lifted a pipe from the table and stuffed the end with thick black pulpy leaves. "Are you familiar with your savior, Azcalaw?"

Sharpe glowered at their table before hanging his quiver on the back of his chair. Diana lowered her head as she slid into her seat. "Say nothing," she whispered. She glanced at Apondra and repeated her words. "Say. Nothing."

Ken fiddled with his cloak's fringe. "I am not as learned in this person you speak of. Who is Azcalaw?" Diana kicked him under the table.

"Aye," said the lobfolk with blue-painted head. "We are disciples of his greatness. I am Tenor."

Apondra shot up in her seat. Tenor! This was the same lobfolk from the merchant town! She attempted to grab Ken's hand before he could continue the conversation.

"Well very nice to meet you, Tenor." Ken picked up his utensils and then placed them on the opposite side of his plate, a nervous habit noticed by Apondra. "We're going to have just a meal here."

"Ah, 'just a meal' says this one," boomed Tenor, rising and approaching the party. "Azcalaw provides nourishment for the soul and spirit. When he first came to be during the days before kings, he protected the dawning world from the wilds. He provided care for the sick and slaughtered the fiends from the dark places. Some say he tamed humans so they would respect our kind." His antennae twitched, pointed now at Apondra. "But we now live in harmony, yes?"

"Thrilling stuff," mumbled Diana as she slurped her glass of water.

"Thrilling indeed! Long ago, Azcalaw fulfilled his first era of destiny, maintaining the balance of the land and magic. This began the dawn of kingdoms, a time of prosperity … but also the dawn of greed and repression."

Apondra drew her scarf over her head, watching Tenor slowly circle the table until he stood behind her chair. "That's quite a story," she stuttered. His tale ignited her curiosity, but also her fear of the rather dominating individual who spoke to them. Tenor loomed behind her chair.

She felt a tingle, like a hair dragged across the back of her hand. A tiny blue speck, barely larger than a grain of sand, but glowing faintly, floated in front of her face before fading. *Magic! Is Tenor a spellcaster?* Her eyes darted to Diana, who stared down at her plate, her lips still trembling. Mumbling. *She's casting something!*

Apondra quickly glanced to her side, noting two long blades in black sheaths attached to Tenor's belt. "Well, you've told quite a story, sir," she sputtered. "Good evening to you now. We'd like to eat after a long day's travels." He leaned into her spying gaze.

"A story? Is it? I'm sure you've heard the words of the woods, the reports of a giant sea beast that has risen from the dark depths of the very ocean which brings us life. The sea has been corrupted and now spits its vengeance upon the land. Why, just this morning, the merchant town has been shattered in the wake of the beast!" Tenor's associates sat with their heads bowed, nodding occasionally as he punctuated his speech. "The beast, a giant snapping turtle, cannot be stopped unless we turn our faith to Azcalaw, and give him domain over all the lands. Only Azcalaw can protect us after the kingdoms are destroyed."

"Come again?" questioned Sharpe. "*After* the kingdoms are destroyed?"

"Yes! You see it now. We are due. This beast must finish its work, sweeping its cleansing wake over the land. Then, and only then, will Azcalaw return, send the beast to its death, and rule over us all with his love and protection!"

The robed fanatics raised their claws and clacked them in unison.

"Well," said Ken, clacking one claw in response, "that's quite interesting. We'll be sure to think about that. After our meal."

Tenor leaned close, his eyes a dark black that shone like mirrored stones in a river. "Only Azcalaw's chosen will survive. Join us, brother. Humans are welcome, too. Azcalaw loves us all." He closed his blue robe and started back to his table. "Except those who deny him."

Tenor suddenly stopped, straightening his back and looking at some unknown point in the ceiling. Apondra lifted her head and saw another faint blue grain in the air, floating toward his face. He glanced back at their party, scanning their faces, stopping on Apondra's frozen expression.

"Interesting," he hissed. He turned away and sat with his fellow lobfolk. The cultists lowered their heads and returned to eating their meal.

"Well, that was entertaining," snarked Tomas in a low voice. The innkeeper placed a large plate of fried potatoes, carrots, and smoked pork sticks, still attached to the rib bones, in the center of the table. "Thank you, sir. Say, are those gentlemen in the robes staying here tonight?"

"The lunatics?" replied the innkeeper. "No. They're generally not welcome, bad for business and all that, but their kind don't purchase lodging overnight. They'd rather walk in the darkness of the wood, and if a wolf or weasel rips their flesh, they'll say, 'it's a trial of Azcalaw! Hooray!' and then bleed out in some field." The innkeeper jingled the coins in his pocket. "But they pay well, so they can eat during dining hours." He pulled out a pile of black coins, counted them, then slid his profits back into his pocket as he walked back to the kitchen.

"Dirty slave coins," sniped Apondra. "Those zealots are charlatans." Her stomach twisted as she tried to unravel Tenor's final observation. *Could he see magic as well?*

"They speak some partial truths," said Ken. "Diana, are you sober enough to perhaps—"

"—to correct and explain everything I know about Azcalaw from reading lost tomes for the past fourteen years? Yes, sure, once they leave." Her fingers clutched the edge of the table, her knuckles striped in red and white streaks from apparent strain. "Give me a moment." She released her grip, snapped her fingers at a barboy and held up her mug. "Ale, now." She snapped back to Ken. "When they leave, we can talk."

The group ate in silence, muttering only a few scant words of courtesy to each other and the inn staff, waiting for the cultists to depart. After the robed lobfolk cleared their plates, the trio abruptly stood, tossed a pile of blackened coins on the table, and glided out of the inn. Apondra craned her neck to peer through the partially shuttered window and watch their forms disappear into the night beyond the porch lanterns.

"Very odd folk," she said. "Nothing is sitting well with me right now."

"Indeed," noted Ken. "Their facts are, well, besides not being actual facts, are accurate in respect to the myths I've read. Diana? What say you?"

"I say they know more than they say, and we should be much more careful." She lifted her ale, sniffed it and shook her head, then opted instead for her water glass. "Azcalaw. Some say he's a god. Some say he's not of this world. He's both man and lobster, not lobfolk. He's a beast himself. Tall as a house. And gushing with magic." She interlaced her fingers and looked to the fireplace, pausing to watch a log crackle and split in half with a small burst of ignition. "He was born, or created, whatever, at a nexus of time and magic. By that accord, he would be immensely powerful as a spellcaster. Allegedly, he pulled at the magic of the land, and sucked it from the air from vast regions, to defeat the first great destroyer, a giant snapping turtle. And magic, once used, cannot be replaced easily and instantly. It burns like a log in a fire," she said, with another nod to the hearth, "but it releases things; raw magic goes back again into the world, but loose and wild, gliding like the winds wherever it blows."

Ken raised his hand. "So, if Azcalaw drew magic into himself to defeat an ancient creature, the magic was eventually put back into the world. But this recycled magic is just not as easy to … catch?"

"Correct. So, the magic that spread through the world, the magic around us now, are the bits and pieces of Azcalaw's great farming of magic." She dragged her fork across her plate, scraping bits of gravy and drops of grease into a tiny puddle. "Then he used it." She placed the fork in the middle of the puddle and dragged it in a spiral until a tiny sheen of food grime covered the plate. "So, to gather all of the magic, or enough of it to use, would be, well, like grabbing all of the winds with a single sail."

Ken leaned over her plate. "I have paper and charcoals. You don't have to keep drawing with your food." Diana smiled, then frowned at him.

"Diana," Apondra interrupted, "did you sense anything from Tenor?"

"Magic? Yes. I felt it before we crossed the threshold. I tried to remember a spell I had read, something like a void, a blanket, which conceals one's magic from detection."

"I saw something, I felt something, when he stood next to me," Apondra said, her voice cracking. "Does he know about us?"

"I tried, Princess. But I'm not experienced." Diana stared into her mug.

"I don't think I was successful. I felt him, like tendrils slowly wrapping over me. I think I protected you with my spell, just enough."

With her heart in her stomach, Apondra sighed. There was no way she could have known that other casters would be traveling around the wilds, nor the reason why it seemed so much more prevalent here, far from home. The vizier never mentioned this to her despite being a former spellcaster. And Tenor! The tension in Tenor's tone implied that he was a lobfolk of dangerous intentions. She needed to refocus.

"Ken," Apondra interrupted, "where did the sea beast, the first giant turtle come from?" She placed her thumb on her chin in thought, talking now to only herself. "Was it … summoned?"

"Who would do that?" said Tomas. "Surely, in old legends, some first king or tribal ruler would want to summon a beast to crush his enemies, but, as we've seen firsthand, the beast in the wilds did what it wanted, driven by no single master."

"Aye," said Sharpe. "And who would summon the beast *now*?"

"A king," replied Diana. "Or a cult." She pointed her fork at Sharpe. "Are you going to finish your potatoes?"

"No. Here. Eat up. Stay sober a while longer." He winked at her. She stuck out her tongue.

"Ahem." Apondra stood. "Do you have any type of spell you can cast that would help right now?"

"Like a 'spy on the cultists' or 'track the giant turtle'? Hardly. I've read thousands of spells and words of the ancient tongues, but it's not all in my head, and I still don't know many of the words, or conjugations. Plus, I only memorized what I thought were the most useful ones that could help me liberate myself, and for protection."

"Like a disguise spell?" Ken asked.

"Well, possibly. My head's a bit foggy. Perhaps if I were to write down some of the…" Diana's voice trailed off. "No. None of the words I know will be put to paper. I can't allow that to happen. One rogue magic user with the spells and words I've learned could cause chaos." Apondra nodded in agreement as Diana concluded. "Princess, let's off to bed. Men, you can tie up the animals and bring the provisions upstairs. Ken, go read some books."

Apondra sat up in her bed, unable to sleep, again. Resting her elbows on the window ledge, she peered outside into the dark woods, listening to the tiny huffs and snorts of their animals. An owl hooted, and a shriek in the distance, like a hawk or osprey, echoed in the night. She held the letter from the vizier in her hands, hoping a second letter would somehow make its way to her, telling her that everything would be fine.

Tenor's words and presence still haunted her. His voice weaved syllables through her imagination, sewing a nightmarish tapestry of cultists and beasts lurking under the surface of the sea, waiting to rise and consume the shore. When she could shake the feeling, her mind immediately ran to the image of her father, alone and bedridden while the royal council conspired in the throne room, led by Larold of Ribbed Beach. She knew little of him, just her brief encounters as he traveled in and out of the council meetings that she was too young to attend. Now she would have to deal with these meetings, as Eave Queen, upon her return, if they returned home at all, *if there's anything to even return to*. She then remembered her encounter on the beach with the local councilman, Teelok, and his quiet assurances that she still held the hearts of at least some of the residents of the kingdom.

"Do I even want to be a princess?" she whispered, followed by a deep sigh.

A cold hand smothered her mouth, followed by a breath in her ear that smelled of stale ale.

"Be still."

Diana's words froze her in place. *"Itso sommun, killo summon."*

As the spell finished, a cool blanket of air enveloped the two women. Outside, in the woods, a flash of blue light burst, then quickly extinguished itself. During the flash, Apondra could make out a tall silhouette, shaped like a lobfolk under a dark hooded robe. The lone figure quickly ran back through the trees, away from the inn.

"That was Tenor," Diana whispered. "He came back, he must have sensed us. I cast a cloak over us, which should last into the morning." She released her hand from Apondra's mouth. "We need to leave by sunrise."

"Given how terrified I feel right now, I doubt I'll be able to get any sleep."

Diana handed her flask to Apondra. "Drink this. A lot of this. I'll wake you up before dawn."

Chapter 8

The Lost Farm

AFTER A HURRIED departure from the inn at sunrise, the next day's journey passed quickly through the darkening woods. Diana rode in the chariot with Ken, trading lore and apocrypha from the texts they had each individually known and read. As much as Apondra missed sitting behind Teacup, she chose to ride on the back of Rose, clutching the squire's cape during some of the rougher parts of the path that were overgrown with roots and bramble. She watched Sharpe, riding alone in the lead, separating himself from the group. As they approached the next turnoff for lodging in the woods, she whispered to Tomas.

"Does Sharpe seem, you know, a bit darker today?"

"I think so." Tomas pulled Rose's reigns to make the turn. "You know, yesterday, when we were with the shepherd and the sheep were attacked, I think something happened. When he shot at the weasel, I think he was aiming for the head. He missed, or he second guessed his shot."

"Hmm." She looked for the right words but could muster nothing except a simple acknowledgement through closed lips.

"I've been thinking, Your Highness, about probably the same thing that you're thinking. When we were attacked at the merchant camp, if Sharpe had not fired his arrow, my master would have still been killed by that weasel. That beast already had him in its clutches and was about to tear into his neck." She felt his body tense under his cape. "I have a clearer mind than I did a few nights ago. I don't harbor ill will against Sharpe; I think it was an inevitable end for a champion like Gunnar. Saving lives." His voice broke for a moment, and he paused to regain his composure. "He was a great defender, a selfless protector. A good man."

She took pity on him. Tomas was crestfallen but trying to portray a stoic image for her, having lost someone who was most likely his best friend, brother, and in a way, also his father, yet Tomas took Apondra as his assignment, his *Lady*. The relationship between squire and cavalier was one that the lobfolk did not observe in their military, but she had studied it in written tales and in person during diplomatic meetings that she watched as a child whenever her father took in ambassadors from other kingdoms. She reached one arm around his waist in a comforting hug.

"Does he know?" she said.

"Hmm?"

"Sharpe. Does he know? Have you told him? That you forgive him?"

"I don't think there's been an appropriate moment yet."

"Right now, his confidence is broken. We all need him, and he's chosen to stay with us. That says something about his character. And he is, in a way, our friend. He will be your friend."

"I'm afraid of what he'll say."

"He can say what he wants. You are the one that can help him with words." She remembered her father, sitting in court listening to grievances. "Honest words are more powerful than anything that remains hidden."

Rose trotted a bit as they approached another inn, saving them from a possible night of camping and rationed food. This establishment, like the night before, left no initial impression, just a plain and square squatty building with only one chimney on the side spewing white smoke into the thinned-out branches above. The paddock for livestock was built high, almost twice the height of a man, surrounding two sides of the inn.

A stocky young woman with shoulder-length, straight, brown hair stood on the porch, polearm in hand. "Stop!" she shouted. "State your business." A large gray and white bobcat slithered around her leg and sat in front of her dirty boots.

"Travelers," replied Sharpe. "Hospitality for one night, and protection for our mounts. We have coin."

"I am Carlala. I can only guarantee hospitality. Your mounts can enter the yard, but we offer no promise against the night for anything that lives outside." She reached down and scratched the bobcat who immediately rolled onto his back. "Titus here makes sure that we have a clean inn, free of pests."

"We'll provide a guard," said Tomas as he dismounted. His leg caught on his stirrup, and he fell to the ground, his false limb folding at an awkward angle. Titus sat up and hissed at the commotion.

"Best hope nothing chases you, one-leg," Carlala huffed. "Our menu is stewed meat and potatoes. We have no fish for you, white claws." She pointed a crooked finger at Ken.

"I do like potatoes, miss. Salt, pepper, goat butter, perfection." Ken twiddled his fingers. "And I am a fan of cake, if you have any."

"Hmph." She held the door to let them inside. "We have cake."

As they passed into the inn, Titus rubbed himself against Ken's legs and playfully tapped his tail.

"Does he bite?" Ken shooed the large feline off the hem of his cloak.

"Only when he's hungry." Carlala sneered. "I will warn you that he has a love of seafood, white claws."

"Noted." Ken scooped up the ends of his cloak. "Your rooms have locks, yes?"

A tiny feast of venison stew, potato bread, and sugared carrots sat in the center of the long table in the center of the parlor, a dark room with a low ceiling, but very clean. Carlala sat with the group to eat, stroking Titus next to her and feeding him bits of venison picked from her portion. She leaned over her steaming bowl and folded her large rough hands.

"You're a pretty girl," she said to Apondra, then pointed her thumb back and forth between the princess and Diana. "Both of you. Ladies on the run? Fleeing a marriage or engagement, perhaps?"

Diana laughed. "Not us, no. We're looking for Azcalaw."

Apondra stepped on Diana's foot. "What my companion meant to say, in a more elaborate way, is that we are scholars. From the far south. We are looking for old texts from history and the stories of Azcalaw that may remain hidden." She folded her hands. "Poetry and things like that. Just, you know, obscure things we can bring home. For our studies." She removed her foot from atop Diana's boot.

Ken ripped a piece of bread in half and offered it to Titus. "We're just passing through." He patted Titus on the head. "Innkeeper, just how exactly does one acquire and befriend a wild bobcat?"

Carlala smiled. "Oh, he followed me home one day. I was in the forest to the west, scouting old growth for lumber. Titus was just a kitten and, well, I fed him a piece of my lunch and he just followed me." She snapped her fingers. Titus leapt onto the table, carefully dancing around the plates and bowls, then jumped up to the thick top rail of her high-backed wooden chair, wrapping himself around her shoulders. "He does this when we read together."

"Oh! Are you a learned woman, of sorts?" said Apondra. "I don't see any books here."

Carlala laughed with a deep-bellied roar. "Do you think I'd keep them down here where some of the less trustworthy travelers can steal or damage them?" She smiled as Titus licked her face. "I acquire books from travelers,

I read them, and then I trade them to the next visitors. It's a good system. Always trade up." She nodded toward her polearm, mounted over the fireplace. "Do you know how much that thing cost? I don't. But I was able to exchange some old histories to a merchant from the Kingdom of Swan for it." She glanced at Tomas. "Your kingdom. I can tell by your colors and dress."

Apondra couldn't help but feel impressed by this woman, running a lodge apparently by herself, protecting her business while also keeping up her education. She finished her stew and then raised her hand.

"Carlala, have you read anything on Azcalaw?"

"I have." She crossed her arms, dislodging Titus who dropped to the floor and immediately began grooming his silver fur. "But I have my doubts."

"What do you mean?"

Carlala stood and grabbed a wine flask from her cooking counter. She poured a drink for herself and returned to her seat, her eyes sharper and more focused.

"I've read many things over the years, and I like to piece together my own accounts from the fragments of texts and novellas."

Ken slid a small notebook out of his pocket and a charcoal from his bag. "If you wouldn't mind, can you tell us?"

Carlala sipped at her wine and cleared her throat. "Gladly. I'm much more likely to meet travelers interested in my stockings than my mind."

"What's in your stockings?" asked Apondra. Diana attempted to hold back a laugh, then shook her head. Apondra bolted upright. "Oh! Oh. Go on, please."

Their host smiled. "In the days before the establishment of the king-doms, there was this thing, a being, neither man nor lobfolk. Some said he was made by magic; others said he was an aberration of tainted breeding pools. Still others suggested that he was created by the experiments of those who sought knowledge beyond their comprehension. In the end, what did it matter how he was created? Azcalaw existed.

"The tribes of man shunned him, not only because they found his disfigurements to be grotesque, but also because they feared his size and strength. Azcalaw stood twice the height of a sturdy male, but his strength was well beyond that. It was said he could heave a cow across the water into a sailing ship, smash boulders larger than a house with his clawed fists, or even shout with a voice that could be heard a valley away. I think that is a load of bear scat."

Ken choked on his drink. "That's quite a colorful assessment."

"It's what I think, white claws. But in the stories, men feared him, so Azcalaw sulked alone for centuries on the edge of the lobfolk lands. They shunned him, too, but in those days, any enemy of men was their ally. The lobfolk reluctantly brought him food and wine. The humans hoped to lure him to their side and offered him their women. I know only a little bit about animal husbandry, but I do know certain situations are just, well, *incompatible*."

Ken fiddled with his fork, chasing a crumb around his plate. Sharpe and Tomas both coughed and looked away. Only Diana leaned forward, her eyes widening. "Go on."

Apondra raised her hand. "I don't understand. Were they offering their women to him as food?"

Carlala winked and continued.

"Ahem. Despite these offerings, during the first war with men, Azcalaw sided with the lobfolk. He used his strength to intimidate and deflect the invading armies. It was sung in one of the old hymns that he sat on a stump of a great fallen tree in the midlands and just waited for an entire army of invading men to surround him. He offered them a choice of retreat or defeat, then stood and cracked a juniper tree in two. They retreated. No one died.

"Over time, the kingdoms that we know now took form. The lobfolk offered Azcalaw their throne, but he denied it, saying no single being had a right to rule over any others. After this, one of the landowners declared himself king on the condition that every lobfolk who bowed would be granted security and a parcel, and that if called upon, they would defend their lands together. This first king asked Azcalaw to defend the lobfolk in exchange for a large tract where they would build him a keep, but Azcalaw declined. He said that no one truly owns anything so long as death exists, and that the ship that sailed into the Undersea had no room for our worthless cargo. And so, Azcalaw told the first king that any royal lineage would be under his gaze, and should they turn their backs on their minions, he would bring down their destruction so a new king could rise.

"Over the centuries, both human and lobfolk kings came to reflect on why Azcalaw cared so much about defending the lobfolk. Some say it was his longing for a family, for kin, for friendships, as he was truly alone. Others said he was building generational fealty for his final army, plotting his revenge against humans as he eventually exiled himself to the lands just north of here, beyond Himmelhavets, the outpost town on the edge of the world.

"Great tragedies would define the end and beginning of each historical period. Every turning point was marked by an appearance by Azcalaw." Carlala pointed at Tomas. "In the Kingdom of Swan, a great sea famine depleted the stock of ocean fish. Azcalaw dragged their boats deep into the sea and they fought against a titanic whale that previously decimated the schools of tuna, sea salmon, and cod. That whale's death helped repopulate the seas. Azcalaw asked for tribute, and the king surrendered his daughter to be Azcalaw's bride.

"His bride eventually grew old and died, a tiny sliver of time in the life of one as ageless as Azcalaw, but her passing filled him with sadness, as this was his only love. He sat next to a lighthouse in the south for a year, never moving, just staring at the sea. Then he disappeared.

"Famines, disasters, wars, these things continued. The lobfolk and humans prayed for Azcalaw to intervene, but he seemed to pick and choose when he would manifest. Living as long as he did, one can guess he grew weary of these disasters and found the civilized world trite. This was when the Cult of Azcalaw was born."

"The cult!" Apondra said. Diana stepped on her foot under the table. "Oh, a cult, you say? Why, that's interesting."

"The cult formed when desperate scholars and priests tried to summon him, believing that he was an elder god stranded here, and perhaps their act of worship would show him that he was loved and bring him to the land in their hour of need. Offerings were made, caravans of goods, and living things, hoping they would sustain and engage him. Sometimes, these things seemed to work. But again, the time between his appearances stretched longer and longer. Sacrifice was suggested; sacrifices were made. Blood was spilled.

"Over this time, men receded from their begging; they stopped asking Azcalaw for aid. They found their own champions and gods to worship. The lobfolk learned to rely on themselves in times of crisis. He faded into legend, and tales of his acts became folklore, things told to children, and prayers for good harvests and blessings.

"But for the cult, he became some kind of twisted messiah and their prayers for Azcalaw's return became the cult's entire existence. It was taught that his return would right the ills and injustices of the world. You can see how this would attract many who were without family or station, without nation, without purpose. Is your life terrible? Azcalaw will fix it." She snapped her fingers.

Ken interrupted. "You have no family or nation out here. Are you in his cult?" Carlala raised an eyebrow, her lips forming a thin straight line.

"No. I choose to be unbound, living beyond the boundaries of kingdoms. Just an innkeeper and her feline friend."

Diana tapped the table with her spoon, her eyes wide. "Well? What happened next?"

"Nothing. Azcalaw never returned. He just became a mythical hero to some, and an apocalyptic savior for others."

"He's a hero to us," said Apondra. "Back home, the little lobfolk would paint their shells blue with flower dyes and pretend to be Azcalaw, fighting monsters and doing good deeds. If you were a good little lobbie, maybe Azcalaw would come to visit and take you on an adventure! There was no harm in making him a hero. From the stories I knew, his appearances always ended with the world becoming a safer place."

Carlala scoffed. "I say it is a more dangerous place. The zealots, the members of his cult, they captivate lost souls with their promises. I can't imagine how many hundreds or thousands of them are just sitting in the woods up north around campfires crying to Azcalaw to come save them instead of building their own life."

"Are you building your own life here, alone? Does that make you happy?" Apondra asked.

"It does. And I'm not alone, I just get to meet new people from time to time and build my nest of coins. Someday I'll pack my things, grab Titus, and settle somewhere in the west." Carlala pushed out her chair and stood. "And speaking of coins, it's time to settle up. I am running a business, after all."

⁓

After their meal and payment, the group retreated to the single room they shared. No other travelers arrived to stay for the night, but at the advisement of Sharpe, they conserved their coins by renting just one room. He took the first watch outside, to be relieved by Apondra three hours later. She chose to take a turn, as it was "only fair" by her own decree.

After another restless sleep, she stepped outside for her watch, the squire's dagger tucked in her belt. Sharpe leaned on the porch railing, his bow slung over his shoulder.

"Warmer than I thought tonight, Your Highness," said Sharpe with a hint of a smile. "If anything comes up, just yell. Better to be woken for nothing than to sleep through a slaughter."

"Hmm." She searched again for words. "Have you spoken to Tomas?"

"About?" He stood, stretching his arms before stepping off the porch, turning his back to her. "I don't think he wants to speak to me."

"Listen, it's not my place really, but, for the benefit of our group, I just think you should know he doesn't blame you for what happened to the cavalier. That weasel already had Gunnar in his clutches."

Sharpe said nothing.

"And I don't want you to bear this burden or have it affect your reputation."

He spun on his heels and marched at her, stopping inches from her face. "My reputation," he whispered, "is a lie. My family and the family farm were lost to a terrible storm years ago. The only way I could survive was to run away from my charred homeland and head north, offering my services as a trail escort. See this bow? I pulled it off some dead man in the woods." He fumed. "There it is. That's my secret. Are you happy? You've outed me. I'm just a homeless man carrying a bow who can sometimes hit the side of a horse at twenty yards and murdered a hero of the Kingdom of Swan."

"It wasn't murder, it was an accident! I can give you an endorsement from my kingdom when we are done, and attest to your bravery. That is why you're still guiding and protecting us, yes? To be sure you have a clear name?"

He sat on the porch step and laid his bow at his feet. "I've no purpose. I'm just a drifter. Not a grifter, just a drifter." He let his quiver slide off his shoulder, rattling to the porch as his arrows spilled out. "I will help you get to the outpost, get to Himmelhavets. I *will* help you. And I would be grateful for your royal endorsement when this is done."

Apondra nodded. After hearing Carlala's story of Azcalaw, and the origins of the cult, she could see how under different circumstances, Sharpe was the type of person who would be recruited, a lost soul with nothing in his pockets, desperate for shelter and belonging. She picked up his fallen arrows and restocked them in the quiver. "Can you teach me to shoot?"

"Are you serious? Now? At night?"

"Sure, why not?" She smiled.

Sharpe accepted his quiver from her. He pulled up his sleeve, revealing a tattered piece of leather wrapped with a fraying cord tied around his forearm. "I took this from the body of the same man where I got my bow. I like to think there's a story behind it. Maybe his wife bought it for him with her saved coins as an anniversary gift. Or perhaps he stole it from a thief after killing him." He smiled, something she had not seen very often; his deep dark laugh lines now exposed a kind face. "For now, it's my only advocate. People see the wear and tear on it and assume my experience."

"It fooled me, *archer*," she said with a wink. "And might I say, you speak rather well. Your tongue is as sharp as your mind."

He tapped his temple with his finger. "You figured me out, Princess. I'll teach you how to shoot when we have time during daylight."

"Alright. Well, I enjoyed our conversation, but now I think I should relieve you of your watch. Off to bed."

"If it's okay with you, I'll sit back right here and close my eyes. If I sleep, I sleep." He handed her his bow and stretched on the porch, resting his head next to his quiver. "I'm used to sleeping like this. Outside. With my arrows."

Apondra let him lay in silence until Sharpe's slowed breathing joined the chirps and creaks from the birds and boughs around the inn. A short huff from Teacup, a whinny from Domino, but nothing else. Sleep pulled at her eyelids, but she shook it off with a short walk around the porch, then a few practice pulls of the bowstrings. *I best not break it; I don't know what I'm doing.* She withdrew her borrowed dagger and carefully passed it from one hand to the other, getting used to the balance and feel of the worn leather handle. She sat on the step next to Sharpe. *I'll close my eyes for just a moment.*

A voice shocked her awake, whispering in her ear. *Sharpe.*

"Don't move."

Apondra opened her eyes, his hand clutching her shoulder. In the darkness just beyond the porch, a large black form, the size of a man or lobfolk, drifted over the grass at the edge of the trees, not more than fifty feet from the inn. It glided slowly with no rhythm, a dark robed figure with no feet or appendages to touch the ground. She attempted to speak, but no breath escaped her lungs, paralyzed by fear. The robed figure continued to wander, floating above a patch of leaves, undisturbed in its eerie motions.

"What is it?" she finally said in the lowest voice she could manage.

"A spirit? A ghost?" Sharpe moved very slowly behind her; she could feel his weight shifting as he released his hand. Such supernatural beings were hinted at in stories, but never confirmed. Had her journey far from home brought her to the edge of a realm that pierced the underworld, some fissure into the Undersea? She shivered in fear. Out of the corner of her eye, she caught the glinting tip of an arrow as Sharpe set his aim over her shoulder. "Don't move."

The robed being paused, hanging in the air momentarily before … *reversing?* It floated backward, retracing its path across the edge of the woods. Apondra and Sharpe held their breath as it glided, a tiny hiss now audible from the figure. It lurched to a sudden stop, hanging on a wisp of the wind. From each side of the property, two more figures emerged, floating above the ground, unmoving, stuck in the light breeze.

"What do we do?" Apondra whispered. Sharpe slowly moved his bow from target to target. The three robed figures remained still, floating in the air. He exhaled, releasing his shot; the arrow sailed cleanly through the robe of the central figure. The pair held their breath as it remained stationary, unfazed.

The door to the inn burst open behind them. Carlala and Titus emerged; she wielded a long pole with a metal hook as she stomped off the porch. "Wretched things," she yelled. She strode to the central specter and jabbed her pole into the air above its head. Titus growled as he leapt onto the robed form, frozen in midair. After a loud grunt from Carlala as she yanked at her adversary, the figures began to move again. Apondra could now make out a thin cable running from tree to tree, laced through an almost imperceptible wooden block attached just above head height. Carlala returned to the porch, polearm over her shoulder, beaming. Titus rolled in a pile of leaves before bounding back and playfully diving between her legs. With a hearty laugh, she scratched him along his back and shook her head.

"My ghouls. Nighttime defense against wandering rogues and some of the less aggressive beasts who hunt in the dark."

Apondra splayed her hands across her chest with a mixture of disbelief and relief on her face. Now discernable as floating scarecrows, the robed figures continued slowly sliding along their aerial cable tracks. Sharpe breathed a sigh of relief and let his quiver slide to the porch with a dull thump.

"You could have told us, innkeeper," he said.

"You didn't ask. You could have wrecked my decoys with your arrows, you know." She held the inn's door open with a huff of disdain, shook her head at him, then pointed inside. "Come on. Back to bed. Don't insult my knowledge of these woods with whatever you thought you were doing."

"We were keeping guard," corrected Apondra. "You said—"

"I said that I can't guarantee safety outside the yard. Your kyloe and your horses are safe in my paddock. Now go to bed and be on time for breakfast an hour after sunrise. And bring your coins."

The morning meal of pan-fried potatoes, grits, and eggs passed without incident, except for Apondra's concern over their lack of taste until she was shown the miracle of sweet tree sap sauce made by hand by Carlala. She asked for two jars of the delicacy to take with them, which aroused the concerns of Tomas as they packed.

"Eave Queen, I would just like to point out that we should be traveling light, for the sake of our mounts and our speed. We're already carrying two bags of your books this entire way, you know."

Apondra held the jars against her chest as she mounted the chariot, spying on Diana as she sat on Domino. "We have a mage who can make bitter potatoes, so I think these bring us a little bit of flexibility if we can't find an inn."

"That's not how magic works," quipped Diana. "They don't just come out of thin air. They're just, I don't know," her voice trailed off, "brought here by something." She crossed her arms across the stolen bedsheet she now used as a makeshift anorak. "Okay, maybe I don't know where they come from, but maybe it would be common sense to not eat magical potatoes."

Ken gripped Teacup's reigns as the group prepared for the day's journey. "I will second that. I was up half the night trying to read your shellbound tome and see what it said about conjured foods. I could barely understand it; half the text is written in the old languages, and it shifts from word to word with no logical pattern."

"Best be careful," said Diana. "Those words are the codex to unlocking spellcasting. If you are magically inclined and speak the wrong ones, you may turn yourself into sand, or summon a swarm of giant crickets."

Apondra leaned back against Ken's claw that gripped the side of the chariot. "Or perhaps summon a … turtle?" An idea blossomed in her mind. "I think we may need to directly speak with these cultists, someone who isn't a recruiter like that Tenor fellow."

Titus bounded off the porch and playfully tapped Diana's leg. As she tried to brush the cat away, Carlala emerged from the inn, her thick arms crossed in frustration.

"Are you forgetting something, miss?" Titus swung at the edge of Diana's anorak. She hung her head and pointed to Ken.

"Ken, pay her for the bedsheet."

He scrounged through the depths of his coin purse. "I'm a bit short, I think. Here." He handed her his remaining coin and a book from his bag. "Well, you said you like to use books as barter. This is a guilty pleasure of mine, it's a romance, a story of a boy who travels the woods alone and then finds a girl trapped in a well."

"I like romance," Carlala replied softly, snatching the book. "I don't get many tales of romance out here." She carefully opened the cover and ran a finger down the page, her lips moving as she read quietly. Her eyes began to well. "Thank you, white claws." She wiped her eyes with a meaty hand. "I can't wait to read this with Titus on my lap tonight! Thank you."

"You're welcome?" Ken tugged Teacup's reigns. "Well, that was unexpected."

Apondra waved goodbye as they rode off, and for a moment, she thought that Titus lifted his paw to return the gesture.

Several days passed with barely any encounters with beasts or merchants on the road as they trudged north to Himmelhavets. The first few nights provided sanctuary in the form of rundown inns and one generous merchant camp, where barter and trade provided much needed replenishment of their food stocks; Apondra reluctantly exchanged one of the jars of delicious sap sauce for more salted meat sticks. Diana used the time to practice spells that generated blue butterflies made of light, providing entertainment at an inn to earn additional coins and refill her wineskin. But the inns now disappeared from their route as they pushed forward at first light into the last stretch of unknown rolling hills and scattered woods. Apondra and Sharpe discussed the misleading distance they were told by the shepherd; only "three days" to Himmelhavets turned into a week with no outpost in sight.

The current day's travel ran into the dimming light of dusk when the group set up camp for the evening on the edge of a deserted farm. Their small fire, hidden by a pile of large stones from the barn's view, burned slowly next to one of the few sections of fence that remained upright constructed of interlocked tree boughs. The further north they had traveled, the more frequently they had passed abandoned cabins and huts, signs of the gradual recession of the population from the stark dry forests and fields on the northern edges of fallen kingdoms' boundaries under the shadows of the mountains. Ken glanced through his journals for additional histories on the former populace.

"It says the harsh winters gradually pushed the humans and lobfolk south. Many moved east to the coast where the fish farm fleets operate." He grabbed the shellbound tome from Diana's small pile of belongings and gently feathered through the pages. He itched his elbows. "Hmmph."

"What does that mean?" asked Tomas, chewing on one of the remaining meat sticks.

"It means," replied Ken, as he nibbled on his own stick by the glowing campfire, "I'm thinking." He flipped back and forth in the tome. "There's a story in here about another village that witnessed Azcalaw when he saved them from some kind of wild animal. They don't go into detail, but it sounds like a wild beast with feathers and fur. And here," he pointed to a set of words written in one of the old languages, "he agreed to be paid for his services with twelve children."

Apondra wrapped her blanket around her shoulders and leaned over Ken. Her breath created a slight cloud as she shivered, both from the chilly air and the thought of children as currency. She could not recall seeing any in the working quarters in the merchant town, but now her eyes opened to the possibility that slavery could also afflict and affect children. "Ken, what would Azcalaw need children for?"

"I don't know. He could be asking for a sacrifice, or food, and yes, my mind quakes at the thought of him devouring humans as payment for his almighty deeds."

Tomas joined their huddle. "Is it only humans? Has he ever taken lobfolk children as … tribute?"

"Not from anything I've read," said Ken. "But our lifecycle is slightly different. Our females lay eggs in birthing pools, not too different from our lobster kin of the seas, but we use the pools to cultivate the youth who survive. They often stay in the pools for a year or so until they are old enough to breath air, speak, and walk upright."

"You are fascinating creatures," Tomas said.

"Aye, we are only interesting to things that are not us." He pulled his cloak tighter as Apondra wrapped her blanket around him.

"Ken, should we venture to that farmhouse for shelter?"

"I wouldn't," interrupted Sharpe, returning from his patrol of the perimeter of the farm with a handful of radishes and a rabbit stuck with an arrow. "I didn't like the look of it. Cook these, Ken."

"Thank you, archer. What did you see?"

"Signs of a forced entry into the farmhouse, just beyond the barn. The door was torn off its hinges, the wood looks freshly splintered. Someone recently made it their den. I could see through the entryway from the path that there were fallen bookshelves and an overturned table in the great room."

Apondra and Ken stood in unison and spoke with the same voice. "Bookshelves?"

"I regret speaking that word in front of you two."

Apondra slung her booksack over her shoulder. "We must go! Family journals, records of farm business, anything would be useful!"

"And entertaining!" said Ken.

Sharpe rubbed his hands in front of the fire. "Not until daybreak, Your Highness. Anything, or anyone, that might be in there will leave at dawn. We're protected from sight here, except for the animals, but they may wander as they feed, which should throw off our exact position." He held his hands closer to the flames. "We should wait."

Teacup meandered close to the fire and lay down behind Apondra. She placed her bag on the ground, frustrated by the delay of adventure, and nestled against his fur. "We should investigate that house as soon as possible," she muttered with crossed arms. If she was going to sit around until she fell asleep, wouldn't the time be better spent reading the books from the farmhouse? Sharpe crouched next to the rabbit over the firepit, his gaze reflecting the red and orange flames, a predator on two legs. He stared and shook his head.

"Princess, caution will keep us alive." Sharpe's features softened, his eyes still ablaze from the fire. "This is what I'm good at. Let me be good at this."

It was now that she noticed Tomas, sitting upright against his stuffsack, gazing at the rabbit as it charred. She nodded to Sharpe.

"Your expert counsel is welcome, and appreciated. We will wait until after sunrise."

Teacup sniffed Apondra's ear with a tickling blast of his breath, and pressed his torso against her as she knotted his fur around her fingers before falling asleep.

The night passed quickly and without interruption as each took their turn on guard. Apondra studied the house as soon as the sun rose, and then left the camp with her bag and dagger before the others woke. Her curiosity and impatience pulled her toward the structure. *I can be in and out very quickly if I go alone.*

The field around the house lay rutted by old plow lanes and the empty holes where potatoes and radishes once grew. She stepped and skipped over the terrain, past the empty barn, missing one entire wall that she assumed was lost to entropy and weather, and into the front entrance of the abandoned residence.

The house itself, a one-story tiny cabin, contained two closed interior doors, one Apondra assumed was the bedroom, the other perhaps a small second bedroom or large storage pantry. Closed shutters with broken boards allowed light to crisscross the main room and had prevented some of the elements from disturbing the contents. She turned a small table upright and set her book bag in the middle. Along the same interior wall that supported the closed doors of the small rooms, she studied the narrow handmade bookshelf that rose from the floor and touched the ceiling. Each tier of the bookshelf overflowed, stuffed with boxes, papers, and leather journals in disarray. She ran her fingers over the spines; hand-pulled and sewn leather binding as was prevalent for handmade or artisan books of the working class. She grasped the largest one, a light brown buckskin leather tome about as thick as four fingers, from the middle shelf and set it on the table.

If this was a journal, she prepared herself to uncover the details of a life long removed from the farm. Something about this book, the disrupted house, and the dead fields that no longer bore crops provided a gravitas that other books from Apondra's studies did not. Libraries provided a barrier, a distance from the tragedies of factual accounts. She looked away from the book at the tattered remnants of a faded blue curtain that clung for life on a nail next to the window, the stiches large and rough, visible from a distance. Someone had made it by hand, with love, perhaps the same person who filled these pages.

The first pages of the buckskin book contained ledgers of crop production over the seasons with diminishing returns. Apondra imagined the family struggling to pay their bills, or trade for supplies as each year's harvest soured more than the last. She wondered when they decided to leave. But wouldn't they at least sell the farm, she asked. *Is this something I don't understand in the business world of the common people?* She blushed, a tiny bit ashamed of her class, and the assumptions she made based on it. Royalty had provided her with safety from dangers and struggles she had never perceived, and now she was uncovering and witnessing more of the real world, and the challenges of the ruled, than she had ever imagined. Apondra pulled the neck of her sweater over her chin. She was a voyeur, and she didn't like admitting it even as she delicately turned each dry page in this book of the deceased.

Blank pages met her fingertips now, then a sudden change in penmanship and content. Brighter, rounder, more … *feminine?* … writing took over as the family business ledger now mutated into a lonely diary. She bit the collar of her sweater, a mix of dried sweat salt and dirty wool in her mouth, and read the new author's text silently at the table.

> *My husband is dead. He hung himself in the barn after lamenting how our daughter was taken by that creature. He, that bastard beast, said our son was not suitable. I don't understand why; they were just a year apart in age, our little Jacob barely a year older than Jillane. Jacob died over the winter, first a cough, then the blood sickness. I believe his heart was broken when his sister was taken, but*

father insisted it was a disease cast by Azcalaw when he 'saved' our dying village. Many others grew sick. Starvation has crept into every barn and hearth. The merchants, foul thieves, bought everyone's remaining livestock for a pittance, then a new caravan of sellers followed on their heels with overpriced food from the south. Greedy merchant sea scum. Damn the lobfolk.

Apondra turned the pages further, skimming stories of neighbors who died or had moved, and the madness of illness that took one family when the father butchered his kin. She continued to read.

Azcalaw! How I regret knowing the word, the name, the beast. Nothing but ruination since the cultists approached us offering to bring him back as our savior. When he first arrived in our village, his giant blue bulk wrapped in his cloak of eels, he promised to 'do what must be done' to save us. So he said! And our daughter, my sweet Jillane, undoubtedly placed on a spit or in a stew to feed his gluttonous hunger. Why would I entertain these cultists after all these years to bring him back unless I wished for death?

I regret settling far from the colleges of the south. I regret falling in love with my husband. I regret not leaving our farm earlier with only a handful of coins rather than having none to buy my way out. And I regret summoning Azcalaw. We have damned ourselves with the worship of a false god, replaced by a nightmarish reaper for the Undersea.

Apondra threw the journal into her bag and ran out of the house, knocking down Tomas who approached the porch. She helped him up and clutched his shoulders, her eyes frantically scanning his face. Her breaths grew shallow, not from her sprinting but from the reckoning the mysterious author had documented.

"Tomas! We've made a terrible mistake! We are running into danger, and we are damning ourselves if we seek Azcalaw and his help!"

"We have larger and more immediate problems, Eave Queen!"

He pointed back to their encampment across the field. The tree line at the edge of the forest shook, a rolling wave from west to east as the trunks and limbs shot into the air. A guttural thunderous roar pierced their ears as the great snapping turtle's head rose above the forest, oblivious to the tiny camp in the field. They watched its back rise and fall above the trees as it continued its path of destruction through the forest. Apondra squinted, shielding her eyes from the rising sun. When the turtle finally left her view, a herd of enormous white mountain elk broke from the forest and trampled over the field, past the two humans, and beyond the abandoned house. Even with their immense size, almost thrice that of a horse, armed with sweeping antlers like saplings, the mountain elks still ran in terror to the forest on the other side of the farm.

"Stunning," Tomas whispered. "Mountain Elks. I've never seen them before."

"Neither have I," Apondra said, still spellbound by the sight of these majestic mountainous animals running in fear.

The human duo scrambled back to the camp, Apondra leading with her hand wrapped around his. The asymmetric footfalls of his wooden leg as he dodged the holes in the field replaced the snapping beast's roar in the distance as it finally faded.

Sharpe, already mounted on Domino with Diana behind him on Rose, rode to meet them, followed by Ken and Teacup. Diana yanked Tomas up.

"Come on, squire boy, get on!" She held her hand over her head. "We should be safe for a while if he chooses to turn around."

Ken folded his map as Apondra took her place in the chariot. "Eave Queen, we need to make haste to the outpost. We need to warn them."

"Ken! I have so many things to tell you about!" She held up the buckskin journal. "In here! Azcalaw is not our savior!"

"Well, you can tell me about it on our way," he said with a flick of the reigns. "Teacup, trot hard!"

Chapter 9

The Outpost at the End of the World

THE ROUGH ROLLING hills of neglected farmlands slowly repopulated with large orange and gray speckled stones at the foot of the northern mountain range. Ages ago, noted Ken to the group, the seas had pushed far inland to the foot of these mountains, and the stones were a reminder of the soil's past life as a rocky beach. A wide hardpacked stretch of sandy terrain decorated with dried hoof scuffs and footprints announced the final approach to the outpost of Himmelhavets.

Tall wooden walls created by placing logs between existing great trees, not unlike the structures of the lobfolk's Castle Homarus, loomed before them. Large orange and black uncut stones stacked as tall as a human created a cuff around the bottom of the barrier and the living trees. A solid wooden door, wide enough for a flock of sheep or a small cattle drive, blocked the entrance to the outpost's interior. Apondra stood in awe of the wall, stretching hundreds of yards in each direction. At the tops of the living trees, small hammocks swung in the breeze, rope ladders dangling from them for an unknown length until their bottom rungs landed somewhere inside the wooden battlements. A shape moved in one, a human archer, lazily dangling his legs as he waved to the group.

"I expected something more, I don't know, akin to a village?" Apondra said. She waved back.

"Himmelhavets is an outpost," said Sharpe. "It's the last sanctuary before the wild north. No kingdom has the right of law here. We need to find the legion constable and register ourselves as merchants or we'll be picked clean by thieves."

Diana tucked her wineskin under her shirt. "If anyone asks, I'm dry."

Ken laughed. "Quite the opposite, but your secret is safe."

A small human-sized door on the side of the great gate opened. A lobfolk in a red cloak and wrapped in black and white leather-pocketed straps approached them, a large-handled weapon in his hand; axe blade on one side, a hammer on the other. His large claws, covered with leather sheaths decorated with metal studs, flexed and clacked as he greeted them.

"Hello, travelers. This is Himmelhavets. I am the constable of this outpost. You may call me Captain Wolf." He reached into a pocket and handed a notepad and charcoal stick to Sharpe. "Names. Point of origin. Final point of landing. Profession." Apondra pulled her scarf over her face, forgetting that her identity was best concealed from anyone who may have seen her in the royal court in the past. Wolf held up his hand in protest. "Keep your face uncovered until you are signed in, please."

Sharpe scribbled on the paper and handed the pad back to Wolf. "You'll see we are merchant scouts, looking for samples to bring back to our respective lands. Kingdom of Swan, the lobfolk of the south, and my islands." Apondra noted his keen lie. "We need immediate lodging and security for our animals."

"Granted," said Wolf, running his fingers over Sharpe's handwriting. "But I have one more query I must ask you, new procedure." He held his weapon in two hands at the ready. "Are you affiliated with the Cult of Azcalaw?" He pointed his hammer-axe now at Ken.

"I am not, Captain Wolf."

"Your pallor—"

"—is how I was born. Not of magic or religious decoration." Apondra noted how Ken's shoulders slumped and heard the embarrassment in his voice. "I ask you please not to stare."

"I stare because it is my job," replied Wolf, turning his eyes to Diana. "You, lady. You are … a mage." He held out one hand, beckoning her to touch his. "I have the gift of channeling. I can sense these things." He turned to Apondra. "You, you're a *channeler*, too, like I am. I must caution you: the use of magic inside these walls is forbidden. Even parlor tricks."

Apondra's eyes widened. She glanced at Diana, who met her gaze with the same look of confusion and revelation. The tales from the vizier said that magic had been swept up from their lands back home. She had assumed this meant all lands, and now she truly understood the scale of the aberration that was her kingdom's lack of magic. "A channeler?"

"New magefolk, hmm? Self-taught without a mentor?" He twiddled his antenna before glancing at the rest of the party. "Clearly, I need to discuss this with you in private so that we don't have any incidents. Enter the gate, follow my legion captains to your lodging and animal protection, and you two, the magefolk, will meet me at the gatehouse tonight for a meal and an explanation. No one," Wolf said, punctuating his words now and pointing with the index finger of each of his four hands, "is to use magic inside these walls."

Beyond the mighty gates, the avenues of Himmelhavets stretched for several blocks in each direction, a repetitive and unvaried array of square buildings. A central paddock for animals was laid out in a grid of new wooden fences, and a central citywide aqueduct fed into the animal watering troughs. Apondra picked an area where other kyloe stood together as Teacup's place to rest and feed. He'll like being with friends, she affirmed as she unlatched his chariot and secured it inside the pen.

He immediately lumbered over to another kyloe with black shaggy bangs and stood silently, nose to nose. Apondra smiled. Their inn sat across the street, and she would be able to watch Teacup from the window of each of their two rooms, one for males, one for females, as they were told was the law for unmarried people in the outpost. Ken, Tomas, and Sharpe agreed to eat at the inn while the two young women made their way to Captain Wolf's residence.

The setting sun fought against both lobfolk and human lamplighters running from point to point, igniting tiny bales in metal buckets on top of brick pillars on each street corner. Diana clutched her wineskin in one hand and Apondra's in the other as they entered the plain gray gatehouse walled in square stones. Inside, smaller versions of the streetlight torches adorned the walls of the main room where Wolf sat at a circular table set with clay plates and a steaming stewpot. He gestured for Apondra and Diana to sit across from him.

"Thank you for coming. It is imperative for the security and functioning of the outpost to have no use of magic inside. And civil discourse leads to mutually beneficial positions."

"I see," said Diana, helping herself to a decanter of wine and filling her glass. "I'm guessing you have some other information or diatribe to unleash."

He tapped his fork on the side of his plate. "Who trained you, girl? Magic users are few and far between outside of royal courts."

She shifted in her seat and poked at the stew simmering in the bowl on her plate. "No one. I trained myself."

"As I suspected. How." He did not ask a question, Apondra noted by the authority in his tone. "How." His repeated command echoed briefly.

"I was the slave of an antiquities merchant. I transcribed rare books. I read. I learned of the art of spell casting, and spell creation, from what I could piece together during my servitude. When I showed a high proclivity for magic, my owner, the merchant, tricked me into transcribing and casting a binding spell."

"Parents."

"None." Diana looked to Apondra. "I don't know where I'm from."

Apondra read a sadness in Diana's face, tired bags under her eyes and slight pout in her lip, a reminder that she was just a girl, like herself, and an orphan, also like herself, but that destiny and fate had played two different hands. Wolf continued.

"Your escape. Your liberation from the bonding spell."

"I used … my friend here … and tricked her into assisting with recasting the binding spell. I didn't know she was a channeler. I just thought that the spells would work when anyone said the right words. We accidentally transferred the binding to herself, but we were able to escape after binding to a decoy."

"You call her a friend, but you also say that you tricked her. Deception."

"She wasn't my friend at the time." Diana's features softened as she turned to Apondra. She clenched her hand. "She's my friend now."

"I see. You're lucky to be alive, you know. Self-taught mages often end up dead. For some reason, it's almost always the result of fire. Or madness."

"Madness?" Diana lifted her glass and stared into the wine's burgundy depths.

"Accidents and a lack of comprehension, or a fruitless pursuit of words to complete a spell. The use of magic includes many moments of *accidental* magic. That is where a trained channeler is also of value; they detect and feel vessels like yourselves. It took me only a moment to *sense* upon our first meeting that you are both untrained and uneducated magic-capable individuals."

Apondra sat up. "Me? I am magic-capable?"

"Not like your spellcaster friend. As I said, you are like myself, a channeler, a being who is sensitive to magic, in tune with the forces that surround us, but unable to wield it on our own. A channeler is like a rag and a bucket, someone who can absorb and contain it, or divert it. And that, dear, is a very dangerous thing in the wrong hands, almost as dangerous as an untrained mage." Captain Wolf glared at each of them. "And we cannot have *trained* mages in these walls, so you are a liability of high interest."

"Oh?" Apondra sat back in her seat and shot a glance at Diana who nodded slightly in reply.

"Why is a channeler dangerous?" asked the young spellcaster.

"They can be manipulated. Used by those who wield magic to increase or amplify their abilities. A poorly trained mage with a journeyman channeler can unleash extraordinary power." He folded his hands and placed his antennae on his fingertips. "You see, in the past, there were individuals who would track and capture channelers, using them for their own schemes. A mad mage once assaulted an entire town by using a procession of chained channelers to pull his war cart. He destroyed the local ruler's stronghold and seized the treasury's riches. Balance of power, high thievery, these are things that we can't allow here in the outpost. And so, it is illegal to show any use of magic, not just for the safety of the town, but to protect individuals from being kidnapped. Or worse."

"I see," said Diana. She pushed her glass away and reached for a cup full of water.

"You do not see. You stumbled in the dark and ended up here. Dangerous outcomes for the ignorant. And you too easily disclosed your magic ignorance."

He sipped from his glass and stared at Apondra. His dark eyes made her uncomfortable as she noticed the fine cracks in his shell, a brown hue that now revealed a fine red lattice of his undermolt. It struck her that this was not a lobfolk to toy with or deceive, as he was not only the organizer of law and executor of punishment, but also a lobfolk who might have no issue killing two young humans now to avoid trouble later. She spied his hammer-axe handle peeking above the table next to his chair.

"Captain Wolf," Apondra asked in as diplomatic and pleasant of a voice as she could muster, "you permitted us entry to your keep."

"I did."

"You've asked us to join you in your residence."

"I did."

"And yet you seem to imply with menace that we are some sort of danger or are in danger. Your exposition is appreciated, but I want to know why I am such a danger to your outpost." She folded her hands, her knuckles white. "I demand full disclosure and answers."

His eyebrows twitched. "A channeler, when properly attuned, can sense magic. He, or she, can tell which individuals have been touched by the mystical world. You, *we*, live in tune with the flow of magic. So, when I sensed a mage and channeler traveling together, I needed to investigate and intervene." He tapped his fork again. "Especially when one of them is Eave Queen of the lobfolk." He folded his hands under his chin. "I know who you are."

Apondra gasped. Diana sipped her water before placing a friendly hand on Apondra's shoulder.

"You're quite the celebrity, Princess."

"Your albino companion wears the same cut of his robe as the lobfolk royal court; he is no soldier or scout or merchant. I can assume you are here as an envoy for something bigger. *Secret.* This outpost was built on the trade of secrets, outside the laws of kingdoms. But no one keeps secrets from the constable." Wolf placed his claws, still sheathed in their leather-studded gloves, on the table. "And, young pretty spellcaster, if you attempt to fling your magic, I must warn you that as a *master* channeler myself, I will just redirect your spell into your companion here."

"You can do that?" asked Diana. Her query was met with a silent affirmation. "Well then. Alright. No flaming potatoes."

He clanked his fork on his glass and summoned a lobfolk corporal carrying a plate of tiny cakes glazed in bright colors. The soldier placed an assortment of the pastries on the clayware in front of each woman, and a long thin dagger in front of Captain Wolf. Diana stirred in her seat.

"Are we being threatened?"

"No. Terms and conditions. A full disclosure, as per the request of the princess here." He smiled slyly, and delicately pointed the dagger at each of them. From beneath the table, he revealed a yellow letter, secured by a wax seal of the kingdom of the lobfolk. He held it out to Apondra, and then withdrew it when she reached, placing the dagger in her hand instead. "You'll need this to open the correspondence. It arrived shortly before your party. The courier said that the Eave Queen of the lobfolk, a fair human, would be arriving with a large party including an albino. Either his definition of large is suspect, or something happened to you on the way here."

Apondra swallowed. "We had a challenging journey." Her throat tightened. "So yes, you have drawn the right conclusions."

"The courier's horse dropped dead after he arrived, so I assume this must be of high importance."

Apondra's eyes narrowed. "You have an odd feel for diplomacy. You withheld an official letter for a member of the royal house until you vetted us for information."

"That is my right as the constable of this town and how I ensure our security." He studied Apondra as she slid the dagger through the wax seal. She stopped.

"I would like some privacy when I read this official dispatch." He ignored her words, as his eyes continued to wander up and down her face, her arms, her sweater. She reached for one of the pastries and slid the letter next to her plate.

"Princess, I assume you have heard of the rumors of the giant snapping turtle's emergence. And perhaps this is why you are here." He stared at the letter now and the partially broken seal.

"We have seen it," said Apondra, tasting one of the tiny cakes. Hints of strawberry and blueberry danced in her mouth until Diana grabbed her wrist and pulled the fork from her hand.

"Are you serious? This little weird warlord is basically holding us hostage and you just ate his poisoned cake or whatever else he did to it!"

"You drank his wine!"

Diana raised her eyebrows. "True, but I switched to water."

"Ladies," interrupted Wolf, rising from his seat, "if I wanted you dead or imprisoned, it would already be done. I needed this meeting to evaluate the threat of your magic, reiterate the rules of the outpost, and deliver your official letter. And I provided you with fruity sweet cakes, which, I might add, are very rare in this region."

With no regard for his office or his weapon, Apondra stood and walked over to the captain, her confidence resting on a shaky foundation of uncertainty and Wolf's intimidation, then seated herself in the chair next to him. The corporal attempted to stop her but was met by a raised claw of protest from Wolf.

"Captain, I am on an urgent mission. That snapping turtle is threatening many kingdoms. It has destroyed the merchant town to the south. My companion from the Kingdom of Swan has said their fishing boats have already been attacked." Her eyes narrowed as she pushed the limits of her false bravado. "I need access to your histories, your travel logs, anything written down that happened before today."

"Tell me, honestly, why you are here, noble. Do not obscure your needs or intentions." Wolf placed his hand gently on hers. His black eyes darted to Diana, then settled on Apondra as he lowered his voice. "I know what that snapping turtle means, and I think you do as well. A ravaging beast like that would destroy all kingdoms and commerce and set back our towns and villages to a time of war and chaos. You are here for Azcalaw." He reached for a small white cake and plunged the entire confection into his mouth.

"I am." Her voice shook. "Please. Help us."

Wolf swallowed his pastry. "*Azcalaw is dead.*" He clapped his hands. His corporal placed the remaining sweets in a small basket, covered it with a cloth, and presented it to the guests.

"I suppose we are being told to leave this hall," Apondra said, grabbing the letter. Her hand shook as she placed the dagger back on the table.

"I have much business to attend to." Captain Wolf rose and picked up his hammer-axe. "Now pardon me, *Your Highness and Lady Mage*, as I must return to my duties."

As he exited the hall, Diana leaned back in her chair.

"'Lady Mage'. I do like how that sounds."

"I don't like how anything sounds right now." Apondra opened the letter, then turned to the corporal, still standing at attention after the departure of his captain. "We will be gone in a moment. You don't need to stand over us." She wiped a tear. "We'll be on our way soon."

The corporal stepped back to the entrance to the dining room and planted his feet. "Guests may not be unattended in the hall."

She sighed and then carefully opened the letter, stained with spots of dirt, dried mud, and what she determined by smell were droplets of sweat. Apondra instantly recognized the vizier's handwriting. Diana rested her chin on her shoulder to read along:

Eave Queen Apondra,

Your father is in good spirits, but still bedridden. An envoy from the Kingdom of Swan arrived to deliver an herbal extract to ease his body, which was tested thoroughly before application. We are grateful to the humans for their concern.

Larold, the Ward of Ribbed Beach, continues to lobby aggressively

for the removal of the king. He has also said he has been researching
the proper path of succession when the king passes, and I strongly
feel that he is trying to generate public support for his cause.

Please make haste with your quest to find and petition Azcalaw.
We hope this message falls on deaf ears as you are on your way back
to the Kingdom already with aid. Please return soon.

Apondra crumpled the letter, her heart racing. "This, this is all insane!" She rattled the ball of paper in Diana's face. "Insane!"

"I don't understand," Diana said. "Literally, I don't know how this works in your kingdom."

"Larold is on the council of our royal court. He's trying to get my father removed so that my claim to the throne is illegitimate, and to do this, Larold is trying to manipulate the public without any evidence! This is madness!" She dropped her hands to her sides, exhausted by her own words. "We should just go home." She smeared the new tears across her face. "You can come with us if you like. Or venture out on your own."

"What good would that do?" Diana held Apondra's hands lightly, pulling her close. "We were on the verge of finding Azcalaw, or at the very least, the truth about him. And some ornery old guard that you just met tells you Azcalaw is dead so you just stop? We are so close to finding out something, I admit I'm not sure what, but something that could be of value to your kingdom's defense, and stopping that giant sea beast that is destroying everything in its path." Her eyes steeled. "We're so close, Appy! All of those deaths in Merchant Town, and the things we've learned so far, they have to mean something." She paused, looking down at their interlocked hands. "You, Tomas, and Ken. You are the only ones left of your group that began this journey. And Tomas, what he did." Her eyes welled. "Tomas gave his mentor's sword for my freedom, before he knew anything about me. That means something. You mean something." Diana's lip quivered. "To me."

Tears now streamed down both of their cheeks. Apondra pressed her cheek against Diana's face.

"I can't do this, it's just too much. And I don't know what to do." Her chest heaved as she threw her arms around Diana. "I'm just a child. I may be eighteen, and have a title, and a coral tiara, but I don't know anything about the real world. It's terrible, and it's cruel, and maybe this isn't something I can change. I can't make a difference."

Diana shoved her back and smacked her. Apondra clutched her cheek as Diana stared her down. "You saved me. You, and Tomas, and Ken, and Sharpe. I am not repaying a debt. I am not some royal servant. I am your *friend*, Apondra." She shook Apondra's hands, her eyes unblinking, two blue spears stabbing through the princess. "And if that means I have to be the one to yell at you to stand up, to press onward, to keep moving, then that's what I'll do. And you're not doing this by yourself. We're all part of this now."

"How can you be so cavalier, so strong?" Apondra smiled through her veil of tears. "You're just, so, you know, tough. Gritty." She recalled her word banter with Ken. "*Resolute.*"

"I know how to work through tough circumstances, even when you see no end in sight. I've sat in literal darkness praying for moments of sun. We push on a little further, a little longer. We don't lose sight of our goal. And we do it together. Come on."

⁓

After returning to the lodge, Apondra paced in a circle in Ken's room, waiting for him to finish poring over the buckskin journals taken from the abandoned farm, the shellbound tome from Diana, and the books he had brought from their library on their journey. She lost her patience with his fastidious note taking and stomped to his desk.

"Ken, please tell me something, anything. What do you think?"

"I think you need to drink a glass of warm goat milk and settle in for the night."

She smirked. "Tell me something I can use."

"Timelines, Appy. Here. See this?" He laid out a folio of papers written in his own hand, scribbles and doodles spanning multiple sheets. "It's the dates, or approximate historical periods, tracking the appearances of Azcalaw. Yes, every time he shows up is in response to a crisis on some level. Yes, many of these are from the eras before the dawn of the modern kingdoms, so the exact calendar day is suspect, but also, this." He circled a number. "This is how many children he has taken over the years, and the intervals of their capture."

"What does it mean?"

"It means I am tired, and we are missing information. Why would Captain Wolf say Azcalaw is dead? Surely, someone with this many legends and documented appearances, even exaggerated, would have spawned some record of his passing." He tapped his baleen pen against his forehead. "Curious."

"Death by old age does not warrant a tale for the ages," Apondra replied. She grabbed a rag and wiped an ink stain from Ken's shell brow. "Your quill left a mark when you did that thing."

Ken slowly grabbed her hand and placed another hand on top. His cool crisp touch calmed the storm in her heart and mind, but also unleashed another crashing wave of sorrow. She suddenly convulsed, sobbing, falling into his arms, her head tangled in too many strings and strands from her web of conflicts. He wrapped his claws behind her back and held her.

"Appy, it's alright. You've done so much. You've learned so much. We can take a moment to catch our breath, and then we'll gather supplies and perhaps an escort and head back south in a day or two. It's alright." He ran his fingers through her hair; she loved how the tips felt like a brush as he made long strokes against her scalp. "It's alright, my friend."

"We tried. We failed." She sniffled, attempting to compose herself. "We did our best."

"That's a horrible epitaph," he said with a tiny laugh.

Apondra shoved him back, her eyes wide to match her sudden smile. "Of course!"

"You want that on our graves?" Ken said, his antennae fidgeting.

"An epitaph! A grave marker! If, if, if," she stammered, "if Azcalaw is dead, wouldn't there be some grave marker, or monument? And I would guess these cultists would certainly know where it is so they could pray or worship or leave tributes." She scrambled to the pile of books and papers. "Perhaps their temple is where he's buried! It's the last thing, *the very last thing* we haven't looked for!"

"Appy, what would it prove? What use would it be?"

"I don't know. Yet. But remember when we arrived? Captain Wolf asked if we were in the cult. There were no consequences to our answer that we were not. There's something there. I can smell it!" She mimicked inhaling; Ken placed two palms on his face.

"How about if you have a glass of warm goat milk like I had recommended, get some sleep, and we'll get back to work in the morning?"

⁓

After breakfast, Apondra, Diana, and Tomas agreed to meet with Captain Wolf. Sharpe, on his own, left midmeal to seek a guide into the northlands for the Temple of Azcalaw as well as inquire about transportation back south to the lobfolk homeland. For the last of their assignments, Ken would continue his work, but he required a plate of wheat cracker cakes and a pitcher of hot honey tea for focus. A courier provided by Wolf brought the appropriate food for Ken and then escorted Tomas and the women to yet another unremarkable stone building on the north end of the outpost.

Captain Wolf greeted them at the entrance and led them inside, revealing a long smooth stone hallway full of wooden doors, each decorated with a small circular window and a single cross bar. *This is a prison,* Apondra realized as the stink of bodily waste saturated the damp air. Wolf unlocked a door near the end of the hallway and beckoned for all to enter.

"You have visitors, Markos," he announced. A small lobfolk, his narrow claws pinched closed by metal cuffs, sat up in his straw bed and nodded. A short chain bound him to the bedframe.

"Hello," Markos said, sniffing at the air. Apondra gasped at his eyes, two dull gray orbs that focused nowhere. "Magic. Magic users. I can smell them."

Wolf held his hand to the humans and nodded. "He has a flair for the dramatic. Markos here is also a channeler. He was caught stealing coins from an innkeeper."

"And for that you put in him prison?" Apondra scoffed. "A handful of coins?"

Markos cleared his throat. "I also punched a horse."

"Tell them what else, prisoner."

"I killed a traveler. For Azcalaw."

A silence floated in the air. Any pity Apondra felt for Markos evaporated with his confession of his crime. "Are you a member of Azcalaw's cult?"

Markos smiled. Some of his antennae around his mouth hung limp as he wiggled them toward her. "Aye. I am a believer in him, and we will bring him back to the world from the Undersea."

"How so?" Tomas held his hand toward Markos' forehead, then recoiled. The prisoner bent forward, revealing the finer lines of his skull shell. Faded paint stripes and old scars covered the top of his head. Tomas attempted to kneel with Diana's help. "Markos, how will you bring him back? Prayer? Sacrifice?"

Markos fidgeted on his bed. "We summon. We believe. And we sacrifice for the world."

Diana spoke next. "What do you mean? What do you sacrifice?"

"The believers. We recruit. We believe. And we sacrifice to bring forth the messenger."

Apondra reached instinctively for her book satchel, forgetting that all her materials were with Ken. She reached under her sweater to her belt pouch for a small notepad and charcoal.

"The messenger? Who is the messenger?"

"We don't know him by name. But we know his form. When he arrives, or when he has arrived in the past, Azcalaw returns to defeat him. We summoned the messenger, and waited, but Azcalaw did not come." Markos stood and raised his bound claws into the air. "Azcalaw must come now to save his believers!" His voice changed from a shout into a loud growl. "Azcalaw will not turn away from us once he sees the apocalypse created by the great beast, the messenger, gnashing the sailing vessels, crushing the cattle in his beak!" He lowered his claws and stared at Apondra with his dead eyes. "Only Azcalaw can defeat the beast. And he loves us." He smiled in the dim light. Long wads of spittle dripped from Markos' mandibles. "That is why he will return. He loves us, and he will love us more for the souls we will gather for him. This is what Tenor has promised us."

"Tenor?" Apondra gasped. "We met him!"

Markos bolted upright. "He did not smell the magic on you? Curious."

Diana leaned forward and peered into his gray eyes. "Curious indeed. Say, Captain Wolf, are you sure I cannot use magic within the town? Perhaps I can coerce this gentleman into providing more information?" She rolled up her sleeves and cracked her knuckles. "Someone get me a drink."

"As much as I would enjoy seeing what you have in mind, no." Wolf shoved Markos back onto his bed. "Law and order only work when no one is above it. No one."

He herded the humans into the hallway. After shutting and locking the door, he turned his back and spoke in a soft voice.

"Lady Mage, you would not need to coerce him into divulging further information. He has been more than willing to tell me what I need to know over the past several weeks. I did not believe him until the report of the great snapper's attacks on merchant ships trickled in with the terrified travelers and merchants. I shut out the cultists at once and exiled them from the city, especially Tenor." He turned around, his antennae drooping. "Some of the cult members still slip inside these walls, seeking converts, surveying our security."

Apondra tucked her thumb under her chin. "So where is the temple? How many days of provision would we need to journey there?"

For the first time since their initial meeting, Wolf spoke with frittering antennae, his large claws dangling at his sides. "It is only an hour north of Himmelhavets. It is almost literally at our back door."

Apondra could barely contain her excitement. "Providence! Then we'll go right there and be back just after lunch!"

"Princess, your naivete is charming. This is not a garden park where you can stroll in and smell the flowers. The cultists and their temple are at the base of the north mountains that divide us from the Kingdom of Ice Lake. Only those in the cult can approach the temple's grounds. Since my decree to evict the cult from Himmelhavets, they have established a large camp around the temple. I sent a band of volunteer guardsmen to watch their pilgrimage from afar. Blue robes dotted the landscape, all wandering around the base of the mountain, praying for a mythical hero to save them from the beast they summoned with their own dark magic."

"Dark magic?" Apondra asked.

"It's a turn of a phrase. All magic is magic. It can be used for good or evil. Tenor, I surmise, has used it with a darkness in his soul. I believe he is the only one capable of summoning the sea beast."

The group stood silently as Apondra took in all of the new information, sorting it as best as she could on top of the ever-expanding mound of truths and lies she had learned since leaving home.

"Did you not ask for aid?" she asked. "My father, he would send help. Much more help than us, as his envoys and researchers."

"We asked some of the closest kingdoms for help. I petitioned the provincial council of the Kingdom of Ice Lake and begged for their army so that we could arrest and break up the cult. They laughed and ignored me, such is their isolation; they have no need for any lands or resources south of the mountains." Wolf walked toward the prison's entrance, gesturing for the group to follow him and exit. "Then the ships began to disappear from the trade routes. The small fisheries ran empty very quickly, and some of the tiny villages flocked to us for food. Merchants began lingering, asking about buying or renting houses in the outpost as business was already showing signs of slowing down. The most desperate ones? Ripe to be plucked as recruits for the cult."

"This is horrible," said Apondra. "No wonder the cult is so appealing."

Wolf placed his hands on the door to exit the prison block. "And those who were attuned to magic would wake in the middle of night screaming Azcalaw's name. So I am told. Those stories go back as far as Tenor's arrival here."

"And when was that? When did he arrive?" Apondra asked. She felt a hand holding hers. Tomas.

"Before my ascension to captain. I once tried to search the visitation logs but found nothing, which is why everyone is thoroughly documented and vetted now. By me."

"Could we see those older records?"

"No." He crossed two of his arms and placed his free hands on his hips. "It's a rule, and as I've said, my rules are absolutes for the security of this outpost."

"Thank you, Captain Wolf," Tomas said. "We have much to think about. It may take us a day or two to gather our information and secure our provisions for the long journey home. If that is alright with you, that is."

"You can stay as long as you like or leave. Either way, it is a high certainty you will face death from the cultist legion or the beast they have summoned."

A somber lunch reunited the five travelers. Sharpe found no escorts willing or currently able to take them back south, but a retired trapper sold him a map of his old side roads and hidden routes beyond the outpost. Apondra unwrapped her scarf to eat; her thoughts distracted her too much to feel hunger. Diana stared at the mug of ale from the bar, but only dipped her finger through the surface of the amber liquid and licked it off the tip. Tomas looked over Ken's shoulder as the librarian scribbled and clawed at his journal pages.

"It's too much," Ken finally announced. "These cultists have twisted the legends of Azcalaw. He's a legendary hero, albeit a rather dark and scary one. He's not some slave spirit to be summoned on a whim into the world." He paused to close his books and place them in an organized tower on the table. "But, also, I ask you: what if we are wrong?"

"What do you mean?" Apondra said.

"What if Azcalaw is not any of these things? Hero, villain … or real."

Tomas slid his chair back from the table. "Then we make a plan." He looked to Sharpe, who shrugged. "I don't have a plan, exactly, but whatever we're doing clearly isn't accomplishing anything at this point." His voice rose with frustration. "Maybe we need to think about going home and focusing on how we defeat a snapping turtle the size of a small mountain."

"We kill it," replied Ken. The group turned in unison. "What? We just figure out how to kill it. I hope you weren't expecting some accidentally humorous quip, as I've run out of those. We kill the damn turtle and send it to the Undersea. If that's where turtles go when they die, that is."

"Tenor," Tomas said, slamming his empty mug on the table. "It's him.

He arrives, the cult appears, and then we have a giant turtle. We need to know more about him." The squire's frustration shocked Apondra. If Tomas was breaking, then she was not alone in her feelings of helplessness.

"But we know *nothing* about him," Apondra said, straightening her back and folding her hands as she would in court. "And we're not assassins. We can't just find him, kill him, and wish that everything disappears."

"You're right." Tomas stood and tightened the belt that held his dagger's sheath. "But we are smart enough to sneak into the outpost's archives and do a better job looking for Tenor's arrival in the visitor's logs than Captain Wolf, aren't we?"

Diana pointed to Apondra. "We are. Or to be more specific, she is."

Across Himmelhavets, dark tattered cloaks and patchwork anoraks adorned many of the visitors and denizens, humans and lobfolk displaced by shared and unique circumstances. Apondra pulled her scarf low over her eyebrows and laced her arm through Tomas' own. The streets, busy but not crowded, smelled of overcooked meat stews and wet woods, and the presence of impending snow hovered over the rooftops in gray clouds as far as the eye could see, cutting off the tops of the mountains past the northern walls. Tomas clutched his dagger handle in its sheath.

"I have decided that I don't like this place," he muttered, his head snapping from pedestrian to pedestrian as they walked to the office of the registrar. He tightened his loop around her arm, protective, but comforting. She rested her hand on his forearm, grateful.

"I miss home," Apondra sighed. The sheen of adventure had finally worn off. Her clothes smelled like soot and sweat, and perhaps a little like Teacup's fuzzy coat, which she didn't mind too much. If she had more coins, she would locate a proper bathhouse, then find a shop at which she could buy a new outfit, but the luxury of a wardrobe was beyond her depleted budget now. As they stood on the stoop of the registrar's office, Tomas pulled a pine needle from her sleeve. She tugged the strap of her book satchel taut over her shoulder and across her body.

"We should be as presentable as we can be," Tomas said, adjusting his cape. "We certainly stand out less than you and Ken as a traveling duo. Do I look, you know, 'knightly'?"

She pulled a dirty handkerchief from her pant pocket and gently rubbed his cheek, remembering how her father would clean her face when she returned from playing in the fields. Tomas still wore the reflection of his master, Gunnar the mighty Cavalier, in his posture and prose, but his own voice slipped through in drips and drabs. His aura exuded safety, not just from physical harm, but from perhaps the jealous and scornful eyes of those who recognized her through her thin disguise as being of noble heritage.

"You look like a captain. A short one," she said with a wink, "but someone with a rank. Someone to be respected."

"Thank you, Eave Queen," he whispered. "*Appy.*" They entered the office arm-in-arm.

The registrar, a beefy bald human with a thick red beard braided into four points, looked up from his desk smothered in journals. His ink-soaked hands, attached to sinewy forearms larger than loaves of bread, reached for his goose feather plume and a lightly stained sheet of yellow paper. His voice was much softer than to be expected by someone of his immense size.

"Names, please?"

"Apondra … Wetflowers. And this is Captain Rosethorn." She cocked her head and pointed her chin at the ceiling. "We represent the Kingdom of Swan." Tomas turned to her and mouthed *Rosethorn?*

"Nature of your business?"

"Merchant buyers. We are here for business."

"What kind?"

"You know," she stuttered, "*business*. Buying of wares, previewing goods, and soliciting of possible contracts." She gritted her teeth. "I am a lady of business."

He looked up from his papers and blinked rapidly. "Merchant *buyers*," he said with a loud exhale. "How long will you be staying?"

"We're not sure," said Tomas. "I mean, until we secure our contacts and contracts. It can be quite time consuming."

Good one, Apondra thought. She nodded in agreement. "We would ask, or rather, we *request* that we gain access to your ledgers, the visitor logs. *Captain Wolf* told us they could be useful to us, so that we could see a list of the visiting merchants. It would help us speed things along."

The ledgerman placed his quill in his ink bottle and folded his hands. He stared at her, then Tomas, then slowly back and forth. He pursed his lips and continued his survey. *What was he waiting for?* Apondra tapped her foot. After a long minute, he separated his hands and drummed his fingers, again not looking away.

"Well?" said Tomas.

"I can't ask," said the ledgerman, his voice small.

"Ask what?" replied Apondra.

"I can't." He lowered his voice further. "I can't ask you for, you know." His fingers twitched in a beckoning gesture.

"Oh, right, yes, yes, yes," Apondra said, shuffling through her pockets. "Ahem. Would this help us gain access?" She slid a single coin across the table.

"You know that's barely worth a sandwich."

"Oh, right. I forgot to bring out his friends." She winked and placed another coin on top, then another, then another, until the ledgerman smiled.

"Miss, you're really bad at this, you know." He stood up and scooped the coins into his desk drawer. "The door behind me, on the right. The registrar logs are in chronological order, oldest are on the bottom rows on the left, then it goes up to the top, then back down, around, around again, and comes up back up."

"Got it," said Tomas with a highly uncertain tone.

The ledgerman blinked rapidly. "Newest ledgers are the top row. That's where you'll find the current visitors."

"Thank you."

The sight of the shelves reinvigorated Apondra, back in her element of researching and reading. She fluttered from volume to volume, scanning pages of sampled books before reshelving them and moving to the next row. She marveled at the handwritten strange names, lost towns, esoteric occupations; all these simple fragments ignited her imagination into fiery narratives of people and lobfolk living their lives and all somehow converging on this outpost, oblivious to each other. She continued to leap backward in time through the ledgers. Tomas followed behind her in silence, checking their exit back through the office for any obstructions.

"Princess, how will we find the record of when Tenor arrived?" His whisper simmered into a hiss. "Princess! What if he used another name! We didn't think this through."

"I don't know, but perhaps anything that looks out of the ordinary will be our clue. Maybe something related to an influx of the cult, or a world event." Her voice trailed as she saw … something. On the bottom bookshelves, a dark leather ledger. She would not have heeded it if it weren't for the unusual shine on its spine, the crisp corners on the cover. She guessed by the dates on the surrounding books that the records inside should be about eighteen to twenty years old.

"This is out of place, it's a new book but in the old section," she whispered. "This is a new book." The crisp pages turned easily between her fingertips, the ink bold and dark. "But the entries inside contain old dates."

"Perhaps they needed to replace a damaged copy?"

"Why would just one book be damaged? If there were flooding, or a fire, surely the whole shelf would have the same remedy of being rewritten and rebound."

The smooth paper and clean penmanship continued throughout the book. The quality of the spine, clean and tight leather, tickled her palms as she caressed the pages, kindling a tiny tingle in her fingertips.

A tingle.

At first she thought it might be her hands finally warming to the building's interior, but then the book pulsed lightly in her fingertips, like dipping her hands into a fine sandy beach. When she placed the book on the floor, the feeling evaporated. *Magic?* She confirmed the sense as she picked it back up.

"We need this," she whispered. "I'm taking this."

"Won't they notice?"

"Not if I do this," she said, carefully sliding each book on the long shelf over by the width of a thick hair. "I'll respace them! I'll close the big gap with tiny, tiny gaps between the other books. I used to do this in the library back home when I 'borrowed' books from the restricted shelves. Now keep quiet and keep an eye out for the ledgerman."

Tomas put his hands on his hips, flaring his cloak over his elbows to provide cover. The heavy footsteps of the ledgerman announced his approach. Apondra continued to slide each book over, one tiny slot at a time, to erase the gap.

"Excuse me," said Tomas, intercepting the ledgerman, "you mentioned buying a sandwich for just one coin, and you look like a man who certainly knows good food." He pointed to the ledgerman's girth, only to be met with a confused expression. "Could you recommend the best place for a cheap meal for weary travelers?"

The ledgerman smiled. "Ah, do you like lamb?"

"Love it," Tomas replied. "Can't get enough." Apondra heard Tomas swallow hard.

"Ah, I've got the place for you! Fresh slabs of lamb on acorn meal bread, and a layer of melted goat cheese, ah! You'll want to go to the eastern side; there's a little place called The Bloody Plate." He slapped Tomas' arm. "You should ask for seconds, lad. And thirds!" The ledgerman's laugh echoed as he skirted past Tomas. Apondra rose, clutching her bag.

"Ahem, *Captain Rosethorn*, we should go. I think I found the names of some good wool traders we can track down."

"Yes, Prin—Miss Wetflowers—we can go now."

"Have a nice day," waved the ledgerman as he rounded the corner into the bowels of the archives. "Enjoy the lamb!"

The duo rushed out of the office and broke into a hurried jog down the block, dodging travelers and tiny flakes of snow.

"Princess, what if he finds out we stole that book?"

"He would have to look for it first, then figure out who took it, and, let us not forget, he has to even *care* that we stole an old ledger from nearly twenty years past!" She gripped the strap of her bag, tugging at the weight. "To the inn!"

⁓

Apondra stormed into her shared room with Diana and tossed the bag on the bed. Diana sat up on her blankets, rubbing her eyes.

"Can I just get some sleep? It's still early."

"Early *afternoon, Lady Mage.* Come. Here!" Apondra pulled the stolen ledger from her bag and held it toward Diana. The spine tingled under her fingers. "Here! Look at this!" She ran to the door and closed it firmly.

Diana recoiled as soon as her fingers touched the ledger. A blue sparkling web sagged momentarily between her hand and the cover before fizzling into nothingness.

"Magic," she murmured. "Appy, we could get in trouble! How did you know?"

"I felt it!" Apondra's eyes widened. "I touched it, and I felt it. *I felt it!*"

"I suppose that's an effect from your channeling ability," Diana replied. "And you've never felt that before?"

"Well not from an object. I felt something when we met Tenor, but you were casting your dampening spell, or whatever it was. But this book? The feeling reminded me of when I helped you with the unbinding spell in Merchant Town. I just, you know." She held her fingers in the air and wiggled them.

"Hmm." Diana laid the book on the nightstand and pulled at her lip. "From what I know, what I think I understand, a heavy part of magic use is belief. Confidence. Since the constable, Captain Dog—"

"Wolf."

"—*Wolf* said you were a channeler, your belief was affirmed. Maybe that's why you were able to manifest it without trying. Interesting." Diana held her hands up, palms forward. "Sit on your bed. Hold your little paws up and mirror me."

Apondra complied. She put her hands, palm forward, into the air. A coolness, like a breeze on wet skin, floated into her hands. "I feel something," she whispered.

"Aim at the book."

Apondra pivoted, slowly, her hands trembling. As the book came into her direct path, the sensation churned, like feathers tracing circles in each of her palms. She closed her eyes; the feeling intensified.

"Is this channeling?"

"Beats me," said Diana as she reached for her wineskin. "But let's say it is. And I think you're right. This book was bound different than the others, much more recently, and with different quality of pages than the others; that's something I know probably as well as you, book construction. And now we know it's magical in nature."

A knock at the door preceded Ken's pale hand waving through the opening. "Are you decent, ladies?"

Diana laughed. "Your question just inspired a volume of questions. You may enter!"

He quickly closed the door behind him. "It's just a respectful habit; I'll be sure to barge in unannounced in the future. But listen! I have an urgent development. There are cultists outside soliciting members. We can perhaps ask them some questions."

"But Captain Wolf said they were not permitted in town!"

"Whatever he said, it's not being enforced. Or at least, not yet. Let's hurry!"

At the corner where several taverns competed at the same intersection, a blue-robed lobfolk stood on a potato crate, surrounded by three other cultists and a small throng of mixed company. The orator's face and claws, painted with yellow and blue stripes, swirled with his grandiose gestures and animated speech.

"You have all heard of the merchant town disaster!" he shouted. "The great snapper of the sea, the beast of myth and legend has returned with its message to judge us! But its judgement is flawed, you see. We are all worthy! Worthy of the love and protection of Azcalaw!" Dissenting voices replied in kind.

"I heard the beast destroyed the timber growths!"

"It's not safe to fish!"

"Azcalaw is dead!"

The cultist paused; his mouth hung open. Apondra, Ken, and Diana, now joined by Sharpe and Tomas, blended in at the far edge of the crowd, huddling behind a cart selling hot bags of nuts and dried berries. Ken yanked his cloak and hood over his head. "I can't wait to hear his reply," he grumbled.

The cult's speaker stepped off his box. "Azcalaw? Dead? Who said this?" He stretched out his claws. "Who would dare say this? He is not dead. He sleeps! He slumbers in the places between our dreams, tethered to this earth by our love, but imprisoned by the lack of faith!" He crossed his arms over his chest, clutching his heart. "But you have not filled your hearts with the love for him that would summon his mighty powers to save us! That is why you, humans and lobfolk, you all need to join with us to praise him!"

Sharpe cupped his hands around his mouth. "And where would we go to find Azcalaw?" Diana slapped his wrists, eliciting a shrug and a smirk. "It can't hurt to ask."

"Ah, young man! I see you are of the southern kingdom, the South Islands. Azcalaw's temple is just beyond this lawless outpost town. Come, come with us, meet our high priest Tenor, and share in his love!"

"See? Not a bad idea," said Sharpe, slinging his bow over his shoulder. Apondra grabbed his wrist.

"What are you doing?"

"Contributing," he said with a smile, then drew his mouth into a stern line and gently freed his wrist from her hand. "I don't have magic, and I'm not a bookworm. I'm doing what I can."

She nodded. He strode through the crowd and shook hands with the cultist. Apondra observed their mouths moving, words exchanged at volumes well below the crowd's dissonance as the lobfolk quickly covered their blue robes with plain gray blankets and capes. The speaker handed a bundle wrapped in brown canvas to Sharpe in exchange for his bow. Tomas clutched Apondra's arm; she attempted to run toward Sharpe as he returned to the group, beaming from ear to ear.

"Well, it looks like I have safe passage through the north gate to their temple." He held out the canvas parcel. "I had to renounce my worldly goods to their cause in exchange for this."

Apondra, mouth agape, grabbed his collar. "Your bow! Why? I don't understand."

He slowly unwrapped the package, revealing the blue cloth of a cultist robe. "It's the only way one of us can pass through their camp undetected. I was told to head to the north gate wearing this when I am ready to begin my pilgrimage."

Apondra felt the robe's cloth, a thick weave like a sail, held by tight stitches consistent with the quality of the lobfolk clothiers from back home. She folded the parcel and glanced at the leather bracer on Sharpe's forearm.

"The sacrifice was unnecessary. You might need your bow if there's trouble during your investigation."

"I'm not the one who should go," Sharpe said, nodding to Ken. "An albino is too obvious, too memorable. And I would not be of much use if there were any engravings or clues that required a learned mind to read and decipher them."

Diana spoke next. "Apondra, my magic leaves a stronger trace than your channeling."

"Oh." Apondra held the parcel against her chest. "Right. I should be the one to go." She looked to Ken, then Tomas, his head on his chest and hands on his hips with resigned acceptance.

"It makes sense, Princess," Tomas said. "If it takes just a handful of hours according to the maps Sharpe bought from the trapper, then you should leave soon so you can be back by nightfall."

"The night comes more quickly here in the north," Ken said. "Squire, give her your dagger. Appy, when the sun begins to set, we'll head out the north gate so we can intercept your return. That will minimize the time and chances of being alone in the dark." His antennae fluttered. "I do not like this plan, but it is what it is."

Apondra scanned their faces. Reluctance, fear, doubt; only Sharpe wore a smile.

"Princess," he said, "this is going to work. Let's get you into costume and on your way."

Chapter 10

A Grave Revelation

THE AFTERNOON SUN dipped below the tops of the tallest trees as Apondra stepped outside the safety of the walls of Himmelhavets. The northern gate opened and closed frequently as trappers and hunters made their way through, as well as groups of two or three men and lobfolk, silent packs that shed their canvas cloaks to don their blue robes of the Cult of Azcalaw. Tomas had carefully cut the parcel that contained Apondra's blue robe into a blanket-like covering to conceal her disguise. She donned the hood and unrolled the bottom of the robe tucked under her sweater.

The path north, a well-worn trail of soil and sand, wound through the tall old spruce trees straight toward the base of the closest mountain. The other pilgrims and converts kept their distance from each other in silence, many of them with heads bowed. Their shapes, human and lobfolk, moved steadily toward the unseen destination. Apondra pulled her scarf over her nose to fight off the stench of rotten apples on the breeze that grew stronger as she continued on the path.

After over an hour of walking, the trail began a slow descent toward a glowing clearing in the woods. The orange luminescence of tiny camp-fires danced in the high limbs over the unfolding temporary settlement; dozens of tents and makeshift shelters made of torn sails, pine boughs, and tiled pieces of bark clustered with no formal layout. Murmurs of small conversations whispered in the shadows as cult members ambled about, sometimes laughing or eating some charred meat on a stick as they passed close to her.

Apondra pressed her hand to her stomach, affirming the handle of the dagger tucked inside her belt. A lobfolk meandered next to her, his face painted with white stripes. He nodded; she nodded back. A faint glowing blue sparkle floated from his face into the air.

A fellow channeler?

She stopped, scanning the tents to her right; another sparkle from a human next to a campfire, then another, further away, floating above a lobfolk carrying an armful of arrows. As she stopped to look further across the camp, the blue lights, like fireflies, drifted in and out of the crowds. *So many channelers!*

The lobfolk carrying arrows turned ahead of her on the side path, tempting her to follow. Another lobfolk sidled up to him, carrying long, black-sheathed daggers in each of his hands. They chatted quietly until they could deposit their weaponry on a table cluttered with maces, arrows, and bows. The arrow-laden lobfolk suddenly turned toward her and waved.

"Have you any more for this brigade?" He smiled as he pointed to the table.

"No," she said, making sure her scarf still covered her face. "I'll bring any as I get them."

"Good. Praise Azcalaw!" The lobfolk turned and left, disappearing into a crowd of thatched-roof shelters.

Apondra counted the weapons, trying to guess the human-to-lobfolk distribution. Lobfolk did not use bows, and she counted twenty. The daggers and maces could be for humans or lobfolk, so she estimated between six and twenty-four individuals could be armed with hand-to-hand weapons from this table alone. She shuddered as she realized the tables stretched in a row deep into the camp, dozens of tables of weapons for an army of Azcalaw.

Deeper into the camp, the tents thinned, replaced by a small crowd of robed figures that filtered in and out of some central gathering. She crept closer, one hand under her robe on the dagger's handle, another hand tugging her hood over her brow. Her stomach grumbled, unsettled by a tiny early dinner interrupted by her nerves. Quiet chants hummed from the center of the group. As she wedged herself between the shoulders of other robed figures, the center of their gathering revealed itself: a squat square stone half the height of a man and just as wide.

One by one, the robed figures approached, each one given the respect of solitude, and knelt, or bowed, or sometimes simply stood and placed a hand or claw on top of the stone. A lobfolk hand suddenly grabbed her wrist.

"I'm sorry, miss, but I was next," said the cultist. Two of his arms ended in stumps, bereft of hands. "I'm going to pray for just one hand to return."

"Oh, yes, of course." She nodded. The lobfolk stepped up to the stone, lowered his head, and then shouted, "Azcalaw! Please heal my hand so I may do your deeds!"

Apondra stood for a minute, allowing another human to approach the stone and say a blessing. She moved around the circle, studying the stone and listening to the conversations as well as the offerings made by the other cultists. She took in the words, the hints, and finally pieced together the clues as the crowd slowly receded, just a half dozen left as the last rays of sun disappeared behind the trees. This was no stone; it was an altar for Azcalaw! This was his temple!

"Sister," said a human voice, "no prayers after dark. Hurry up." The man to her side, a pale but friendly face with dark eyes, gestured to the altar. "I see your robe is clean, so I'll assume you are new. Welcome."

"Yes, thank you." Again, she adjusted her scarf. "You're correct. I'm a bit nervous. It is my first time."

"Everyone has a first time. Just make it quick. It's bad luck to pray at night over his grave."

His grave. She attempted to hold back a gasp that still forced its way past her lips.

"Right. Yes."

"There will be plenty of souls to pray to once our work is done. We'll be spared as humans, of course."

"Of course?"

The man turned, leaving Apondra alone to approach the stone. *Azcalaw's grave,* she repeated in her head. She bit her lip and touched the stone. Neither cool nor hot, with a surface worn from hundreds or perhaps thousands of hands, the stone retained the engraved words on the top:

HE OF THE BLUE

She trembled, her breaths now shallow as her throat tightened around the air that she forced in and out. This was him, this was his place, his final place. She traced her finger into the letters, heat slowly rising in her cheeks. A tiny blue flare fluttered under her palm as she ran her hands along the edges.

"So much loss," she whispered, her voice weak and tired, "so much loss. All the people we lost trying to find you, all the people killed by that beast in an attempt to summon you. And all these misguided lost souls hanging on to myths, desperate for a savior." She frowned. "They're building an army. In your name."

An angry tear fell from her cheek onto the stone. Her hands trembled as her fingers curled into fists. Gunnar. Diggins. So many others, dead because of *him.*

"I don't need your help. I don't want your help." Her voice shook. "I will save my people without you, Azcalaw. And I will save them from your followers as well. Stay dead. The world is better off without you."

The tingle left her hand. Her jaw tensed as she turned and strode back into the camp, her anger boiling, her adrenaline surging. Azcalaw's grave, his tomb, and all these ignorant fools amassing weapons in his name for what purpose? To slaughter the turtle if Azcalaw did not appear? To conquer the outpost on their doorstep? To invade and loot the devastated merchant town?

She froze, the heat of her rage washed away by a chilling terror that replaced the blood from her toes to her fingers.

They're amassing an army for sacrifices for Azcalaw. They're going to slaughter my kingdom!

Apondra stomped back through the camp, past table after table of weapons. She paused by a barrel stuffed with crude arrows. Next to them, a table of freshly carved longbows. She grabbed a black birch bow and scowled.

With a glance over her shoulders at the blue robes massed around their orange fires, she lifted the edges of her cloak and ran as fast as she could back to the path to Himmelhavets.

Her pounding footsteps matched her breaths as she sprinted through the darkness. She slipped and fell on a sandy patch, then stumbled upright to continue her run. Her sides ached; her head now covered with a layer of sweat. She pulled down her scarf and lifted her hood, then tossed her blue robe behind her. She wished she could run straight through the walls of the outpost and back home to Castle Homarus.

"Appy!" Ken's voice broke through her haze. "Appy!"

A group emerged ahead of her in the shadows. Ken leaned to the side in Teacup's chariot with Diana, and Sharpe and Tomas stood in the stirrups on their horses. Barely able to breathe, she held up the black bow to Sharpe.

"Yours now," she said. "Army. Cultists." She doubled over, caught by the gentle hands of Diana.

"Easy, Appy. Get into the chariot."

"Hurry. We must hurry back," Apondra panted. She leaned forward and rubbed Teacup's flanks. She nuzzled his fur. "They're coming for my kingdom."

Ken tapped her on the shoulder. "Let's get you home and then get something to eat."

"Do we have enough coin left?" Tomas asked.

"For potato soup and drink, yes. For dessert, I'm afraid we'll have to use our imaginations."

In the morning, Apondra and Diana sat in their room with a bowl of oats and a pot of honey tea huddled over the stolen book from the outpost registry. Diana occasionally held her hand over the cover, staring at blue specks that hovered over the leather. She opened her mouth, moved her lips, but failed to emit a sound. After several iterations, she slammed her hand on the book and stood. She kicked at the bedpost.

"Dammit. If I could just find the word." She huffed and opened the shellbound tome. "What was that word?"

"Looking for a spell?"

"The right spell." A knock at the door interrupted her, followed by Sharpe poking his head inside.

"Am I interrupting?"

"No," said the women in unison. Apondra extended her hand toward the tea. "Come in. Drink?"

"No thank you. I just wanted to take a moment and, you know, thank you for stealing a new bow for me." He rubbed his thumb in the palm of his hand. "I was ready to move on from being a sellbow, truth be told."

Diana closed the shelltome and tucked it under her arm. "I'll leave you for a moment. So that I can concentrate."

She closed the door behind her. Sharpe sat on the bed across from Apondra. He splayed his hands, opened his mouth, then closed it.

"Everyone is having trouble with words this morning," Apondra said.

"I must confess. I know my most recent occupation involved providing protection to travelers, but I've only killed wild animals." It was now that Apondra noticed his bracer was missing. "I've wounded men, but never killed one. Before, you know."

"I know." She placed her hand on his shoulder, searching for something her father would say. "We are all going through our own challenges, but we have our combined strength to support us."

"I killed him," Sharpe stammered. He covered his eyes. "I see it, every night. I see the arrow, the straight shot." He drew a slow breath. "I see Gunnar's face. I've tried to justify the events; I've told myself it wasn't my fault."

"It was an accident."

"But it happened." He uncovered his face, his brown eyes tearing. "Tomas forgave me, I know that. But I can't forgive myself. I can't do it again." He stood and smoothed his hands down the front of his leathers. "I am not a sellbow. I am not an archer. I'm only a man who knows the roads."

"But also a smart man." She scraped her memories of farmers standing before her father with mangled limbs, fisherman who lost their tails. Even the vizier, with his half-claws, who still found meaning in his role. Something in her experiences would find its way to her tongue. "You're a good man, and that is something." She looked at her lap. "It is something, indeed."

Sharpe shook his head. "I know you're trying. And I appreciate that. And I just want you to know how much I appreciate the gesture of finding me a new bow. I'll treasure it as a gift of friendship. I truly will." He turned his back and walked out of the room.

Diana leaned in through the doorway. "I didn't go far. Come with me outside."

The two women walked downstairs and out to the quiet street corner. The pedestrian traffic thinned considerably over the past day, attributed by Apondra to the cult's continued recruiting and the reduction in merchant traffic from the wilds of the south. Diana sat on the stone curb and watched Sharpe walk down the block and disappear into a side alley.

"He'll come back," Diana said. "This is a very hard thing for him."

"Are you close? To him?" Apondra asked, sitting next to her.

"I think," Diana said softly, "I am growing fond of you all." She kicked her worn leather boots into the stones in the gutter. "I didn't have any friends, save a handful of transcribers, back at the merchant town. But they were more akin to associates." She shook her wineskin and sipped. "Actually, there was one friend, but he went away."

"What happened to your friend?" Diana shrugged and looked toward the far walls of the keep, holding her silence. Apondra sensed there would be no answer forthcoming. "Anyway, what about Sharpe?"

"Sharpe is a free man, he can do what he likes, and he's been that way for a long time. I'm jealous of his life." She rested her lips on the wineskin again. "He found a purpose, even if he's doubting himself right now. He can always work as a merchant guide, even if unarmed."

"Well, I would say … you, and Sharpe, are part of our special group of friends. Friendship is a purpose."

Diana stood. "Princess, let me ask you something. Do you have many friends? Real friends, not just us in this adventure party."

"Well, I do, I suppose." The lie became evident as it passed her lips. She was royalty, and many of her interactions were bound by duty and protocol. From the vizier down to the courtyard merchants she spoke with every day; she knew them, but they were not friends. Even her relationship with Diggins, poor Diggins, was constrained by her duty as a royal guard.

Only Ken was a true friend. Ever since her schooling began, Ken was her tutor, but also spoke with her at length about life, history, and their little shared joys like bird watching and tasting desserts. "Diana, are we friends? That is, when this is all done, will you remain my friend?"

"I don't see why not," Diana said, taking Apondra's hand. "I won't disappear on you." She uncorked her wineskin and poured out the remaining drops. "Let's go check on Teacup. Maybe that will help jog my memory for some spell words."

The outpost paddock now held only a handful of animals as a clan of fur trappers loaded their empty sacks on their horses and mules and departed. Apondra fed Teacup by hand, stroking his broad nose and whispering tiny affirmations of affection. Tomas attended to Rose and Domino. The squire's leg gave him more trouble today, locking sometimes in the knee and ankle joints, causing him to stutter-step and hop from the hay bales to the horses.

"Does that happen a lot?" Apondra asked, nodding at his leg.

"It needs a cleaning, and I could probably use a new set of leather straps. I have to replace them every season as they eventually stretch. I'm not a terrible leatherworker, so that worked in my favor in hindsight. Gunnar said I was rather skilled at crafting with leather, even when my stitches were crooked."

"Ah." She admired his resilience. It was not her place to ask him about the minute details of having one leg, but still she wondered. He was such a gifted caretaker with the animals, barely speaking as they acquiesced to his motions and single words, especially Rose.

"Squire, do you think about him? Gunnar?" An obvious and silly question, she reminded herself.

"Of course, My Lady. Every day I wake up, and I think of doing a good job, doing my best. That was how he lived." His tone grew somber. "He was a good man. There was a lady at home who pursued him before we left, a widow with child, but he refused her hand in marriage because he still loved his first wife with all his heart. He gave the widow a bag of coins before we left."

"We should all be so lucky to find a love of our lifetime. Or someone so kind."

Tomas tied the horses back to their posts and ran his hand along Teacup's shoulder. "If I may, Princess, have you been in love? Besides Teacup here. I know he's fond of you." A soft smile followed his words.

"You know, I think I have been too young and too busy to look for love. And my father was adamant that I would not, should not, marry for political purposes. I've read so many tales, romances of history, fiction from other kingdoms. I like those." She blushed, feeling his eyes as he looked into hers. "I will be in love. I have time."

"I hope you do not wait too long," he replied. "For some, life is short. And time is never on our side." He kicked his wooden leg free of a mud clump and made his way out of the animal pens. The kyloe snorted and nudged Apondra.

"Well Teacup, I'll be back later." She kissed his nose. "And you are all the love I need."

The next hours passed slowly. Apondra and Ken spent some of the late afternoon walking with Captain Wolf on his patrol, studying the history of Wolf's position and the changes of regulations, very rigid now, but over the past several decades evolving with flexibility. The head constables were free to uphold and change the laws as they saw fit, depending on the dominant populace, but over time a united rulebook was created. Apart from heads of state, the surrounding nations and towns agreed that the constable's word was final law within the confines of the keep's walls, and that it was best to not interfere. Merchants could use the relative freedom to negotiate outside of taxes and embargoes, which trickled into more commerce down in the merchant city, and eventually throughout the rest of the lands. They talked and walked, crossed the center of the outpost's streets, and started their loop along the north wall.

"Captain," Apondra asked, "how did you start here?"

"Like many, I was lost, without a country or family. I found myself here after a year or so as a sellsword and joined the outpost guard for free food and lodging. I did such a good job that I survived my patrols and became the captain."

"Survived?" asked Ken.

"Some leave on their own. Some die during fights with thieves, or skirmishes on the roads with giant weasels, bears, and colossal ospreys. I knew one guard who was gored by a giant mountain elk. Some just disappear. They may wander in a drunken state outside the walls in the cold, or join the cult, or just resign without any word and hop on a trapper's wagon out of town."

Apondra looked up at the top of the walls, and one of the guard hammocks swinging gently in the breeze. She could make out the details of a human gazing into the distance through a monocular while eating some type of ration on a stick. No one outside of her kingdom had a homeland, just a job. Everyone that came into Castle Homarus was made comfortable by her father, independent of origin. Captain Wolf, in his own way, did the same for her. The guard in the hammock tossed his food stick over the wall and whistled down to the streets. Wolf adjusted the studded leather gauntlets over his claws and nodded toward the north gate. "You may want to stay back."

A small circle of guards swarmed the door next to the large gate. A loud pounding ceased when they opened it, followed by the blur of a tattered man in scraps of brown clothes, a black scarf over his face, as he rushed inside. The man pointed to Captain Wolf as he collapsed.

"Captain!" he said, his voice hoarse as he struggled to remove his scarf, revealing his brown thin strip of hair on his head.

"Sharpe!" cried Apondra, rushing past the captain. She looked upon the former archer, his details coming into focus, his hands caked in mud and blood, his clothes tattered. A bloody stain seeped through the fabric of his sleeve. Ken followed close behind and caught him with his claws as he attempted to stand but fell forward.

"Aid! We need aid for this man!" Captain Wolf cried.

"I will be okay," Sharpe said with a breathy exhale, "I ran. I just need water and rest."

They laid him down right on the stone walkway. Apondra whisked her clean scarf around his head, the captain donating his cloak as a blanket.

"What happened?" she asked, running her hand over his forehead.

"I went outside the walls, to the north trail towards the temple and camp. I thought I could spy on them further, bring back some more information. I was recognized as a recruit who never showed up and they beat me." He put his head between his knees. "They said it would be useless to kill me, because 'only the dead souls of the kingdom of the lobfolk will bring about his return.'" He threw up on the stones. "They are mobilizing already. Wagons piled with supplies are already rolling around the outpost walls to the east."

Wolf squatted next to Sharpe. "They must be taking the coastline roads to accommodate their numbers, and there will be less scouts that could discover them on the water. That giant snapping turtle's presence has practically brought the mariner traffic to a standstill." He raised his antennae and snapped his fingers. "Princess, we can warn your kingdom if we head to the ports and take my swiftboat. There will be no one in the shipping lanes to slow us down."

"But how long will the journey take?" Apondra bit her knuckle. "Even with a swiftboat unladen by cargo, a week? Two weeks? We need every day possible to prepare! We need to get word south." She glanced to the west and watched the sun drift just above the mountains on its journey into night. "I have to warn my kingdom."

Sharpe lay on an improvised cot in Captain Wolf's office while Diana dabbed wet strips of cloth on his arm to clean the cuts and scrapes. Apondra studied Diana's methods, the wringing and reapplying of clean bandages, self-taught, she was sure, during her imprisonment. Sharpe's hand clutched Diana's own, and Apondra watched the spellcaster place a silent kiss on his forehead. Wolf sat at his desk, surrounded by Tomas and Ken as they huddled around a large linen map of the outpost. Sharpe interrupted their studies with a raspy voice.

"Are you able to secure the outpost if the cult attacks?"

Captain Wolf ran his hands over the map. "We do not have the means to stop an army of delusional untrained zealots. Even if we are not their target, we will at a minimum be able to lock them out and prevent them from using my outpost as shelter."

Ken outlined the walls of Himmelhavets on the map, and then drew an imaginary line south. "How long would it take us to send a messenger home over land?" He counted on his fingers, using all four hands. "Even a relay of riders trading horses nonstop would take several days."

Apondra sat quietly, letting the information continue to work through her brain. Words, actions, resources; she catalogued them and put what she knew, what she learned, what she believed, into scenarios real and imagined. Could they send a message by sea? Yes, but every day of travel equaled one less day to prepare. A relay bird of some sort? That would be unreliable due to the critical nature of the message. Was there some magic that could be used?

Magic?

"Diana. I need you to think," she said, leaping to her feet and grabbing the spellcaster by the shoulders. "Can you send a message somehow? Cast some communication spell?

"I don't know such words to send a scroll or letter to somewhere I've never been before." Diana pointed at Apondra's satchel and the edge of the stolen outpost ledger. "I'm still trying to figure out a spell for the—"

Apondra slammed her hand over Diana's mouth. "Yes, well, that can wait." She glanced sideways at Captain Wolf. Diana nodded as Apondra uncovered her mouth.

"Right. That other thing can wait. But for our problem, I don't know what words we could use for a message spell."

"What words do you know? Speed? Haste? Quickness? Do you know any spells of that nature? What *do* you know?"

"Speed? Maybe I can make a letter tied to an arrow change its target. Probably. Maybe." Diana looked down. "I don't know. I might be able to make a horse run faster, but there's a problem." Apondra leapt to her feet and clutched her friend's arm.

"What's the problem? We can enchant a rider to take the warning south! Right? You can do that?"

"If we knew the right spell." Diana dug under her fingernails. "I don't know the words."

Apondra crossed her arms and narrowed her eyes at Ken. "Quickly, to our books!"

Chapter 11

The Ride Home

APONDRA PACED BACK and forth in the bedroom, the shellbound tome open in her hand, scanning for any passages that contained snippets of the elder languages. She wasn't entirely sure what she was looking for, but at least when she came across a word she didn't recognize, she could bring it to Diana in the hopes of translating it into something useful. Seated in her chair at the edge of the bed, Diana looked up wearily from the ink-filled pages on the nightstand, a steaming pitcher of white tea next to her. Apondra had asked her to write down as many words as she could remember, in hopes of completing a spell for fast travel, but the process grew tedious as the hours of night wore away.

"I can't find it," said Diana, slamming her fist on her notes. She downed her tea and tossed the cup on the bed. "I can't do this."

"We must. It's the only plan we have." Apondra sat and reached for her own tea. "Let's look again at the wording we have available."

"I can't! I can't! It's one thing to read books for Clem while chained in a room, it's another to be under this kind of pressure!" The spellcaster slumped her shoulders, then craned her neck and stared at the ceiling. "I just realized something. We're doing this so that we can get the word south before the cult army arrives. But whatever we do, people will die." She looked now to the window, and the animal paddock just in view. "Appy, you know that, right? It's your army against the cult. People will be killed. You can't save everyone."

The shift in pronouns was noted. *"You"* can't save everyone. Apondra put her head in her hands and let the frustration run down her cheeks in soft wet streams. "But I have to stop it. The people, those who were slaves and trapped laborers, the ones who saw a chance at freedom and have now been tricked into joining the cult for a false savior who lies dead under a stone? They shouldn't have to die. And I don't want anyone from my kingdom to die defending it."

"Appy, look." Diana moved from the chair to a space next to her. "You're a princess, an 'Eave Queen' or whatever. You're going to have to accept these types of consequences, even if it's not your fault, even when you do your best. It comes with the crown. And if no one else will tell you these truths, I will."

Apondra wrapped her arms around Diana and hugged her. "This world is filled with more suffering and sadness than I ever imagined. What if I don't want to be a ruler? Or what if I'm a bad ruler? I'm useless if all I'm good for is crying when things are bad, and smiling when nothing is wrong."

"Here's what I know: you care." Diana brushed a strand of tear-soaked brown hair out of Apondra's eyes. "You care about people and things and places. All the nouns," she giggled. "You're smart, too. But it is important for people who *care* to be in charge, because they can weigh and bear the consequences of decisions. And being smart is the icing on the cupcake."

Apondra appreciated the compliments, the *confidence* that this former slave had in her. It was true, Apondra did care. She wanted Tomas to find his heroic purpose and duty. She wanted Sharpe to find his peace. She wanted Diana to have opportunity. And she wanted Ken, wonderful Ken, to read and laugh and ponder wonderful things for the rest of his days.

As if her thoughts transmuted into acts, Ken knocked on the door as he entered. "I assumed you were decent. And the door was ajar." Apondra quickly wiped her cheeks on her sleeve.

"What did you find, friend?" Apondra asked.

"I have some words I found, some adjacent texts, and a few other things, but, well, here." He handed over his notes to Diana. "What do you make of this?"

The spellcaster ran her fingers over his handwriting, her lips barely moving as she attempted the phonetics of the interspersed old language. "It's something. These parts here, they reference something flowing over the hills. It's almost like a rainstorm. Something to move the winds. Or move with the speed of the wind." She looked at Apondra. "This is good, this is close, Princess."

"There is one other problem, though," admitted Ken, his fingers from all four hands twiddling. "I can't seem to find a word for 'horse'. And I would think that would be very useful."

Apondra sighed. The plan would fall apart if they couldn't find a way to travel back to the kingdom far in advance of the cult to ensure that they could prepare, or evacuate, which she accepted as a possible short-term solution. If only she had a way to predict the future. She reached for her saucer and glanced at the tea leaves that had escaped the pitcher's spout, resting in the bottom of the teacup.

Teacup.

She shot up from the bed, scaring Ken and Diana with her outburst.

"What's the old language word for 'cow'?"

Dawn's early beams of light floated through the trees growing through and above the outpost's walls. A speckled pattern of tiny, jagged shapes created by the filter of leaves on the lower boughs decorated the outside fortress walls and illuminated Teacup's breath as he exhaled outside the southern gate. Tomas tightened the last straps of the wide saddle cobbled together from bits of the chariot harness, leather saddle, and canvas pieces donated from Captain Wolf. The assembled group encircled the kyloe, packing thin supplies into saddlebags. Sharpe used a tiny blade to trim the light brown tuft of hair hanging over the animal's brow.

"He's going to need to see, right?" he said, standing back to marvel at his barbery.

"He always knows how to go home. They are a very smart breed with excellent navigation," Apondra replied, mounting Teacup's new saddle and pointing to the stirrups. "Squire, if you would, please."

Tomas adjusted the improvised straps. She caught a smile crossing his lips as he examined and adjusted the saddle one more time. "The anatomy is generally the same, but some dimensions are slightly different, of course." He tugged at a strap, eliciting a snort from Teacup. "Sorry, fellow, I'll loosen this one a hair." He ran his hands over his finished work and grinned. "Your steed is ready, Eave Queen."

Ken held his notebook and ran his fingers over the words one more time. "Alright, let's go over the order. First and foremost, everyone stands to the side. No one in front or back. Diana, when you're ready, please place one hand on Apondra's leg for channeling assistance, and the other on Teacup's flank." He looked up to Apondra. "Well, channeler, you'll need to pull as much magic from the air as you can feel."

Captain Wolf gently seized Diana's wineskin. "There is magic in this land outside the walls. I will help channel as much as I can, draw it from the sky and soil toward Apondra. Princess, that should make it easier for you to grab the concentrated magic and funnel it for Diana."

Apondra looked at her assembly of friends and felt a pinch in her heart. "If this doesn't work, we'll just have to take our chances with the swiftboat. That's all there is."

Sharpe crossed his arms high on his chest and nodded to Tomas. "Eave Queen, if this works, we will be right behind you, but traveling by sea."

Tomas nodded. "There's room on the swiftboat for three mounts. Teacup, Rose, and Domino will all travel well if the spell doesn't work." He looked at Sharpe. "But this will work. We believe in you. And Diana."

Apondra pulled her scarf from her neck and handed it to Tomas. She straightened her shoulders and tucked a loose strand of hair behind her ear. "Tomas, Squire of the Kingdom of Swan, I will be thinking of you, and your bravery. If something happens, I will tell your story." A tear streamed down her face. "Please be careful, my friend." She saw the sheen of tears forming on his eyes.

"I will do my best, Eave Queen Apondra." He wrapped her scarf around his neck. "I will return this to you."

She reached down and held his hand for a moment; a moment she needed to affirm the duty she was about to perform. "I look forward to seeing you again."

Ken approached, his eyes downcast. He fidgeted with a small black stone. "Appy, I don't know what to do when you go."

Apondra froze. Her life was divided into two fragments; one era as a tiny child before she had met Ken, and every single day after that when they became best friends. Not a day passed that didn't include a lesson, a story, or a meal. Some days they would meet wordlessly at the lighthouse and sit back-to-back to read together. On one hectic birthday for the king, Ken made sure to knock on her door before bed to make sure that she had a marvelous day. Her eyes stung as she cried softly.

"I won't see you tomorrow."

He nodded and extended his hand to Apondra. "My friend." She grabbed it and squeezed.

"Ken, you are my best friend. My oldest friend." She tasted her own salt as rivers streamed down her face. "*Just stay alive*, and when I see you again, we'll have a table of pastries and books all to ourselves to celebrate. *Stay alive.*"

He pressed the black stone into her hand. "I found this next to the gate. I thought it was pretty. It's for good luck. Or something." His antennae quivered. "I'm having trouble saying something profound. I want this stone back someday." His claws reached around her and squeezed. "Be safer than you've ever been. And do your duty."

The weight of her task felt heavier than their kinship, but both mountains rested on her shoulders as her knees shook. She steadied herself and put on a stern face. "I am your Eave Queen. I will serve you. And I will be safe."

They held hands for a final silent moment, the smooth black stone between their palms. "I love you, Appy," he whispered.

"I love you, too, Ken."

She wiped her tears on her shoulder and looked to Diana, who met her somber gaze with a quick nod. Diana flipped to the last page of spell notes and raised her hand. "Oh no, no, no. Complication." She reached for the saddle and attempted to pull herself behind Apondra. "The spell may need to be cast again. It's not permanent. It fills the vessel and then the magic drains as it's used. I'll need to go with you." She glanced back at Sharpe. "Don't get killed."

"The same to you." He winked; she replied by lowering her head. Apondra heard Diana exhale loudly and slowly.

"Diana, are you ready?"

"I'm fine. I'm fine."

Diana wrapped her belt around both Apondra's waist and her own, then placed one hand on Apondra's shoulder, the other behind her on

Teacup's rear. Tomas gave a final yank to cinch the belt tight. Captain Wolf nodded and raised his arms and claws, closing his eyes.

A soft mist of blue lights bloomed in the trees across the field. Tiny glittering droplets made their way across the grass and through Wolf's claws. Apondra lifted her hands, focusing on the tingling that now spread through her body. *We have to succeed.* The tingling slowed and the blue glow began to fade.

"Confidence," Diana whispered. "You are a channeler, you know this to be true. *Fact.*"

I will succeed.

A cold chill rushed into her blood, a quick vibration in her muscles and bones, more intense than any of her previous moments siphoning and sensing raw magic. The blue mist flashed white, swirling into her chest; a nearly suffocating weight pressed inside her lungs.

I must succeed!

A sudden hot flash from Diana's hand clawing into her shoulder drew the cold out of Apondra's body. Diana shouted in a raspy voice.

"Light and wind, rain and storm!
Light breaks darkness in the dawn!
Cast the river, on wind be fleet,
Crashing waves beneath my feet!
Light my kyloe, feet of flame,
Chase the land like quickened game!
Fast and quick to light the gala,
Accra denalum ..."

Diana paused. She inhaled.

"... BOVINALA!"

The riders looked down at their mount. Teacup stood still, continuing to chew on a long blade of grass.

"I don't understand," Diana whispered. "I felt it. I know I did the spell correctly."

Apondra leaned forward and pulled back Teacup's ear.

"Teacup, please go home."

An eruption of blue flames burst from Teacup's hooves. He stomped forward, surging into a raging gallop. The initial shock twisted Apondra sideways, and she caught a glimpse of the outpost in her periphery, already tiny and fading into the mountains behind them. The cold rush of wind forced her to press her body snuggly against the kyloe's neck and shoulders, with Diana crushing her ribcage from behind. Against the roar of the wind and a thunderous mooing from Teacup, her own laughter flooded her ears.

A wall of blue fire blazed directly ahead of Teacup, shattering trees and brush as he hurtled through the forest. Shrieking birds were barely audible over his thunderous hooves, stomping the stones of the trails into scorched dust. His orange-brown coat shivered, emitting tiny blue stars that burst into the air behind them. The tips of his horns blazed white, sparkling like tiny lightning bolts guiding the way.

Teacup leapt out of the woods, his illuminated footfalls bouncing and prancing now through a wide rolling field. In his wake, the grasses lay flat, blades ground into the soil.

"We're going to die!" Apondra cried. Diana laughed.

"Can you enjoy this for a moment?" The wind bit at her words. "I need you to get your head back in order for when I recast."

"And when is that?"

"Whenever we feel like we're slowing down?"

The minutes and miles grew in a dizzying whirlwind. Apondra lost any reference of how far they had traveled until they leapt over a landmark from their original journey. The deep dirt ravine of the sea snapper that they had crossed on their initial trek north now came into view. Teacup shook his head, then lowered his horns.

"Teacup? What are you doing?"

With a loud snort, the kyloe crouched and leapt, launching himself into the air. The blue flames under his hooves flared, tracing a glowing streak in broad daylight across the sky and over the ravine. As they crossed the apex, Diana slid her arms under Apondra's sweater and dug her nails into her skin.

"Uh, Appy? Is this going to hurt when we land?"

"Hang on and we'll find out!"

Teacup landed beyond the rut with a bounce, arcing again into the sky for a shorter airborne span. He touched down again in the woods and continued his frenetic pace.

"Good boy," Apondra said, rubbing his neck. "Don't do that again! And keep heading home!"

The blur of trees and fields continued, as the wind assaulted their senses. Apondra pulled the collar of her sweater over her mouth and nose, squinting against their speed to check their location. A decrease in wind told her that Teacup was slowing down.

"We're getting close to home," Apondra shouted.

"But we're losing speed. I'll cast again," announced Diana. "Brace yourself."

The kyloe stomped to a sudden stop, Diana slamming against Apondra's back. Teacup bent his head down and drank greedily from a small creek that crossed their path.

"I didn't think of that," Apondra said. "Good boy." The riders took advantage of the pause to stuff their faces with salted meat strips and dry cooked potato slices from their single sack of provisions.

"Where are we?" Diana asked, unbelting herself from Apondra and sliding off the saddle. The forest showed a break in the trees to their right, a wide area devoid of growth. Apondra dismounted and skipped to the timberline.

Another rut, wider than several houses, plowed across the forest, leaving splintered logs, jagged rocks, and craggy roots clutching for the sky. Apondra glanced in each direction, noting the position of the sun in the sky.

"This rut runs north and south." She placed her hand in the fresh mud, warm and wet. "This is new. I think the giant snapper is heading back to the cult." She dragged her hand through a deeper singular scar in the earth. "I know this. These are the claw marks, pointing in one direction. I think it headed back north."

Diana shaded her eyes. "I wonder how fast it can travel."

"I don't want to find out." Apondra grabbed her companion's hand and dragged her back to Teacup, now finished with his drink. "Time to make haste again!"

They mounted their ride and fastened their belts and stirrups. Apondra lifted her hands, reaching out with her mind for magic. Nothing. A moment of a tingle in her hands, then nothing.

"I can't feel anything here."

"We have to get going," Diana snipped, shoving a last piece of potato into her mouth. "Let's see what Teacup has left in him, and as we ride, keep your focus on pulling and dragging any bits of magic along." She spread her arms wide, her fingers curled like gnashing claws. "Think like you are dragging a rake while running and collecting leaves."

"I can visualize that, yes, but what if it's not enough?"

Diana wrapped her arms around Apondra's chest. "Whatever you have will help me. Don't doubt the amount of magic you can find. Even if this part of the land *appears* devoid of magic, it still exists in tiny drops and sparks. Just collect what you can."

Apondra tapped Teacup on the head. "Please go home, Teacup!"

Another blue blaze lifted his feet as he leapt over the creek and thundered further into the woods.

The frigid headwind chilled Apondra's skin, but her bones also grew cold with her siphoning of magic. Small short icy flashes continued intermittently as they rode, whisps of magic misting behind them. After another hour, she glanced back, seeing a long frosty tail of blue stars sweeping behind them.

"Are you ready, Lady Mage?"

Diana spoke the incantation, ending it with a shout. The wave of blue surged into Teacup, igniting his speed, albeit slower than the initial spellcasting, as they burst through the trees into a field that opened next to the junipers. A low rumbling ahead and to the right diverted their attention.

"Thunder?"

"Not with these skies," replied Diana.

The crown of a gigantic head resembling a large stony mound broke the forest ceiling to the east, parallel to their track. It rose and fell in intervals, the thunderous cacophony increasing. A deep stink of trash and stagnant water filled Apondra's nose.

"The snapping beast," Diana whispered, "it's horrifying."

The turtle's head rose, revealing its beak and eye. Teacup blazed forward, easily outpacing the menacing monster that now lumbered behind them.

"It's turning south!" Apondra felt a swelling dread in the pit of her stomach, already unsettled by their tiny snack and the jostling of the racing kyloe. Not only was it urgent to arrive in time to prepare for the cultist army, but possibly the defense against the giant snapper. How, exactly, to fight such a thing was foremost on her mind, but also the sad admittance that she knew nothing of how a military or defense force would begin to counter its devastating attack. Not even the entire lobatorium guard could possibly slay this titanic creature.

"Princess, look!"

A merchant caravan blocked the trail ahead. Several carts lingered as one overturned, spilling cabbages and large wooden drums across the path. Teacup juked around the congestion, sweeping his head to the side to grab a small cabbage and swallow it whole.

"Bad Teacup! Bad!" Apondra nearly slipped out of her stirrups as he shook his back in protest of her reprimand.

"He's a special one, this one," said Diana. "A very special pet."

"He's not a pet," Apondra corrected her, a smile leaking over her lips, "he's my friend."

The riders pounded through alternating patches of trees and plains, continuing at a slowing but nonetheless terrific speed as the sun crept lower. Slight wisps of salty sea air tickled their noses, signaling to Apondra that they were closer to the center of the kingdom, the castle, and home. Teacup's strides slowly softened from wear, lessening magic, and what she hoped was a recognition of the end of their tenacious ride. Diana's grip tightened around her waist.

"Are we almost there?" Diana poked her head over Apondra's shoulder.

"We should be, the forest is thinning, and I see a large break of light through the junipers ahead."

As Apondra spoke the words, Teacup surged through the tree line into King's Plain, bounding onto the well-beaten road through the outer field. The walls of Castle Homarus loomed ahead; Teacup slowed his gait to what had been a normal sprint in anticipation of running into the lobfolk legion standing before the mighty castle doors. A captain with leather epaulets and studded sashes on his claws held his banner to signal her to halt.

"Eave Queen! We have been waiting anxiously night and day for your return!" He lowered his banner. "I am to be the bearer of grave news."

"Captain Terra," she hailed, slowing the kyloe to a standstill before leaping off Teacup's back, Diana by her side. Teacup whipped his tail and chomped ravenously on the field grass.

"Your father's health, Princess, has taken a turn for the worse over the past day. The vizier is doing what he can to ease the suffering."

"Then I will see him at once!"

"There is more," said Terra, extending his claw to block her strides. "A merchant group came through here a few days after your departure. He informed us of an attack on an encampment." Terra's eyes darted. "A scouting party confirmed the identities of the fallen and recovered what bodies they could, including Diggins. Moe Murr is distraught over the passing of his sister, and the lack of proper burial. He asked to be assigned to the southern lighthouse."

"I see." Her acknowledgement was met with a stern gaze.

"Eave Queen, I understand this is a trying time for you, but when a solider passes, the monarch passes condolences personally to their family."

"I understand. But I need to urgently see my father." Terra raised his hand as if to place it on her shoulder.

"Moe Murr is a good soldier. Greif can claim just as many lives as battle." He sighed. "There are things a council advisor won't tell you that are just as important as meetings and pageantry."

She nodded and searched the horizon. Far off to the south, the glinting pyre of the lighthouse sparkled in front of the reddening sky. She sighed deeply.

"I understand. I need to go. But Captain Terra, if I should forget—"

"I will gently remind you of your duty, Your Highness."

Diana grabbed her hand. "Go, Appy. See your father." She turned to Terra. "Captain, if you'll show me where to go, I can relay all the news we have gathered to your council of the giant snapper and other happenings. Apondra cannot be in two places at once." She whispered, "Appy, go!"

Apondra leapt up the grand staircase, three steps at a time, tearing down the hallway to her father's bed chamber. The door, already ajar, yielded to her shoulder as she burst into his quarters. The vizier sat on a small stool next to the bed-hammock where Abbasdah rested on his side under a white sheet, his shoulders and claws wrapped in a purple wool blanket.

"Eave Queen," said the vizier, "so much has happened." Her father raised his head, his shell molting in tiny thin bits that fell onto his pillow.

"Oh Father," she said, grabbing his hand and kneeling next to him."

"Apondra," Abbasdah wheezed, "my beautiful treasure. Thank Azcalaw you have returned! My illness has continued to sink the black claws of the Undersea into my lungs. I prayed for your safety, hoping that no news meant you were still alive. Please, my dear, tell me what you have learned."

"I searched, and there were so many tragedies. I did not find Azcalaw except in myths and tales. And I suspect he is not the great hero and savior that we had been told for all our lives." She wiped away a tear. "I saw his grave. Azcalaw is dead. We are on our own against the giant sea beast, and the cult of Azcalaw is mobilizing."

"What? His cult?"

"Yes, and they are on their way here to sow blood across our fields. I don't know what we'll do."

"It's alright," her father whispered. He managed a small smile. "It's alright. I am still proud of you. I know you did your best."

"I'm not sure I know anything anymore." This truth tightened in her chest as her father coughed. What was the point of searching for Azcalaw at the expense of not being with her father in his last days? Her jaw tensed. "Father, I am an adult. I am the heir to this kingdom. I have encountered more truths, horrible truths, than I was ever able to imagine. Slavery, death, horrible people. And Azcalaw? The stories I read painted him as a destroyer, a glorified mercenary by some accounts. We must triumph without his aid, real or imagined. But I don't know how." Again, a tear streamed down her face, her confidence receding. "I'll figure something out."

The vizier nodded. "We are running out of time." Abbasdah sighed heavily, his crown slumping on his head.

"Indeed. We are running out of time, and there is no more time for secrets. Apondra, let me use my final breaths to tell you the truth I have hidden from you." The vizier shook his head in protest, but the king continued. "If you are to lead, you must know who you are."

"I do not think this is the appropriate time, King Abbasdah," remarked the vizier.

Apondra whipped her head back and forth between them. "We have no more time. And no more secrets. And I proclaim this to you, Grand Vizier, *servant of the court.*" Her desperation bubbled, boiling to an angry froth. She wiped her face and furrowed her brow. "I have important decisions to make to lead my lobfolk."

The vizier feigned a smile and walked to the window. He glanced out to the courtyard where the unsettling quiet echoed without the hustle and bustle of sellers and buyers, the shouts of barter, the laughter and songs of children. Apondra had seen this sullen posturing of the vizier only a handful of times, and each time was when he would talk of the former queen, the bride of her father.

"Apondra," the vizier said, "you were found on the shore as an infant. But you have never asked for further details on your parents."

"Yes. Should it have mattered? They died. But this lobfolk here is my father, dying in this bed, for every intent and purpose."

"Your father," he countered, "King Abbasdah, that is, found you on the shore after a terrible storm and shipwreck." The vizier turned to face her, his shoulders slumped despite his efforts to maintain his royal posture of folded hands and swept back claws. "Your parents were still alive."

"What?" She turned back to the bed, Abbasdah's eyes telling her all she needed to affirm these new truths. "Father, what happened?" The vizier stepped to her side and placed a hand on her shoulder.

"To understand what happened, what we did, I must tell you the true fate of the queen, the bride of King Abbasdah. She was beautiful. Her shells radiated wonderful rainbow rings along the edges, a mesmerizing unique pattern only surpassed by the love of their marriage. But alas, she was not able to bear her own eggs for the birthing pools. This saddened her. Your father, as you know, is a lobfolk of great care and great love. He never asked her to leave, never once looked to abdicate her crown in exchange for a bride who could bear his offspring. *Because he loved her.* And this is the same love that the humans fail to fully comprehend, but spin into their folk tales that lobsters mate for life. Your father would always love his wife.

"But this sadness was too much for her to bear, as she loved him just as much, if not more, than he loved her. Her sorrow became an illness that infected her heart and her will to live, until one day she could bear it no more and passed on from this world." The vizier drew a shuddering breath. "Your father sat for a week in her chamber, unable to speak.

"You may know that viziers throughout history are often, but not always, the spellcasters for their kings. At the time of her passing, I was such an individual, a mage. By no means was I a masterful wizard, but I was a spellcaster of some renown. My power was not enough to bring her back from the Undersea.

"I journeyed to the edges of the known world. I discovered words, ancient spells and tomes, and I learned some of the more esoteric tales related to Azcalaw. But I was younger than I am now, and with my magic, much less intelligent. And more headstrong.

"I returned to the kingdom with the words and phrases and knowledge to cast a formidable spell, one that would deplete me, and a large portion of our lands, of magic." He lowered his voice. "For it takes an enormous amount of magic to breach the Undersea."

Apondra reeled. She began to see the pieces of his tale, his apology, his confession, all weaving into one cloak that she would wear when it was complete.

"So you depleted the land of magic to try to bring back the queen?"

"No. The king and I spoke at great length, but he chose to have a broken heart rather than risk sucking our kingdom dry of its magic. Heavy is the heart who wears the crown, and your father decided he could bear that weight."

"Oh Father," she said, squeezing his hand. "I am so sorry."

"It's alright, my love. Let him continue."

She turned her attention back to the vizier's face, his antennae drooping as he sighed.

"Apondra, a year after the queen's passing, we withstood the storm that brought you to our shores. A merchant vessel lost the battle with the seas and crashed just north of Ribbed Beach. Not knowing what kingdom they represented, your father and I joined a royal guard to bring aid and show our compassion to these strangers.

"The father and mother were gravely injured, and you were on the verge of death. The mother, your birth mother, passed quickly. The father begged only for one thing: to save the life of his daughter. But you were already slipping into the waves of the Undersea. Your injuries were dire."

Apondra gasped. "Did I … die?"

"You were … adrift, slipping away from this world. I looked to King Abbasdah, his eyes full of tears, holding the hand of your dying birth father. These two, human and lobfolk, understood the unspoken bond of losing their wives. Abbasdah turned to me and nodded." The vizier folded his hands. "He asked me to try the spell, the spell that returns a soul from the Undersea. And I did what my king asked."

"For me? Why for me?"

Abbasdah loosened his grip on her hand. "For love, my daughter." He labored against his thin breath. "I promised the merchant, your birth father, that I would adopt you, see that no harm would come to you. And he placed his hand on your head and said, 'I love you, my dear.' And then he was gone."

Apondra wept. She never realized how much tragedy, and love, could be tied to the story of her discovery. The annual retellings hid these moments, the sadness and the duties of kings and fathers and strangers. Her father had no reason to do any of these things for the dying merchant, yet he did. The vizier handed her a kerchief and continued.

"As I cast the spell, the trees swayed, the grasses tingled, and a hurricane of magic struck your almost lifeless body. In that moment, your eyes sparkled blue before returning to their brown hue, and I realized you had become a channeler, a vessel so overwhelmed by magic that you would someday be able to feel and divert it into a true spellcaster. But as the magic was sapped from our land, it passed through my body and left me hollow. *Burned.* I watched Abbasdah cradle you in his arms, overjoyed at your life, while I held back my sorrow that I could no longer feel or control magic. I was a spellcaster no more."

"I am so sorry, Vizier. If I knew that my life was spared in exchange for your loss—"

"What would you have done? What could you have done?" He stood and walked to the window. "I was distraught. I asked the king to grant me leave of office so that I could search for my own cure. I traveled north again. Far north."

Apondra clenched her fist. "You went to the outpost. And the temple of Azcalaw."

"I did. I knew a great lobfolk sorcerer who lived in Himmelhavets. His name was Aarch Conch. I kept my secrets close to my shell, obscuring the details of your near-death. I only told him that I had cast a dark spell that depleted my magic, and the magic of my land.

"Aarch Conch said that if my lands were devoid of magic, we could be susceptible to a rogue mage or invading army. Specifically, another fanatical spellcaster, a lobfolk who lived in the north, could take advantage of this if he knew our kingdom was without a magical means of defense."

"And was his name Tenor?" Her eyes blazed. He nodded and continued.

"It was critical to keep my arrival, and my point of origin, a secret. Aarch Conch and I crept into the registry of the outpost and obscured any record of my visitation, so Tenor would not be able to identify the kingdom that lost its magic."

Her hands recalled the tingle of the ledger book in Wolf's archives. "What happened next?"

"Tenor only knew that I was a soul on a pilgrimage. I was devoid of magic, so he suspected nothing of my former abilities. He tried to recruit me for his cause, to join his cult. Aarch Conch tried to intervene, and Tenor killed him."

The vizier again lowered his head, his words quiet. "I fled. Tenor had no means to follow me, and I prayed many blessings to Aarch Conch's soul for having the foresight to hide my entry in the records." He paused, glancing at the king for approval to continue. "I returned home. I told your father. Abbasdah decreed that henceforth I would only be known by my title, Grand Vizier, to obscure my identity should Tenor ever find his way here. Over the years, it would be possible to slowly erase any mention or trace of my birth name, *Fyrr Conch.*" His voice broke. "*Son of Aarch Conch.*"

The vizier knelt and placed his hands, all four, onto the four hands of the king. She had never seen such an outpouring of emotion as he began to weep. A surge of pity overwhelmed her as she placed her hands on his back and rubbed his shell, a sign of affection she had never used with the vizier before. He stuttered, then cleared his throat.

"Apondra, Eave Queen, you can see how much we have sacrificed and believed in your future. But eventually, the future becomes today."

Her knees buckled, her chest tightened, and she sobbed. Her father raised his voice to her distress.

"You are loved, my daughter. Ever since the moment I set eyes on you as a tiny pink human child, I have loved you. And that is how your greatness has been forged; the love of a father, the love of a parent, and the love of a servant of this court and duty." He nodded to the vizier. "And that, my dear, is also why I know this is your kingdom and you have been given every ability needed to rule, *for you are my heir*, and you were crowned by the love of your family."

Apondra reached across her father's chest and continued to weep, the weight of her very existence pressing on her back like a beach boulder from the north shores. So many losses littered her life's journey, and she could not repay those debts created in her name. Now the vizier's father was added to her tally. In this moment, she hated everything. She hated her life. She wanted nothing to do with a title and throne that would remind her every minute for the rest of her life that she was the vessel that sucked the magic out of the land, a magic that could have now saved them from the looming threats marching and trudging toward the kingdom.

"Eave Queen." The vizier placed his hand on her back. She smacked it away.

"Just leave me be. I do not want my crown or the blood that stains it."

The vizier stood slowly and smoothed the front of his skirting and sash, his head high. "It has always been my pleasure and duty to serve you." He paused. "And it always will, Your Highness." He turned and left.

"Daughter," Abbasdah said, his voice weakening, "I know this is much to hear, much to bear, but the crown must be passed."

She glanced toward the window, imagining the townsfolk waiting to see her after her return. "*An omen. I am the omen.* My birth was the harbinger of dark days which have now dawned. We have no magic, and a dying king. And we have a heretical murderous cult on its way to our fields and villages."

Abbasdah narrowed his eyes, a look she had never seen before. Was this anger, from her father, directed at her?

"Child, you are the sum of many things. You were naïve in your youth and narrow-minded from your inexperience. You were stubborn. But you were never indignant. You treated others as your kin and peers." His voice firmed, his whispery rasp disappearing for a moment. "And now I see your fire, your complexity and grace. You are the heir, my heir, to my throne. And you are responsible for the lives of every lobfolk in the kingdom. What matters right in this moment, is that you choose to save them. Because you love them." He gasped, exasperated. "Apondra, love conquers fear, death, and hate. Love is the champion we look to in our darkest hours. My crown is no longer mine. You are ready." He slipped back onto his pillow and closed his eyes. "Conquer, my love."

His chest slowed until it lay still under his sheet, his eyes unblinking as his last breath evaporated into the room. A light breeze lifted a tiny piece of molted shell from his cheeks. Her father lay still. The king was dead.

Chapter 12

Friends and Despair

HEY, FRIEND, GET up."

Apondra opened her eyes. She awoke sitting on the top step of the grand staircase, unsure how many minutes or hours had passed since she blacked out, her knees tucked against her chest underneath her sweater. Diana crouched next to her, rubbing her back.

"Hey, Appy." Diana's eyes showed a light sheen of tears. "I am so sorry. Terra told me about your father. Can you stand?"

"Yes," she sniffed. "Yes. I can stand. But I want to lay down."

"I don't think you will be afforded that luxury for a little while longer. Come downstairs." Diana held Apondra's cheek in her hand. "I spoke with Terra and the guards, I explained the cult, the turtle, Tenor. All of the nouns."

"Thank you." Apondra smiled weakly.

"They seem a bit curious about my spellcasting abilities. I didn't give them a show."

"I appreciate that. Thank you."

"It's night, and we should eat. Come on."

Apondra held Diana's hand, worn and calloused, yet tender, against her cheek for a moment before rising. She smoothed her sweater and brushed off the dirt that remained from their frantic ride before the duo descended to the throne room.

Along the walls, guards stood in nervous but attentive poses, holding spears upright in ceremonial postures. A small selection of foods sat in the center of the small table, and two clean plates. Apondra picked at a selection of berries, then settled down for a slice of roasted ham and a finely whipped potato. She picked at her meal, pondering each bite.

"Diana, in a way, I miss the stew from those dirty inns of the north."

"Some of it was good. A lot of it was better than what I've eaten for the past few years." Diana held up her cup, immediately filled by a lobfolk attendant from a wine decanter. "I could get used to this. You must have been quite the privileged child."

A slow tear rolled down Apondra's cheek. "My father wanted nothing but the best for me." She stood and gestured to the attendant. "You, servant, what is your name?"

"Loretta," said the lobfolk, smiling with her antennae.

"Well, Loretta, please take this home to your family. It was all excellent, it truly was an excellent meal, but my appetite is small, and my head is too stormy to eat anything else. But it was excellent. You deserve to have this. I'm grateful."

Captain Terra stepped forward quietly. "Tomorrow will be a day of public mourning. I would suggest you and the fair Diana here retire to your quarters. We'll have your bath ready, and some proper attire for you both." He glanced up and down at Diana and leaned close to her ear to whisper. "I will ask my wife for a selection of perfumes for you to choose from, if you are not offended."

Diana pulled her shirt collar up to her nose and inhaled. "No, I understand. That's a good idea."

After their baths, Diana and Apondra retired to the bedroom suite, down the opposite end of the hall from her father's bed chamber, now guarded by a royal sentry in a black cloak. Apondra nodded to the sentry, who returned the gesture with a salute. The silence upstairs was deafening, and she hastened her steps so that she could shut the door to her room and just sit with Diana.

A selection of dresses was already laid out upon Apondra's bed. Diana walked past each one, feeling the fabric between her fingers before settling on an off-white one of delicate cotton.

"These are beautiful, Appy. Clem had told me that lobfolk were the most extraordinary loom masters, but words do not do these dresses justice."

"Choose what you like," replied Apondra, sniffing a tiny glass bottle from the perfume tray stocked by Terra on the dresser. She looked back at the dresses, the white one now missing from the display. She allowed herself a small smile. "Ah. I approve."

With a delicate rustle of the fabric, Diana held the dress up to her chin, letting the soft cloth drape over her figure in front of the full-length mirror. She posed for a moment, running her hands down the sides of the skirt against her legs.

"Have you been in love?" she asked Apondra.

"Why would you ask that? Tomas asked me about that as well."

"I was thinking it was something we could talk about that didn't involve, you know." Diana waved her hand around the room. "Everything else going on. A distraction."

"I don't have the time to pursue it, nor have I really been interested," Apondra replied, crossing her arms uncomfortably, then resetting her hands on her hips. "Even before everything that's happened since I set off on this journey. Where would I find the time? When I'm here, I'm very busy with my schooling and duties." She stomped over to the bed and dropped in a heap on top of the plush duvet cover. "Why? Have you?"

"It happens when it happens, I think," said Diana. "So yes, I think I might have, once."

"I suppose you're going to expand on that." Apondra picked at her nails.

Diana smiled at her reflection, clean and bright, a sight Apondra was sure Diana had not seen in many years during her servitude. "There was a boy. Or a young man, I should say. He would deliver food whenever Clem asked." She held the dress away from her figure and then draped it over the mirror's frame. "He was nothing extraordinary, but he had a quiet smile. Stormy gray eyes and rough brown hair. A bit taller than me, and he wore faded blue and gray work clothes. I thought his eyes changed color to match his outfits sometimes, as if they had a magic in them."

"Such attention to detail." Apondra reached out to one of the dresses on the bed, a green velvet top with black trim. "Is this a true story?"

"The only things I had in that prison were my thoughts, so sometimes I filled them with the details of things that made me happy." She touched the green velvet. "Once each week, this young man would come and deliver some wine, a few loaves of bread, and a jar of jam from his family's farm. Clem paid him a moderate wage for his tasks. We didn't exchange names, as I was a slave and he was a farmhand, two people of inconsequential existence to most of the world. He would ask me sometimes what I was working on, and I often thought that he didn't understand half the words coming out of my mouth. He was uneducated, but smart. Perceptive. *Inquisitive.*" She smiled. "He liked to ask me what I thought of the people in the stories and histories I translated, who they were before their story was written, what happened to them after the ink had dried." Diana looked at her feet, now adorned in clean socks without holes. "He asked if perhaps someone like him would ever be written about. He said that was a nice thing to ponder on his ride to the warehouse."

Apondra sat on her hands as Diana moved to the window. Diana's eyes held a glimmer of a recollection that wasn't scarred with pain or solitude. A soft breeze filled the room, lifting Diana's clean golden hair and knocking the dress off the mirror frame. She quickly picked it up and returned it to a hook hanging on the wall. She looked to Apondra for a nod to continue.

"One day, he stayed a little longer and we ate together. That was the day he told me his name. He asked me mine, and when I told him, he said it was as beautiful as I was." She blushed. "I had never been complimented before. I told him he should leave, and so he did. The next week, he brought me a sugar biscuit, stolen from his own kitchen. We shared it." She bit her knuckle, the corners of her mouth turning up. "We didn't use our hands."

"How did you? Oh." Apondra now blushed. "You kissed him with food in your mouth?"

"I held it between my teeth and put it to his mouth. We didn't know what we were doing. But it was fun. It was special."

"I see." Apondra's cheeks flushed, a bit of jealousy mixed with her curiosity. "What happened next?"

"We continued for several weeks this way. If we had five minutes, we hung on to every tick of the clock. Each word we spoke burned precious seconds. One week, he threw the bag of food on the floor as soon as he entered and kissed me without stopping until my master's footsteps came to the door thirty minutes later. We said not one word."

"It sounds romantic. Daring. Forbidden." Apondra chose her words based on some of the passionate plays she had read in the deep fiction of the library's archives, unsure if they were truly appropriate descriptors. "Well? Tell me what happened next!"

Diana sat on the edge of the bed and gazed at herself in the mirror. "One day, he arrived and was visibly shaken. He told me that his father had sold the farm, for quite a profit, and they would be moving to the Kingdom of Swan where he would work at a new grain mill that his family purchased with their windfall. He would be a farmhand no more."

"Oh my! What a pleasant surprise!"

Diana shrugged. "He would be well-off and have comfortable wealth, enough to buy new clothes and a horse. But he did not have enough money to buy my freedom." Apondra stared at Diana's reflection in the mirror, and the small tear that ran down her face. "I didn't say anything. I kissed him, and I never saw him again. Whenever I was sad, that was the kiss I held on to, the only one I could still feel."

"What was his name?"

"I won't tell you," Diana snapped, then whispered, "sorry."

"I'm sorry if I offended somehow."

"It's not that. It's just … it's my secret. And when you have nothing, secrets are the most valuable possession you have."

Apondra rubbed Diana's shoulder, wishing she could suck the sadness and pain out of her friend. Diana's lover, hidden from the world, a very different path to the same outcome as the vizier's tale, a name erased from history. Diana reached back and clasped Apondra's hand.

"Somewhere, in the Kingdom of Swan, is a young man who I like to think stares across the ocean and dreams of his first kiss, his first love. I always thought that if I was going to die a slave, at least I would live on in his dreams."

As she heard these words, Apondra sank back into the bed. "When you put it that way, I would like that. To be in love like that… Someday."

"Someday." Diana rolled over on her back on the bed, her arms above her head. "When you liberated me, my first thought was to beat you for your coins and buy passage on the first ship to the Kingdom of Swan."

"Thank you for not doing that."

"You are welcome," Diana smirked. "But in that moment, I realized that if strangers cared enough to help me escape, that maybe, you know."

"I'm not sure I know."

"I thought that maybe I was worth saving, and it was for a reason, or a role I had yet to fulfill."

"You have been more than a valued member of our group." *More than me in many ways*, Apondra admitted.

"Would you," Diana paused, "would you come with me to find him, someday, if there is a someday?"

"I promise. Here." Apondra pulled down the duvet cover and smoothed the bed sheets. "Thank you for telling me your secret. I needed a moment to think about something else."

"You have a lot to do." Diana rested her hand on Apondra's shoulder. "Get some rest. No more crying for the last minutes of the day."

The two women slid into the bed and closed their eyes. Apondra felt Diana's hand holding hers until she drifted away into dreams.

The morning passed in a blur. As per ceremonial protocol, lobfolk burials were held within a day of death. Good King Abbasdah was laid to rest in his purple woven burial shroud in the undercrypt, a sacred private hollow next to the library's depths beneath the castle where only the royal family was permitted. Apondra and Captain Terra went alone with two black-robed burial sentries. Only a short prayer completed the ceremony; Terra's hand remained on Apondra's shoulder during the entire ritual. She flinched each time Azcalaw was mentioned in the prayer.

Apondra and Terra returned to the courtyard and were greeted by Diana and a throng of noble lobfolk who praised the king and passed wordy condolences to the Eave Queen. Apondra smiled, wiped her tears, and accepted from each visitor some trinket, a bundle of flowers, or the occasional tribute scroll. At the end of the receiving line, the vizier stepped forward, dressed in a plain green cloak and matching tunic.

"Eave Queen," he said, tripping over the two words, "I have brought you this." He handed her a folded piece of parchment.

"What is this?"

"My resignation. It is customary for the current Grand Vizier to resign upon the death of a monarch. The new monarch then chooses to retain the prior vizier or appoint a new one." He flashed a short apologetic smile. "There is no ill will if you accept my written resignation. Given the circumstances."

"Hmm." Apondra held the paper, then placed it unread into the pocket of her skirt. "I will be taking a new vizier. Diana, what do you think?"

"Appy," Diana said, "I know very little about being a vizier, but I do not think I could take his place." The now former vizier lowered his head.

"I understand if you take her as my replacement," he said. Apondra nodded.

"Your counsel … is noted. Which is why I am choosing Fyrr Conch, Son of Aarch Conch." She lifted her chin and smiled.

"Eave Queen!" His antenna stood up. "No one has spoken those words in many years in these halls."

"From what you told me, Fyrr Conch so loved his kingdom and his king that he sacrificed far more than anyone could imagine. That is who I want by my side and in my ear."

He gasped. "Thank you, Your Highness."

"You can take as much of the day as you need to mourn your king, Fyrr Conch. King Abbasdah was my father, but he was also your friend."

"I serve the kingdom, and the Eave Queen. The needs of the kingdom outweigh my own. I appreciate your offer." The vizier, Fyrr Conch, bowed.

Apondra gave him a quick hug. "Now gather your wits and we'll reconvene later, Fyrr. Be early for the council meeting this afternoon," she said with a short smile. "Or the lady mage over here may take your job after all."

"I should hope not," replied Fyrr, looking Diana up and down. "But if it pleases you, I can take her under my claw and educate her on the finer points of the court. She is a bit rough."

"I am a refined lady!" Diana said, giving him a playful push. "Appy, put on your boots and let's away to the lighthouse! Remember, Terra said you have another duty to perform."

The flat stones that formed the path to the lighthouse rumbled underneath the chariot wheels. Apondra and Diana took the lead with Teacup, followed by Captain Terra as her bodyguard in his own chariot. His kyloe, Blackwood, huffed as they began the slow ascent toward the outcropping where the lighthouse sat for nearly a century undisturbed by the lobfolk of the closest village. Pine and spruce trees grew at odd angles out of the craggy faded orange rocks and boulders that dotted the shoreline cliff.

Apondra loved the smell of the sea, especially at this height where the salty mists were pure and not mixed with the odors of seaweed and fish rotting in the sun, torn by gulls after the waves slammed them on the shore. But now, her thoughts drifted toward the upcoming council meeting. Diana had provided a synopsis to the guards when they arrived yesterday, and they in turn presented their readiness report to the individuals who sat many times with her father during times of struggle. She hoped someone had a plan; she had none. A confrontation with Larold of Ribbed Beach would be inevitable but had to wait until the confines of the council. Apondra pulled Teacup's reigns to stop, and the trio quietly dismounted at the base of the lighthouse.

The building itself was a squatty, rotund structure, only two stories tall, made of old, irregularly cut stones layered by hand and claw with hard mud and sap for mortar. The final construction resembled a short cylinder wrapped by a wide exterior stone staircase that ran right to the edge of the cliff, several stories above the crashing sea. The top of the lighthouse lay flat with a small partially covered roof for the open hearth where the assigned attendant would keep the burning blaze alight each night and during storms. Apondra learned the work to maintain the fire was very lonely, and that many sad souls volunteered to tend the flames during times of personal mourning. She had heard her father discuss dispatching a new caretaker whenever the current one had fallen, sometimes by their own choice, dashed upon the rocks below. She now shielded her eyes from the sun and spied the outline of a lobfolk standing silently next to the smoking embers of the previous night's fire.

"Moe? Hello!" she called. The silent sentinel turned and nodded.

"Maybe Terra and I should wait here," Diana offered. "I think this is a private conversation, even if it is within your official capacity."

Apondra nodded and carefully wound her way up the stairs. She selectively placed her feet on each weatherworn step, dodging mossy and lichen-covered patches on the shady side of the lighthouse. She leaned her shoulder against the wall as a cold gust blasted the tower. A large tan claw reached down and pinched her sweater.

"This is not a safe place for a noble," Moe said. "You should not have come."

"It's my duty. Thank you." She took the final step and immediately sat as close to the central hearth as possible. "This is a beautiful view."

"Aye." Moe stood next to her and gazed out across the sea. Small whitecaps were born and died in the distance, and an angry gull floated next to his head, riding the wind, squawking in protest before descending to the short stony beach. "That yappy fellow, he immediately took a liking to me when I first arrived."

"Well at least you have company, then." She bit her lip as she rethought her words. There was nothing to do for his pain, so she chose not to ease into her visit. "Your sister was a fine lobfolk. Diggy told me as she lay dying to tell you how much she loved you."

"My sister and I did not always see eye to eye." Moe leaned over to grab his spear, then placed it in his claws. "But we both shared a love of the kingdom. And our duties with the guard."

"Is your family from a long line of guards? That is, did your father and his father serve?"

Moe shrugged and she caught a small smile cross his face. "My *grandmother* was a high-ranking officer. She fought alongside *Prince* Abbasdah in the bandit raid battles long ago. When she lost one of her claws, she was given a retirement purse and spent time raising us so our mother could work on her potato farm."

"That's lovely. That's a nice memory."

"I haven't thought of that in a long time," Moe said, twisting the spear in his claws. "Thank you."

"I am not very good at this."

"You are fulfilling your duty to the family of a fallen solider, as my sister fulfilled her duty." He sighed. "I am … not fit for active duty at this time, so I volunteered to relieve the current lighthouse keeper so she could spend time with her family."

"We have to find ways to keep ourselves busy in times of mourning, or grief will consume us, atrophy our souls. At least that's what I've read." She looked at her lap, the fine spray of the sea forming tiny droplets on the thick canvas cloth of her skirt. "I did not come here to distract myself, you know. I came because I care. Diggy was my friend."

Moe exhaled and continued staring at the water. Apondra stood carefully and reached toward him.

"Moe, I—"

A tiny blue dot drifted from his shoulder to her fingertip, then evaporated as it caressed her skin. A cold tingling ran up her finger, and then disappeared.

"Moe, can I bring my friend Diana up here to meet you?"

"I don't see why not."

Apondra scurried to the edge of the lighthouse tower and whistled at Diana. She turned and waved back, then nodded and skipped up the stairs with the ease of a mountain ram.

"Diana, this is Moe Murr. Would you please introduce yourself formally to him?"

"Formally?" Diana raised an eyebrow and extended her hand to Moe. The two women watched a trickle of floating glowing dots drift between them. Moe stepped back, aghast.

"What is that?"

"Moe," Apondra smiled, "you have been touched with the gift of magic!"

"You're a channeler," Diana said. "And I'm a spellcaster." She smiled. "Consider yourself gifted with being a sidekick for a mage."

He held his hands before his face, then turned to the sea. He extended his claws and all four hands, his mouth agape as a slow sheet of blue dots drifted through the air, glistening in the sun. "It's beautiful. What does it mean?"

"It means," Apondra proffered, "that magic is returning to the land. Or at least can return to the land. And if we have channelers, we can use it!" She grimaced at Diana. "Right? If we have any magic, then we have something to use against the cult and the sea snapper? Right?"

"If we can find channelers," Diana countered. She extended her thumb and watched a tiny blue spark settle on the tip before dissolving. "A lot more channelers."

"Moe, I know you said you are not fit for active duty, but I have a request. If you're ready for a special task, that is."

"Diggy always bragged about how much more important she was than I, because she was at your beck and call, part of our sibling rivalry." A short smile crossed Moe's face. "I can't turn my back on one more moment to rival her for your attention. What is it?"

"Will you help me find more channelers throughout the village? Diana can explain as we go. After I send your lighthouse relief, of course."

"I am duty bound, Your Highness." He bowed.

"Thank you." She gently grabbed his hand. Her heart swelled, closing the rift torn by her father's passing and the death of Diggins just a little bit.

"This is quite peculiar," noted Grand Vizier Fyrr, flipping through the texts he recovered from the library. He circled the council table, still being assembled and set by the court attendants. The castle staff diligently cleared the great hall after lunch except for the long table and seven maple chairs, with the eighth, Apondra's now, but formerly her father's business seat, set with a high back carved with scenes of craggy rocks and crashing waves. She had only sat in it as a small child when she worked on her academics with Fyrr; now his lessons were more important than ever. "I have found scant references to prayer circles and, yes, cults, where a chain of channelers fed into one sorcerer, but the words for the spells are obscured."

"Do you mean erased?" asked Diana, leaning on the table with both elbows. The vizier cleared his throat and tapped one of her elbows with a free hand.

"Be mindful of your etiquette, apprentice. No elbows. And if you think you're having trouble with two elbows, imagine how challenging it is for me, with four arms and two claws." He placed another hand under his chin. "Elbows on the table. I don't know why that is considered a rude thing, but nonetheless, it is. So please follow my example."

"Fine."

Apondra paced around the hall, bounding up to Captain Terra upon his arrival through the great doors, followed by a small group of six lobfolk escorted by Moe Murr. She welcomed the visitors.

"Ah. So these are all channelers you've discovered so far, and who agreed to help." Apondra pulled one of the bench seats lining the wall toward the table, surprising some of the assembled lobfolk with her hospitality. "An Eave Queen serves her people," she said. "Light food and drink for all while we discuss."

For the next hour, Apondra relayed the tale of her journey and her uncovered clues about Azcalaw. The assembled channelers clung to her words as she described the devastation of the giant snapping turtle, and the looming threat from the march of Cult of Azcalaw. A small gray lobfolk, a teenaged smith apprentice named Jison, raised his claw.

"How are we going to defeat a turtle? I can conceive how our army would fight a rabid and untrained cult, but a giant snapper?"

Diana nodded at Fyrr, and then stood. She cleared her throat and placed her fingers on the tabletop.

"Potatoes. A field of flaming potatoes." The silence in the room prompted her to continue. "They're quite effective, based on our prior experience with them. We can use them as our ballistics and long-range weapons."

Fyrr nodded. "We will need many more channelers if we want to draw every single speck of magic from the land and sea. All that we can gather." He gestured to Apondra. "Eave Queen?"

"I will need you all to be my advocates. Go out into the village, find your friends and family. Now that you know you are channelers, you will, how do I say this? What you know now as fact removes doubt from your mind. You will be more receptive to those who channel, and you must use this as your leverage to find them, show them, rally them." She breathed heavily, her nerves and bones aching as the stress of the past day whittled away at her. "There are some who do not see me as the rightful queen. I understand that. But this is not about me, it's about you. And your families. And the future."

Diana stood and applauded, then slowly stopped and receded into her chair. "Well, I thought it was a rousing speech."

Jison joined Diana. "It was good enough." He turned to the others. "Do what we can, to the best of our abilities." He smiled with a youthful face full of hope. "And how do we lure a giant turtle in range of the potato farms?"

Fyrr tapped his fingers. "This is an evolving plan. But it is a plan."

A bell sounded in the back of the hall announcing the attendance of the royal court officers and advisors for the start of the official council meeting. Fyrr motioned for all to stand, except for Apondra.

The collection of lobfolk wearing varied garments of wool stoles and aprons of leather hurried around the table and seated themselves. Fyrr sat to Apondra's right; on her left, a short stubby lobfolk named Oskar who oversaw the kingdom's finances. He spoke first, his red and brown spotted face huffing as he flipped through the pages of his journal.

"Eave Queen, while I understand the security of the kingdom is our top priority, we must at some point discuss the trade revenues so that we can secure extra food for the winter." He glanced at Captain Terra seated opposite him. "But I cede the floor to the captain."

"Thank you, Oskar," said Terra, standing first to bow to Apondra. "We have three scenarios, Your Highness. One: the great snapper attacks before the arrival of the cult. Two: The cult arrives first."

"And what is the third?" Apondra asked, already weary of sitting and listening. Terra swallowed hard.

"The cult and the snapper arrive together."

"Oh."

A silence fell upon the table. Apondra looked at the Captain of Farms, a large lobfolk with a deep brown shell and green appendages. She couldn't recall his name. Fyrr leaned into her ear.

"I believe *Dustfind* has something to contribute," he said with a wink.

"Yes, of course. Captain Dustfind?"

"Your Highness, this plan that was provided in summary prior to the meeting, to weaponize the potato field into magical artillery, it is rather dangerous and will reduce our winter food. As Oskar will attest, this will be an additional financial burden." Dustfind reached into his apron, a worn leather piece covering his entire chest, and retrieved a dead worm. "The soil is not aerating as we had hoped, there is some illness with the worms. We'll need to send a party to dig and transplant more worms for the other fields." He delicately placed the worm back in his pocket. "I'm sorry, but I cannot support this plan."

"Oh. I see." She sipped on a cup of tea presented by an attendant. "What else?"

The next three ministers, each one a territorial ward of the village, began to shout concerns and protests on behalf of their precincts. Their words blurred into a cacophony of suspicions and indirect slander against her position and the looming crisis. She listened, but stared into her tea and watched the brown liquid ripple as one of the wards pounded the table. Apondra looked up and saw a seething rage on the face of a gray lobfolk, the ward of Ribbed Beach, Larold, and his distrust for her legitimacy oozed between his words.

"Eave Queen, precious girl," he snarled, "what will we do? What will *you* do?"

Apondra sensed that Larold was testing her, pushing her to make a decision that he could pounce upon to dissect her solution and show her as unfit to rule, in addition to his claims of her illegitimacy. Under the table, Fyrr placed a hand on her knee, a small gesture of empathy, but also an indication to her that he could help steer through the objections, with her permission. She nodded silently.

"Captains and assembly, as Grand Vizier, I will politely remind you that the Eave Queen is in a complicated situation. She has just returned from an immensely draining journey. We have not had to fully mobilize our military in several years, a challenge to any ruler." He paused. "And her father just died. Not just the king, *her father.*"

A wet sheen drew across her eyes. *I must not cry now*, she told herself. *I need to show strength, especially in front of Larold.* She cleared her throat and stared at him, sitting up a little in her chair. "Larold? You wish to continue, yes?"

"With my apologies and empathy, Your Highness, as the Ward of Ribbed Beach, I mean no disrespect." Larold sneered and stood slowly, placing his claws on the table with a firm gesture. "I put forward to the council a vote to enact the Sojourn of the Monarchy."

"What is that?" Apondra gasped. Fyrr held up one hand as he placed another on her forearm.

"Eave Queen, the Sojourn of the Monarchy is a vote that must be unanimous by the council, whereby our monarch is relieved of power for thirty days. If any member of the council changes their vote, or dies, during that time, the monarch is reinstated. This is a measure to ensure balance of power during a crisis. It ensures that no member can scheme for power, as one member changing a vote reverts power back to the monarch. It is used sparingly in times where the king or queen is incapacitated or otherwise unfit to rule."

Larold spoke next. "It is not a displacement, or rejection, Your Highness, but for our current situation, I feel it would allow more experienced captains to steer our kingdom through the crisis. Efficiently."

"I see." Apondra stared again into her tea. She couldn't recall if she had been taught this procedure and forgot about it. Fyrr leaned close.

"This rule is so obscure that it has not been enacted in well over three hundred years, and as such I did not prioritize it in your studies." He lowered his voice to a whisper. "I apologize. I am sorry."

"And I have no way to counter this?" Her eyes remained fixated on her tea.

"Only by murdering us," said Larold. She looked up at his frozen expression; he did not smile.

"Oh."

"Eave Queen," said Fyrr, his hands resting on her forearm, "you have been thrust into a situation where you have no experience, and too much is as stake. I know this is not a personal attack." He leered for a moment at Larold. "Let us, the council, take over the planning and quibbling. It is only for a moon cycle and two days. Thirty days total."

Apondra pushed back her chair, the legs dragging and squealing across the floor. She pulled the cuffs of her new sweater over her hands. "Well, I will not object. Since I cannot." A single tear ran down her cheek. "I just want to do the right thing. For the lobfolk." Her voice shook, her feet burned with the urge to run far, far away. "Captain Terra, thank you for your service. You are relieved of your duties as de facto bodyguard."

"You cannot relieve him," protested Larold, "you do not have those powers during the Sojourn of the Monarchy."

"Did you vote yet?" Her eyes flashed as she snarled. "Did you vote?"

"Well, no. I have just put the motion to the council just a moment ago."

"Then, in this moment, my word is law and binding." She picked up her cup and threw it against the wall. "If I order one of you to clean that up, *until you vote*, you will do it." Her chest heaved, her sobs welled. "*But I would not do that*. I love this kingdom. I love all the lobfolk, and the fishermen, and the farms, and the kyloes and the chickens! *I am the Eave Queen*, and as my father told me over and over again, the monarch serves the kingdom!" She bent over and began to sort through the jagged broken pieces of ceramic. She grabbed a napkin from the table and wiped up the remaining liquid. "I serve the kingdom," she whispered.

A large claw extended next to her, and Dustfind whispered in her ear.

"You need time to mourn. And we need time to prepare. These events should not overlap, but unfortunately, they do." He removed the cloth from her hand, his gentleness belaying his size. "We shall give you thirty days. Please be well."

Apondra brushed off her skirt and nodded slowly. This was not the time to be a child, but she was not mature enough to wear the crown other than in ceremony. She glanced at the doorway to the inner sanctum where a cluster of attendants now leaned against the stone archway.

"Captain Terra," Apondra announced, "you are reinstated. I apologize for using you as an example. That was wrong." She looked across the faces at the table, still frozen, awaiting her next words. "Oskar, twenty coins bonus for Terra this month."

"But our budget, as I've stated, is thin, Your Highness." Oskar's plea was met by her upturned nose.

"I await the results of the vote, my advisors." She stumbled as she retreated from the great hall.

Apondra lay on her bed, still wearing her sweater and skirt. Her feet dangled over the side as she was too tired to take off her boots. The light hooting of an owl outside her window snapped her attention back to the darkness of the room, the plush duvet under her exhausted frame, the small raglobster from her childhood tucked in the crook of her arm. A knock at the door startled her, followed by Diana's voice.

"Can I come in?"

"I don't see why not," Apondra said, sniffling as she sat upright. "It's your room, too, while you're here."

"Hey." Diana lit a candle on the dresser and then flopped into the bed next to her. "I'm not the best person to give advice on a lot of things, but I can see you're breaking."

"I have a lot to do." She tucked her ragdoll under her skirt. Diana reached over and slowly slid it out of hiding. She held it with two hands and sniffed it.

"Appy, I miss everyone. Tomas, Ken." Diana paused. "Sharpe. I know you must be missing them as well. Especially Ken."

"I'm trying not to think about him. He hates traveling on boats, you know. Odd thing for a lobster to dislike." She looked around the room, so large, but so empty despite the ornate carved furniture, the bookcase, and the plush linens and clothing folded on top of a chest brought by the royal staff for Diana. "I needed a vizier, Fyrr, to stand up for me. I've never felt more helpless, and I must do everything by myself now."

"And yet, you don't." Diana handed the doll back to her. "Appy, you have an entire staff, a court of officials, an army of guards, all these people who not only serve you, but care about you. In my short time here, I can see that for the most part, these people, these lobfolk, they all care about you."

"But the stakes right now—"

"—are not your burden to bear alone." Diana slid her hips next to Apondra before giving her a final shove with her shoulder. "Lay down."

Apondra slid back on to the bed and closed her eyes. A quick dry kiss on her cheek surprised her.

"You are a good person. You are trying. And that's all you can do." Diana slid her fingers through Apondra's hair. "I never knew my father. It's okay for you to cry. Just cry, Appy."

Apondra tucked her head into Diana's chest and sobbed. Her eyes burned as her tears stung, a painful crying wail bursting from her lips. She missed her father, and his last days were spent in his bed as she traveled in search of a tainted myth. Her shame burned inside her. *I should have stayed with him! I was a fool to go on an adventure!*

"I didn't know," Apondra whispered. "I didn't know how close to death he really was. It would have been better if I had just stayed."

"Appy, if you didn't go out on your own into the world, I would still be locked in a room full of books."

This was true. Apondra lifted her head and saw the tears now slowly dripping down Diana's face, swollen and slick from crying, visible even in the soft moonlight. Apondra traced a finger down Diana's cheek, following a tear. Her friend smiled.

"Appy, I think we both learned a lot in our first time out in the world. It's full of pain, injustice, and other terrible things. But it's also full of beauty. Hope. I came from a place where I had nothing. You came from a place where you have everything. I think we met in the middle."

"That's a new way to look at it."

Diana shook her head. "No, Appy. It's not a new way. It's the way it just is. And I'm grateful for the journey. It led me to your friendship." She mirrored Apondra, now tracing her finger across her cheek.

"Thank you," Apondra whispered, giggling. "I hope you don't take this the wrong way, but right now, you remind me of Ken."

"I've been compared to much worse than an albino lobfolk," she replied, "not that there's really anything wrong with that. He's very charming."

"A good listener."

"He's very smart."

"I miss him." Apondra squeezed Diana tightly. "I am so worried about him."

"He'll be fine. They'll find their way home. All of them."

"Home."

"Home."

Apondra slipped into sleep, the warmth of Diana's arm her last thought as she closed her eyes. She woke once, startled awake by a nightmare of tidal waves crashing through the walls of Castle Homarus that evaporated as soon as she rose, but found comfort in the quiet droning of Diana's snoring.

Chapter 13

Solitude and Sojourn

AFTER AN EARLY breakfast alone, Apondra waited for the council meeting. Diana was notably absent from the morning meal, summoned by Fyrr Conch for some secret assignment. Apondra stared into her empty teacup as a battalion of servants cleared the table and reset the room for the council. She remained seated in her chair, her father's chair, as the attendants whirled around her, laying out baleen quills, candles for wax seals, and parchments for the royal secretary.

Larold arrived first, never taking his eyes off her, sitting at the far end of the table in silence. Dustfind, Fyrr Conch, and Diana entered next, and stood in wait for the final council members as they proceeded in a funeral march to their spots.

Fyrr raised his hands. "Be seated. We commence the Sojourn of the Monarchy proceedings." He reached under the table and grabbed his satchel, retrieving an old black leatherbound book. As he handed it to Diana, Apondra caught her winking at him.

Apondra's ears hummed as each member stated their impressions.

Dustfind's words were incredibly kind and thoughtful as he pointed out her commitment to academics and history but acknowledged that she was a sunflower that "needed more time to attain a dizzying height" as he voted in favor of the Sojourn of the Monarchy. Fyrr abstained, as per the minutiae of the process: no vizier, although having the most intimate insights into a king or queen's temperament and cognition, was permitted to vote lest they show preferential treatment in self-interest.

The other lobfolk around the table continued their cases, each one concluding that they saw the Sojourn of the Monarchy as a necessary albeit painful moment for the kingdom. Larold continued to stare into Apondra's eyes during the few moments that she could lift her head and survey the assembly of conspirators. *Is that too strong of a word, "conspirators"*, she asked herself. The sudden scraping of Larold's chair diverted her back to the matter at hand. He stood.

"Eave Queen Apondra. I will spare you from further humiliation and degradation as everyone here has pointed out your flaws and shortcomings. I vote my approval to enact the Sojourn of the Monarchy." He folded his hands and reclaimed his seat at the end of the table. A lone tear rolled down Apondra's cheek. "Don't cry, Princess. This is what is best. For the kingdom."

Dustfind stood and leaned his claws on the table. "The vote is unanimous. The power of this kingdom resides in this council for the next thirty days—"

"—At which time," interrupted Larold, "we shall reconvene to evaluate the removal of the ruling monarch and potential replacement by the largest landholding family in a peaceful transition of power."

Apondra did nothing. She said nothing. Not even her sadness could move her to shed another tear. The faces stared back at her, each one a mixture of pity and sadness, except for Larold, who sneered … and Diana?

"Ahem," boomed Diana, bolting upright with the black leather book open in her hands. "According to the lore and law, of which this council must abide," she said, pausing to wink at Apondra, "there is one more condition."

Larold growled. "What would that be?"

"I'll read this for you so you don't have to worry about any big words. 'In a time of war, unless the monarch is acting as an agent of the opposing faction that invades our land, the monarch's sovereign rule is unquestioned if proven through victory in battle in defense of the Kingdom of Lobfolk.' That, Mister Larold, means that if Apondra has not been permanently removed before the Cult of Azcalaw arrives, then her claim to the throne is iron-clad."

"In battle." He placed his claws on the table. "You just read the words yourself. *In. Battle.*"

Fyrr placed a hand on Diana's shoulder and then bowed to Apondra. "It would seem that the Ward of Ribbed Beach who has initiated these proceedings didn't read far enough in the laws."

Larold fumed. "Then so be it." He tossed back his chair and stormed toward the exit. "Good luck on the battlefield, Princess!" he shouted as he unsuccessfully attempted to slam the large wooden door during his exit. "On the battlefield!" he yelled.

The remaining council members sat silently until Dustfind found his voice.

"Eave Queen, we'll do our best to continue preparations. If you need any weapons training, I can assist."

"Thank you." She stood and smoothed the front of her skirt, her neck tightening as she reached up to adjust her coral crown. "I no longer have the power to dismiss the meeting. If anyone should need me for the rest of the day, I'll be in the library."

Apondra leapt up the stairs to her room. With a sweep of her hand, she knocked a small pile of coins into her booksack, then crammed a textbook on geography and a notebook inside. Diana bounded into the room, stomping her foot onto Apondra's boot to hold her in place.

"What are you doing?"

"I'm not sitting around, that's for sure." Apondra reached for the scarves next to her mirror and wrapped one around her neck. "I'm cold. I feel a chill."

"Appy. Appy. APONDRA!" Diana grabbed the bag from her hands, spilling the books onto the floor. "What is the plan?"

"*There is no plan!*" She knelt and shoved the spilled contents back inside, then slung the strap of the booksack across her body. "I'm going to the library because it's the only place where I won't feel the stares and verbal stabs of those idiotic council members. You have a purpose here. You're needed to help train the channelers." She knew the real reason she wanted to hide deep in the shelves.

"Appy, you miss Ken. I understand."

"What do I do?" Apondra folded her hands, slowly wrapped by Diana's own. She looked at the faint traces of stubborn ink stains on her friend's fingernails, contrasted with her own pink and white unworked fingers. Diana's pale hands reminded her of Ken, gently sorting his index cards and reshelving borrowed books, holding each one like a precious child or finely crafted ceramic bowl. Even when he dusted the legendary artifacts, his care and attention to detail was that of a parent cleaning a babe. "Will you come with me, just for a little while?"

"Whatever you need. My loyalty is to you ... *Eave Queen.*"

⁓

The dust accumulated rapidly in the library on the shelves and relics during Ken's absence. The general staff of Castle Homarus only arrived to clean every other week, much to Ken's dismay, and with a lesser attention to detail than he would have preferred. Apondra reached behind the counter and handed the willow duster to Diana.

"Appy, what are we doing?" Diana sniffed at the duster.

"Thinking logically. Taking care of what we can. Being around books always gives me good ideas. Maybe there's another idea in here. Plus, you can search for anything that might be of use, newborn Lady Mage." Apondra curled the corners of her mouth. "I just feel happier here, even when it's a rainy day."

"But the sun is out. Oh, right." Diana lowered her eyes. "Sorry. I get it."

Apondra immediately set herself to task and descended into the lower level. She tapped the lamp pomp on every sconce, pausing to admire the contrast of yellow-green light from the glowing algae with the black shadows cast over stone and wood. In the history section, she located a pair of books on war strategies and famous battles and set them down on the reading tables. An hour, then another, passed without finding anything of use.

Nothing.

She replaced the books and returned to the main level. Something looked amiss in the artifact display. The Bounty Shield hung in its place, a few old spears sat upright in their stands, but something was missing. Suddenly, she jumped at a loud thud from behind.

"Appy! Look at this!"

Diana stood, legs wide, dressed from head to toe in leather-studded armor: a central scaled tunic with oversized pauldrons and a round helmet, each component adorned with shell-shaped metal studs, a legendary piece that should be displayed on the stand next to the Bounty Shield. Apondra gasped and grabbed the dome-like helmet from Diana's head.

"Take that off! Do you know what that is?"

"According to the display, it is the armor worn by Freya Rock, who was the first female captain of the Lobfolk guard, 'a magnificent warrior who inspired the wives of the farmers to rise and supplement the lines in the Battle of Everbeach.'" She extended her arms to display the excess leather that draped over her hands. "If I had claws, I suppose these would cover them."

"It's a historical relic!" Apondra hissed, carefully but quickly removing each piece from Diana and putting it back on the display rack. "It's amazing that it survived this long, given the exposure to sea water!"

"How would I know that?"

"You wouldn't. The Battle of Everbeach was between the lobfolk and a united number of human tribes outside of any of the modern kingdoms. The humans marched toward the castle in large numbers, untrained hungry barbarians, and the guards positioned themselves outside the walls. Freya Rock, a chariot builder by trade, recruited her own army and took an impromptu legion of female lobfolk into the sea to lay in wait. At daybreak, the humans charged, configured for a frontal attack. However," Apondra arched her eyebrow, "Freya's battalion rose from the sea, intercepting the unprotected flank."

"They attacked by boat?"

"No, they rose from the sea. Some lobfolk embellish the story by saying they sang as they rushed through the breakers, a 'chorus of death', but there are no official records of that or the songs they sang." She traced her fingers along the seams of Freya Rock's helmet. "Anyway, it was a tactical move of genius and changed the perception of female lobfolk who joined the guard. Many human armies still exclude female warriors."

"You have a rich history."

"I know." Apondra held her hands over the armor's cracked chest plate. "Sometimes, as a child, I wondered if it was my history. Now that I know more about ... the world ... I have more questions than answers about those lobfolk from the past."

"Maybe one of those invading humans was my relative," Diana said with a weak smile. "Or yours."

Apondra gazed around the room, examining each piece of the history of the lobfolk, each one a relic of war. "It's a shame I can't be like Freya Rock. If the cult of Azcalaw marches on us, they'll come through King's Plain, and there's no beach for us to lie in wait."

"The potato fields are not within sight of the castle, you know, so there's your flanking maneuver. That plan looks like it might be a failure before it can even be tested." Diana flopped to the ground and pulled her legs under her skirt. "I'm sorry. It still feels like it could be a good plan."

"It's alright." Apondra sighed. "Diana, can I ask to be left alone for a while this evening? I'm sure Fyrr will tend to your needs. I'll bet he's still very curious to discuss you and your abilities."

"Appy, is anything wrong? Something not related to your crown, that is."

"No, nothing's wrong." Apondra inhaled the tiny specks of dust and the barely perceptible dry musk of the library. "I think I just need a little more time to clear my head. I haven't thought much about Azcalaw, but now I'm just wondering what would happen if he was able to help." She examined the library one more time, fixating on the Bounty Shield. "But we don't need him. He can stay dead in his grave. Somehow, lobfolk always seem to find a way to be clever and take care of themselves."

Night fell quickly with a blanket of cool air over the village outside Castle Homarus. A small shanty radiated light through the seams of the shutters as voices of children mixed with laughter and direction from their parents. Apondra paused before disturbing the joyous clamor with her knocking, the voices receding as Dell the baker opened the door.

"Hello, Your Highness! You have been missed! Come in, please," he said with a sweeping gesture. His children, a boy and a girl lobfolk, stood at attention next to their mother, adorned in a tattered but clean apron.

"Good evening, friends. I was out on a walk and thought I would stop by." She bit her lip. "What are you all doing this evening?"

"Well, Eave Queen," said Dell, "we just finished supper and were about to start baking some of the breakfast goods for tomorrow's market." Dell nodded to his children. Their antennae twitched as they waved.

"Oh my, such young bakers! Or do they bake yet?" She knelt and offered a hand to each of them. "Hello, little lobbies!"

"Jed and Jen are both learning the craft. But if they show some skills in another trade, I'd be happy to see them pursue it."

Jed nodded and puffed his chest. "I join guard! I soldier when big!"

Apondra smiled. "My, such ambition! You can always train for the trials. When you are older." She winked and smiled but knew the criteria for joining the royal lobsters was more befitting of the children who grew up strong in families that worked the fields or other physically demanding trades. "But wait, you are baking? Now?" She glanced back at the closed front door. "It's already nightfall."

"We bake when we can so we make what we can." Dell hobbled over to his small oven. She hadn't noticed his limp during all their interactions in the market. "My queen, would you like to choose what we bake?"

"Oh no, surprise us tomorrow!" She watched the children clear the tablecloth and replace it with a thicker, coarser sheet of clean canvas, followed by flat pans and an oiled board. Their efficiency and politeness were beyond charming; tiny workers helping the family as best as they could with their limited abilities. She crossed her arms in thought.

"Princess? You have a question?" The baker held his mixing bowl and an old spoon with a slightly bent handle. "Something must bring you here this late that we can assist with."

She examined the rest of the main room. The multipurpose table had been cleared of the four wooden stools with carved kelp decorations on the legs. A fire burned in the hearth as well as a second fire for the oven. A small shelf of stacked dishes, apparently the family's own for dining, and then another shelf of pots, pans, jars, and cans of baking supplies. A tapestry hung on the wall depicting a great lobster holding a cooking utensil in each hand and claw. Something was missing.

"Dell, do the children keep their books in their room?"

"Books? We haven't time for books, Eave Queen. They help me and my wife, Gertrud, now."

"Where do they do their schoolwork and keep up with their studies?"

Gertrud curtsied with her apron before speaking. "Your Highness, our children finished their primary education, but now we need them to work. They will learn the trade. When we have time, we recite the learning rhymes and sing the history songs." She lowered her head. "They don't really read. Or, should I say, they barely know how."

"Oh." Apondra leaned over the table, unsure of what she could do to help, so she chose to straighten the cooking pans. "Would they like to continue at school?"

"Princess," Dell said, "they would like a lot of things. And if we continue to bake and sell well in the market, we will get there. Hard work does pay off." His wife shot him a look. "We try to save money."

The fire of the oven crackled and sparked as Dell added a new log. Apondra cleared her throat. "Well, I should like to say something about hard work paying off, but I'm … not exactly a role model." She sat on the farthest stool, hands folded in her lap. "I was born lucky." The death of her parents underscored her half-truth.

"Princess, you are very valuable and do many things to help the kingdom."

"Lid tight," Jed said, holding a small jar in his tiny claws before placing it in her hands. "You can?"

"Oh, why yes, little lobbie." She unscrewed the wax cap with a dry smile and gave it back. The baker placed a sack of flour on the table before resting his hands on his hips.

"Honestly, what brings you here? Not that we object to a visit from the royal family, but how can we help you?"

Her head sank. She shuffled her feet under the stool. "I just wanted to say hello to my friend."

"Oh. Oh! Well, certainly, you are welcome to visit any time." Dell tapped on Jen's head as she scurried around him. "We're just very busy and short of entertainment this evening."

"I don't need to be entertained." Apondra sighed. His gestures resonated with a nervous energy she had not anticipated just by stopping in to say hello. She was his ruler, and he was her subject, and that relationship would never be removed by chitchat and introspection.

"Dear baker, *Dell*, I just, well, I just wanted to see how you were, you know, outside of the market. I enjoy your stories and anecdotes of your family and wanted to visit. If I am intruding—"

"You are not, Eave Queen—"

"Apondra." She stood, surprising herself with a darker tone than expected. She quieted her voice. "How about whenever I come over, and it's just us, me and your family, you may just call me 'Apondra', and your children may call me 'Appy' during my visits." She smiled at them. "That's what my friends call me."

Gertrud placed a basket of fresh eggs and a wood whisk on the table. "If that's so, then tell me, Apondra, would you mind cracking these eggs into a bowl for me?"

"Yes, I think I can manage that."

She sat quietly as she worked, carefully breaking each shell and watching the gooey contents drip into the bowl. The candlelight brought out new yellow and orange hues in the yolk that she had never seen before in the kitchen of the castle. Apondra located a wood whisk and began to stir. Gertrud slipped a gentle hand over hers on the handle.

"You'll want to flick it, like this, less stress on the wrist."

"Yes, thank you." The baker's wife watched her work for a moment, then leaned in close, out of earshot of the children.

"Are the rumors true? Are we are going to war?"

"It is … not war. There is a faction that has been on the march from the north. They belong to no nation or kingdom. They are a cult. They mean to disrupt our peace. And we shall turn them back."

"The Cult of Azcalaw?" Gertrud twitched her antennae. "That is the rumor we hear. And yet, Azcalaw will not protect us, nor dissuade them?"

"It's complicated." Apondra folded a napkin, pressing the creases to get the lines just right. "But our guards will take care of us. You can certainly count on having a big day in the market when they return victorious with hungry bellies."

"Your propaganda is excellent," said Gertrud. "My husband cannot fight, and I am grateful for that. I say, 'if we are to die tomorrow, then we die together as a family'. The children will never sleep in fear; we are grateful for your reassurances."

"I am doing my best."

"We know you must be trying."

Apondra placed the remaining napkins on the shelf and sighed. "You have a lovely home."

"We try."

For the next hour, they made small talk, discussing breeds of chickens, which time of year yields the tastiest wheat, and what Jed did when a small frog had wandered into the house one morning last week. Apondra found herself finally laughing, happily unburdened by the crown. Dell stopped to place an array of small bottles of sugars and spices on the table before the tray of uncooked pastries, now almost ready for the oven.

"Apondra, if I may," he said with an air of caution in his tone, "before I add the final touches, this is when my family and I pray. We pray for a successful day tomorrow in the market, and to express gratitude for what today has already given us." He glanced at his wife for a nod of approval. "It is a private moment."

"Oh, I see." She brushed her hands on her skirt and stood.

"We mean no disrespect, Your Highness."

And there it is, she thought. Despite her hopes of friendship, the crown and her adopted birthright would always be between them. She felt her eyes sting, her throat swell. "It's alright."

"Appy," said Jen, "we love you." Jen threw her tiny arms and not-as-tiny claws around Apondra's waist. "Mama says you are pretty sometimes, even if you are different pretty."

Apondra ran the back of her hand across the top of Jen's head, the smooth and shiny shell of a youth. A trickle ran down each of Apondra's cheeks. "Thank you, beautiful lobbie." She wiped her hand across her face and turned to the door. Dell politely halted her as she reached for the knob.

"Princess," he said, "*Apondra*, thank you. This was a pleasant surprise."

"I shall see you in the market."

"Yes, bright and early."

She thought about the lines of soldiers that would march through the castle gate eventually when the cult arrived. Some of them, she assumed, would be leaving spouses, parents, and children they would never see again. These were her subjects, her people, even if they were not her friends. Each and every lobfolk was her responsibility. She smiled at the lobchildren; Jen and Jed clacked their claws in farewell.

"Children, be good. And maybe I'll bring you some books and read with you next week."

She closed the door behind her and pressed her back against the wooden frame. The outside air bit into her with chilly teeth, nipping into her confidence, already raw. Tears flowed freely as she began to walk back to the castle, alone. She stopped once to look across the other homes in the village, lighted chimneys spewing funnels of smoke into the air, obscuring the moon.

Chapter 14

A Clawful of Returns

A TRIUMPHANT CLAMOR RANG through the courtyard, rising above the dissonance of the merchants and their customers bartering and laughing through exchanges of commerce to start the day. Captain Terra hurried through, his arm locked around Apondra, his claws pushing and shoving the villagers and visitors out of their path.

"Clear way! Eave Queen!" he shouted.

"Captain, what is all of this? Why was I scooped up from my breakfast with such haste?"

"Visitors at the gate!"

The mighty doors of Castle Homarus opened before them as they passed beneath the stone and wood archway. Ahead, past the entrance clearing, a small party stood within a small huddle of guards: she could make out among them two men, a brown paint horse, a black and white horse pulling a wagon, and a pale lobfolk gentleman waving his claws at her.

"Ken!" Apondra lurched away from Terra and sprinted into King's

Plain. Her breaths came quickly, her pulse rose, and she leapt into Ken's arms as they collided.

"Oh, Appy," he cooed, "you are the best thing in the world to see right now. Oh, how I've worried about you!"

"You too, I mean, me too," she said, holding back tears so that she could see his face. Apondra kissed his forehead, then closed her eyes. His antennae traced tiny circles on her cheeks. "I am so grateful, so grateful, to have you back. How did you all get here so quickly? I expected a few more days."

A pair of large claws, covered in leather-studded armor parted the group. Captain Wolf strode forward, his hammer-axe in his hands.

"No ships on the sea, not a one. We went full speed out of port. The sails and paddles of the swiftboat cut the sea just beyond the breakers and hugged the coastline." He nodded at Tomas, lurking in the rear. "This one, he came up with a pulley and barrel system. Rose and Domino were able to walk in a circle and crank the paddles nonstop."

Tomas nodded, then smiled. "It was an idea I had. The boat became powered by horses. Like a grain mill, but different."

Apondra opened her arms to embrace him, only to be intercepted by Diana as she tackled Tomas and kissed him on each of his cheeks. When they finally stood, Sharpe gently pushed Tomas aside and wrapped his arms around Diana.

"Hello, Lady Mage." He nuzzled his face in her hair for a moment. "I am glad you are safe."

Apondra laughed as her friends exchanged various hugs and handshakes. Tomas bent at the knee to present her scarf. "This, I believe, is yours." He grunted as he tried to stand. She grabbed his arm and lifted him up, kissing him lightly on the cheek. "Thank you, Princess." He stepped back, his face ruddy.

Ken grabbed his sack from the wagon still attached to Domino. "Did I mention to you that I hate riding in boats?" He tapped the ground. "I will never disparage you again, dirt." Captain Terra raised his spear to redirect their attention, then pointed it at Captain Wolf.

"As a member of the lobatorium of Castle Homarus, I will ask you to lay down your weapon in the presence of the Eave Queen so that we may discuss—"

"He's fine," Diana said. "I mean, if you want to practice your guard speech, go ahead, but he's with us. We've vetted each other."

Wolf nodded, then placed his weapon on the ground.

"I am here as a trained soldier, a captain of Himmelhavets. Your librarian convinced me to come here so that my skills in defensive tactics can shore up your castle in the limited time that we have."

"Our castle is safe," said Terra, crossing two arms and brandishing his spear in his other limbs. Wolf scoffed.

"Your eastern wall is at a slightly obtuse angle, making a siege ladder more stable when leaned against it. Those branches growing on the northwest side are too low, able to be climbed by two lobfolk standing on a barrel. Your gate hinges are exposed on the right side—"

"We will take your advisement to the council," Terra huffed, then smiled. "Later, I want to observe your hammer-axe skills."

"Well, this is grand," Apondra interrupted, "but for now we need to get inside, get my friends some food and beds, and prepare a planning meeting."

A bell clanged from the interior of the court, followed by a rolling thunder of shouts and screams. As a shock of icy cold shot through Apondra's chest, she turned to Diana, frozen in place, her eyes a roiling blue that matched a sparkling mist that surrounded her hands.

"Diana, do you feel that?"

"I do," whispered Diana.

A swarm of guards ran out of the castle, surrounding Apondra, as a second horn blast from the castle courtyard reverberated behind a thrall of soldiers preparing spears and shields. Terra raised his spear and charged into the commotion in castle courtyard.

"What is going on?" Apondra asked.

Moe Murr stepped forward from the freshly assembled lobatorium, his eyes peering out from under his metal helmet. "Princess, we have an unannounced visitor ... *inside the royal chamber.*"

"Who? And how did they get inside?" She surveyed the faces of the guards, antennae nervously twitching, hands tightening around the shafts of the spears. "And wouldn't this be a matter for the council?"

"No," said Moe, tightening his grip on his own spear's shaft. "*Azcalaw asked for you by name.*"

Captain Terra paced in front of the grand hall's doors as Apondra approached. A throng of villagers, some cheering, others praying, parted as Apondra waded toward Terra. He rang the exterior bell on the hall and pointed his spear at the crowd. "Make way for Eave Queen Apondra!"

"Let us inside to see him!" shouted a deep red lobfolk clutching a scroll. "Let us pray to Azcalaw!"

"No one enters except for the Eave Queen!" shouted Terra.

The crowd moved around her as she approached. She now noticed a blue fog seeping through the cracks around the door, a creeping cloud of icy cold that evaporated as it moved out of the shadows into the sun. She tasted salt in the air and the smell of dead kelp as she approached.

"What happened? How do you know it is Azcalaw?"

"He simply ... appeared on these steps. He said he was going inside to wait for the monarch, and then the doors shut behind him." Terra's eyes darted. "Only a few of us actually saw him. And it was him. There is no doubt." He leaned close, his antenna almost touching her cheek to shroud his whisper. "I am not a lobfolk of faith, but when a god speaks to you, you become a fast believer in many things." Terra offered her his spear; she declined. "Be careful. He asked for you by name, Princess."

As she stood at the door, her ears rang with a white silence. Terra gripped the handle of a short dagger in his belt.

"Will you come with me, Captain?"

"No," he said, his hands twitching over the great iron handle of the door to the royal hall. "Azcalaw is not someone I think we should challenge with our protocol. He asked for you. Alone. I should wait outside, but I will be at the ready if needed."

Apondra bit her lip, her eyes widening. She extended her hand toward the great door and immediately felt the tingle of magic accompanied by tiny blue glittering stars leaking through the wood. She glanced at Terra again, impatiently waiting with his hand on the handle.

They nodded together and opened the door.

Nothing could have prepared her for the shocking beauty that engulfed the inside of the castle's great room, a lattice of widely spaced and barely perceptible blue threads radiating from the throne and filling the great chamber from its stone floor tiles to the wooden ceiling beams, as if a thousand loom workers spent a thousand years weaving all the blue thread in the world. Each filament of magic sparkled like a gem and dissipated with her touch, every strand a cool tingle but unique sensation. She forgot where she was, and, momentarily, she forgot about the visitor that had summoned her as she walked slowly through the web of magic. As she moved closer to the royal dais, the radiant blue strings faded. There, sitting sideways on the ancient chair, a giant blue man, or somewhat of a man, clacked the claws on the end of each of his massive muscular arms. He swung his giant leg over the armrest, his thighs massive thick barrels of muscle wrapped in blue segmented crustacean shell pieces. He rose to his full height, twice that of a normal lobfolk.

Azcalaw.

His face resembled a human but was crowned with a shell scalp. Patterns of rigid shell patches scaled his cheeks and chin. He smiled widely as he peered down his crooked human nose and bore his black eyes into Apondra with sternness and absolute authority. Jagged gray teeth filled his smile with malice and decay.

"Eave Queen Apondra," his voice boomed in a high tenor tone surprising for his size. "Princess of Castle Homarus. Lady of the Land of Lobfolk. I assume you know who I am, as you have been pecking about in the world, speaking my name."

She knelt on one knee, lowering her head but keeping her eyes locked on him from under her brow, then returned to her standing posture. A slithering swarm of eels curled over the back of the throne and attached themselves to the giant's shoulders, draping over him as a living oily black coat of quiet hisses and bubbling breaths.

"Azcalaw," she said. Her fingers began to tremble. "I would request that you make yourself comfortable in any of the other seats or benches in this room, out of respect for the deceased king."

He turned to the throne behind him and held his claws in the air, now revealing the human hands fixed in the joint of each pincher. "I like this one. It almost fits me. It is a pragmatic decision, not disrespectful. Perhaps I can be your acting regent. Your father has passed, and you are not his blood heir." He smiled, his lips cracking, tiny black drops of blood rolling down his chin. "Should I be concerned about the masses outside? Any mages who might try to manipulate me?"

"We have but one spellcaster here, and you need not worry about a conflict. With you."

"A single spellcaster," he purred, marveling at the glowing lattice in the room as it receded into the corners of the high ceiling. "There are so few of us left in the world. Less than a hundred." His hand glided through the air in a motion not dissimilar to a parent testing hot bathwater, followed by a single blue gaseous orb as large as his head that floated toward Apondra. Suddenly it jerked left, then right, and dropped to the ground at her feet before fizzling into the floor. "Just checking to make sure you weren't deceiving me. You are a channeler, not a mage."

Her whole body quivered, standing before such an intimidating figure. She withdrew her fingers into her sleeves and looked for something she could use to steady herself.

"Sit, child." Azcalaw gestured to a chair that slid across the floor, led by magic threads from his claw hands. "Sit. It has been a long time since I have walked the earth. Perhaps I am intimidating you unintentionally." He held his hands in front of his chest and splashed a shower of blue mist over his face. When he lifted his head, his features had changed; his eyes now a beautiful light blue, his teeth straight and glistening white. Azcalaw's facial structure had changed as well; his chin and cheeks refined, nose gently sloped and ending in a small point. He was now handsome and welcoming. "Better?"

"Less intimidating, yes." She swallowed.

"The eons have granted me malaise. Boredom. Sometimes, I feel a depression of unfathomable burden."

She swallowed. His gaze, unblinking, stabbed at her as if he knew her, her insecurities, her fears. Apondra shook her head and straightened her posture.

"I should like to call in the council of the royal court to consult with you, Azcalaw. I am being put on … a sojourn … while I grieve for my father."

"Grief is a reminder of something lost. Something of value." He squatted down to her height. "Your council has made no effort to seek me out. You did. But that is not what brought me here. You came to my grave, or rather, my resting place. And then you did something no one has ever done in any of my memories."

She shuddered. "And what was that?"

"You said you didn't need my help. 'I don't want your help,' that's what you said. You spoke from your heart and said you will save your people without me, and you would save them from my misguided followers. Is that what you uttered over my resting place with a tinge of anger in your voice?" He smiled again. "I hear so many things when I'm trying to sleep."

She inhaled a shallow, nervous breath. "I am sure, wise and powerful Azcalaw."

"No accolades. I've done nothing to earn those words from you." Her heart surged. Something in his tone had changed, but she couldn't place it. Was it some sort of humility, or eagerness to hear *her* speak? His eyes softened to match his short smile. "Tell me. Why did you say that? That you didn't need me?"

"There is a threat to not just my kingdom, but all kingdoms, and a cult that is killing in your name. I thought you could be, would be, the savior from the stories we learned here for generations, the hero of the lobfolk, a deity made flesh in the legends we sang as children." She crossed her arms. "I went to find you. But the more I learned, the more I realized that we do not want your help if it is to come with a heavy price. And as we are running out of time, I needed to decide what was best for my kingdom. The lifetimes of these people are but a blink in yours."

"I am aware of this." He stood, again, rising to his immense height. "I don't have the same sense of time as you do, as I have lived for longer than I can remember, but I see the urgency of your situation." He walked over to the door, his footfalls absolutely silent, and gestured to the iron handles. "I can see that you are not at ease here, in this room. The specter of your father is guiding your words with an invisible hand. Why don't we take a walk to discuss our situation?"

"'Take a walk?'" She blinked rapidly, her mouth agape. "You're asking me to go for a walk?"

"Yes, it's how humans have conversations of a more relaxed nature. So I've observed."

He opened the door, revealing an enormous crowd packing the courtyard. The lobfolk immediately fell silent. Guards staggered themselves in various poses of readiness and gawking. Apondra slowly lifted her hand to wave. Azcalaw extended a finger into the palm of her hand for her to hold.

"Your Eave Queen and I are going for a walk," he announced with a beaming smile. "Please allow us some space."

The villagers and guards stepped back to create a wide lane. Apondra and Azcalaw nodded silently as they walked past the frozen faces towards the castle's gate. Lobfolk folded their hands, kneeled, and prayed quietly as the princess and the giant passed. Some of the assembled gawkers stood completely still, awestruck by the very sight of her gigantic escort and his unnatural features.

"They fear me," Azcalaw remarked. "I was a savior and hero from tales of long ago." He nodded to a frozen lobfolk, who immediately walked backward away from the procession. "It will do you some good for you to be seen with me; negotiating, planning, whatever the lower caste needs to imagine in order to instill hope and faith in you."

"How do you mean," Apondra hissed, "and do not call them *lower caste*." She looked up at him. "Please, if you don't mind, great Azcalaw."

"I will soften my language," he said. "I have no doubt you have heard many tales about me. Legends, songs, whispers. And all of them are rooted in basic truths but spun into tall tales and maleficent myths." He stopped to grab the heavy chain to the front gate of the castle before yanking it effortlessly and opening the doors that led out to King's Plain. "You must of course know that any paragraph out of context would be ruinous and disrespectful to the story being told. And my story has not been properly, how would you say?" He laced his claws together. "Edited?"

As they crossed under the great arch of the gate of Castle Homarus,

Apondra's hand still wrapped around Azcalaw's finger, her friends stood in a tight huddle. Ken cowered behind his hands, peeking between his fingers. Sharpe and Tomas stared, and Diana uncorked her flask, her mouth agape. Apondra shook her head.

"These are your companions, yes?" Azcalaw stopped to wave. "Albino, what is your name?"

"Ken. K'Ken Darloch Ambertide." He lowered his hands. "It is nice to meet you, sir, I think?"

"It is nice to meet you," Azcalaw said. He glanced at Apondra, then back to Ken. "I can feel the bond between you two. Very strong. And almost as old as your lives. Would you like to come with us, K'Ken Ambertide?"

"Not at the moment, but thank you for the offer, uh, Your Greatness."

Apondra blushed. "He is a special friend, yes. May we continue our walk, if you don't mind?"

Azcalaw nodded and they strolled out into the King's Plain, beyond the flat outer pavilion where the northern forest paths and merchant trails intersected the side roads to the village and mills. His demeanor continued to soften, as if Apondra's anxiety fed his relaxation. The slow, cool, tingles of magic continued to flow from his hand into hers, calming her with every step. Azcalaw paused. The sun floated just above the tree line. A strong wind from the east carried another surge of salty smells from the sea, which he inhaled deeply.

"Are you a god?" Apondra finally asked, breaking the silence.

"I once thought so, but no. I am from the earliest days of this world, when only a few beasts had access to the power of magic. Each of the first beasts was birthed from one of the corners of the world; the great snow serpent of the north, the fiery owl of the forest, the great swan of the eastern shores, just to name a few. I was one of them, an avatar of the places where the sea meets the soil."

"Where are these great beasts you mention? Where are they now?"

"Hidden. They act on animal instinct. As I am part man, yet not a man, I am imbued with a man's curiosity and a thirst for intellectual pursuits. Part of my nature is ego, happiness, and tragedy."

Apondra glanced back at the open castle gate, and the crowd that dared not venture forward.

"They do fear you."

"And yet they stare. Curiosity. An admirable trait shared by humans and lobfolk."

He extended his arm, palm up between his pinchers. A tiny sparkling blue light floated like a dandelion seed into his hand. "I see there is still some magic here. It is part of the air, part of the land. When magic is used, it leaves a place, but like the tide that rolls out, it will come back." He waved his hand over the grass by their feet, blue and green sparkles glinting on the blades. "Magic has been returning here slowly, after something sucked it dry. I would guess about eighteen years ago." He winked at her. "Give or take a few weeks."

She nodded. Her acrimony rose as she focused on the current crisis. "So, have you come to help us, to save us from this giant beast that was summoned by your cult to bait you? Job well done by your cult, by the way. And now here you are."

"Here I am." He smiled.

"From what I have learned about you, it is in our best interests to do this thing without you. We do not want to pay your fee."

"As you stated over my resting place."

"I learned many things, Azcalaw." She stuttered as she tried to speak, her frustration and fear mixing with rising courage. "There is a tale from a place in the far north. I read the journal of a farmer, a firsthand account. They had a harsh winter. Their food became blemished and depleted. The people, the people of the soil, *good people*, pleaded for your help. You provided relief but requested payment in the form of their children." She planted her feet and crossed her arms. "*Children.* You did that. According to the journal, and according to the other legends."

"'According to the journal, and according to the other legends.'" He flashed a smirk.

"Oh?" The tempest of her emotions refocused as confident aggression. "What is your version? Tell me. In your own words."

"My own words would be the truth. And understand this truth above all else and listen for it in my tales. I am not a killer. I cannot choose to kill."

"But the stories, the accounts of crushing your enemies?"

"Embellishment. History is told and recorded by the conquerors, and to brag of death is to imply power. I do not, and I cannot kill."

"Go on, then."

"The story of that farm in the north, yes. I remember the winter was harsh, the worst in a century. The farmers, spoiled by years of healthy harvest surpluses and mild winters, grew lazy with their storage. Spoilage, yes, they had that from their lack of cleanliness and maintenance of their silos, bakeries, and butcheries. And that was all that was needed to allow disease to be born and thrive. A plague." He looked for a place to sit and lowered himself to the dirt so that he could meet her at almost eye level. "The children, raised on soft grains, sugars, and simple foods, were yet to be sickened by the plague that infected their parents. I took the healthy children so that they would not die from the looming pestilence."

"You took the children but not the adults?"

"I took everyone who was not ill. Mostly children. But the villagers, many of whom were illiterate workers, would not understand my explanation. They didn't understand disease, and assumed it was some supernatural blight. Or *omen.*" He let the word float in the air between them for a moment. "I told them that taking the children was *payment,* not my attempt to provide sanctuary to those who might live. Otherwise, they would not have let me save them. As I gathered the healthy children,

I also asked the few adults who were not diseased to join me in escorting them to safety." He looked toward the now descending sun. "They lived long and happy lives in my care, and I had companionship for several decades. I did not ask them to, but they worshipped me. I asked nothing of my new children. And their bloodlines were able to continue as they found husbands and wives, moved on to the established kingdoms, and bore children and grandchildren."

Apondra kicked at the dirt. "Why did you decide to help them at all?"

"If the disease was allowed to spread, the sickness would creep unabated across the kingdom. I closed off the circle, let the village damn itself, and the disease killed its remaining hosts before it could spread. I did it to save the world of a cruel and agonizing plague." He held an open claw toward her in a gesture of understanding; she understood. "My greatest power is my mind. To study disease and sickness was a challenge I accepted, but it was how I was able to save a handful of people in the short term, and humanity in the long term." He placed his claws on his knees. "And of course, the lobfolk, the brothers and sisters of humanity."

She nodded, appreciating his apparent love of knowledge. "So you are not here to take from us? Are you here to stop the sea beast?"

"The beast is not what I fear." Azcalaw stood. He opened one of his claws, revealing his smaller blue hand tucked inside the joint, and picked a long strand of grass, his human fingers gently bending the blade. "It is the aftermath. I see things but I am not a seer. I see possibilities. A cult that murders and weakens the kingdom of lobfolk, a sea beast that rises and lays its eggs, disrupting the natural law, eclipsing the top predators." He paused. "You can comprehend this, I assume. You ask questions."

Apondra nodded again. Looking back to the castle, she watched the crowd slowly thin, perhaps as fears and doubts were allayed by those who observed her and Azcalaw sitting in such a beautiful scene as the sun painted new hues across the grasses with each minute of its descent.

"Princess Apondra, this sea beast, the giant snapping turtle, is not truly of this world. It was brought about by magic that blasphemes my name."

"And what good is your name?"

He stood to full height between her and the red sunset that now bled behind the trees. His shadow covered her in darkness, his blue eyes glowing against the black.

"My name is all that keeps your kingdom from being conquered by fearful and weak men from across the sea to the east, and the tribes beyond the mountains to the north, and the alliances of the islands to the south. Legends of my existence are what prevent the great war of kingdoms, for none would dare face my wrath, fictional as it may be." He closed his claws and pointed them at the ground. "I am not a god; I am not a hero. But I am nature. I am balance."

"So you did not come to help us; you just came to observe the funny little girl who shouted at your incorrectly labeled grave and make sure the scales of nature stay level."

Azcalaw laughed. At first, it resembled a short yipping like a dog, then grew into a hysterical deep booming guffaw. She cocked her head and was met with his surprised reaction.

"I like you, Princess Apondra. Here you are being rather accusatory toward an immensely powerful being who has watched the birth of glaciers and their inevitable deaths."

Her eyes narrowed. "My father is dead. My friends and I outran an army of zealots who are thrashing their way here to murder us all *in your name*. A titanic beast has destroyed towns and killed many people because it was summoned *in your name*. I don't have any more time to be afraid of you or stare in awe." Her head swam, trying to find the right logic and reason, and a simple plan. "Now we have had a nice chat, but if you do not mind, if you're not here to help me and you're just going to observe, I need to work on a plan to, well," she huffed. Apondra squared her shoulders and stepped toward him. "I need to work on a plan to clean up your mess!"

"Well," he said, scratching his chin with his claw. "Well put, Princess." A flash of light caught her eye as Diana approached from the castle, carrying a small lantern. Apondra gulped.

"Azcalaw, you speak of keeping the world in balance. If this was your duty, you would simply perform it. The people would not have to beg for your help, leaving you to be distorted by their tales." Apondra's mind churned, a smile crossing her lips as Diana joined them. "It is not us that needs you, for you would do this deed without us eventually. It is *you* that needs *us*, isn't it?"

His blue claw reached toward Diana; she froze, a small blue wisp fluttering from her chest to his hand. "Your mage? She has potential."

Apondra held her hand to Diana, motioning her not to speak. "Yes, she is our mage. We have a plan, and we will do this on our own."

"And yet moments ago, you were trying to convince me to help, to keep balance." He leaned forward, his features relaxed and reassuring. "You cannot wear two faces. I know that burden. So are you asking me to stay or to go? Actions, and inactions, have consequences."

Apondra poked her finger upward toward Azcalaw's face, her eyes ablaze with the fire that ignited inside her mind. "That's right! Actions, and inactions, have consequences. And right now, we are facing a crisis like we have never seen in our lifetime because of *your actions and inactions*. You have consequences, Azcalaw." Diana exhaled slowly and put her hand on Apondra's shoulder; she shrugged it off. "You, He of the Blue. You, mighty Azcalaw." Her voice broke. "And people died, people that I knew, and hundreds if not thousands of strangers I will never get to know, because you slept under a stone at the foot of a mountain. So if you don't mind, I think we are done." Her last words erupted in a ragged voice torn by her shouting.

"Well then," he said, his face frozen.

"We are done, Azcalaw! I'm going back to my home to figure out how to save my people, a people, *the lobfolk*, who don't even want me as their ruler. And why am I doing it? Because unlike you, I care about this world and am not afraid to take action." Her legs shook. "My father taught me to care, because a good heart is incapable of making the wrong choice."

The giant blue god sat. "No one has ever spoken to me like that before. Only you, little Lobster Princess." He rested his chin on his claws.

The adrenaline crested in her arms, now hot, burning, as her frustration boiled over. She reached up and felt a tear in the corner of her eye. "Diana, we're done here. I'm hungry."

"Should we offer him anything to eat—"

"He can make it rain cupcakes and beef broth whenever he chooses," Apondra snapped, her anger redirecting at Azcalaw. "He's a god, a false god. He can do whatever he wants. And so can I."

She grabbed Diana's wrist and stormed back toward the castle, now draped in dark browns and the deepest green hues. The long shadows of the forest around the King's Plain finally surrendered to the dark of dusk as Azcalaw sat alone.

At daybreak, Apondra and Ken tended to the livestock paddock where Teacup stood patiently waiting for his morning bale of hay. Apondra added a mix of fresh pine needles and oak leaves to his trough.

"Hello friend," Ken said as he tussled the hair on Teacup's head. "Oh, I've missed you."

"He slept for a full day after we arrived. And he's been eating everything I feed him since then."

"Pine needles as well?"

"Kyloes do eat fresh needles, although I don't recommend trying it yourself," she said, donning a sour face. "They taste very nasty."

Fyrr and Tomas approached, each one carrying a stack of books.

"What's all this?" Ken asked. "Are those from my library? And you've brought them here where they could fall into the paddocks?"

"I brought them to Azcalaw this morning," said Fyrr. "I thought an introduction and an offering of an activity might break him from his pouting."

Tomas readjusted his stack of books. "Apondra, you do realize we have a very large dangerous child sitting outside the castle? And it's your fault?"

She attempted a smile. "We don't need his help. I do admit that even without his magic or powers, his size alone would make him a wonderful warrior." She ran her hand through Teacup's hair again. "Except Azcalaw doesn't kill. He told me that during our discussion." She paused to help Tomas with his teetering stack of books. "How is Captain Wolf doing?"

Fyrr shook his head. "He and Captain Terra are getting along like two wolves."

"Oh that's good," noted Ken, grabbing a book in each of his hands.

"Two wolves chasing the same lamb, that is." Fyrr shook his head. "They have different styles of motivation, and the soldiers are not quite coming together."

"This is concerning," Apondra noted. She gestured for the group to head back toward the castle. "Very concerning. I suspect that our lack of wars over the past few years has taken some of the urgency out of the guard. Many have never faced true combat."

"Agreed," said Fyrr. "A blessing of peace can ultimately be a curse. The council is doing their best, but I think their inexperience is now exposed."

"Some of the soldiers are not attending the drills," Tomas said. "They are either afraid of war, or in some cases have said they are not in the service of the Eave Queen." He looked to Apondra, his lips loosely frowning. "An illegitimate queen, some are saying."

She knew this dissent was possible, but Apondra lifted her head, trying to convince herself and her friends that she was no longer hurt by the accusation. "One good soldier is worth more than ten cowards. Or something like that."

Fyrr scratched his head, his antennae fluttering. "Apondra, after we return these books to the library, perhaps we should head to the lighthouse."

"What for?"

"Fresh air." He sighed, a more common occurrence observed by Apondra since her return.

"Hail to the Eave Queen!"

A young green-shelled lobfolk waved his claws from the roof of the lighthouse, Moe Murr's replacement. Apondra returned his salutation and climbed the stairs with Fyrr.

"Hello good sir," she said, minding her steps. "What is your name?"

"You don't recognize me? My apologies for not making a better impression. I am Teelok's son, Teeron." He clutched his spear. "I'm in the guard now."

"Yes! Of Ribbed Beach! A thousand apologies, I have had much on my mind."

"Yes. My condolences, Your Highness. Your father was a great king."

She nodded and sat on a stool by the embers of the prior night's fire. "Yes. He was a great father, too. Your father, as well, he's a good lobfolk."

"Aye." Teeron leaned on his spear. "My father and I don't see eye to eye recently."

"Oh? Why is that?"

"I apologize, I should not trouble the Eave Queen with petty family issues."

Fyrr stooped over the tiny remaining flames of the beacon and extended his hands. "There are no petty family issues."

"Well, Grand Vizier, my father and I discussed Larold. We both dislike him, that much we have in common, but I told my father I wanted to join the guard to protect the kingdom; many soldiers are defecting. My father said it was best for me to not join at all, and to let others fight as the army of Larold's council."

"Oh. Larold's council," Apondra said. "I see." She watched an ember on the edge of the fire flare orange with the breeze, then turned black as the mist blowing from the sea extinguished it.

"I told him that I am not fighting for the person in the throne, but for the land underneath it. He didn't understand." He gazed across the churning waves. "I am looking forward to the end of the Sojourn of the Monarchy so you can return to the throne."

"Thank you." She quietly walked around the fire, carefully stepping over burnt logs that spilled outside the ring. "Keep a tidy fire, Teeron. A tighter circle. I learned that recently while I was away."

"Yes, Your Highness." He immediately began rearranging the logs and kindling. "I'll do better."

"You don't have to do any better than your best."

He paused and smiled. "The people in Ribbed Beach, those who believe in you, always say you know the right things to say because you're so smart."

"Do they now?" She shrugged.

Fyrr stepped to her side and laced his arm through the crook of her elbow.

"Come, Eave Queen. Let us leave this guard to his duties." They turned to head back down the stairs.

"Princess Apondra?" called Teeron. "Everything is going to be okay, isn't it?"

"Yes," she said, tripping over the simple word. "Yes. I believe so."

The next several days fell into a repetitive schedule for Apondra. She woke early, walked through the vendors, and checked on Azcalaw, still silently seated in the middle of the field outside the castle. A guard rotation was assigned to report any changes in his demeanor, and to manage the small trickle of villagers that came to gawk and pray before him. Children left tributes of painted shells and flowers, building a circle around his silent sentry.

After her one-sided visitation with the blue giant, Apondra would attend the morning military drills led by Captain Wolf and Captain Terra. They contradicted each other during formation drills; Wolf insisted on looser formations to allow quick movement into fighting stances, while Terra insisted on tighter lines to avoid penetration by unseen charging foes. It was agreed, after a compromise proposed by Apondra, to keep the front line tight as a wall during defensive marches complimented by a loose second line to fill gaps more quickly. During offense, Wolf and Terra agreed that a wider spacing on the first line allowed for swift attacks, backed by a claw-to-claw wall ready to fill the places of any fallen soldiers. Wolf reminded all that time was not on their side; by his estimates, the cult would be at their door within five to ten days.

Following the drills, she made herself a simple lunch of peppers and goat cheese on potato bread, the food of the commoners, alone in the castle kitchen, shunning the help of her attendants. If she was to be removed from her royal duties, she insisted on spurning the help of the staff so that they could focus on the needs of the council. She often took her half-eaten meal to the potato fields to spend the afternoon with Diana and Fyrr as they worked with the channelers on simple magic gathering and casting. Magic trickled back into the land, perhaps, Apondra guessed, because of the presence of Azcalaw, but nonetheless they used the magic sparingly during the channeling studies. Every day that passed yielded the sense of a small but steady growth in the blue stars buried in the soil and floating in the air. Per one particularly heated late night strategy session, Diana agreed to reduce her wine consumption. Ken applauded quietly for her sobriety when she acquiesced.

For Tomas and Sharpe, Apondra assigned each one a highly specific duty. The squire studied the armors on display in the library archives, measuring and cutting new leather to match Apondra's small frame and the girth of Teacup. Sharpe advised on the armor's most vulnerable penetration points, and practiced with his black bow, not for battle, but for use as a signal bearer during the inevitable battle that marched closer every day. She respected his insistence that he could not bring himself to kill another being, an aside that he repeated in confidence whenever Tomas left the library to gather more leather or metal buckles.

She counted the cycles of the moon, each day and night bringing the Sojourn of the Monarchy closer to its end, and the Cult of Azcalaw closer to their door. Her routine only deviated when a scout returned with a sighting of the cult members approaching Ribbed Beach. The town evacuation culminated in several dozen families relocating to the village precincts south and west of Castle Homarus, and the extension of gracious hospitality by the lobfolk who took them into their homes.

During the twenty-fifth evening since the enactment of the sojourn, Apondra wandered to the paddock where Teacup stood silently under the glow of the moon. Ken asked to meet her there for an undisclosed reason and arrived shortly after she did. He placed four hands on the paddock gate and waited as Apondra brushed her kyloe.

She caressed Teacup's nose and ran her hand along his horns, broad beyond his shoulders. She touched the dull points on each horn. "You're not quite fit for battle, my friend."

"I think that is an understatement," Ken said. "I mean, look at my claws."

"I was talking to Teacup." She glanced back at the village, and the forest beyond. She returned her attention to her kyloe, examining the tiny knots where Tomas' improvised saddle had matted his fur during their manic ride. Next to Teacup, a large barrel adorned with boards and branches formed the guide used by Tomas to craft Teacup's new leathers. "I don't need to fight to keep the throne, you know."

"You don't, and you don't know how." Ken reached over the paddock and tapped Teacup on the nose. "And neither does he."

"I just have to show up, be there on the line in the morning, ready when the cult arrives." She reached both hands over Teacup's back and rubbed him. "It's all I have to do to regain my crown. Show up in battle. And watch people die." She pressed her cheek on her cow. "All I've done since my birthday is watch people die, you know."

"I know."

Ken lifted the latch and entered the paddock, carefully stepping over clumps of mud until he was next to her. He touched her hand lightly with his finger, then his thumb, and finally wrapped the rest of his fingers around her hand.

"Appy, the reason I wanted to speak to you, alone, is to tell you something. Ever since we began this quest, adventure, or whatever you call it, we've been in danger." He traced an antenna along her cheek. "*You've* been in danger, more specifically. And I just needed to tell you, before tomorrow, that I have never been more afraid, more terrified, than I was when you rode home from Himmelhavets." He drew a long breath. "Because I was alone."

"You were with Tomas and Sharpe and—"

"I wasn't with you."

"Oh." She lifted his hand and placed it on her cheek. His hand trembled for a moment on her face as her lips rose into a smile. "I felt the same way."

"I just needed you to know, in case something happens tomorrow. Your friendship, our friendship, is unlike anything I've encountered in fiction and nonfiction. And of all the words I've ever read, I think there's one word that feels correct, and yet, it doesn't quite suit us. Even though we've said it before."

"I know." She fought to breathe, her chest tightening as she attempted to speak. "We, you and I, are bound by our hearts to each other, and no one will ever sever that bond."

"Except for the poor unfortunate lobfolk lady that I trick into marrying me someday," he said with a tiny laugh.

"I want to be there, standing next to you, on the happiest day of your life."

"And I hope to return that favor. I hope you find the love of your life as well. Just take your time. But not too much, mind you."

She laughed and let go of his hand. Teacup huffed. "Goodnight, Teacup." Apondra kissed her kyloe on the head and led Ken back through the paddock gate, making sure the latch was secure.

They walked silently, hand in hand, back to the castle and the entrance to the inner halls. She stood on one leg to kiss him on his cheek. Ken nodded and took one step back, bowing.

"Goodnight, my Eave Queen."

Chapter 15

The Battle of King's Plain

EAVE QUEEN ON the line!"

Captain Terra raised the red banner tied to his spear as the clip-clop of Teacup's hooves announced Apondra's arrival at King's Plain. The guard regiments stood four rows deep along the entire length of the castle's wall in front of the gate, waiting for her inspection. Under different circumstances, she'd be more interested in the morning birds that skittered from nook to nook along the trees embedded between the stones of the battlements, chirping over the short quiet banter of the soldiers. With his hammer-axe over his shoulder, Captain Wolf walked the line ahead of her, tugging at one guard's armor apron, nodding silently.

"Captain Terra, they are ready," Wolf said. "As ready as they can be."

Teacup shook his head, his tuft of fur covered by a thick leather pad that matched the barding around his neck and shoulders. Apondra stood in her stirrups, revealing the leather armor copied to match Freya's design from the library's relic collection; Tomas had worked through the night to finish tailoring the pieces to her tiny frame after the protests of Ken. She touched the last-minute addition, an engraved rose in the upper left of the tanned chest plate. The arms and shoulders made of segmented leather bands resembled lobfolk tails in another homage from her uniform. She borrowed the black boots of a smith from the village and Tomas hastily resized them using brown straps and light blue tethers torn from one of her bedsheets. She felt the weight of the Bounty Shield strapped to her back, the legendary piece designed for a lobfolk much larger than herself.

Terra nodded once, lowered his spear and shielded his eyes from the sun.

"Have you spoken with him, the big blue spectator, Your Highness?"

"Azcalaw still sits."

At the center of the plain, Azcalaw remained motionless. The sprawling array of flowers and trinkets reminded her of a giant blue frog sitting amid a pond covered in lily pads, or a crayfish from a southern river that had wandered out of the water into a patch of clover flowers. He would surely be run over by the approaching army when they arrived this morning per the guard scouts' reconnaissance.

"Princess, he's a lost cause." Terra pointed to the line of soldiers. "These lobfolk are our saviors now."

Apondra stood again in the saddle and lifted the Bounty Shield over her head. The freshly polished surface glistened in the sun as her arm shook.

"Lobfolk of the greatest kingdom of the land! Today is our day!"

A silence fell across the regiment. Captain Terra dug his spear's pole in the dirt. One of the guards in the front line coughed. Apondra glanced up at the birds on the battlements, as well as a small murder of crows resting in the branches along the living wall, and then back across the field to the edge of the forest, and the trail that led into the woods. A pair of guards relocated to the castle gate and waited for her.

"Princess," Terra said in a low voice, "I know what is at stake, but you don't belong here, on the line."

"I belong here, with the sons and daughters of those who came before us. These are my sisters and brothers. My family."

One of the guards on the line gasped, pointing beyond her to the plain. She turned, her eyes stung not only by the sun but by the sudden movement in the middle of the field.

Azcalaw rose.

A glittering dark blue web sprouted from his back, reaching into the blooms and buds that surrounded him. He lumbered toward the castle, his sparkling cape woven with the tribute bouquets and a rainbow of single petals. The soldiers stood in complete silence as he lumbered toward the line. After several minutes of silent gawking by the lobatorium guard, he arrived, standing next to Apondra.

His facial features had changed again. While he still bore the handsome symmetry and jawline of his more approachable form, Apondra saw the newly etched deep wrinkles and furrows in his forehead, the rough patches on his cheeks, and the bags under his eyes, still sparkling blue like the midday sea.

Azcalaw's cape of flowers floated behind him, supported only by his magic. It curled to his sides, allowing him to pick a single daisy from the starry weave. He placed it on Terra's shoulder, then turned to walk down the front line of soldiers.

One by one, he plucked a flower or bud and placed it on the armor of a guard or into an outstretched hand. Through the open gate of the castle, a crowd of villagers and townsfolk displaced from Ribbed Beach watched, still and silent, while Azcalaw continued to return each of the tribute flowers to a lobfolk.

Apondra remained silent, without fear or resentment or anger, only bewilderment, as the god-being walked among the lobfolk. When he finally emptied his cape of blooms, he turned back toward her, his head low to avoid her gaze, and lumbered to her position. Teacup huffed as the blue giant stopped in front her.

Azcalaw opened his mouth and lowered his massive frame to one knee before her.

"I serve Princess Apondra," Azcalaw whispered. He drew a deep breath and shouted with a thunder that echoed across the plain. "ALL HAIL THE EAVE QUEEN!"

The guards at the gate suddenly dove to the sides as a crowd of villagers poured out, armed with shovels and axes, braced with shields crafted from barrels and wagon wheels. The civilian army raised their weapons and shouted a single whooping cry. At the front of the assembly, a familiar face held a fishing spear.

"Teelok of Ribbed Beach brings his clan and claws for the Eave Queen!" He stood next to a green lobfolk in a fresh guardsman's armor, his son. "Our family fights for the Kingdom of the Lobfolk!"

Behind him, a large, brown-shelled lumbering lobfolk held his green claws in the air, his hands each wielding a short hammer-axe. Four similarly hued large farmers stood behind him.

"Dustfind brings his clan and claws for the Eave Queen!"

Another group of lobfolk, all female, slipped out from behind the farmers. Gertrud, Dell the baker's wife, stood defiant with a large wooden club in her hands. She raised it and clacked her claws.

"We fight for our families," she cried. "Our clan and claws for the Eave Queen!"

The assembly of soldiers straightened their backs, their postures upright and focused. Apondra looked to Azcalaw through teary eyes.

"Thank you," she mouthed.

"They believe in you, not me," Azcalaw said, standing back up.

"Why did you decide to stand with us?" She fumbled with the Bounty Shield as she tightened the strap on her forearm.

"You put your kingdom above yourself. You put these lobfolk's safety above your own needs. You have every right to be angry at them for attempting to take your crown. You could choose to disavow them after your father's death, as they are not your blood. But still, *you love them.*" Azcalaw searched the field beyond her. "Their tributes showed me that they are a nation capable of love. And there is only one thing in all this land, and the lands beyond the sea, and in the Undersea itself, that should always be unbalanced, and multiply in everblooming abundance. And that is love."

She fought tears as she recalled the dying words of her father, staring at her tiny hand wrapped around the shield's leather strap. "But you will not fight or kill," she whispered. "You have said that."

"I will mitigate the actions of the cult that bears my name."

With her shield raised above her head, Apondra led Teacup down the line. She smiled into the faces of every eye that met hers. Her chest shuddered, her throat dry and dusty, but she drew a deep breath to force herself into the moment.

"This armor I wear, this shield I hold, are reminders of our greatness. My father taught me that to be a ruler is to serve, not command. I serve you. As my family—"

"Incoming!" came a shout from the top battlement.

A flaming arrow landed several yards from Apondra, its origin the forest on the other side of King's Plain. A large mob of blue-robed men, humans, emerged from the tree line, set their longbows and aimed their weapons into the air. Azcalaw clacked his claws.

"Apondra, I'm afraid you will not be privileged to provide a rallying speech for the histories."

The cult's human archers parted the middle of their line as a lone robed lobfolk stepped forward. He walked methodically toward the middle of the plain.

"Should I meet him?" Apondra whispered to Azcalaw.

"Let them come toward us, into the open field."

As the cultist drew closer, another cadre of robed warriors, lobfolk and humans, followed him with black-bladed swords and crooked spears. They shuffled along slowly, and Apondra could make out some using their weapons as canes and walking sticks, fatigued after their long march south. She tugged Teacup's reigns again.

"Azcalaw, I am going to meet their emissary," she said. "Let's see what we can negotiate." Captain Terra shook his head. Azcalaw raised a finger to him.

"Let us try. She is safe with me, Captain."

The cultists bowed as the pair drew close, some trembling and smiling as they stared at the blue titan walking next to the human on her cow.

"It's him!" one of the cultists shouted.

"Azcalaw! Oh, the mighty savior of our souls!" cried another, dropping his spear and raising his hands to the sky.

When they came within several yards of the procession leader, Azcalaw drew a long breath and scanned the mob of followers. He looked to Apondra, then back to the collective. He filled his lungs and unleashed his voice against the army.

"GO HOME!"

He smiled at Apondra, turned around and headed back toward the castle. She pulled Teacup in a circle and trotted up next to Azcalaw.

"Is that it? Is that all you're going to do?" she snipped.

"The believers in their ranks will listen to me. If I told them to dance and sing like a drunken crab, they would do so. Any bloodshed that can be avoided, should be avoided."

Apondra looked back at the cult army. A significant number, but still less than the majority of the men and lobfolk, dropped their weapons and returned to the path leading back through the timberline. The remaining cultists stood, dumbfounded. Some picked up the discarded weapons and slid swords into their belts or jabbed their surplus spears into the ground. Their envoy leader remained frozen, his hands extended to match the confused look on his face.

"Azcalaw!" he yelled. "Don't leave us! Our tribute is yet to be made! Ignore the cowards in our ranks, for the believers will bring you souls to feast upon!" He clanged his daggers. "MORE SOULS FOR AZCALAW!"

A slow dull crunch echoed beyond the edge of the forest, followed shortly by another. Then another.

"Azcalaw?" Apondra tapped him on the elbow. "The trees are moving."

He turned at her provocation and crossed his arms.

"Ah. The turtle."

The high pines and junipers swayed, then whipped back and forth, followed by thunderous snaps. A dark and craggy mound rose above the tree line, then fell again, a rhythmic pattern that moved closer accompanied by the rising volume of old trees twisted and broken by the looming juggernaut. A shrill cry echoed from the forest, followed by a booming low rattle of air hissing through the beak of the monstrous snapping turtle.

Apondra whipped her head to the battlements. She put two fingers against her lips and blew a shrill whooping whistle.

"SHARPE! FIRE!"

The archer popped up from behind the central battlement, black bow in hand. He nocked an arrow, leaned back, and drew the string as far as he could before releasing his shot. His arrow, adorned with three long yellow ribbons, arched through the sky over the battlefield.

"Captain Terra!" Apondra shouted. "Move the line!"

As the words left her mouth, the remainder of the cult army surged across the plain. Ferocious faces followed their dark blades and spears, shouting in a guttural rage. The front row of the castle's defenders rushed toward them, claws clacking, their hands full of spears, daggers, clubs, and axe-hammers. Captain Wolf raced ahead of the pack, his antennae dancing with his hollering and chest thumping.

"Wait," Apondra whispered to herself, "draw them closer." She tapped the etched rose on her chest plate and steeled her eyes, raising her shield.

"Wait." She looked up to Sharpe, her arms shaking.

"Wait." He nocked another arrow, decorated with long red streamers.

"FIRE!" She slashed the air with her shield.

The next arrow soared over the plain. Several of the cultists stopped, watching the red-plumed streak against the cloudless sky. A distant popping and hissing crept across the battlefield.

"SHIELDS UP!" Apondra screamed. Her army stopped and swung shields strapped to their backs over their heads, some extending their defenses to their fellow countryfolk who were without cover.

A shimmering blue wave erupted from the west, a tidal wave of blue light over the tree line, blinding even in the sun's rays, followed by the intensifying crackling of flames. The cultists froze and stared at the wave of flaming projectiles arching over the edge of the King's Plain in their direction. Shouts and screams exploded from the advancing army.

"Well played," said Azcalaw.

"Let's hope so," replied Apondra.

The battery of magic-infused potatoes bombarded the cultists' positions, exploding on impact, igniting their robes and the wooden poles of their spears. Cries of pain and agony erupted as humans and lobfolk of the cult fell to the ground, rolling in their flaming apparel. Apondra turned to the western edge of the plain and saw Tomas emerge from the woods on Rose, waving a small red flag attached to the blade of his dagger. She whipped her attention back to the castle and again bleated her shrill whistle at Sharpe.

"Volley two is ready! SHARPE! FIRE!"

Again, he drew his bow and fired. As they had planned the days and nights before via Fyrr's advisement of the council, once Diana, positioned in the farmland behind the tree line, could see the red plumes of the arrow in the sky, she would draw the magic through her channelers to launch the bombardment. Tomas was to ride to the edge of the battlefield and signal when Diana was ready to recast her spell.

The second bombardment scattered more cultists from the plains. Some of the initial deserters retrieved the wounded and maimed, dragging them into the woods.

"Hup, hup, Teacup!"

Apondra kicked Teacup into a run, charging along behind the advancing line of the lobatorium. The kyloe zigged and zagged around the combatants, the kingdom's lobfolk surging against human swordsmen and lobfolk spearmen in blue robes, the random hissing of an arrow past Apondra's head reminding her of the danger in every direction.

"Here! Aid!" she called, circling a wounded lobatorium guard, an arrow protruding from his shoulder. "This one!" Two villagers ran to the fallen lobfolk, one with a shield, the other with a bag of rags and herbs to tend to the wound. Apondra shot back across the field to another body.

"This one!" she called, then realized the body of the lobatorium soldier lay still. "No! Go back!" she yelled, waving away another group of responders.

Teacup obliged every command, starting, stopping, running hard from point to point. Another lobfolk, face-down on his stomach but flailing his hand in the air, caught her eye.

"This one!" she called. Teacup pulled to a stop, and Apondra leapt to the ground. Every soldier she could save would be one less stain on her crown.

"Where are you injured?" She placed her hand under his claw to roll him over.

"To the Undersea!" hissed the wounded lobfolk, slashing with a broken dagger at her chest. He leapt to his feet, his muddy blue robe's remnants dangling from his neck. Apondra slipped in the mud, falling backward, her heels kicking at the air. The cultist laughed.

"All the glory to me, for killing the Eave Queen!"

As he thrust his broken dagger at her face, a white flash tossed his hand aside, then another slash as Teacup's horns thrashed at him. The kyloe roared a mighty moo and rammed his head into the cultist's chest. Apondra crawled across the mud and grabbed the dagger.

"I can't," she whispered. "But I must."

She stood, hands shaking, the broken blade glinting in the sun.

A thunderous rumbling shook the ground under her feet. She stumbled backward as a branch shot from the ground, sprouting vines and leaves that encircled the cultist. The plant grew into the air, weaving a cage around him that glowed with blue light. Azcalaw stepped out from behind the magical tree, his hands raised into tight fists in his claws.

"I do not kill," he said, then lowered his hands. "And I see your heart. It is not in you to kill, either."

"Thank you." She grabbed hold of Teacup's saddle and stepped into the stirrup. Another tremor surged across the field. "It that you, too?"

Azcalaw shook his head; Apondra gasped as the head of the giant snapper suddenly burst through the timberline. The colossal turtle slowly waved his head from side to side, hissing like a storm's wind, his black tongue greedily lapping at the bodies before him. The snapper dug his claws into the ground, the bulk of his massive body still buried in the forest. Apondra kicked at Teacup and rode west along the battlefield, waiting for Tomas to reappear.

"Tomas, where are you?" she muttered. The snapper paused, its head and front legs fully emerged from the timber and creeping into the field. She estimated that the entire shell was larger than her castle, its foul maw wider than the front gate. It roared again, timidly approaching the smoldering bodies and small fires between it and the open plain.

"My magic ballistics are suddenly missing," Apondra said, searching for Tomas.

Azcalaw stood by her side. "And you cannot defeat this thing without me."

She bit her lip. He was right; a force ten times the size of the lobfolk military regiment would be no match for the mountainous snapper. She doubted the magic of Diana, who was now inexplicably and critically absent from the attack. They could, as was just proven to both sides of the battle, handle the swarm of the cult, but this behemoth was superior to anything they could muster.

"Azcalaw, these people, even the misguided ones, all deserve to live. If you can make this stop, what is your price?" She leapt in front of him, the Bounty Shield at the ready. "What is the toll I have to pay for these lobfolk to be saved?"

"You." Azcalaw stooped and brought his face to hers. His shining blue eyes darted, his mouth showed no sign of frown or smile. "You must perform a task for me. It is a task that only you can perform. But I know you will do it."

"What is it?" she said, clutching the shield now between herself and the godlike giant. "What am I to do?"

"You must promise me first. You will oblige my request without explanation when I complete my task."

"What is it?"

Azcalaw inched closer, his breath a chilly wisp across her face. "If you love your people, if you truly love them, including the ones who shunned you and voted against your right to the throne, the ones who abandoned the guard, the very cowards who called you an omen, then you will pay any price for their sake. These people called you an illegitimate heir. They distrusted you." His words carved menacing chills into her skin. "They are not your kin. *They hate you.* Would you still do something, blindly, for them?"

"I cannot bargain if I do not know the price!" The snapping turtle roared, stepping on a fleeing band of cultists.

Azcalaw pressed the tip of his finger to her forehead. A white light filled her eyes. "I know the history of this world, Apondra, and I know you were saved by a foolhardy, overconfident mage who paid dearly. You were saved by a father who lost his wife. Your friends rally around you, because you have touched all their lives so dearly." The blinding white light faded. He pressed his face closer, filling her field of vision with his features, barely a finger separating them. He opened his lips to produce a dark whisper. "Failures of love, blind love, and lost love are what made you into a champion of love."

Her throat tightened as she fought the bubbling urge to cry. An image burned in her mind: her father, on his deathbed. His skin flaked and fluttered into the air of the room as his shell cracked. Abbasdah's last words, in his voice, floated into her ear.

"Conquer, my love."

"Azcalaw," she said, her tone resolute, lowering the Bounty Shield. "I serve this kingdom with love in my heart, a love like the sea that stretches beyond sight and sings with its waves every second of every day for all of eternity. And if I can just perceive a moment of the concept of eternity, then I understand you. And I trust in you."

"And so, Lobster Princess?"

Her heart pounded in her chest; her head ached. "*I accept your price.*"

Azcalaw smiled. "Good."

He stood back to his full height and stretched out his claws. A thin blue fog passed from Apondra into his chest. Her lungs constricted, her heart slowed; she attempted to speak but no words passed. When the fog cleared, she gasped and filled her chest with air.

"What was that?"

"Channeler," Azcalaw said, "you have been told that belief is part of the ability to cast and control magic. And I needed you to believe with absolute *purity*, more than anything in the world, in your heart and your convictions. Now follow me!"

He opened his claws wide and stormed across the field, his footfalls like the crashing of boulders, his arms cutting the wind as his speed increased. The lobfolk soldiers and cultists sprinted and dove out of his way as the ancient hero flattened the growth beneath his feet like an apocalyptic hurricane. Teacup charged behind Azcalaw's magical wake, Apondra standing in the saddle with the Bounty Shield slung across her back.

The snapper held its ground, huffing through its enormous beak, eyes watching the flames in its path. Something stirred on the top ridge of its shell, a menacing lobfolk figure swathed in loose blue robes. His black eyes leered across the plain, surrounded by jagged blue stripes of face paint. The figure opened his claws and arms wide, a black blade in each of his four hands as he spoke.

"I am Tenor, High Priest of the Cult of Azcalaw! We sow death for eternal life!" He pointed two blades at Azcalaw and Apondra. "Approach me and be consumed by this dark creature that I have summoned to destroy this world so that we may rebuild our souls in the light!" He cocked his head, sheathing his daggers. His mandibles dripped with spittle. "Azcalaw, you have denied us your presence! You have mocked our belief in you! You have erased all meaning from our toil and strife! And for this, your followers demand you lead us to the Undersea! You shall die first!"

Azcalaw slowed his pace as he passed over the last smoking robes and bodies, the snapper snorting as they met. Apondra nudged Teacup closer to the flames, but the kyloe reared up, throwing her onto the field on top of her shield. She leapt to her feet.

"Azcalaw! Why did you stop? What are you doing?" Apondra said, kicking his shin. He widened his eyes to match her own surprise at her outburst.

The snapper lowered its head, its breathing slowing to a gentle breeze of heat as it passed over Apondra. Its eyelids closed slowly over the burnt yellow of its irises. Apondra glimpsed a faint blue sparkling deep in the depths of its black pupils.

"This creature is under his power," she said.

Azcalaw nodded. The mighty blue giant extended his hand, touching the tip of the snapping turtle's beak. It rested its chin on the ground. Azcalaw brushed his hand against the monster's cavernous nostril, a tender gesture of affection, then stepped back and spoke in a booming voice that echoed into the woods.

"From earth, to sky,
To swim and fly,
To field and stone,
To safety of home.
By my peace,
Be gentle, beast.
In dimini te sallah paciva."

A warm blue light enveloped the snapper. Apondra clutched her chest as an icy wave passed through her, over Azcalaw, and into the giant turtle. It opened and closed its eyes, and then curled its legs under its shell, glowing brighter, wrapped in the web of magic that squeezed the beast into submission.

The snapper began to shrink; first to the size of a large mansion, tossing Tenor off its back, then the size of a cottage. Smaller and smaller, pressed by a lattice of cold white magic into a diminutive form. Apondra clung to Azcalaw's side until the turtle's shell collapsed to the size of her tiny human fist.

"I told you," Azcalaw said dryly, "I am not a killer." He staggered and picked up the diminutive turtle. "He'll be safe here for now." Azcalaw placed the tiny creature next to a broken log. He whispered incoherent words to the snapper, then fell into a heap, his breathing labored. "I have no more magic to give."

A cadre of lobfolk guards charged from the western tree line, led by Moe Murr and accompanied by Tomas and Diana. The spellcaster and the squire broke off from the soldiers and raced to Apondra and Azcalaw. Tomas dismounted Rose and supported the lady mage as she stumbled forward.

"Are you hurt?" asked Apondra.

"I'm okay," Diana said. "I can barely stand; I ran through the magic much faster than I expected. It disappeared too quickly from the land."

"I know why," said Apondra, snapping her attention back to Tenor.

He stormed toward the group, his mouth frothing under his antennae, blue sparks sputtering from his fingertips. "Azcalaw! You have siphoned the magic from me, and this land! You have forsaken us! Forsaken me! You defy the old texts and legends? You are the balancer; you must cleanse this land with your death and save the devout!" He clashed his blades against each other. "I am the devout! I am a believer, but you are a hoax of a deity! You are no god!"

"True, I am no god," Azcalaw replied, his head sinking to his chest. Apondra saw a sadness in the blue titan's eyes that surprised her. "I just am."

"And you," Tenor growled, accusing her with an extended blade. "You have corrupted this, my inevitability! You are a sickness that needs to be purged!" His anger curled into a sneer. "*Asphixus Mortem!*"

Tenor extended a hand toward Apondra's throat. Invisible needles stabbed her neck, drawing her breath as she vomited a blue cloud of mist. Had Azcalaw drained Tenor's magic during the giant snapper's defeat, or had he merely siphoned it? Tenor still had enough magic to hold her in his grasp and steal her very breath. She clutched her chest, suffocating as his spell floundered. The blue fireflies of magic floated out of her and into his hands. *He's using me to channel my own death spell!* Darkness crept into her periphery, blackening spots as the air left her body. The icy knot in her chest continued to feed Tenor's spell.

Tomas surged forward, knocking Tenor to the ground and releasing his deadly grasp of Apondra. They rolled together, the squire's leg falling off in their melee. The sinister mage rose first as Tomas drew his dagger.

"Step aside, pathetic boy!" Tenor kicked Tomas in the face and turned toward Apondra, slowly unsheathing all four black blades that hung on his belt. "To your death, Eave Queen!"

Apondra fumbled with the shield as she tried to protect herself. She shut her eyes, bracing for Tenor's blades to penetrate her leather armor.

Diana's scream filled her ears.

Apondra opened her eyes.

Tomas faced her, his expression frozen, his eyes wide. He looked down at his chest, and the tips of four black blades protruding through his tunic, surrounded by a growing stain of blood. He stumbled as he turned away, the hilts of Tenor's daggers thrust into his back. Tomas' mouth fell open, but no words followed.

Tomas dropped to the ground, then onto his back. His eyes stared toward the sun as he passed.

"NO!" Apondra cried, as Tenor stepped back from the body, his face a twisted mix of glee and anger.

Apondra knelt over Tomas, weeping and convulsing as she stroked his hair. If there was one person on her journey who never thought of himself, it was Tomas, and now that beautiful flaw in his character had killed him. She clutched his hand, peering into his lifeless eyes staring into the sky. Gunnar's ring hung from his neck, covered in Tomas' blood.

"My friend… my friend." She reached for his belt and clutched his empty sheath.

"Your friend is dead," Tenor growled, raising the fallen squire's dagger, "but you will be reunited in the Undersea!"

A searing hiss and a flash of red whipped past Apondra's face, followed by a dull *thunk*. Tenor, frozen in his attack, teetered as a long arrow decorated in red ribbon pierced his right eye. Another shot, a second arrow, pierced his left socket. His body collapsed backward, dead.

Apondra glanced back across the field. Sharpe charged, his black bow raised, and another arrow sailed past her, puncturing Tenor's chest. The archer fired another shot, and another, and then his last arrow, each one into the dead body of the spellcaster.

A gentle hand wrapped itself around Apondra's waist and lifted her up. Diana's voice resonated in her ear.

"Look away, Princess. Just look away."

Sharpe joined them, wrapping his arms around both women and clutching them to his chest. He bawled, his knees buckling, and the three collapsed into a heap in the muddy and bloody grass. A short distance away, Teacup sidled next to Rose, the two mounts standing silently. Teacup nudged Rose toward a patch of untouched field to graze.

Across the rest of the King's Plain, cultists knelt, hands over their heads, as guards rounded up the invaders. Several lobfolk rushed to and fro with improvised carts and stretchers, and small huddles knelt in prayer over lifeless bodies. Apondra attempted to wipe her face with her leather-armored sleeve; Diana offered her own to dry her tears.

A chariot rattled toward them, pulled by a black kyloe, carrying Ken and Fyrr Conch.

Diana rushed to meet them and immediately hugged Ken, his claws drooping at his sides and his head shaking back and forth furiously as

Diana attempted to console him. He scurried over to Apondra and threw his arms around her.

"He was a good friend," Ken said, his face wet from tears. "He was so brave."

"He was," she replied between gasps as she cried.

Fyrr knelt next to Azcalaw, who lay motionless in the place where he had cast his spell on the snapping turtle. The vizier placed his hands on Azcalaw's head, leaning close for a moment, nodding.

"He is very weak." Fyrr stood. "Apondra, he is calling your name."

She struggled to walk, each step heavier as she approached the blue giant, his chest slowly rising and falling.

"What is happening?" she whispered.

"And now, Eave Queen, you will pay your toll."

Azcalaw stared into her eyes, his pupils manifesting glowing portals into his eternity. She saw sadness, and grief, the sorrow of a burden. The faces of all those he saved, all those he lost, every beautiful sunset and sunrise, and the clearest night of stars she had ever seen, in image from the dawn of time. All of his memories flooded into her, the pages of his long life, overwhelming her. Then, a glimmer, a flicker of tiny white light as his eyes turned black.

"You must write my story, my lore, and ensure the world knows my love. Never again will my name be wielded by the misguided. Write my truth and be my advocate. This is your toll."

"I understand." She blinked through tears of joy and wonder. "It's already leaving my mind, these memories. I'm sorry. I'll do my best."

The blue titan attempted to smile. The lines on his face darkened, his teeth fading to gray. "I gave myself for the binding of the snapping turtle, shedding most of my magic like the shell I have never molted. And the magic that remains inside me must flow into your land."

He whispered an incantation, a spell only he could hear. As the final words escaped his mouth, he closed his eyes one last time. Tiny blue flower buds rose from the soil around him, each bloom opening and releasing a sparkling pollen that glided on the wind up in the air, to the castle and the forest, and out toward the sea. Each single spore grew into another bloom, and the process repeated several times until suddenly all the blossoms wilted and floated away into dust.

Fyrr extended his hands. "Diana! Lady Mage! Do you feel anything?"

Diana stood before Fyrr and mirrored his gesture; a volley of sparkling fireflies danced between them.

"Your magic," she said, "is back?"

"No," Fyrr said with a deep sigh, "but you can feel the magic here, yes? The land is bubbling with it, is it not?"

She closed her eyes and smiled, then frowned. "I am sorry," Diana whispered. "It's wonderful, this feeling. I know what you lost once upon a time." She traced her hand over the right side of his face. "Thank you for saving Apondra all those years ago."

Fyrr stood slowly and brushed off his robe. "The world is full of magic. I will be alright on my own, as I have before." He stepped forward, stumbled, then righted himself and cleaned his robe again. "It was well worth it so the Eave Queen could stand before us today, as our champion." He bowed.

Apondra sat quietly, taking in her friends and the losses that came with their victory. She peeled off her armor, first the sleeves, then the chest piece. She stared at her boots, the muddy blue ribbons from Tomas still tied tight around her calves, choosing to leave them alone for now. A pair of farmers covered Tomas after a conversation with Sharpe and placed the body on a small cart. The archer placed one hand over the sheet, his other hand, a fist, against his heart, before the cart wheeled away.

Ken quietly collected Apondra's armor and placed it in his chariot with Sharpe's help; she knew that Ken would spend all night cleaning it and preparing it for the antiquities display. Sharpe then hugged him, a gesture she had rarely seen between the two, and the archer delicately placed his black bow into the chariot. He walked back toward the castle, alone. She wished she could find a way to heal him, but he was now one of many lines she added to her list of broken things to mend. Ken secured the last items and signaled to bring it back to the castle.

Terra, his head low, returned to Apondra with his hands carefully wrapped around a tiny object.

"This seemed important."

He extended a simple cord, a necklace, adorned with Gunnar's ring, retrieved from Tomas' body.

"Thank you."

Apondra clutched the ring, feeling the perfect circle against her dirty palms, then placed it around her neck. Ken put his hand on her shoulder as she cried. The clouds drifted in front of the sun, cooling the air. Now unarmored in just her tunic, she shivered for a moment, then squeezed Ken's hand.

They waited for the clouds to pass and cried together. The sun returned.

"Appy, I'll see you when you are ready."

Apondra nodded as Ken wandered back to Castle Homarus. She closed her eyes, sat, and leaned back on her palms, momentarily forgetting the mud. A tiny sloshing noise from behind startled her.

"Oh, it's you," she said, picking up the small snapping turtle. His tiny feet clawed at the air. "Azcalaw said he could not kill, and truth be told, you were only a tool manipulated by Tenor." The turtle's beak opened and closed slowly. "Do you want to go down?"

She placed the snapper back in the mud. It turned and faced her, then cocked his head.

"What is it, tiny sir?"

The turtle walked toward her boot and poked her toe.

"I'll pick you up again."

She lifted it carefully, bringing it closer to her face than she normally would, given the reputation of normal snapping turtles in the wild. It blinked at her with its dark eyes.

"You are not terribly ugly, you know."

The turtle's eyes flashed blue, sparkling between blinks. For a moment, she thought she saw a beautiful sunrise from a thousand years ago, a memory from Azcalaw.

"Oh." She scooped up an empty helmet from the field and placed the turtle inside. "I think you need to be taken somewhere safe. Perhaps later we'll sit somewhere quiet, watch the waves, and we can say nothing together." The turtle chirped, its eyes flashing blue again.

Chapter 16

The Ascendance of the Eave Queen

THE DAY FOLLOWING the battle left Apondra drained, but she knew that her responsibilities continued through the bureaucracy of the kingdom. She only had a moment of peace with Sharpe, sitting by the lighthouse with him and her snapping turtle, until last night's supper. Now she returned, again, to her royal duties. Her heart stormed with a mix of fear and anger as she entered the great hall of Castle Homarus for the council meeting.

The council stood for Apondra, every seat filled except for Fyrr Conch's and her own. Apondra brought Diana with her as vizier pro tempore. She, too, was weak, but Apondra needed someone by her side for the meeting, someone she knew she could trust outside of the voting members, if for no other reason than to listen to any details that might slip past her weary ears. Larold and Dustfind sat on opposite sides, staring in silence at each other.

Captain Terra pulled out their chairs and then resumed his place. "For the benefit of the council minutes, please introduce yourself." He gestured to Diana.

"Um, hello. I'm the attendant for the Eave Queen." She looked at the frozen faces, then crossed her arms over her sweater. "Lady Mage Diana."

Larold immediately pushed his chair away from the table. "A human mage and a human queen," he scoffed.

"She is only here while the vizier recovers," Apondra countered. "And she proved her worth and valor in the battle in the King's Plain. Dustfind was there, you know. I did not see your countenance." She bit her lip.

"Many losses, Eave Queen." Larold stroked his antennae, then picked at a splintered edge of the great table. "Many losses. The guard is severely depleted."

Apondra tensed. Her fingers clutched the edge of the table. She drew a slow deep breath before standing.

"I have proven myself and led us to victory in battle. My right to the throne is affirmed. So says the law."

He clacked his claws. Apondra saw his taunt; his mere act of claw-clacking reinforced that he, not her, was a lobfolk. She glared at his dark eyes.

"Larold," she continued, "would a just ruler do what is best for the kingdom? Yes. That is the unequivocable answer. *Yes.*"

"Princess Apondra," he said, leaning forward. "We are still confronted with an inevitable truth: you are not a lobfolk. When you pass into the Undersea someday, a new monarch will be crowned. By law, that is the largest landholder of record at the time of your death."

"Should I be frightened? Am I going to need to look over my shoulder for the rest of my life?" She allowed herself a sideways glance at Diana, who returned the look with a tiny smile and wink.

"Of course not," said Larold. He clapped for an attendant to fill his tankard. "It will take me several years to buy out the farms and lands to increase my already substantial equity."

"And if I should die tomorrow, who would be the largest landholder? Who would swoop in and take the throne?"

A silence fell across the room. Dustfind raised his claw.

"That would be me, Your Highness." He glared at Larold. "And I would like to state for the official records and history that I have no intention of sitting on the throne." Dustfind slumped in his chair. "I'm not as smart as you, Eave Queen."

Diana smiled. "Well, that is reassuring, I suppose."

Larold downed his drink and stood. "I motion that due to the resolution of the Sojourn of the Monarchy and the reestablishment of Princess Apondra to the throne as Eave Queen, that we convene in five days with a full agenda."

Apondra glared at him. "So that you can plot your next maneuver, Larold?"

"No," he said, stepping back and lowering his voice. "So that now, with the threat to the kingdom resolved, you can have a proper time to grieve the loss of your father." He slid a folded piece of paper onto the table. "I'm not a monster. This is a list of flowers available from my gardener. Order as much as your like, as many as you like, whenever you like." He looked up, his antennae still. "Your father was never my enemy, you know. He was a good king."

Larold turned and left the council table. The other members filed out behind him, leaving Apondra and Diana alone with Terra and an attendant who stood next to them with a decanter of wine. Diana looked up and shook her head.

"Tea, just tea for the two of us, thank you." Diana snapped her fingers and watched a firework of blue stars burst and fade. "You know, Appy, the ones who say they aren't monsters are usually the most monstrous ones of all."

⁓

As the volume of needs and grievances of the lobfolk swelled well beyond the capacity of the hall for the scheduled time of the public forums, Apondra ordered a large table and banners set up outside the front gate. For two days, she sat with Fyrr and Diana, listening to the reports of broken and destroyed farm equipment, mild looting of Ribbed Beach during the cult's southern march, and the reports of rogue cultists sleeping in barns, stealing hot pies from windowsills, and one unfortunate altercation between a shepherd and a thief that resulted in murder. The lack of cooperation between lobfolk, now more concerned with their own well-being than the consideration of their neighbors, furrowed her brow with every new grievance. At the end of the second day, she ended the public forum, her hair disheveled, her hands aching from writing, and called for an emergency evening meeting of the council.

Larold arrived first, supplied with his own meal of salted meat cubes and oat stick bread. He kept one arm wrapped around his plate as he ate, eyeing the other members as they seated themselves, Diana and Fyrr settling on each side of Apondra. The last member, a tan lobfolk named Deccan Broen, the Captain of Infrastructure, stumbled into the hall.

"Apologies for my tardiness, Eave Queen."

"Accepted," she said. "But I will address you first. How are the roads?"

"Like a bale of hay tossed in the mud. A mess."

"Hmm," said Larold, pointing a piece of his bread at Deccan. "And the ports?"

"With many shut down for over a month, the ones that were not damaged by the sea beast are in need of maintenance and repairs just to accept the ships now idling at sea and in the bay. We had to ask a large ship from South Islands to route north several miles to a dock that could accommodate their size."

"Well," said Larold, rising from his plate, "these are interesting problems." He began a slow walk around the table. "And, these are very complicated problems. We are quite weak and susceptible to even a moderate invading faction. Perhaps we need to vote for an additional Sojourn of the Monarchy? This may be too much for the Eave Queen's limited experience to—"

"The Eave Queen," Diana shouted, "is still gathering information to make decisions. I don't see you doing anything productive other than counting your money and stuffing your maw with food." Her eyes blazed a fiery blue, embers of magic glowing in a halo around her face. Larold returned to his seat, wrapped two hands around his plate, and ate quietly.

Apondra rested her hand on Diana's wrist. "What my passionate attendant is trying to say is that I have a plan and a purpose that I would present so that we, the Kingdom of the Lobfolk, will be able to continue forward safely, and without providing an opportunity for another kingdom to turn chaos against us. Even though you are plotting to take the throne, Larold, you can at a minimum agree we need to project an outward appearance of organized governance." She waited for a response but was met with silence. "The merchant town has been devastated. Not only does that impact us, it affects all kingdoms. *All of them.* Commerce, trade, supplies. Chaotically disrupted. I saw firsthand how the merchant town works, and there are many eager and able workers without employment, and many slave masters who will look to take advantage."

Larold crossed his arms. "Continue."

"Any of the kingdoms that we believe to be our allies are now in the same desperate situation. Food, lumber, construction goods, loans. None of these will flow in the short term. And that desperation is why, long ago, many kingdoms who are now our allies went to war." She stared at Larold, guessing that he more than the others understood the gravity of the situation, as Ribbed Beach was a strategic location for the lobfolk ships, and a barrier against the northern lands. "War," she repeated. "Everything I have read says we are stirring the ingredients necessary for war."

"I admit I am impressed by your ability to see the scope and scale of the current state of affairs." Larold bit down on another meat stick.

Apondra looked down her nose. "I've read a lot of books."

"Continue," Larold said with a wave of his hand.

"I will assign Sharpe, Archer from the South Islands, to act as a sheriff of the wooded lands north of Ribbed Beach and up to the merchant town. He knows that land like no one else, and he will be able to act as our eyes and ears. I have given him the authority to deploy soldiers as needed to maintain the peace."

Oskar stood and raised one hand, his others busy with scribbling numbers on a sheet of paper. "That will be costly. And we are delegating our policing to a human?"

"His heart is truer than his aim." Apondra crossed her arms and smiled.

Dustfind made his presence known, standing abruptly and raising his hand. "I need to speak, Your Highness. We know the Kingdom of Swan attempted to be our allies during the crisis of the sea beast and the cult, but are we sure they will maintain peace with us? Invasion by sea would be difficult, but we know desperate times are here, and will get worse before they get better."

"The Eave Queen has a plan," announced Fyrr, breaking his silence. "We will send an envoy of the highest rank, the Eave Queen herself, to the Kingdom of Swan to sign a renewed treaty and trade contract. By this example, humans and lobfolk together, we intend to instill trust, and hope, into the hearts of the citizens of both nations."

"And what of the other kingdoms?" Dustfind asked. Fyrr crossed all of his arms.

"King Abbasdah's envoys to the Kingdom of Ice Lake were rejected year after year. Ice Lake is content with their isolation, but Captain Wolf is going to seek new diplomatic ties on our behalf. The Kingdom of High Wood to the west, and the Kingdom of Dark Sea, far to the east of Swan, are of strategic interest, but it is the Kingdom of Swan that remains our immediate potential ally."

"But first," Apondra said, waiting a moment for the nod of approval from Fyrr, "we will head to the merchant town, survey the damages, and curate a plan for the even distribution of goods in the short term, prioritized to those places and industries where it is most needed."

Larold drummed his fingers on the tabletop. Silence filled the hall, except for his continued tap-tap-tapping on wood. Apondra searched his face for an indication of his acceptance, or rejection, of her plans. He finally folded his hands and nodded.

"This is not the way of a free economy, to tell these businesses who and what they may sell to whom."

"These are not times for profiteering." Apondra glowered. "This is about what is best for the kingdom, for all kingdoms."

She lifted her coral crown off her head. She traced her finger along the rough surface, then the ribbon wrapped around it in a simple spiral. She placed it on the table.

"You want this? You will get it, Larold. But only if there is a kingdom at all. And I am doing this with or without your help, so it would be in your best interest, the only interest you ever seem to have, to help me."

"Well played, Eave Queen." He stood to leave. "Oh, and did you take advantage of my offer of free flowers?"

"Not yet," Apondra said. "The offer is still valid?"

"Of course. I gave you that contract."

"Oh yes, you did, that's right." She reached into her pocket and withdrew the paper, raising her eyebrow. "Dustfind, please take this to Larold's employees and tell them we require a bouquet for every lobfolk who perished defending King's Plain. And then a bouquet for every spouse and every child who lost a loved one." She glared at Larold. "And then, a bouquet for every fallen member of the Cult of Azcalaw to be placed in King's Plain. Every. Single. Body."

Dustfind took the paper and nodded. Larold's antennae twitched violently.

"That's preposterous! I will lose a tremendous amount of money on those flowers! A tremendous amount! Why, I may have to sell property to stay afloat." He gasped.

"Your generosity," she said, placing the crown back on her head, "will be added to the recorded history of the battle. You'll be remembered long after you die for this moment." Her pulse quickened; her throat tensed. "Unless you get in my way. Then history will remember you as I see fit. This meeting is now officially adjourned. Diana?"

"Yes, Your Highness?"

"Pack a bag of clothing for yourself. And tell Ken to do the same. Be ready to travel north with me tomorrow after breakfast."

⁓

Each step up to the top of the lighthouse felt longer and longer. Apondra paused to catch her breath before making the final ascent, her bag of books pulling at her shoulder against the winds that blew in from across the rough surf below. She stopped finally at the top, squinting against the sunrise. Moe Murr stood on the other side, leaning on his spear next to the dying embers of the night's fire.

"Good morning, Princess." He reached down to his supply sack and pulled out a half loaf of potato bread. "It is all I have left, but it is yours if you would like it."

"I had an early breakfast," she said, pulling out one of the books, "but thank you. That's very kind, but it's your meal after all."

"Well technically, it's the kingdom's food, part of my rations as a solider, so you have a claim on my bread." She smiled and nodded at him as he continued. "Eave Queen, what brings you here this morning, and at such an early hour?"

"I could ask you the same."

"I relieved Teeron. He asked to work for the Ribbed Beach guard."

"He joined the guard, and yet he works at home." She took a piece of his bread. "And so I ask, why you are still holding your vigil in solitude?"

"Again, I could ask you the same question." He laughed briefly. "I am obligated to answer the Eave Queen before satisfying my own curiosities." She scowled. "But also, you are my friend." Her scowl reversed into a tiny smile.

"Thank you for saying that. Just call me Apondra when we're talking like this."

"As you wish, Apondra." Moe Murr stretched his spear out toward the sea. "Every morning, the ocean decides to be fierce, like today, or it decides to be calm, like it was yesterday. It does what it wants. And we accept it. If I wish to board a one-man bob-boat to fish, I am at the sea's mercy. And I think that is something I've needed to do. Accept things. My sister, Diggins, is gone." He returned the spear to his side. "And every morning, I can be like the sea, and choose to grieve, or choose to find joy, but I can choose. Today, I look at the colors of the sunrise and choose joy."

"That's very comforting."

"And look what it rewarded me with! You! A welcome surprise, someone I can have a lovely conversation with today."

"I brought my books; I wasn't planning on much conversation." She tapped her bag.

"What are you reading?"

"I am looking for history. I want to ensure there is nothing missing from the full bloodlines of King Abbasdah." Her book felt heavy, like an anchor holding her in one place. "I miss my father."

"We all do." He walked over to her and placed a hand on her shoulder, watching the waves beyond the cove rise and fall. "I miss my sister. I wonder what it will be like to meet her again."

"Do you look forward to seeing her in the Undersea after death?"

"I look forward to swimming in the Undersea with her, when my time finally comes." He exhaled deeply. "When the tides of fate decide I am to be washed away, I accept it, because those tides only wash us out to sea. They do not bring the souls of the dead back to the shore." He raised his spear and pointed it along the horizon. "That is the world, and I do not fear death, for this world is nowhere near as grand as the gifts of the Undersea. But while I am here, I will fight every single day to protect this kingdom."

"You do not fear death."

"No."

She reached into her bag and retrieved a worn map, an old piece of parchment obtained for the archives by a cartographer that traveled to the Kingdom of Swan.

"Moe," she said, holding up the map. "Would you like to come with me on an adventure?"

"I'm not sure I'm ready yet."

"Neither am I." She stood, tucking the map back into her bag. "And that is why I need a new royal bodyguard."

"I am touched," Moe said, bowing before her, "that you would make this proclamation. I will oblige your order."

"It's not an order," she said, smiling with the thought of her father's hand on her shoulder. "It's a choice."

A fortnight and four days passed since the Battle of King's Plain. The six lobatorium guardsmen assigned to Apondra's envoy under Moe Murr completed the journey to the merchant town without incident. Sharpe's guidance ensured no animals or thieves attacked, much to the relief of Ken and Diana, although he declined to join their mission, relishing his new role and finding fast friends with the lobfolk guards as well reuniting with old acquaintances who dared travel the rough roads with their wares.

Their arrival at the merchant town was met with little fanfare, as the city council of dock owners found themselves too busy with rebuilding, hiring, and protecting their goods to have a proper meeting. Apondra's entourage crawled along the main avenue to the riverside path, or what was left of it. Diana silently surveyed the far docks across the muddy and trash-filled river. A broken hull of a trade ship still haunted one of the docks, its bow sticking straight up and piercing the sky as the tombstone of the sailors who perished on board.

Apondra stopped to buy a tiny bundle of carrots from a lobfolk grocer. He scoffed as she immediately placed them into a tiny cage at her feet. The snapping turtle inside munched ravenously at the fresh vegetables.

"He's an interesting pet," the grocer said. "Does he have a name?"

"Deet." She tugged at a carrot in the turtle's beak, his eyes blazing bright blue for a moment until he won back his snack. "I like to think that's the sound he makes when he trots. *Deet, deet, deet!*" She tapped his head. "*Deet!*"

The royal party continued down the path along the marina. A charred warehouse frame sat behind a painted sign for Dock Nineteen. Apondra approached cautiously, stepping over broken stones, until she could place her hand on the brittle wood and trace the letters with her fingers. Diana finally spoke.

"Something here?"

"Not anymore," Apondra said, remembering the brief encounter with the quartermaster. "Come on, let's see if Clem is still in business."

They continued further, crossing a threshold where the once giant snapping turtle turned abruptly to cross the riverbank. The fire damage still touched many of the buildings, but the structures survived the devastation. Her guards encircled her now, as the foot traffic around them swelled. Ken stuck to her side.

"I see the book merchant's place," he said, pointed to a building made of stone with charred walls. "It looks like Clem knew the value of his wares, using blocks and bricks underneath the wood. Clever."

Apondra shrugged, then smiled. "Let's see how clever Clem really is."

She led the party to the front of Clem's warehouse and opened the door resting in the warped frame with a shove of her shoulder. Clem scampered toward them, his antennae furiously waving, his hands already clenching his notebook and quill.

"Names, please—oh it's you." His shoulders slumped. Diana smirked.

"Hello, Clem."

"And what brings you all here, Your Highness?"

Apondra gently set Deet's cage on the floor, crossed her arms and looked up at the top of the shelves. An intricate array of boards and clay pots caught the drops of rain that leaked from the ceiling through small holes and cracks. Two central bookshelves sat completely empty; the aisle filled with damp leaves that smelled of rot. Two lobfolk in black canvas aprons continued to sweep them into a pile and load armfuls into barrows.

"Well, good sir, *Clem*, I am here to survey the damage and commission a ship. But you can't help me with that."

"Your Highness, I can recommend a captain and a vessel. For a price, of course."

Diana scoffed. "I don't think we'll be paying you anything in this exchange."

"Oh?" He leaned closer, reaching into his pocket and retrieving an apple. He bit into it, still inches from her, and chewed loudly with his mandibles. "It looks like you're eating well, slave."

"I'm a free woman." Her eyes sparkled blue. "Advisor and Lady Mage for Eave Queen Apondra. And you'd better be respectful if you want our help."

"Help?" He leaned back, stretching his arms wide. "I've had no help from the kingdoms who trade here. I am a wealthy merchant, but even this disaster taxes my finances."

Apondra stepped forward. "I have a proposal, Clem." She circled him, slowly, taking deliberate steps to avoid broken stones on the ground as well as to build the anticipation for her plan. Diana winked and slunk down the aisle toward the back of the warehouse, unnoticed by Clem. "My plan is simple, Clem. No slaves."

"That's your plan?" He blinked rapidly. "No labor?"

"I didn't say that. I said *no slaves*. I have several dozen, if not hundreds, of able-bodied lobfolk displaced at Ribbed Beach who need shelter and food. I can have them assist you for two months, if you provide them with beds and meals; decent meals. That should help you surge back to business in full."

"Oh. I see." He scribbled in his notepad. "That would be a substantial savings in labor cost, if I do not owe them wages, and do not have to hire outside specialists who are doubling and tripling their fees." He dipped his quill for another refill of ink from the bottle dangling from his neck. "Price gouging of labor, can you believe it?"

"You'll save quite a bit." She turned on her heels and walked around him in the opposite direction. "Now, you told me once that your word and your reputation were critical. So as I see it, you will honor this deal. One your warehouse is repaired, the laborers would then be able to work on the next warehouse down the dock, and you'll endorse them, with your word. And recommend a pay rate for them." She stopped. "A *fair* labor rate. Not a slave rate. To be paid weekly."

"Ah I see," he said. "You have an endgame."

"Of course I do," she held up a finger and winked, "but we're not there quite yet." She gestured for his notepad and quill. "If my math is correct, this is the cost of some supplies we would need prioritized for the rebuilding and repairs at Ribbed Beach. We would ask you, here, to act as a broker. And here," she said, scribbling a number, "is what we will pay over the next twelve months to you as our brokering agent."

He glanced at the notepad. His antennae struck straight out from his face. "Well, that's quite a sum." He looked at her and broke into a wide smile. "I'm making out far better in this deal than I thought."

"Not exactly," said Diana, appearing from the end of one of the aisles. She held her hands behind her back. "There's something I needed from your vault. So I grabbed it."

"You—no!" Clem's hand clutched the handle of a dagger in his belt. "How did you?"

Diana's eyes blazed blue. "Magic, of course. It's the best tool for picking a lock." She swung her arms forward, revealing a long leather sheath. "Princess, you may have the honor."

"It is an honor, indeed." Apondra reached for the handle of the sword, a finely woven leather that wound up to a hilt emblazoned with two silvery wings of finely crafted steel. She pulled it out slowly, revealing the graceful neck of a swan engraved onto the blade, and held the sword of Gunnar Brekke, First Cavalier of the Kingdom of Swan, above her head.

"This should make our deal square," Apondra said, lowering the blade, holding it in two hands. She pointed it at Diana. "Here, Lady Mage."

Diana wrapped the sheath's belt around her waist, and then slid the weapon into place. "I think it looks good, yes?"

"Yes, I do indeed." Apondra reached into her sweater and pulled the cord of her necklace, allowing the gold ring to rest over her chest. "So, Clem, I still need a ship. And make sure it has accommodations for my kyloe to come with us."

"It shall be done," he said, grumbling as he headed off to a table across the vast warehouse. "You have my word."

Apondra smiled.

Ken reappeared, running toward her with an armload of books, their covers barely attached.

"Apondra! Look at these! They were going to be thrown out! Just a few loose covers, but I can fix them; I'll rebind them!" He flipped open the first one and ran his finger across the rippled page. "A little water damage, but they're salvageable. You know, I think that innkeeper lady we met might appreciate these. The one with the bobcat? I would really like to properly repay her hospitality before we go."

"Good," Apondra said. "Good."

Clem returned from his desk with a small pile of papers, each freshly sealed with a wax impression.

"Here. Take these to the dock at the mouth of the river. The mariner in charge of chartering all remaining ships will honor these." He placed them in her hand. "Now, if you happen to come across anything of extraordinary interest in your travels, such as a book of antiquities, would you bring it back? I will compensate you, of course."

"Of course," she said, the corners of her mouth turned up very slightly into a polite smile, "you have my word."

Diana spun in a circle, stopping to pose with her hand on the hilt of the sword. "I think this fits me well. At least, until we return it to its homeland."

Apondra fingered the ring around her neck. "Come on now, we have a lot to do."

The group exited the warehouse, the royal guards and Moe bartering with a human baker pushing a cart of confections. Ken held up a finger from a hand unencumbered by his stack of books.

"Do we have a moment to see if he has any cupcakes?"

The sun rested behind them past the western mountains. Far to the east, beyond the edge of the forest, the mouth of the river of the merchant town flowed into the sea, several days journey away from the Kingdom of Swan. A pair of seagulls cawed and frantically flapped their wings, following the river toward the ocean. Apondra still held the gold ring between her fingers. Once upon a time, this ring represented a woman, a mother, who died somewhere in a land far away, but left an indelible mark on the lives of the people around her, her own life, and the life of countless strangers across her lands, a circle of good deeds that could perpetuate into eternity, like the true tale of Azcalaw. She tucked the ring and the necklace back under the collar of her sweater.

"Yes, Ken, let's get a few cupcakes," Apondra said. "It'll be my treat."

The End

APONDRA'S JOURNEY CONTINUES IN

The Lobster Princess Book Two

Special Acknowledgments

Thank you to my wife who chose Maine for our anniversary trip, and the nightmare that spawned the origin of Apondra's world.

Special thanks to Vivien Reis. Your artistic vision is a magnet that has pulled so many people into this book before release.

Paige Connelly, you have brought the world to life as the cartographer of Apondra's world. If there is one thing driving me forward to finish Apondra's epic, it's the excitement to see what you'll come up with next. paigeconnellyillustration.com

And Jennifer Gale: you have a special place as the first person to read any text, bringing Apondra into the real world. I would have abandoned ship without your support.